Dennis Dillard was a sensor, a dramatape recorder:

Am I a crusader, a death-or-glory hero? The answer is no! I was in this mess on Hydro up to my eyebrows— and who got me in? Dr. Stanley and your Philosophy Corps. And who got me out? Me. And I'm staying out! I've been clobbered by cold-blooded aliens who saw me as edible protein. I've spent hours underwater and I can't even swim. And that's enough. You want to go ahead and save Earth, you do it.

What's Earth got, anyway? Population, pollution and psychosis—let the Venusians and the Roggans fight for it, and destroy it and themselves—just leave me out!

And then Dillard's spaceship took off without him, turning the political issue into a life or death situation—his life. . . .

Turn thi⋯ ⋯ second⋯

ALIEN SEA

by

JOHN RACKHAM

ACE BOOKS, INC.
1120 Avenue of the Americas
New York, New York 10036

I

HELPLESS, CRIPPLED AND ALONE, the ship cart-wheeled through space. Its rate of tumble was ponderously slow, but its forward speed was as great as anything it had ever achieved under its own power. The gravity-sink of the incandescent star-mass dragged at it with mighty hunger, but its path was such that it was passing, it was in a cometary orbit; any time now it was due to swoop out of its loop and gradually begin to fall away again from that searing nuclear reaction.

At any rate, the hundred people carried within it hoped so. They lay still, sweating and aching, sipping at over-heated air with tortured lungs, blinking agonized eyes, and hoped that the murderous temperatures would start falling soon. It had to be soon, or never. Frantic calculations had been made on a computer only partly functioning, the rest of it obliterated by the fragmentation-bombs that had blasted the rest of the hull like a collander. On the shaky basis of those figures the stuttering, protesting, half-maimed main-drive had been fired. Just one burst, because that was all it had left, and that burst had to be enough to nudge the suicidal plunge into holocaust just that fraction off, to graze and go on by. In ever increasing temperature, with the wounded and injured expiring one by one from heat exhaustion and other things, the survivors had watched, waited, and wondered just how high the temperature could go before they, too, expired.

And, eventually, they learned that they were lucky. The ship *was* to go on by. But luck is a comparative thing and they wondered about it as the more refined observations showed their ship was not going *by*, but *around*. Of the surviving hundred there were many who said, and many more who thought but didn't say, that the dead ones had been the lucky ones, after all. Those who were still rational enough to keep check estimated that it had been a matter of twelve days since the Harpat ship had shattered them with its last-gasp shot. Twelve days of falling helplessly away from their beleagured planet into the arms of the sun. And now, after four days of undiluted hell? The parched-throat rumor was that, with luck, they would spin off, out of the scorching bypass, and tumble all the way back again. But, by that time, it didn't seem to matter much. The only thing that mattered, the only thing anyone could think about was the heat, and whether the environment-complex, the one remaining out of four, would hold out.

Even Jeko Dogran, commanding officer of what had once been *Starga Two*, a fine ship, could hardly force his mind to consider anything else but that murderous heat. He lay limp in the untidy mess and nonfunctional litter of the control room and his weary eyes seldom shifted far from the pyrometer which read the hull temperatures. The needle hung far above the thick black line that indicated safe-maximum. But it hung. At least it wasn't climbing any longer. If only it would start to fall! He moved his eyes painfully to glance across at Falma Herk. She was very still, only the slow rise and fall of her rib cage indicating that she was still alive. One very junior lieutenant, on her first flight, and that was all he had left of his executive staff. Out of five hundred overall complement there could be no more than a hundred or so left alive, and those only because the moment of disaster had found them scattered in those compartments that had not been ruptured and burst by that damned salvo of bombs.

Dogran switched his gaze back to the pyrometer and tried to think ahead. Suppose—just suppose the temperature did fall. Suppose the ship fell, all the way back to Roggan, then what? A pulse pounded painfully at the back of his head as he tried to carry out the function of an executive, as laid down in the training manual. Arrange the data, assess the whole, then extrapolate. The data, then. One fifth, possibly less, of his crew remained. Great areas of *Starga*'s hull were ripped away, or hung useless. The drive-assemblies, both main and guidance, were useless. One environment-complex out of four was still clanking and shuddering away, limping and overloaded in its vain efforts to preserve the proper temperatures and humidities. About one fifth of the hull-sensors were still submitting some kind of information. The computer was still working, but with half its fluidic circuits dead and the rest suspect. And there was, still, ample power available from the central converter unit.

Assemble that into a whole, he commanded himself. If this orbit *is* a cometary, if the ship swings away and down, then? His eyes hurt and he had to squeeze them tight to restore focus as he tried to shuffle what he knew into something worth concentrating on. The ship was a crippled wreck. Not that it had ever been an efficient warship in any case, even after conversion. Before that it had been a totally self-contained mine-and-smelt freighter, specifically designed and built to spend long weeks combing patiently and methodically in and out of the million moonlets which made up most of this planetary system. It was one of ten *Stargas*, and the *Starga* fleet but was but one of ten such fleets maintained by Vercal to dredge the million moonlets and bring back the ingots of metal that nation so desperately needed. The term "precious metal" had no place on Roggan. All and any metals were precious on a planet where only one twentieth of the surface was habitable land. Vercal needed metal just as much and as badly as did Harpat. They were the only two nations Roggan could support, and even they had to struggle. It was inevitable that they should be competitors. Perhaps it was inevitable that they should, in the end, go to war against each other. But it was suicide, and nothing less, when both sides decided simultaneously to escalate the war.

Dogran halted his train of thought a moment to look at that word that had appeared in his mind. Simultaneously? Faced with almost certain extinction and slightly light-headed with heat and privation, he was getting a new and unreal perspective on many things. He was Vercalian, and Harpat was the deadly, treacherous, unspeakable enemy—

surely? Or was it all an illusion? *Had* both sides shifted from sea-battles to air-assaults, to missiles and then to jury-rigged armor and weapons on their spacecraft, at the same time? Had some collective insanity overtaken the entire humanoid population of Roggan? Dogran had read and absorbed some of the propaganda put about in the early stages of the war, and had believed it because he wanted to. Now, all at once, he saw it as false. This war was pointless, was suicidal. He faced this new vision without flinching. Life on Roggan favored the ruthless and pragmatic approach. Life was cheap there, was overabundant. Living creatures were of small account: there were too many of them always. *Living space* was the all-important thing. That's what the war was all about. Room to live, on a planet of which only one twentieth of the surface was solid, the rest sea. And of that twentieth a considerable proportion lurked under the massive icecaps at either pole. Roggan's tilt was so extreme that the poles ached with cold so fierce that even the land-hungry humanoids couldn't live there for more than a week or two at a time.

Room to live! Dogran jerked his feverish mind back from the futile channels it had slid into. What a time to cogitate on philosophy, when the immediate future might extend no further than hours! He squeezed his eyes tight shut again, to clear them, and squinted painfully at the master pyrometer. He stared, blinked again to be sure, and it was so. The skin-temperature was falling. Not rapidly, but it *was* falling. The orbit *was* cometary. The ship was going to swing away, all the way out again as far as Roggan's orbit. Dogran drew a careful breath, disciplined his mind to be calm. Death had receded. But had it gone away altogether, or was it just waiting in the wings?

He reached and levered his couch upward to the point where he could operate the microphone of the internal communication system. He had last used it fifteen hours ago to inform those who could hear just what was ahead for them. He hoped it was still working.

"Your captain speaks. Hear this. The outside temperature is falling slowly. This seems to indicate that we have passed our nearest point to the sun and are now swinging away. Possible, not certain. There will be a wait of one hour, when I will speak to you again." He moved the switch to cut out the microphone, rolled his head and said, "Lieutenant Herk, go and find Dr. Orsini, tell him to report to me, here, at once!"

Falma Herk stirred, sat up, swung her legs to the deck and stood, reeling. Pale blue eyes glazed with near-exhaustion, her long forelock of straw-yellow hair plastered back over her shaved skull with caked sweat, she put a shaky index finger to the paint-band on her brow and said, "Yes, sir. At once."

As she went feebly down the ladder from the control room into the warped guts of the ship, Dogran scowled to himself. All his executive staff dead except Herk, a green junior, and a female at that. It was this damned war, of course. In Roggan's ruthless economy, women were strictly confined to their destined functions as non-skilled, non-opinioned labor, and for breeding offspring as—but only as—economic circumstances indicated. Before the war, women would have flown this ship, would have worked in the smelter, or the detector room, or as labor in the drive-chamber, but never on an executive level. Decisions were made by men, always. Dogran himself had been an up-and-coming merchant-banker until the war had gouged him out of his narrow rut. He had a talent for organization, and that talent had insured his rapid rise this far. He could command people, but now he needed to know just how many people, and what kind of a command he still had. For that he needed Orsini. It was symptomatic of his feeling for the ship's medical man that he had not thought of him when regretting his lack of executive staff. It was hard to think of Orsini as that kind of material. Dogran squinted again at the pyrometer, to see that the temperature was still falling, grudgingly. Here came Orsini up the ladder now, to halt and turn and extend an arm to assist Falma Herk.

"All right? Now, you just stretch out on your couch and relax; it's the coolest thing to do. Forget everything else."

"Orsini!" Dogran edged his voice. "You will refrain from ordering my staff. That is my function!"

"You have no function!" Orsini said it flatly, without emphasis. He stood easily, lean and somehow slouched, yet poised. "That's obvious. Think it over." He moved to sit sideways on the vacant copilot couch. Dogran glared, his anger hurting his head. The man was insufferable. Like everyone else he was stripped down to just a brief black loincloth, enough to provide pouches for his minimum equipment, but

unlike the others, and in sharp distinction to Dogran himself, he looked almost comfortable. There was a thin sheen
of sweat on his brow, where the broad black-and-white band
of a lieutenant-commander crossed, just above his eyebrows,
but that was all.

"I command this ship." Dogran rasped, always conscious
of the red-edged band across his own brow. "I give the
orders. You have never properly appreciated that, Orsini.
I have noticed it, meaning to speak to you about it. I do
so now. I demand your obedience and cooperation."

Orsini did not look impressed, or even interested. "Three
years ago," he said, "the war claimed you. Half a year ago
you came aboard this ship as commanding officer. That was
your function. Twelve days ago that function ended. We
are no longer at war with Harpat."

"Treason?" Dogran offered the word coldly, despite the
heat that was scorching his nostrils. Orsini's tone was that of
logic, a reasoned statement of fact. To Roggan's brood, logic
was a way of life.

"Not treason. Common sense. This ship is now at war with
the elements only. We are not fighting Harpat. We are fighting to survive."

Dogran studied it, and nodded slowly. "But I am still
commander."

"If you insist, but only if you ignore the prime need. You
are the executive of a warship. This is no longer a warship." Orsini paused, then went on as if talking to himself.
"Eleven years ago I first became medical officer on this ship.
I know it from bow-scoop to stern-chute. The commanding
officer we had then had to go aground to learn the arts of
war, and you came. Most of the crew stayed, are still here,
have survived. You probably think the ship a wreck. It
isn't. I have known emergencies almost as bad as this many
times. Ore-hunting is a hazardous business."

As his voice ceased Dogran looked again at the temperature. It was still creeping back. He pondered Orsini's words.
They made sense, were logical. "The prime need," was a
powerful phrase.

"You are suggesting that I surrender my command? To
you?"

"Not openly." Orsini grinned. "Some of your staff still
survive. The rest are trained to think of you as the chief

order-giver. So you should go on giving orders. But I will advise you how, and what."

Dogran frowned, finding a flaw in the reasoning. "You would be doing this in any case. For instance, I sent for you to find out how many people still survive, what their condition is, how many can work. I ask it now."

"The answer is, exactly one hundred, including ourselves. All the injured and disabled perished in the heat. Of the hundred, fifty-two are women, forty-eight are men. But that is not the point now. Of that hundred, forty-three, including myself, are long-service crew of this ship. Those are the people who know what is to be done. None of them are executive, or in authority of any kind. Your first order will have to be to change that, to get those people and put them in charge of every department where repairs are possible. The second order will have to be that everybody works. Everybody will contribute time, and effort, and labor. We can no longer afford any passengers." Although Orsini kept his tone even, Dogran got the point at once, this time.

"I am a passenger?"

"You have been. This was a ship first, a fighting unit second. It is no longer a fighting unit. If it is to become a workable ship again everybody will have to contribute. I include myself, of course. You agree?"

Dogran didn't like it. His military training had not included any course on what to do with a wrecked and crippled ship. Vercal had blithely assumed such training would be necessary only for Harpatian ships, not its own. He did not like, furthermore, the idea of the skulking and hitherto ignored "black gang" taking over and giving orders. But if they knew how to lash-up and jig the ship so that it would work again—he stifled his personal feelings and bowed to logic, like a good Roggan.

"Very well," he said, "I agree. What is the first step?"

"We need information. We will assume that we are falling out from the sun and work on that basis. Assume that we have eleven—twelve days in which to get something going, enough to be able to reestablish control. I know my section of the crew. They need no telling what's to be done, only to be told to get on with it. But they will need help, and that's what we must find out first. So you will call a meeting. Best place is the central smelter, which is big enough and undamaged. You need to know just what skills you have among your staff. I mean skills, not combat training. Anybody who knows one end of a wrench from the other. Anybody who knows how to handle sodium wiring, or radio, or can fix a light circuit. Or those who don't know a thing but can contribute muscles to lift and eyes to watch. Economization."

Another key word. Dogran nodded. Economization was a creed with all Roggans. Maximum results with minimum resources. Waste not. For one crisp moment he contrasted that survival doctrine with the fantastic squandering waste that was war, and his home planet felt very far away and unreal. What insanity it all was. This was what the pitiful little handful of pacifists had been trying to promote all this time. One world! Live together! He wished too late, that he had listened more attentively.

"Very well," he said again, and reached for the microphone. The outside temperature was still falling.

The meeting and the subsequent discussion and working out of survival plans went better than he had expected. In any self-conscious humanoid there must be a nonrational component, an amalgam of the inner and outer values and abstractions which together make up "society." Harpat and Vercal alike had their creeds and beliefs, and shared a stubborn to-the-death hatred of each other out of which had come the final insanity of war. But all were even more fundamentally Roggan, and the evolution of life on that planet had instilled in them values that were far more basic than any cultural implant. Nineteen-twentieths of its surface were trackless sea perpetually torn with storms. Between the twin ice caps and the semitropical equatorial belt where the two major landmasses lay, the temperature extremes were so great that there was a permanent cloud-blanket over the whole planet, through which they saw their primary and the other, scattered masses of the system only vaguely. Out of such an environment the Roggans had grown to be able to put aside odd and trivial things like fancies and fashions, art and delicacy. Survival came first. Dogran himself had accepted it. Now the people under his command accepted it in the same way, once he had made the point.

Starga Two continued to fall back and out, away from the sun. The heat-bleached humanoids aboard grimly reorganized themselves, pooled their resources, forgot about protocol and status, learned not to bother about watches and rest-periods, but came to think, instead, that so long as there was still something to be done, there was no rest. Clothing was discarded permanently, because they couldn't afford the precious resources needed to keep it repaired, washed, pressed and presentable. Marks of respect and rank went too. Those who knew how, did, and showed others. Dogran himself discovered a hitherto unsuspected dexterity with fine wiring, and Falma Herk came to tower above him because she had a gift for grasping the principles underlying fluidic circuits. The drive engineers contrived, cannibalized the beamers to jury-rig control units and, in turn, managed to adapt spares from the drive to lash up several of the frag-bomb projectors.

By the fifth day it was pretty certain they were going to survive and Dogran began, in rare moments of rest, to cast his mind ahead to the point where he could ask, "survive for what?" By the ninth day the question became acute. The main-drive was four-fifths efficient, the navigation-complex adequate for anything but the most strenuous acrobatics. Outside sensors were working to the point where he could, at last, get a fix on the cloud-ball that was Roggan itself. Calculations with the patched up computer told him that it was well within their capacity to adjust their fall so as to intercept. They could get home safely. But what then?

He called another meeting. The habit of assembly for discussion and working out ideas had grown to be enjoyable, but this time the atmosphere was grim as he announced his findings.

"We are fly-worthy enough to make reentry," he told them. "Enough to locate Vercal and get down. We have armament enough to defend ourselves in the event of an encounter, up to a point. If we are unfortunate enough to be intercepted we will fight; that goes without question. If, however, we are lucky enough to get back to home base and set down, what then? The ship, of course, will require a massive overhaul. We will be pulled off and, we must presume, be sent to transfer. To fight again. Is that what you want?" He studied the stern, pale-eyed faces around him curiously.

"What does it matter what we want?" Orsini asked, just to keep the dialogue going. "There's a war on. We have no choice."

The rest gave no sign one way or the other. Dogran took his courage and used all of it at once. "I find a choice in me," he said. "The past days have taught me something. I shall resign my commission. I intend to become a pacifist, to do whatever I can to end this futile waste of war."

"You'll be shot," Orsini told him, flatly and without emphasis. "You will achieve nothing."

"Perhaps," Dogran agreed. "That remains to be seen. All I wanted to say here is that I am your commander until we get down. Until then, we go on as before. But after then—you must all do what you think best. I have told you what I am going to do. That's all."

It was a very unsatisfactory meeting, but it did mark a point. From that moment *Starga Two* was back on a military footing. Falma Herk, reporting to the control room, found herself made a lieutenant-commander on the spot.

"Me?" she demanded, overawed.

"You. You are the only executive officer left. I will make other adjustments in due course. For now, Herk, get busy on the radio and see if you can raise a polar beacon. We should be in range now."

"I should have told you earlier," she said, "but I had a computer-link to finish up. I tried to raise a beacon two hours ago. Nothing!"

"Oh! You're sure about the radio?"

"Almost. I'll go over it again now, of course, but I'm pretty sure."

"Go over it, quick as you can, and report!" Dogran left it at that and busied himself with the job of reverting to combat status, but his mind persisted on worrying. That the polar beacons had failed was unthinkable. One was just a bare possibility, but both was just not to be believed. Ever since the enterprising humanoids of Roggan had taken to the air the better to cross and exploit the vast wastes of sea, the need of permanent markers had been acute. With only a haze for sky, and all the land gathered in two great continents around the equator, it was easy to get lost elsewhere. So, in the one hard and fast example of coexistence ever recorded between Vercal and Harpat, the polar radio beacons had been established. The effort had been heroic, the installations massive and virtually indestructible, needing no attention, drawing their operating power from the thermal range between the icy land and the warmer air-streams that whirled evermore overhead.

Without the beacons, Dogran mused, the whole of Roggan would fall back into semi-primitive conditions, sailing and flying cautiously, never very far from visible land. Fishing fleets would be permanently crippled, space-mining impossible. Economic chaos had to follow. It didn't make sense. Those beacons could not have failed. The radio had to be faulty. But—and he faced it in the same way he had faced other unpalatable ideas recently—if it wasn't the fault of the radio, then the beacons had been taken out deliberately. And that was the logical and ultimate insanity that had to follow the original mistake of war. He felt all his insides sag and go heavy like lead. From this standpoint he could see no end now but annihilation, of one side or the other. And for what? So that the victor could survive and starve?

Half an hour later Falma Herk reported woodenly. "The radio is functional as far as it is possible to check. And there are no beacons."

"Keep trying," he ordered, concealing from her that he was not very surprised. She went back to her board, he returned to his gloomy thoughts. Logic still held. Whichever side had first decided to cut out a beacon as a tactical blow, the other had to duplicate or be at a disadvantage. Logic, yes, but with his new-found and hard-won insight it sounded gruesomely like cutting off a nose to spite a face. He sat on his convictions until the last hours of the eleventh day, when Roggan was a naked-eye disk in the viewers, when clumsy course corrections had been made to intercept her orbit, when the various work sections had reported three-fourths of the stern and midships armaments back in service once more. Then he called one more meeting.

"We shall strike atmosphere in six hours," he told the assembly, "and from that moment we will again be a warship. The drills have all been worked out, you all know your posts, and I could have announced this over the speaker-system, but I wanted this last chance to see you all together again."

The unspoken grimness in "last chance" stirred them to a ripple of restless movement. He waited for it to cease.

"I have to tell you, now that for three days we have been trying to pick up a polar beacon signal. Lieutenant-Commander Herk is reasonably sure the radio is functional, but we have so far been unable to detect any signal of any kind. Beacons or otherwise."

He paused again, to let the implications grow and become apparent. The first to speak was Rackar Gron, the senior of the engine room staff.

"Maybe the war is all over," he suggested, and there was a grunt and growl from his own colleagues as they considered this. Then Orsini stood.

"It's over all right. In the worst way. If they have gone to the limits of bombing out the beacons, then they're all stark raving mad down there. They must be!"

Dogran scowled as their slightly different interpretation offered something to puzzle over. "I hadn't thought of that," he admitted. "I was assuming that one side or the other might deliberately cut out a beacon in order to gain a tactical advantage, if only for a while. I suppose it is just as much possible that one side would bomb out the beacons of the other." He saw Gron shaking his head. The senior engineer was a wizard with machinery but thick-headed at anything else. He obviously didn't grasp the reasoning. Before he could demand explanations Dogran went on.

"No matter what the reason, the effect is the same. For us this means we will be flying blind once we penetrate the cloud layer. Since no one else is using radio, we cannot either. You know what that means. We must be on constant alert if we are to find our way home, and no one knows how long it will take us. At the same time we must also be alert for Harpat ships. And all this with the naked eye. Lookouts and watches will be revised accordingly. If we can strike a free-fall orbit at twenty miles the fuel problem will not trouble us, but we are nearing our limit on food and drink. Ration allowances will be revised in that light. Orsini, I want your help on that, right away. That is all, except for one thing. I may not have the chance again so I will say it now, to all of you. Goodbye!"

"Getting sentimental?" Orsini demanded, as he clambered up into the control room on Dogran's heels. The commanding officer shook his head. A few days earlier he would have considered the comment insulting. Now he was amused by it. In a wry kind of way he and Orsini had grown to like each other.

"Not sentiment. Common sense. It may seem obvious to

you, and it has been heard from our muttering philosophers a time or two, that we should not have time to fight each other. Our real fight is with the elements, and it has always been so, but I never realized the truth of it until recently. And we've lost the fight, Orsini. You realize that, don't you?"

"I know." The medical officer was as calm as ever, but the light in his pale eyes was bleak. "The way we've been crippling ourselves to fight this insane war, and it has to be the same for Harpat, we just do not have the resources, the manpower or the structural metals, to put those beacons back. And without them our whole way of life is finished."

"Back to the primitive," Dogran muttered, and Orsini shook his head.

"Not even that, Dogran. We can't go back. So far as we can tell, it has taken humanoid life something like half a million years to get this far. The last thousand years, the really civilized years, we achieved at the cost of every square inch of fertile soil producing to the limit under intensive technical boosting, and we have long ago skinned out the last metals. I've had time to think about this, in the years I've been riding this old bucket in and out of the moonlet swarm. Without us, you know, Roggan civilization would crumble. So it follows: take out the beacons and you cancel the ore-ships. Take out the ore and you cancel civilization as we know it. Try to imagine life, any kind of civilized life, without metal. We can't go back, Dogran. You can't go back to an empty bag!"

Dogran sagged in his couch. "Sooner or later the crew will realize as much," he said. "By the Great Wave, what's the point of going on?"

"Why do we struggle to survive?" Orsini murmured. "I don't know the answer to that one. No one does. It just happens to be a built-in characteristic of living systems, that's all." His lean face split in a mirthless grin as he added, "It's a drive, and, like any other drive, it can warp. Then the individual goes suicidal. Had that crossed your mind?"

"It had. Pacifism seems a trifle empty, now. Orsini, why don't I just smash this ship straight down into the sea down there and finish it?"

"I can tell you why, but without logic. It's because you are not the type to give in. None of us are. We haven't sur-

17

vived this far on luck, altogether. We'll see it out to the bitter end because it's the type-pattern for us. That does not mean I think it's a good thing, though. Like you, I wish I could head this old wreck straight down into oblivion. But I couldn't. You can't. We have to go on."

They went on. They plunged through the ion-soup clouds in a nightmare of shuddering and buck-jumping. *Starga Two*, her arrowhead shape never very aerodynamic anyway, was now a caricature of a ship and she fought Dogran all the way through and out into the silent skies over Roggan. He ached all the way from wrists to ankles by the time he had leveled her out into the twenty-mile orbit he had predicted. He hit the button to signal "finished with drive" and leaned thankfully back but the thankfulness didn't last long. In a minute or two Falma Herk came up with sun-drift figures for the computer and there was a short burst of trimming-thrust. Then *Starga Two* was flying north-south. Or south-north. By the vast and uncaring deep down there, no one could tell which. All available sensors were on and working, striving to pick up a hint, a clue, a whisper. But nothing came, and Dogran knew, by some inner intuition, that nothing *would* come. His imagination painted for him the torn and blasted ruin of his homeland, the stark and life-less debris from fragmentation bombs and corrosive charges, lethal gases—and there had been some persistent rumor, he remembered, of a new and dreadful device that could yield hell-fire from the partial annihilation of matter.

There would be nothing left. He knew it. With the apathetic calm of total despair he realized that he had known it all along, that millions of other people must have known it too. Yet there had been a war. What was it Orsini had said? A drive, any drive, could warp. Survival, driven too far, could warp into self-destruction? Dogran thought his way through a nonsense mixture of contradictory values and felt old and empty. How, he wondered, had it all happened? To his present regret he had never been much of a historian. Not that it mattered, but he was curious to know just how humanity, with all its wonderful potential, could also carry this suicidal streak. He came out of his black reverie to a startled squeak from Falma Herk.

"A signal, sir!" she gasped. "Very faint, far away. And it's voice-modulated!"

Training asserted itself instantly. Dogran hit the alarm

switch, sat forward tensely, and demanded, "Get a course fix on it, data into the comp at once. Range?"

She took a maddeningly long time to reply. "Just to make sure," she said, at last, "and I am, now. It's a suit-radio. Range about four hundred miles, bearing sixteen degrees left of our present course. And—sir!"

"Yes, what?" Dogran halted with his finger on the speaker switch.

"I'm also getting a kick from the echo-locator, dead ahead. Shallows!"

"Hmm!" Dogran considered this swiftly. Echo-location was useful on any mass less than five hundred feet below surface, and all such "shallows" were charted. It might help to know just exactly where he was by this method. "Very well, we will proceed on course for the moment, Herk. Read that shallow and get me a bearing from it. Fast!" He buttoned the speaker. "Hear this. We are receiving faint signals from a suit-radio approximately four hundred miles away. Condition alert but await further data."

He waited, watching Falma Herk from the corner of his eye and feeling curiously indifferent to all this evidence of warlike normality. His body and trained reflexes were responding, but his inside, his personality, seemed to have stepped off somewhere apart. She had let her pale forelock grow and thicken enough to be tied in a sedate little bow at the nape of her neck. As she craned down over her instruments now he thought she was extremely attractive. She had turned out to be very competent, too. It seemed criminal that all that grace, the beauty, the competence, should be utterly useless and wasted. He caught himself from reverie with a start, amazed to find, for the first time in his life, that he had consciously thought of some other person as attractive. One didn't think of people like that. He didn't, anyway. Other people were useless or not, significant or not, involved or not—but attractive—? She swiveled and looked at him, catching him unawares. Then the wide fear in her eyes cut through his other distractions.

"Sir!" Her voice had gone right back into her throat. "Sir —that shallow is two hundred and thirty-six miles north to south, and seventeen hundred and sixty miles east to west. And there's no such shallow on any chart!"

"There's got to be—" he began to snarl, then the figures

sank home. "Two thirty-six by seventeen sixty? But—but those are the rough dimensions of—of Vercal!"

"That's right," she whispered.

"Rubbish!" he shouted, as much at the chills on his spine as at her white face. "It must be coincidence. You can't sink a continent! Forget it for now. Fix on that radio again."

He fed data into the course computer and the ship shuddered gently as steering jets throbbed. The faint signal grew louder. Herk switched it to the main speaker. A voice began to sort itself out of the carrier mush, a voice that rambled and wavered like a man in stupefied delirium. Dogran took up the signal-mike, cleared his throat.

"This is *Starga Two*, of Vercal, Captain Dogran speaking. Identify!"

"By the Wave!" The rambling death-weary voice suddenly took on life and cut clear through the interference roar. "That was a living voice, or I am really mad at last. If you are really there, *Starga Two*, this is Ral Wentil, second lieutenant of the ship *Colbar*—what's left of it—of Harpat. Where in storm have *you* been, *Starga*?"

"What do you mean, where have we been? How many are you, Wentil? Give your true state and power, or we blast you down!"

"Please do, Captain—Dogran, is it? Please do. We've been trying to do just that for three hellish days now, but we can't. There are sixteen of us, all in suits. The ship is a dead wreck, no power, no control, nothing, and our suits are running out. Make it quick, Captain!"

Dogran stared in bewilderment at Falma Herk, and then at Orsini, who had come up into the control room just in time to hear the plea. The medical officer moved a switch and muttered, "The rest ought to hear this. Something is hellishly wrong there."

"Hello, Wentil." Dogran made his voice obey him. "Do I read you that you *want* to be blasted down?"

"What else is left? Everything is gone, you know that!"

"Everything? You mean—Harpat has been wiped out?"

Wentil laughed, or snarled, they couldn't be sure which. "It's all gone, Dogran. Harpat *and* Vercal. All gone. Drowned. Didn't you know?"

"Drowned?" Dogran's voice was talking by itself now, beyond his control or care. "Drowned?" it repeated foolishly. "But how?"

"It was the hell-bomb. Your side launched it. A missile with a hell-fire warhead." Dogran went numb inside. So the rumor had been true, after all. He heard his stunned voice demanding, "But why would anyone launch a missile at a polar station?"

"Didn't!" Wentil cackled. "That was cunning. You launched it in a sneak orbit, over the pole. But our intelligence was too good. We found out. A four-ship squad intercepted and shot it down. Over the North Pole ice cap."

You can't sink a continent. Dogran's own words came back to him. You could do the equivalent, though, simply by melting the millions of tons of water locked up in an ice cap.

"How long ago?" Orsini demanded, his voice choked with despair.

"Ten days. Silly, isn't it?" Wentil was coming closer to madness with every minute. "Our side had the hell-bomb too, but we tried to deliver ours with ships. *Colbar* was with the squadron covering the bomb-ships. We ran into opposition over the South Pole. Silly, isn't it? We've been drifting helplessly in orbit ever since, watching Roggan drown."

"What about surface ships?" Orsini growled, and this time Wentil did laugh, a hideous sound over the tinny radio.

"Surface ships, in tsunani waves half a mile high? The sea has won out, Vercalians. Roggan is dead. They said this was the war to end all wars, and they were right!"

Dogran sat back in his chair and felt suddenly old. There was no future, only this present moment. There was nowhere else, only this patched up ruin of a ship. There was nothing. He screwed his head around painfully to stare at Orsini, and then Falma Herk.

"What price pacifism now?" he asked stupidly. "Now what about your suicidal warped drive? Now"—his voice boiled up loud in his throat—"give me one good reason why I don't point this ship straight down there and get it all over with!"

"I'll do better than that!" Orsini was savage, the gleam in his pale eyes a terrible thing. "Listen, everybody. You on that ship, too. Listen. We still live. We are more than a hundred, fit and healthy. The world we knew is dead, drowned and destroyed, because it forgot the one thing that matters, the real enemy. They fought each other, and perished. We can live if we work together. Let me tell you how—"

And all that happened, allowing for Einsteinian edicts about simultaneity, about the same time that Caesar's legions were leaping down into the surf to start the conquest of Britain.

II

IT WAS, therefore, about two thousand years later that an alarm-gong sounded in Dennis Dillard's ear, and a quietly firm voice announced: "Your attention, please. We break into norm-space in five minutes, I repeat, five minutes. We will then proceed immediately to make splash-down on Hydro. All passengers are requested to proceed at once to their cabins and strap in according to the instructions printed over each couch. A single gong will mark the minutes. I say again, you have five minutes. Do not delay. Do not leave your couch until so instructed."

Dillard began to pack his equipment rapidly. He had deliberately strewn it over the cabin table only ten minutes before. He had calculated carefully that if he hurried he could pack everything, wire spools, headband, amplifier-module, battery-pack and vernier-panel, and just give himself time to get to the control room before the acrobatics began. This was his way of making sure that his attention was too thoroughly occupied for him to think, and thus to get the cold shakes anticipating what was going to happen. He cursed as, in the delicate act of fitting the battery-pack into its recess, his cabin-visor chimed for attention. Still monitoring his fingers, he crossed to it and knocked the switch with his elbow. A beautiful but carefully aloof blonde gazed at him from under the beak of a black space-service cap.

"Mr. Dillard? You should be on your way, as arranged. Hurry, please."

"I'll be there," he muttered, settling the battery-pack and snatching for the switch. Damn it. That interruption was just enough to break the carefully contrived busy-ness he had built up. Now he had to rush. He grabbed the headband, which went in last because it was flexible, stuffed it in place, clicked the kit-box shut and hoisted the loop over his shoulder as he hurried out of the cabin, up two decks and out through the cross-member tunnel into the central body of the ship. A mellow gong sounded as he began stepping lively up the sharp spiral toward the control room. *Hurry equals panic,* he reminded himself, trying to keep calm. *Why does everybody call this thing a spiral,* he asked himself, *when it's really a helix? Why does Captain Conway call the damned place "the bridge," when bridges went out with sailing ships? What's all the panic about, anyway?* Breakout from Pauli-space was nothing! This was his very first space trip, and you couldn't get much greener than that, could you? Yet there had been three breakouts so far, for navigation purposes, and so what? For a split-second you felt as if you were being turned inside out, sure, but it was all over before you really had time to feel it. And he should know surely. He, Den Dillard, professional "feeler," should know.

But it didn't work. None of his argument therapy ever did. Action was the only effective method. Carefully planned activity, not this edge-of-panic scramble. How many gongs was that, now? He arrived in the control room of *Venture Three* with his knees threatening to let him down any moment and a fine sheen of sweat on his brow.

"Sorry to crowd it a little," he muttered, and Captain Conway took out his pipe to gesture with it soothingly.

"Perfectly all right, Dillard. You have a full minute yet. Here, take the copilot seat alongside me."

"Copilot?" Dillard's voice threatened to squeak, and Conway grinned, biting on the pipe, which was lit and releasing a thin blue spiral in complete defiance of all regulations to the contrary.

"Quite all right, believe me. Matter of fact the auto-helm will take us all the way. I'm just here in case, and should it come to that we'll have you out of *that* seat in ample time. But it won't, you know. It's all right."

Dillard let himself down into the contoured seat and began flipping the catches on his kit-box. His educated fingers knew what to do without help from his eyes, which roamed restlessly around the control space. Richter, over there by the state and auxiliary console, looked bored and probably was. As First Officer he had answered Dillard's questions this far with patience but was unable to keep his contempt from showing. He probably didn't have any nerves at all by this time, Dillard estimated, clipping the headband into place and adjusting the touch-pads to press firmly against the nape of his neck. Over in the far corner, Lieutenant Rogers, blonde, beautiful and icily aloof, concentrated on her communications board and pretended not to know that he was there at all. She owned the mellow voice that had issued the breakout warning, and was the only other person on the ship Dillard had tried to talk to, apart from Captain Conway himself. He had got exactly nowhere with her. Somehow she had managed to make her neat-fitting all-in-one-piece, black and gold uniform a barrier between them, and he hadn't tried too hard to break it down. After all, he wasn't just along for the ride, or enjoyment.

The black needle on the master clock crept nearer zero. Dillard hoisted his vernier-panel on to his knee and made fine adjustments, switched in the lead-wire to sound.

"You say"—Conway leaned across—"that you don't pick up sounds and pictures with that gear?"

"Not at all," Dillard assured him. "Just for this bit now, excuse me." He depressed a button and spoke into a tiny microphone on the board. "Control room of *Venture Three*, about to break out of Pauli-space into norm-space and then go down to landing on Hydro. Den Dillard, recording." He released the button again. "That's all the sound. From here on it's just sensations, *my* sensations. You know, thrust and surge, free-fall vertigo, spin—those are all straightforward neuro-muscular reactions, of course. But also the wire picks up emotional effects like fear, excitement, tension, from the event itself, and the more subtle sensations of being seated, enclosed in here—this room—and stuff like that."

Conway nodded, leaned back to puff his pipe, then shook his head half in wonder, half in disbelief. "Haven't I read about something like this?"

"Not recently." Dillard managed an unsteady grin. "A long time back the idea was written up by a fantasist of the period. Huxley something or other. He called it 'feelies,' but his idea was to record tactile sensations. This is something a bit different; it's the gestalt reaction to a set of circumstances as they happen. When this is played back through the right equipment the audience will feel everything that I feel." He heard Richter snort, quite distinctly, and felt a flush come to his face.

24

"It probably wouldn't mean a thing to you, because you've done it a thousand times . . ."

"That's all right," Conway interrupted. "I can remember my first drop very plainly. Insides like water and wanting to grab hold of something solid to hang on to. You mean you can pick up all that on your gadget?"

"Oh yes. More than you think. Because of me, you see." Dillard made a rueful shrug as he confessed. "Some people are more sensitive than others. They react more. For this job you have to be one of those." Sweat was starting on his face again and he added, in sudden angry complaint, "It's hell, but it's what I'm good at."

Conway nodded, not smiling now. "Sensibilities," he said, "can be the devil, but you can't be an artist without them."

"That's right. That's it exactly."

"And you say this stuff is used in—what d'you call them? —dramatapes? That's the new 'total-television' thing, isn't it?"

"Right again." Dillard settled lower as the needle narrowed the gap. "Background effect. Sound, pictures, music—and sensation!"

On that last word there came a vibrant shiver of sound that screamed up and away out of audibility, the whole universe collapsed in on itself into breath-stopping nullity, then exploded silently and instantly into steady solidity again. In the next second a screen flared into light in front of Dillard's eyes, a neat row of pointers lifted up from their stops and heaved. The air was full of busy clicks and whispering relays, then the solid fabric of the ship began to shudder distantly as reaction-drive cut in.

"We'll jockey about a bit," Conway said casually, "to select the best approach, then we'll go down. Queer system altogether, this one. D'you mind if I talk, or will it put you off?"

"Won't make much difference." Dillard gasped, fighting against the assault on his nerves as the seat fell away beneath him, then slammed back and shoved him sideways. "The technicians can always modify the amplification. Will, in any case. Part of the art. You were saying?"

He wanted Conway to go on in that casually confident drawl. The hell was with him now. Some people *are* more sensitive than others. As Conway had said, artists.

Painter, poet, sculptor, musician, all are people who live
with their sensibilities close to the skin, who suffer and
weep, who laugh, who shake with wonder, at those things
which hardier mortals pass by without recognition. Whether it be chemical or mental, or a combination of both,
if you have it you can't help it, a curse and a blessing by
turns and according to circumstances. Dillard had it, and he
suffered now, nine-tenths of him writhing and cringing,
and lurched to find an approach pattern. The remaining
tenth of him was the hard-won control fraction, that part
which stood aside and watched, which kept a chill eye on
neural-fluxes and skin-sensor inputs, which nursed the ver-
niers and kept rigidly aloof from the shattering nerve-storm
of the rest. It had taken Dillard many years and a lot of
sweated suffering to discipline that much of himself. The
reward was that he was one of the very best sensor-men in
the business. At times like this, that knowledge was only
a tenuous consolation for the panic-fear that racked him.
He wanted Conway to go on talking.

"As I said"—the ruminating captain chewed on his pipe-
stem, cast a skilled eye over the panel, and shook his head
—"this is a crazy system. You see the primary there? Sol-
type within the standard figures. And there's one inner
planet that would pass for Mercury. But there all resemblance
ceases. Instead of the second and fourth planet that you'd
expect, there's a positive plague of minor moonlets averag-
ing six or seven hundred miles across, and in all sorts of
orbits and planes. They fill the spaces where the second
and fourth planets ought to be, if you accept Bode's Law,
that is, and there must be a hundred thousand of them, at
least. Two great gas-giants further out, but they don't concern us. Our problem is that Hydro is lying in third place,
where Earth would be, and putting down on it is quite a
business. If we had to do it by hand and instruments—"
he let the hypothesis hang as if unable to describe just
how it would be. Dillard was not surprised.

On the screen before him there came and went spinning
spots of light, some close enough to show an appreciable
disk, half-cut with shadow, and he was fearfully aware of
the groan and grind of the ship as it dodged its careful
way in and out between the random hunks of rock.

"Queer planet, too," Conway went on, reaching out to tap
a gauge with his knuckles, then leaning back again, satis-

fied. "Slightly less than Earth in diameter, but about the same in mass, and all water. Warm water, too. A pronounced axial tilt, perfectly circular orbit, and with the tidal effects of all those moon-masses, the water is constantly churning. Pretty shallow in spots, so there's all sorts of tidal inequalities, and a constant vapor-haze, which produces rainbows almost all the time. Queer place altogether."

Dillard tried hard to agree, but "queer" was not the word he would have used at that moment. As the seat fell away under him, then slammed back, and screaming masses of rock slid past the corners of the screen, he was grinding his teeth to keep his last meal down, and praying for the nightmare to end. At times like this it felt to him that his stomach-churning panic must surely extend several feet out from his skin, and it was amazing how those around him couldn't feel it.

"Doesn't seem right," he managed to say, through his teeth, "that a whole planet should be just water."

"Cosmology theories are cheap hereabouts," Conway grunted. "I've heard a few. One expert, so-called, tried to explain to me how, if there was a big enough landmass to create air-temperature turbulence, there would be clouds. I've heard 'em arguing that there ought to be ice packs at the poles. If you go in for that kind of thing it could drive you crazy."

"Seems a waste. A whole planet, with no chance for life to develop anywhere except in the sea."

"Waste? I suppose you could say that. Doesn't concern me. All I know is that it's a very handy arrangement for us, since all that water down there represents so much fuel for the taking. Ah!" Conway leaned forward again and extended a finger which weaved a bit as the ship still lurched. "That's Hydro now. See it?"

Dillard saw, and just for a moment the sight was enough to take out some of his panic. There against a black-velvet curtain of space studded with star-jewels was a small disk. Three-quarters of it shimmered silver and ice-blue, the dark side rippling with a rainbow halo superimposed on deep dark violet. It grew larger as he watched.

"Your first time. I've seen it a score of times. But it's still a sight. A pity you can't get *that* on your wire," Conway said.

"Pictures—we can always get those." Dillard forced himself to keep the conversation going. "You can do a lot of things with pictures and sounds. Play tricks with them. All you need is a camera, or a recording machine. But this"—he gulped as the ship seemed to leap and heel in a tight arc—"takes a person. Somebody like me." The stand-off fraction of him was aware of the multiple flow of impulses from the nerve-net that were being channeled into the hair-fine ferrite wire that was now sliding steadily between the gaps of a delicate magnet, and an irrelevant quirk of memory brought back the words of his boss, Production-Manager Elmer Basalt, of Epics Incorporated:

"Sure you have delicate artistic sensibilities, Dee-Dee boy, but who can sell those? That kind of stuff is great for the long-hairs, the intellectuals, the high-Q crowd, but who makes a living from them? We have to deliver where the money is, Dee-Dee, and that is where the people are. And what do they want? They want sensation! Hit them in the guts, make their flesh creep, scare the pants off them, that's what they want!"

What *they* wanted called for Dillard, and a handful of others like him, to suffer gibbering fear, blood-chilling terror, palpitations and repeated dread, just to get it on the wire. And it helped not at all to know, with the sane fraction of his mind, that the horrors were largely unreal, invented by his hypersensitive nervous system. Nor did it help any to know that he was special, and sought-after. Rich. At the top of his profession. Basalt's favorite son. None of it helped at all. The ship shuddered, the screen picture jittered and spun, and his insides became one snarled and tangled mass of shrieking primitive terror, while his trained fraction clung grimly to sanity and monitored the things that were pouring into the wire.

But now the acrobatics lessened and the visible sky cleared of zooming white chunks. The disk of Hydro grew larger and larger. Conway leaned forward again to tap a gauge and murmur, "That's the hairy part done with, Dillard. Straightforward landfall, now. Not that you can call it landfall, mind you, but you know what I mean. All routine. You can relax." He swung his head aside to grin, and then his grin froze into concern. "You all right? You look terrible!"

"I feel terrible," Dillard confessed between stiff lips, swallowing and breathing hard as his viscera swirled and settled reluctantly. "Don't mind it, please. This is what I'm for."

"My God!" Conway breathed. "Is this what landsiders want for their entertainment? Blood and circuses? And they say we're civilized at last! Why the devil d'you do it, man? There must be other ways to make a living!"

"My only talent, Captain. And I have no skills." Dillard gulped, got his breathing steadied, felt the sweat burst out on him now that the tension was easing, and cast his eyes down to the control-panel on his lap. His explanation was true, as far as it went, but it was only a shadow of the reality. There were no words to explain the long years of futility, the hopeless struggle to find some other way of employing his sensitivity in a world where art, any art, had to be explosive, arrogant, stridently crude enough to smash through the barrier of apathy, or cease to exist. Delicacy, sensitivity, those were words without meaning in a culture sated in and numbed by the relentless, never-ending assaults on the senses so essential to an economy of consumption-growth. It had taken him a long time and a lot of grief to discover the one thing he could do really well.

He kept his eyes down now, not wanting pity. He became aware of quick movement, saw slim legs shimmering in skintight black metallon come to a halt beside Conway, and a mellow voice saying, casually, "Billet Fourteen, sir."

A rustle of paper-plastic as she put the radio message down, then the slap of soft feet as she went away again. Walking about, even though the ship was still surging and shifting into attitude for drop. Going back, now, to her seat at the radio-console. He could imagine the look on her face. Conway made movements, busied himself punching the information into the auto-helm, then sat back again.

"Handy place, this," he said. "Just right to break the jump-time for Castor, Pollux and Capella. Water-planets aren't all that common, especially this close to Terra." The sub-audible shuddering ceased suddenly and for a sickening moment the ship was in free-fall. Dillard held his breath until, just as suddenly, the shuddering started again. "That's it," Conway declared. "It's all straight down from now on. You'll see the base in a moment. Not that it's much to see."

Dillard forced himself to take an interest in the picture on the screen. Hydro was big enough now to fill all one corner, and as the image swelled still more, automatic focusing adjustments shifted the view, brought him a close-up bird's eye picture of a thing like a giant many-limbed star-fish, but the whole was silver-plated metal, the arms were double, like two-tined forks, and each pair that starred out from the center held a gray-green mass like a sausage. That, Conway explained, was the desalination and water-processing plant and fueling station. The gray-green blobby things were huge plastic tanks that floated in the water, and a "billet" was the semi-enclosed space formed by the incurved ends of the retaining arms and the bag itself. Dillard counted eighteen billets, and saw that many of them were occupied. The metal starfish grew huge, became a tracery of girders and struts, with a solid mass in the center.

"Five and a half miles across," Conway murmured, "and anchored to the seabed with cables. Shallow just there. No more than seven hundred feet or so. Right on the equator. Warm water, warm air. Pretty place."

He fell silent as the auto-helm piled on the braking power and everything grew immensely heavy. The screen image shivered and blurred in the heat-waves of the retro-thrust. Dillard groaned as he was squashed down in his seat. Just when he felt he couldn't bear it a moment longer, the crushing weight came off, dwindled to a blessed normal, the shuddering died away, and all was peaceful.

"All over," Conway announced cheerily as the gauges on the board fell back to zero in orderly succession, a faint *ping* announcing each stage of completion. Dillard groped in his poncho for the handkerchief he had saved for this moment, mopped his face and neck, felt light-headed as he always did immediately after a strenuous "experience," and shifted uneasily in his seat.

"I can still feel movement."

"Naturally. We're afloat." Conway took a reviving puff on his pipe, set his hands to the sides of his chair and said, "Come and take a look at the view from here. From the bridge-walk. Passenger-view is several feet lower, not as good as this. Not that there's much to see."

Dillard shucked out of his equipment rapidly and expertly and clipped it away into its box, then rose and followed Conway on wobbly legs. It was obviously part of the captain's verbal small-change to deprecate the appearance of almost anything, but this time his apologies were justified. Apart from the desalination plant itself, there was nothing to see at all except rolling ocean. Take the man-made pyramid of steel away, Dillard thought, and one might just as well have been out at sea anywhere. On Earth, even. Then he corrected that. This sea was a different blue. Just how different he could not have said, but it was. And it smelled different, too.

"Certainly is warm," he said, loosening his poncho-string and shouldering it back to let the faint breeze strike his chest and arms. "How long do we stay here?"

"Twenty-four hours, about. You'll have time to go ashore, if you want."

"Ashore?"

"This way." Conway led him along the walk and around the curve of the ship's hull. "Over there, see? Joytown."

Dillard stared. The thing was about three miles away, perhaps more. It looked, and he shook his head as he strove for images to fit, like a great upturned dish, a dome with many facets, and it glittered in silver and gray and blue, catching the sunlight. It sat, rim to rim, in another dish that lay close to the water, and now that his eyes had adjusted to the strangeness of it, he saw dark orifices at regular intervals all around that lower dish.

"Joytown?" he echoed, only half-understanding. "I looked up this planet just before the trip, but this wasn't mentioned in the literature."

"It wouldn't be," Conway growled. "Officially it doesn't exist. If that sounds crazy to you, well, it is crazy. Look, just now I said the water-plant was anchored to the seabed, and so it is. But it also stands on tubular pylons, telescopic things so that it can go up and down with the tide. That is the way it was planned and built. Now, during the business of settling official rights and authorities and all that stuff, the standard old phrase, 'territorial rights,' got a thorough airing. You see, somebody has to take a responsible stand for the planet. You have to have some kind of law and order, after all. And it was decided, by a competent international court, that because the water-plant was in firm and permanent contact with solid ground, it qualified as 'territorial.' So, incidentally, does the Planetary Base and Embassy, over there, see?" Conway extended his arm and Dillard saw, about four miles away in the opposite direction, a slim spire of metal topped by an array of antennae.

"Then some joker, reading the proceedings very carefully,

realized that if you had a structure that was just anchored by cables, and was, technically, afloat, you had something that was outside territorial law altogether. It's been done before, of course. Ships on the high seas and all that kind of thing. Responsibility borne by the country of registration, by whatever flag they were sailing under. But here? There's no country to be registered with. That place there is outside any law, or regulation, or anything. And it's a goldmine, or a sink of iniquity, whichever way you care to look at it."

"That's pretty smart," Dillard said and grinned as the implications sank in. "A monopoly, too. I mean, for those who want to get off the ship, there's nowhere else to go. But I imagine most passengers will stay put rather than visit such a place?"

"Don't get me wrong now," Conway said hastily. "It's respectable—in spots. If that's what you want, you can get it. Peace and quiet, and the odd souvenir and so on. But if you fancy something else—well, you name it and they've got it. But it's strictly illegal. Or nonlegal, I should say. As a matter of fact"—and he lowered his voice to a confidential murmur—"we are all in on it. We bring in the stuff for them, supplies, furnishings, food, liquor, and they pay well. Charge plenty too, just in case you were thinking of trying it. Might be an experience for your records, eh?"

"Not that kind." Dillard shook his head. "Bright lights, noise and organized vice leave me cold. I could afford it. I have a healthy ex-card, but it's not my line at all. In any case I have something else to do."

"Ashore? There isn't anywhere else."

"Yes there is." Dillard grinned and led the way back around the bulge to where they could again see the waterplant. "There. I'm going to call on the big boss who runs that lot, one Dr. Edmund Stanley."

"You know him? Friend of yours?"

"Not exactly a friend." Dillard spaced the words carefully. "I used to know him, long ago. I have a few things to tell—"

"Sir!" Richter came into view with a flapping paper. "Would you pass this watch-list now. And the fuel-up orders." Dillard stood back as Conway took and scowled over the business of paper work. He turned to look at the metal pyramid of the water-plant, and thought about Dr. Stanley. They were cold and unkind thoughts. Dillard bore malice to very few people and never for very long, but Stanley was an exception. The score with him was grievous and of long standing. Doing his homework, as he did thoroughly before taking any assignment, he had been stirred to discover that name and to realize that here was an unexpected chance to settle an old score. His memory was dredging up Stanley's sharp-edged and infuriating voice when he became aware of a new note in the murmur between Conway and his first officer.

"Never seen one before, Mr. Richter? I can well believe it. So far as I know they only have half a dozen ships altogether."

"News to me that the Veenies had any ships at all!" Richter growled, and Dillard swung around to see both men staring away to the left, toward Billet Twelve. Then he saw what they stared at, and stared in his turn, because this was a ship quite unlike any he had ever seen. He inserted himself into the conversation with a question.

"Did you say Veenie?"

"That's right, Mr. Dillard, a Venusian ship. Clumsy looking barge. I'll get these orders out right away, sir." Richter strode off. Dillard moved to belly up to the guard rail.

"I'm no expert on spaceships," he said. "All I've seen are those we use on film or projected background shots. And in the newscasts, of course. But I never saw anything like that before. And I didn't know Venus had ships."

"Odd, that," Conway murmured, around his pipe-stem. "Typical though. The way people would rather not know things that are unpleasant. And, of course, the Venusians aren't given to advertising themselves, which is natural. But that's one of their ships, all right. And why not? They discovered this planet. One of their ships was the first one ever to splash down here, and it was the Venusians who built the basic foundations for everything. Water-plant, Port Office, Planetary Base and Embassy—and Joytown."

"You mean—Venus owns this place?"

"No no! That's not on. Earth government wouldn't stand still for that; you know that as well as I do. No, they just found it, laid the foundations, then turned it over to Earth. But they collect a hefty kickback. I can only tell you what I've heard, but it runs something like fifteen percent of all profits, after expenses and taxes. And that is something, when you realize how many ships come in and out of here."

A Venusian ship! Dillard stared, and the story of Venus, as it had been told him in history lessons, made a background to his wonder.

"I wonder what they're really like," he muttered, and Conway chuckled.

"You've heard the stories, I'll bet. You'd be a fool to believe them. Humans don't mutate into monsters in five generations. Of course, when they were deported a century and a half ago it was fashionable for everybody to believe they were monsters already. But they were human then, and they're human now."

Dillard felt a trifle disconcerted and hoped it didn't show. Despite himself he *had* been thinking of long skinny humanoid "things" with greenish skin and goggling eyes. Only a couple of years ago Epic had done a space-opera tape with creatures like that in it, denizens of a warm planet perpetually swathed in vaporous clouds. The script hadn't *said* it was Venus, but the implication was there.

"They must have changed a bit," he protested. "After all, five generations in a hot house atmosphere and without UV must have done something to them."

"Why don't you pay them a visit and find out?" Conway suggested, and he spoke half in jest, but the suggestion lodged and caught fire in Dillard's mind. It provoked the twin conflicting emotions of desire and fear. It would be a hell of a scoop to get a sensory recording of the interior of a genuine Venusian ship, and the real "presence" of living, breathing Venusians. But it would be, even in prospect, a terrifying experience too. He could feel the squeamish shivers just thinking about it. It was the trained one-tenth of him that turned eagerly to Conway and say, "Why not? If it's possible. Is it?"

The other nine-tenths of him quailed and shrank away, screaming soundlessly against such a foolhardy undertaking. Conway must have seen something of the turmoil underneath, for his grin faded.

"You really work at it, don't you, son. You'll drive yourself over the edge one of these times. But, if you really do want to go aboard that ship, I might be able to swing it. Can't do any harm to ask, and there's no reason why they would refuse a request from another ship. You want that?"

Dillard couldn't back down now. "If you would," he said.

34

"I'd be very grateful. How long will it take? Do I have time to call on Dr. Stanley first?"

"Look." Conway consulted the chronometer on his wrist. "To get to the water-plant laboratory anyway you'll need a hydrofoil—"

"But we're alongside!"

"Yes, but you can't go strolling about the de-sal gear. That's against regs. You'll need a 'foil. You step inside and ask Lieutenant Rogers to call one for you, on the radio. I'll get a signal off to that ship, and I'll pass the reply along to the 'foil, all right? And good luck. Excuse me!" He stood away to lean over the rail and bawl down to someone far below an adjectival suggestion to shake it up a bit with the qualified hose-pipe.

Dillard went inside and over to where Lieutenant Rogers was busy with her radio board. As she looked up coldly he asked, "Miss Rogers, would you call a hydrofoil for me, please?"

"There's one coming alongside right now, Mr. Dillard, requested by one of the other passengers. If you're quick you can catch it. Shall I ask for it to be held?"

"Please!" He nodded. "I'm on my way." And as he turned to run he heard her call out after him, "Gangway Three!"

He hurried, down the ladders and across the connecting-tunnel into the Section Three passenger quarters, and thought as he hastened that it was just his luck, or her luck, whichever you like, that his request should be so very promptly and efficiently granted. He could imagine her saying to herself, "That's how we do it in the Service, civilian!" And just when he had a good legitimate excuse for talking to her!

III

HE KEPT HIS trivial complaining mood as he trotted down the gangway to water level, as a device to avoid thinking about the awesome thing he had let himself in for, but trivia receded into limbo as he halted there and got this new perspective on things. All at once he felt horribly tiny. The great up-thrust mass of the ship loomed over him from behind. To the right the massive water-bag container bulked grossly. In front of him the twin-hulled hydrofoil surged and strained against the rolling waves. And all the rest was just sea, vast, restless and green-blue. In that moment something of the immensity of it came to him. A whole planet, as big as Earth nearly, and all water! He gulped, eyed the pitching hydrofoil, clung to the rail of the gangway and tried to estimate one heaving motion against another. Just a step, that's all it took. He nerved himself, leaned, stepped off as the foil was rising, and almost fell as his leg gave under the strain. Then he had made it, and was aboard.

The two hulls were flat-topped and easy to walk on, with seats ranged athwart in fours. The pilot, in the stern space, gave him an impatient look and held out a hand.

"Card! Where to, mister?"

"To the desalination plant laboratory." Dillard handed over his credit card, watched it being slotted into the meter and scanned, took it back and stowed it in his pants pocket. The pilot gestured.

"You sit up front. Stay midships. Helps to keep trim."

Dillard interpreted that as a request to distribute his weight somewhere along the center line of the craft, and staggered away forward. Then he saw someone else already seated, and remembered, belatedly, that there was someone else traveling with him. She had settled herself on the very front seat. He weaved his way to slip down beside her just as the engines cut in with a cough and roar, and a fine spray-shower rattled off the transparent bow-shield. She gave him one quick glance, then edged fractionally away to give him room.

"Hope I didn't keep you waiting long," he offered. "I got down here as quick as I could." His sideways look told him that he had seen her once or twice before, on the trip, but only at a distance.

"You haven't gained anything by hurrying," she said coldly. "You might as well have waited a few moments for the regular ferry."

"Ferry?" he echoed, not understanding, and she gestured with her arm as if making a sword-thrust. He saw a much larger craft, by the spray-wake a cushion-effect vessel, moving rapidly in toward the gangway they were now leaving behind. And there was a crowd of passengers streaming down the gangway, ready to board the thing. The ferry.

"But that, surely, will be going to Joytown," he objected, drawing the obvious conclusion.

"Where else?" she demanded. "Now you're going to have to wait until the pilot has put *me* down first."

"But I'm not going to Joytown. I'm going to the water-plant."

"Oh!" Her voice, cold before, became hard now, as she turned around in her seat to stare at him. "You are? May I ask why?"

"I don't see where it's any of your business," he retorted, meeting her stare with a frown. Her eyes were dark blue, very intent, and her face was regular, a trifle too square-jawed for beauty, but attractive. At least, he temporized, it could be attractive without the gimlet-eye stare. Jet-black hair, close-cut and glossy with health, clung like a cap to her head. Her dark blue cape was caught at her throat with a white metal clasp in the shape of a bow. The glitter and the dark cloth emphasized the clear pallor of her skin. Her eyes stayed steady.

"I'm afraid I shall have to make it my business," she said, putting out a hand to grasp the seat-back as the 'foil began to surge into the waves.

"I don't see why. Who are you, and what business is it of yours that I want to visit the water-plant laboratory?" Dillard could feel a cold wall of defense around her, and a sense of hard power that went strangely with her amply feminine form.

"My name is Mara Hunt. The water-plant is very much my business, mister—?"

"Dillard. Den Dillard."

"Mr. Dillard. I am on my way to take up a post as Dr. Stanley's assistant. He is the scientist in charge of the desalination plant laboratory."

"I know. He's the man I want to see."

"Indeed!" The defense wall was almost tangible now. "What are you, Mr. Dillard, a newsman?"

"Hardly." He slapped his kit-box affectionately. "I'm a sensor-man. Not that it has anything to do with anything. My business with Stanley is purely personal and private. Needn't concern you at all."

"I find that hard to believe."

"That's up to you." Dillard ducked as a running wave spouted foam up against the plastic shield, and began to feel mild irritation. The same gust of wind caught her cape and sent it fluttering back over her shoulders, to reveal a torso as pale as her face but beautifully contoured. The odd contrast added to his irritation. A woman with a figure like that, but cold and ruthless, didn't seem right to him. Out of his irritation he said, "You're not all that easy to believe yourself, Miss Hunt. Assistant to Dr. Stanley? I checked up on this business as far as I could before coming this far, and the way I heard it, Stanley's appointment is one of those things, a sinecure. Figurehead. People who crave a little peace and quiet to do some personal research and get paid for it, those are the kind who land a job like that. Right? So for what would Stanley need an assistant?"

As far as he could tell she wasn't shaken in the least by his veiled accusation. If anything the glint in her eyes grew harder.

"You're not a scientist," she said, "so it's rather pointless trying to explain. But, truly, Dr. Stanley has run into something exciting in the field of water chemistry and needs assistance. If only to keep worries and routine chores off his mind while he works."

Dillard was tempted to retort, "I am neither a worry nor a routine chore," but instead he muttered, "I'm going to see him anyway. To talk to him for a few minutes. You going to try to stop me?"

That remark earned him the kind of smile he could well have done without. There was mirth in it, of the kind that an adult might feel when faced with a truculent child. It said, more plainly than words, that she could brush him aside without exertion, if she wanted to. But she said, mildly, "Very well, see him, so long as it *is* only for a few minutes." Then she turned her face forward and stared into the breeze, letting it ripple her cape stiffly back over her shoulders. Snubbed and smarting, Dillard looked away, and found himself staring full at the mysterious Venusian ship, now slipping past as the small craft circled it to reach the inlet lane to the water-plant center. That ship looked enormous from here, on the water level, and he felt a cold chill as he remembered what he had let himself in for. It loomed hugely, totally different in shape from anything he would have classed as a spaceship. It was hard to believe such an awkward thing could fly at all.

Venture Three, now, like any other cargo-and-passenger ship, was of the triple tube construction, three mighty cylin-

ders joined by a set of Y-sections, where cargo, human
or otherwise, rode in reasonable comfort, lifted, powered
and driven by the drive-and-power unit which was a slim-
mer cylinder up the center. You could think of it as engine
and crew quarters, plus cabins all around, and it was a
logical arrangement. Police, military and courier ships, of
course, were just the one cylinder. But this Venusian wasn't
even a cylinder at all, nor anything remotely like it. Dillard scratched his memory until it yielded up the term
he wanted. Teardrop, that was it. An upended drop, like
a huge metal pear standing on its stem. He scowled up at it,
trying to rationalize the design in his mind as the 'foil
scuttered by.

Drive, he knew, consisted of fusion-power plant, reaction-
mass for the uncomfortable business of planet-fall, and Pauli-
drive for the space-bending leaps in between stars. And
the drive unit as a whole, plus the auxiliaries, had to lie
along the center of gravity of the whole thing. So, in this
ship, it must run right up the middle like a core, but you
couldn't tell that from the bulging top-heavy outside. This
thing seemed to wallow in the water like some obscene
growth. And yet, he mused, it had buoyancy, much more
than *Venture Three*, which would have submerged almost
out of sight had it not been for the magnetic girdle that
held it up. Dillard nodded to himself as the answer came.
Buoyancy was a logical thing to build into a ship that had
to land and take off from the swampy semiliquid surface of
Venus. And for a water-planet like this, too. He recalled
Conway saying that Venusians had discovered and opened
up this planet. And why not? A place like this would be
more homelike to them than to any ordinary human.

That phrase led his thoughts into a shivery byway. Just
how un-human were the Veenies, after five generations? He'd
never seen one, nor had anyone of his acquaintance. Were
they really monsters? Conway hadn't thought so.

"Ever see a Venusian ship before, Mr. Dillard?" Mara
Hunt's cool question broke in on his thoughts, and he turned
to see her blue eyes mocking him.

"No. I didn't even know the Veenies had ships until
Captain Conway told me. You seem to know." Her expression
stayed scornful, and a wild notion came to him. "Just so
I won't put my foot right in my mouth," he said, "you're
not one of them, are you?" Now for the first time he saw

the ice break. She laughed, and he was astonished at the transformation.

"I am not, Mr. Dillard. Nor are you. I've met quite a few Venusians, and you obviously haven't, or you wouldn't have said that."

"You mean, they really are different from us? I've heard all sorts of things. Who hasn't? But if you've actually met some—are they really tall and skinny with hairless heads and green skin?"

"I said you weren't a scientist." She laughed again, delightfully, and shook her head. "They are as human as you or I. And why not? After all, it is only one hundred and fifty years since we put them away on Venus."

The "we" rankled suddenly. "Not me!" he denied. "Oh, by association, if you like. I will own that kind of guilt, for what it's worth, but I am not responsible for what my predecessors did all that time ago."

"Not as a person, no," she agreed. "But then, neither were the individual persons of that time responsible. They never are. The guilt slips away onto the anonymous shoulders of some government or group, always. Mankind, as an abstraction, can and does commit crimes that no individual would ever dream of. And, as you say, it was a long time ago. You are not guilty. And those people there"—she pointed a sword-like arm again, at the towering ship—"are not responsible, either. But they have to live with it. They are the descendants of those people we banished all that time ago. They have suffered. You can't expect them to shrug it off quite as easily as you do."

"Suffered?" he echoed, stung by her mockery. "Come now, they survived, didn't they? They should have been executed for what they did, no doubt of that. Never before can there have been a criminal group so well aware of what they were doing. And when they were rounded up they admitted guilt, expected to be executed. But no, they were dumped on Venus with ample survival gear, and left. And they survived. So let's not go too strong on the suffering!"

"You said that very well," she retorted, still scornful. "Even on Earth, where the various races of men have learned to live in the most unlikely spots, the mild temperate areas are still favorite. A man *can* live in the desert, on top of a mountain, or among ice and snow, but at what cost?

And it's worse just as soon as he knows there are better places. When he knows he is being robbed. The Venusians were robbed, and they resent it. They have learned to live with it, just as their deported ancestors learned to live with perpetual humidity and swamp-heat, in half-darkness, but you can't expect them to like it, and they don't."

"But they've adapted now, surely?" he insisted, unwilling to surrender all his myths of queer people.

"I said you were no scientist." She was openly laughing at him now, and he had time to marvel at how attractive she could be, even while her scorn irritated him. "In five or so generations no true adaptation is possible. But there has been a degree of selection-pressure, which is not quite the same thing. As a result, Venusians—and I have met and spoken to many—tend to be leaner than average. You can't carry a lot of body-bulk when you have little or no opportunity to dissipate body-heat by surface evaporation. They tend to be extremely fit and healthy, in a smoothly efficient way. They are pale, with bleached hair, because they encounter virtually no ultraviolet. Because of constant humidity and a lessened rate of oxygen exchange they tend to be deep-chested, with a large lung capacity, and low-pitched voices. They swim as much and as readily as we walk. And they have large violet eyes."

She added the final sentence in a flat calm tone that caught him for a moment. Then he snorted.

"You're putting me on. Big violet eyes?"

Her lip curled in a derisive grin. "You'd be an easy man to confuse, Mr. Dillard, if such was my intention. In fact that last item is absolutely true. And fascinating. Geneticists, those few who have been able to observe the phenomenon, are highly intrigued. Sight is the youngest of the senses, and, it seems, the most flexible. I've heard a number of theories, but without a flow of volunteers for study they will remain just that. Apparently the human eye does have a capacity to detect ultraviolet, and as there is virtually none at surface level on Venus, their eyes have become considerably more sensitive to what little there is. We are violet-blind by comparison."

By now they were far away from the ship that had started the whole subject, and circling around the stark end of a steel arm, to enter a long and dark waterway, bounded on both sides by the great bulks of plastic water-tanks, and roofed over with spidery grids of girder-work. At the far end, standing back from a metal platform and landing steps stood a tall round tower of bright chrome steel. At the very top the chrome gave way to windows. The 'foil slowed now as it made its way in and alongside the steps. The two passengers rose and went back to the stern end to dismount.

"You'll hang on for me," Dillard said. "I don't expect to be more than about half an hour."

"Right. What about you, Miss?"

Mara Hunt gripped her traveling-case firmly, extended her card and said, "Check me out. I expect to be staying here." Getting her card back from the machine she stepped ashore and strode away toward the tower, leaving Dillard to follow. The landing platform had a slope, and then a barrier with a door, beyond which was dark and weed-smells, and round tunnels leading off in many directions. He squinted through one in passing and saw a stretching expanse of catwalks and pipes. All around this dark enclosure were curving pipes, color-coded in some systematic way that meant nothing to him, and a great number of massive wheel-valves, each with its motor and buttons. There was no one in sight, but the whole structure shook delicately to the throb of some mighty machine laboring somewhere nearby. Right in the center of the cavern stood a polished curved surface and elevator gates. Dillard felt relief at the sight. He hadn't fancied lugging his kit-box up several flights of steps, and he was far too attached to it to leave it anywhere about.

With her palm on the call-button Miss Hunt asked, "Aren't you going to record anything of this, Mr. Dillard? It must be a novel experience!"

"Not right now. Maybe, after I've done my business with Stanley I'll have a scan over the plant. Depends." The elevator came and they stepped in, sending it skyward.

"You still haven't said why you want to contact Dr. Stanley. Do you know him at all?"

"I once knew him only too well." Dillard had to exert control over his voice, now that the crucial moment was close. "He cost me three years of life, three precious years."

Her fine black brows came down in a hard line of unbelief. "Surely not," she objected. "You must have the wrong man."

"Not a chance. I checked, here and all the way back.

Dr. Edmund Stanley was on the Vocational Advisory Board when I came up for assignment to university. Because of him I had to slog through three lousy years of general science. I didn't want it. I said so, good and loud, but he had the casting voice and made a big play about my academic record, and potential, and all the rest of it. I caught it. I suffered, because of him."

It was her turn to say, "Oh come, Mr. Dillard. Suffered? Three years of general science couldn't hurt anybody."

"You don't understand, any more than he did."

"That's the oldest craven cry in the world, that nobody understands."

"Go ahead and sneer!" he invited angrily. "Maybe I couldn't explain it myself, at the time. Not properly. But I've grown some since then."

"You're trying to say you're not interested in the facts of life?"

"I knew you didn't understand. Of course I'm interested in things. I was then. I still am. But what he couldn't understand then, and you won't now is that I'm not interested in facts. Not minutiae, details, about things. They only get in the way, for me. I'm curious, just as much as anybody and more than most, but I don't want to know *about* things. I want to know the thing itself, to see and feel and experience it, not a collection of data and symbols and explanations. Take this elevator. You probably know exactly how it works, a lot of stuff about cables and motors and so on. I couldn't care less. I feel I'm being lifted up, going up. I feel it. I don't care how it is done. I'm sensing what is actually happening . . ." He caught himself and let the sentence fade as he saw the baffled look on her face. It was quite impossible to explain to her the difference between living and knowing about life. The explanation didn't sound very convincing even to himself. All he knew was that it was true, that Stanley, by insisting on three years of general science for the young Dennis Dillard, had created a monstrous barrier of data between that sensitive soul and the life he wanted to sense directly.

"Anyway," he muttered, "I made it to where I am now despite him."

"And where are you now?"

"Top man in my field," he told her. "I doubt if there

are a hundred really good sensor-people altogether. The backwoods are thick with hacks, sure, but the real artists are few. And I'm up around the top, in an income-bracket Dr. Stanley will never reach. And I aim to tell him just that, to rub his nose right in it."

"Dear me!" she murmured. "All this, just to gratify a childish spite?"

"I quote you," he growled. "I had to live through it, and with it, and fight my way out of it. No thanks to him."

"I doubt if he will even remember you."

"You may leave that safely to me," he said. "I'll remind him!"

The elevator hissed to a halt, the doors slid open and they moved out into a small but bright hallway, anonymous in muted green plastic. Of three doors, one stood half-open, affording a sight of a domestic interior, an automated kitchen, a dining room and, beyond, a living room. The other doors, closed, bore legends. On one LABORATORY; the other, OFFICE. Dillard looked, and sniffed.

"This is living?" he demanded caustically. "This dump?"

Miss Hunt ignored him. She seemed to be listening for something. Then she moved away to the door marked OFFICE, and knocked, waited a moment, then pushed open the door and went in. Dillard stayed where he was. Imagine being stuck in this monastic retreat for two years' service! There was nothing to be done, he knew that. The desalination plant was virtually self-operating, and what little manipulation there was to do was done by a staff of semiskilled laborers under a technical foreman. Connect, disconnect, check levels and output, make out balance sheets, monthly reports, and pass them along here for Dr. Stanley to initial. And that was all he was for. A figurehead. So all right, he had all day and forever to potter about with research into water chemistry, good luck to it! Dillard couldn't imagine anything he would enjoy less. But what gave him particular joy was his knowledge that this post was regarded as very much a backwater, a convenient slot for some third-rate test tube waver who would never rate anything better. The great Dr. Stanley!

He saw Miss Hunt come out of the office again and cross, with quick strides, to the laboratory door. Again she knocked, then went on in. All at once Dillard felt uneasy. It was too quiet. The place didn't feel right. He put the thought away with the rationalization that it was simply because he was being kept waiting for his moment of triumph, but it came back. He stepped to the laboratory door and looked in. It was full of gadgetry but empty of persons, apart from Miss Hunt, who stood now in the middle of strewn apparatus and was scowling to herself. All at once she marched back to the door.

"There's something wrong," she said, brushed past him and went on to the third and last door. Dillard followed on her heels. The living space, too, was empty. Miss Hunt wasted only a moment in there, then came out, hard-eyed.

"There's something wrong," she repeated. "He's not here. And he should be. Not only is there nowhere for him to go, the rules are quite strict. He is not supposed to quit this space unless he makes special arrangements or leaves some word. I don't like it."

"Maybe he left word with the foreman?"

"It's possible. I'll check." She marched swiftly now back to the office, Dillard following, to see her sit down at the visor-phone and begin dialing. His uneasiness returned tenfold.

IV

LOOKING OVER her shoulder he found time to wonder how she came to know such a lot about rules here. That thought led to another. She, from what he had seen, was hardly the assistant type. Much more likely to be dominant. He didn't fancy being Stanley and having to boss her around. As the visor screen opened into activity he was on the point of shifting allegiance, going over to Stanley's side. He was, after all, a man, and probably hated bossy females as much as any other man. The screen showed a jowly-faced man of about forty, registering surprise.

"Jacoby here. What's up, Doc? Uh? Sorry, Miss thought you were Doc Stanley. Who . . ."

"I am speaking from Dr. Stanley's office. My name is Mara Hunt. I have just arrived to take up a position as Dr. Stanley's assistant. But he is not here. Have you any idea where he might have gone?"

"He ain't there?" Jacoby scratched his sagging jaw and frowned in bafflement. "He must be. You sure?"

"Yes, I'm sure. Unless there are more than three subdivisions here. Laboratory, office, living area. I've checked those."

"That's it, then. But why would he leave? And where would he go?"

"I'm asking you!"

"Yeah. But—unless he went for a stroll around the works. And why would he do that?"

"Will you make inquiries, please?"

"What kind? Oh!" Jacoby's face struggled to register eager desire to help. "I'll pass the word around the gang to look out for him."

"Do that. And would you please tell me who I should get in touch with, in case this is something serious?"

"Huh?" Jacoby was floored now.

"Who is the supreme authority on Hydro? Law and order?"

"Oh! That'll be the Port Base. It's a radio number. You want Port Admiral Bredon. But what can he do?"

"I'll know that when I ask him. Please make your inquiries and call me back, here." She cut the call vigorously, then expelled a breath of exasperation. "The man's an idiot!" She swiveled her seat around to stare up at Dillard, looking right through him as if he were furniture. "There's something very wrong here. Very wrong."

"Maybe he went for a stroll and fell in the water." Dillard was nudged into facetiousness by the way she ignored him. It got her attention. She drilled holes in him with her blue eyes.

"That was not funny, Mr. Dillard."

"Not to you. But look, this is a big layout, and why wouldn't he go for a stroll around it? Maybe he wanted a close-up look at one of the . . ."

"I will repeat, for your benefit." Her tone would have curdled milk. "This plant is sealed; is fully automatic; is so designed that human contact with any of the preparatory stages is avoided, is discouraged. There are a series of monitor stages that permit close examination of any part, a relay of tappings that permit an extracted sample from any stage. There is absolutely no reason whatever for Dr. Stanley to leave this area, even if the rules did not specifically forbid such a thing. It is one of the conditions."

"You mean he couldn't even get away to pay a visit, maybe, to an old friend on one of the ships? After all, I came to call on *him!*"

"He could leave, but only by arrangement with someone responsible. You don't seem to realize, Mr. Dillard, that this water-plant is vital to Hydro."

"Maybe he left a note of some kind."

"That is extremely unlikely. Jacoby would have known."

"Can't do any harm to take a look. There might be some indication . . ."

"I shall do that, of course." She surged up from the chair, unfastened the neck clasp of her cape and swirled it into a drape over the chair back. "But there's no reason for you to linger now, Mr. Dillard. This is my business. I can handle it." As she stood bolt-erect, assuming authority as if by heritage, he was spurred by some irrational demon to oppose her.

"I'll help you," he offered. "After all, Stanley was something to me, too. Not an old friend, exactly, but something."

"Are you deliberately trying to be obnoxious, Mr. Dillard?" She glared, edging forward as if to crowd him out by her physical presence. In that one instant he had the peculiar sensation of being able to see beyond the barrier she had erected between them. As an armor it was chill and unyielding, but inside that was a flame, a tremendous vitality, and he had the irrational conviction that if he did anything to crack that shield her inner self would explode out and consume him in a flash. He knew abysmal fear, and fought it.

"I'm just trying to help," he protested. "What's wrong with that?"

"A blind man will help me to look?"

"I'm not blind. Thanks to your Dr. Stanley, I can even find my way to and fro in a laboratory with some skill."

The phone squealed for her attention. She turned, hit the switch, and sat. Jacoby's face came on, his eyes widening, then shifting upward with a visible effort to concentrate on her face.

"I've checked around," he announced. "All the gang. Not a sign. Never have seen him wandering around, come to that. I have also checked with water-taxi center, and all ships presently on planet. Nothing. You want to call Port Base, now?"

"Not immediately. I want to look around here more. Thank

you, Mr. Jacoby. I'll keep in touch." The screen blanked again and she scowled at it. "That man was agitated about something. . . ."

Dillard chuckled, and she whirled on him abruptly.

"No, wait!" He put up a hand to halt the fierce words on her tongue. "Don't blame Jacoby too much. Lord knows how long he's been here, or how long since he saw—what you just showed him!"

Her black brows came down in that hard line again, then, all at once, she glanced down at her naked torso and back up at Dillard.

"You don't mean . . . ? But how ridiculous! We're not back in the dark ages!"

"No? It's my guess you haven't had much to do with people of Jacoby's class, or you wouldn't say that."

"Class? That old myth. Class distinctions went out before you and I were born, Dillard. And don't try to argue with me, either. I have degrees in socio-dynamics."

Dillard drew a breath in readiness for a hot retort, then let it ease out again. What was the use? This, he thought, was what science did for you. All the facts and formulae, the studies, the conclusions—but no actual sense of experience. She had done her social science courses, maybe even some field work to get her diploma or whatever, but she had never *been* lower-class, as he had. With her background and abilities, she could never know what it felt like to be inferior, insecure, unimportant to anyone, dependent on a web-work of simple values and shallow certainties, needing something to lean on, some given set of "right" things. She would never know, for instance, that unless a woman had inbred self-confidence, tremendous courage, or total innocence, it would be a physical impossibility for her to discard her protective clothing in the presence of strangers. She would never know, because it wasn't in the book, or in any formula, but was something you felt. This was the class that still existed in this so-called classless society, the division between the self-confidently aware and those who were just not up to it.

"Forget it," he muttered, and began unzipping his kit-box. "Where do we start looking first?"

"And what do you think you're going to do?"

"Make a recording, of course."

"A recording of what?" she demanded.

"Of what it feels like," he said patiently, as he clipped the headband into place and snuggled the neck-contact firmly down, "to search through a strange laboratory for clues to a mysterious disappearance. Thing like that is bound to come in handy for all kinds of story-material."

She looked unconvinced. "What kind of recording?"

"And you a scientist!" he jeered gently. "Mean to say you don't know? Back on the boat I told you I was a sensorman. Didn't I?" He felt a small triumphant glow of superiority. First her socio-dynamic innocence, now this. "My apparatus records, on a wire, all the physiological and emotional reactions I feel during the session. Not pictures, nor yet sounds, except for the lead-signature, which I will now do." He thumbed a switch, held the box close, and recited, "Conducting a search for possible clues to a mysterious, possibly sinister, disappearance. Laboratory interior. Male subject. Also present and assisting, one attractive female personally involved with missing person. Chief stress on curiosity, sense of mystery, novel surroundings. No immediate awareness of personal danger. Den Dillard recording." He released the switch, cocked an eyebrow at her. "That will cue in the technicians when they come to use the wire. Of course they will boost this or that, play down the other, just as they want it, that's their job. All I get is the raw reactions. Now, you'd better scan this office, and maybe the living section. I'll do the laboratory."

"Why did you say 'sinister' like that?" she demanded.

"Why not?" he countered, with a shrug. "Any laboratory is slightly sinister, for me. Look, I examine my feelings. I know them, I use them, but I do not analyze and edit them. I'm an artist. It's a poor old word, but it happens to be the only one that fits."

In some strange way it was as if her barriers had come down. She looked at him oddly. "You said 'attractive,' meaning me. Was that—just for the technicians, or did you mean it? You said Jacoby was bothered because he saw me—uncovered. Does that affect you, too?"

He looked her up and down deliberately, not unkindly, all the way from her glossy black hair to her glossy shoes where they showed from skin tight dark blue pants, and back up again, taking in all her sculptured contours. He saw a faint pink start up under his scrutiny.

"Of course I'm affected. Whether you've stopped to

think about it or not, that's what it's for, isn't it?"

She started a denial but he put up a palm. "Maybe not in any deliberate sense, no. But you register on me just by being here. Just as I register on you. So I react. *How* I react is something else again, is up to me. But, because I am what I am, I'm aware of reacting. Most people pretend not to notice, or try to ignore, things they can't handle. Not me. It's my job!" He frowned over the futility of language, caught at an analogy. "Look, a man who writes a cookbook, with all the specific details, is a scientist. The man who takes the book and from it concocts a tasty dish, is a technician. But neither one is a cook. A cook is one who just goes ahead with the ingredients and processes, by feel, and produces a tasty meal. Who *does* it. A scientist knows what. An artist knows how. You can't mix 'em."

All at once she smiled, and it was a totally different smile from any that had gone before. "Your world is completely alien to me, Dillard, but I'm obliged to you for trying to enlighten me. And flattered. I've been complimented before, but never quite like that." The unguarded moment lingered just a breath longer, then she switched, briskly, to efficiency. "All right, you take the laboratory. I don't know what you're looking for, but if you see anything unusual, call me."

The laboratory was easily the largest room of the three, with two long benches splitting it into three slices, and a shorter bench taking up almost all the far wall space under a solid bank of glass windows. Dillard spent a long moment staring out of those windows, out over the pipe-and-girder pyramid of which he was now the apex. *Venture Three* over there. The Venusian ship on the left. Away in the distance, Joytown. Other ships lying still. Far away over there the spike-spire of Port Base headquarters. And where was Dr. Stanley? Somehow, as he swung away from the window and began surveying the sparkling glass and chrome, it didn't seem to matter anymore to Dillard. His desire to confront his one-time teacher with his present success seemed childish now. Adjusting his input controls with the casual ease of long experience, he started a methodical tour. Most of the hardware was familiar enough to be given names, and he had no intention of lingering over it anyway. If Stanley had left any clues at all, they would more likely be among the paper work in the filing pigeonholes which lined the outside walls. So he moved fairly briskly along the benches, going through the motions of stopping to inspect every now and then, simply to gather the skin-sense effects of being close to complex glassware and gadgetry.

The equipment showed all the signs of being under the control of a tidy and orderly mind. Dillard found his thoughts wandering despite himself. Odd about Miss Hunt. Highly intelligent and educated, yet utterly naïve about subjective matters. Oddly, too, that was true of so many women. One tended to accept the old assumption that the female was closer to unconscious and intuitive matters, but it wasn't true. He'd discovered that for himself. You take, for instance, that matter of dress. By tradition it was a woman's subject, and yet not one woman in a thousand had any real feel for it. They went as fashion dictated, hoping to put on or take off some attribute or other along with this, that, or the other arrangement of clothes. And it wasn't like that at all. The effect, the charm or otherwise, was inside, and it came through no matter how much, or how little, a woman wore. There she was, now, in nothing more than a tight-fitting pair of dark blue pants. And she had a shape to catch your breath. But that's all it was, a shape and a movement. Like an elaborately beautiful lamp, not switched on.

Dillard halted, shook his head, then found what it was that was catching his attention. Water trickling, gently and steadily. He looked, and saw a thin stream of water jetting from a pipe and trickling into a basin. An oversight, among such orderliness. He put out his hand, looking about for the tap-source, intending to shut it off. Then he came fully alert and stared. There was no tap. He traced the pipe back with his eye. It was the drain-outlet for a glassite tank. One wall of that tank was a grayish silver screen, square, about nine inches a side, with the water forming on it constantly like heavy sweat, then coagulating and running down into the bottom of the tank. Running away. But where was it coming from? He moved a step or two, to get beyond that screen, where he could see the other side. And it didn't make any sense at all.

He knew what he was looking at. That wasn't the problem. In common with almost everyone else of his generation, Dillard knew something of the Yatsu-Kono desalination process. He remembered, wryly, that Stanley had carefully omitted to assign him a paper on *that,* because it was so fundamentally easy. And this thing was a miniature model of the plant. The duplicate of it stood in every high school laboratory on the face of the Earth. The reverse of the condenser screen, where he was now staring, was a dark mass of allotropic carbon-on-copper, shimmering under a maze of hair-fine silver threads of a printed circuit. And the whole thing stood boldly on a solid block of clear plastic. Fine! But where was the input? Dillard scowled, scratched his jaw, walked back to stare, then came to his second position again. As far as his memory served, this was almost exactly half as thick as the conventional unit ought to be. There should be as much again, on this side, with a water supply of some kind. He stared, in imagination hearing the thin acid of Stanley's voice saying, "Don't just stare, boy! Explain!"

"The hell with it!" he grumbled and moved on. Some new refinement or other, no doubt. Just the sort of thing Stanley would delight in. His mind pulled up for him all the details he had so unwillingly learned so long ago. Water, the wonder substance, had become one of those examples so dear to the heart of science-philosophers, a perfect instance of one chance discovery leading to a whole new insight into a whole clutch of problems. Water, the weird stuff that everyone took for granted except those few who tried to explain it. The only substance, for instance, that becomes *less* dense when it changes from liquid to solid. And at the other end of the scale it was equally perverse. You heated it and it got hotter, up to a point. But beyond that point it got no hotter at all, no matter how much heat you poured into it. Instead it transformed into a gas, at the *same* temperature! You called that "latent heat," in order to have a name for something you couldn't explain.

And so on, until the late nineteen sixties, when certain scientists began investigating the notion that perhaps liquids have structure. At this same period there was a terrific pressure to discover some cheap and efficient way of desalinating water, because the whole of human civilization was facing an acute shortage of this hitherto taken for granted commodity. Then the key breakthrough, in the Yatsu-Kono laboratories, by a couple of scientists who were innocently investigating the precise nature of osmosis—or why does a water molecule eagerly migrate from a weak solution into a dense one through a suitable membrane? The answer they found—or refound—was that water is not just simply H_2O, but is in fact a long chain polymer of the same basic formula, linked into complex knots by a strange and little-understood thing called the "hydrogen bond."

And then all sorts of oddities started falling into place. This was why water had such a high boiling point, for instance. By analogy it should have been slightly lower than a similar liquid, hydrogen sulphide, which has a higher molecular weight, yet it was one hundred and sixty degrees higher! That was where all the heat went. And why it expanded on freezing, because the knotted skeins of polymer had to straighten out and regularize into crystals. And this, also, was why a long chain molecule could slip through a permeable membrane like an eel, whereas a compound molecule had bumps and knots in it. And, of course, by this period in the history of science, there were people who knew quite a lot about polymerization and its effects. So, in very little time after, there was a well-developed technology for stripping the bumps away from water—otherwise to be called desalination. And, as a stupendously serendipitous bonus, if you knew how to depolymerize water—and they did—you got, for free, quite a lot of energy released. Water to drink. Water to burn! The ideal fuel.

The facts rattled around in Dillard's head, threatening to spill over into the second advent of space flight, socio-ecological revolutions, the banishment of the Wicked Politicians to Venus, and he growled under his breath. Facts! What the hell did he want with facts? Epic Dramatapes were paying him to get emotions, sensations, reality—not textbook data! He came to the end of the bench and went one step beyond before his laggard eye telegraphed a message. He went back. There was the other half of the Yatsu-Kono unit, as innocent as if there were nothing wrong with it. There, now, was the steady run of seawater going into the separation chamber. But no outlet. It was impossible to avoid the conclusion that it was going in here, and coming out over there, with some thirty feet of thin air in between! Dillard glared at the offensive thing for ten seconds, then snarled and stalked away. It was exactly the kind of childish trick he might have expected from a confirmed Torquemada like Stanley. Again in memory he heard that high-

pitched infuriating voice saying, "Don't just stare, Dillard.
Look! See it. Engage the brain and never mind the subconscious!"

"Maybe the old fool did fall in the water and drown,"
he muttered, and was angry enough to hope it was true.
He came to a halt in front of a solid array of notebooks,
labels stuck along their spines and inscribed in some kind
of private symbology. He took one at random, more for
something to keep his fingers busy rather than from any desire to find anything. That intention had long since faded. He
riffled the pages idly, then turned to the flyleaf to check.
There was a heading in angular script: *Artifacts native to
Hydro. Some notes, descriptions, theories.*

Dillard read it again, was just beginning to grasp the
implications when Miss Hunt's voice intruded, from the
region of his right shoulder.

"What have you got there?"

"Just a notebook. Some nutty theory, it sounds like, about
a planet-sized Atlantis. You find anything?"

"Nothing at all." She took the notebook from his hand
and looked at it, turning over a page or two. "How much
of this have you read?"

"Enough. I'm not all that interested in the whacky work-
ings of Dr. Stanley's mind, thank you. And if he left any
kind of forwarding address, I didn't see it. What do you
do now?"

Her barrier had returned. She chilled him with a blue
stare, slid the book back in the gap it had left on a shelf,
and said, "I don't think that really concerns you, Mr. Dillard. I'm obliged for your help, but I think it's time you
went. Remember, you have a hydrofoil waiting for you."

"That's right, I do. Well, see you around sometime."

"I doubt it. I understand *Venture Three* lifts off for
Castor tomorrow. And I have enough work here to keep
me busy for quite a long time."

"I suppose," he agreed, switching off his equipment and
shedding it with quick movements. "Matter of curiosity,
Miss Hunt. Just what was old Stanley working on, here?"

"Nothing very spectacular." She kept her bleak stare. "Just
further research into water chemistry. May I correct a small
point, Mr. Dillard. I would estimate your age about the
same as my own. Thirty-ish? For your information, Dr. Stanley is forty-seven. Hardly old! He was twice your age when

you were a student, admittedly, but it's about time your outlook matured a little, don't you think?"

"Why don't I grow up, eh?" He grinned at her, no longer cowed by her assumed superiority. "In my book a person is as old as his habits. One of mine is the firm conviction that I do not yet know all the answers, and that I still have a lot to learn. I doubt if I'm likely to do it here, or from you. Goodbye now. Have fun!"

All the way out, into the elevator and down, he was engrossed in studying his own reactions to Miss Hunt. She was physically attractive. He was attracted, in that sense. She was intelligent and competent. He was impressed, in *that* sense. But she was also insensitive and conceited. Aggressive. Critical. And yet, somehow, he felt sorry for her. He couldn't shake the notion that she was afraid of something. As he ran down the steps to the 'foil he had to grin at his own fancies. *It must be this equipment*, he thought, *beginning to get me turned on!* That was not altogether fanciful, either. According to reports from other experienced sensor-gatherers it seemed that frequent exposure to the minute electrical stimulus had the effect of sharpening up the sensory network, toning up the nervous system until they were aware of and reacted to things an ordinary person would never notice.

"Hey!" the hydrofoil pilot hailed him, dispersing this intriguing flow of speculation. "Your name's Dillard, ain't it?"

"It is. Why?"

"Got a radio-call for you. Fifteen minutes ago, from Captain Conway, *Venture Three*. Made a note of it."

"I think I can guess what," Dillard said, all his confidence draining away out at his feet.

"It said," the pilot read off, ignoring the guess, " 'All arranged your visit Venusian ship, compliments, Conway.' All right?"

"I suppose so," Dillard said dismally.

"You want me to take you there now?"

"I suppose you might as well." Dillard stood by the pilot, listened to the engine roar into life, and wondered, as he always did, why he had to pick *this* kind of living. It was insane. He was the hypersensitive nervous type, automatically building horrid phantasms about anything new and strange, so he had to go and get himself famous for always running into something new and strange. And recording it.

All his fine talk about being an artist came back hollowly now. But—this was no more than a repetition of what always happened just before a recording session, and trained reflexes drove him on as if they were something separate and apart.

"All right if I sit back here with you?" he asked, and the pilot shifted over a fraction in silent assent. "Know anything about Venusians?" he asked, seeking company in his misery. The pilot snorted.

"I've seen 'em. Not close to, mind, but I've seen 'em. You want to go aboard that ship, and I'm taking you, but better you than me, brother!"

"What's there to be afraid of?" Dillard retorted perversely. "They're just as human as we are."

"Not the way I heard it. Nor by the look. Long skinny green beggars. No hair to speak of. No clothes, either. And would you just look at that ship! Human?"

"Oh, I don't know," Dillard argued. "Isn't that just a lot of idle talk? After all, just because a man's umpteenth great-grandfather was exiled to Venus for some political misdemeanor, that doesn't make him a fish!"

"Idle talk, huh?" The pilot advanced his throttle now that the 'foil was clear of the channel, and the small craft began to bounce over the waves in a long-radius arc. "That's history, mister, and it was no political whatdycallit, either. Dictatorship of the elite, that's what they were planning. The big-domes in charge, sitting back and getting fat, and everybody else slaving away for them like a lot of termites. They wasn't even human then, if you ask me, never mind about now!"

Dillard sighed. This was the way the story had been tailored, by all kinds of media, to suit the masses. Epic Dramatapes had contributed their share to the universal canard, so he had no real reason to feel angry, but he did nevertheless, because it wasn't true. Those people hadn't planned anything like enslavement of the masses, quite the reverse. Quietly, with determination and insight, they had prepared their coup. They were going to unite the highly intelligent of all races into one coherent body. Yes, an elite, if you liked the term, but a responsible elite. A group with a master-plan to really put scientific potential to work, to create, at last, the perfect ecology, where machines and technology would do the drudgery automatically. Abundance for all, no longer the survival-need to work, a chosen handful to steer the whole thing, and all the extended resources of modern computer-wisdom to insure a stable and viable whole.

Dillard had called it a political misdemeanor, and it was, because it aimed to bypass the politicians, and they didn't like that, when they found out. And so the Anarchists, as they had been called, were caught and proved guilty. No feat, that. They were only too willing to confess, to explain their plan, confident that it would be immediately approved once known. But the politicians, the statesmen—and the news media, too—destroyed that faith. In a world without strife and conflict, without grief and horror, with no injustice, no war or threat of war, what future was there for the politician, the statesman, the great newspaper? And so the Anarchists were tried, condemned, and deported to Venus. Water-power had happened along just in time to make it possible. Dillard smiled wryly, and let it go. He had neither the time nor the ability to correct the pilot's version, now sanctified by a century of repetition and acceptance.

And then he forgot it entirely as the bulbous silhouette of the Venusian ship began to loom up ahead. His nerves tightened again. The fear, so recently elbowed out of consciousness, came back anew. The ship itself was enough to tickle the nerves along his spine. It bulged. It looked incredibly top-heavy. Around its girth, just below the maximum spread, a series of dark ports seemed to stare down at him balefully and his hyperactive imagination peopled those blind holes with shivery monsters. Down in the slow-tapering stem there was a conventional hatch, and a conventional ladder extending down to a pontoon that floated on the choppy surface. Dillard shortened his attention in to that reassuring sight. The pilot eased his engine as the 'foil headed in to the pontoon.

"You'll wait for me again?"

"How long you going to be?"

"Hard to tell," Dillard muttered. "I'd say about half an hour."

"All right. I'll be back in half an hour. But I'm not waiting there, mister. I don't like your friends."

Dillard had to be satisfied with that. He stood up, stepped off, and before he could catch his balance the hydrofoil was roaring away in a tight sweep, out to sea. The pontoon heaved under his feet. The seaweedy smell was queasily strong just here. He stared up at the enigmatic hatch, a tall black oblong in the slime-green hull, and felt horribly alone. Practical considerations drove his fingers to get out and put on his recording gear and cut the lead-in.

"About to go aboard and inspect a Venusian spaceship, at anchor on Hydro. Den Dillard recording."

Green fear melted his bones, attacked his balance, so that the platform under his feet seemed to heave enormously. The small, pragmatically practical part of him stood off and lashed him with its cold sanity, commanded him to stop making like a jelly and get up there. He went, striding heavily up the treads and hoping his shivering didn't show. He knew that this overpowering dread was worth its weight in platinum wire to him, but that didn't lessen it at all.

The hatchway *was* dark. As he hesitated before stepping in he saw that it was bathed in a reddish glow. Forcing his imagination away from thoughts of blood, he rationalized hurriedly. Miss Hunt had said "sensitive to ultraviolet," so this red tint must be some kind of compensation against the bright sunlight outside. He went in, treading across the air lock space, and came face to face with a monster. His throat closed and his knees locked as he stared up at the man who waited there. Man? Six foot three, he stood, and he had the usual arrangement of arms and legs, and face, but there the similarities ended. The face was square and bleak, like nothing so much as one of those weird Easter Island heads, and maybe the eyes were deep purple but they might have been any color, under those red-black lenses he wore. Hairless, not even eyebrows, and his only garment a glossy black plastic loincloth. Dillard glanced down hastily and corrected himself. Shoes also, glossy black things that ended snugly just above the ankle. Over and above everything else was a sense of otherness, of complete and unmoving stillness. A man of stone, but breathing. Dillard summoned his reserves and went forward two steps. The stone-man made a harsh throat noise that could hardly be speech, but Dillard chose to accept it as such, having no choice.

"I'm Dennis Dillard," he said, hardly recognizing his own voice. "I have permission to visit you."

The stone-man spoke again, and it *was* speech. Dillard

recognized it, barely, as the one word, "Visit?" Miss Hunt had said their speech tended to be low-pitched. She had not said that it was almost all scrape and no noise.

"That's right, visit. I want to look around."

"Wait!" This time it was clear, even if it was a sound made simply by passing air through the throat. The Venusian extended a long arm to take up a thing like a flashlight on a cable. Where the light should have come out was a metal grille. He pressed this to his throat and made more of the harsh, nonvocal noises, rapidly. Throat-microphone, Dillard assumed, wondering about the reverse process. Then he saw, as the man moved the grille to press it against his jaw-bone and stare into nowhere. Bone-conduction speaker, he deduced, and wondered what it was about Venusian atmosphere that made such an inefficient device necessary. In a moment the guard put the instrument away.

"Wait," he breathed again. "A guide comes."

Dillard waited, speculating meanwhile about perpetual hot humidity and what it would do to electronics. And how else could you have a communication system that had to be totally sealed? It made sense. He stared about, straining to see details in the red glow. The passage ran right and left, that much he could make out, but if the rest of the ship was no better lighted than this part he wasn't going to see much. Maybe his eyes would adjust in a while. He comforted himself with that thought, then started as he heard a soft tread at his side and a low, throaty, purring voice ask, "You are Mr. Dillard, spoken of by the captain of *Venture Three?*"

There was a quality to that voice that made him shiver even before he turned to see who was speaking. But not a shiver of dread, at all. A cello note muted through warm honey and furry smooth, it baffled his attempts to analyze even as he half-shrank from seeing the person, who *had* to be a disappointment after such a delight. But she wasn't. She was perhaps two inches shorter than himself, making her five-ten, and she wore only the black-plastic loincloth and boots like the guard, but she couldn't have been more of a contrast to him if she had spent the whole of her twenty years in trying to do just that. Delicately sculptured, she was lithe and lean where muscle was appropriate, but abundantly curved in other ways. Her hair, pale as silver silk, was caught into a plume that curved forward over her right shoulder, and the skin there, and elsewhere, was so transparently pink in this light that he knew, instinctively, she would be marble white in ordinary daylight. But what caught and held him, after that first comprehensive glance, was her eyes.

They were large, steady, and glowing violet, and they seemed to channel to him a surge of seething aliveness. Where the impassive guard was stone-cold to him, this girl was a flame, a flame that licked into fire as she smiled, her white teeth gleaming against the pink of her face. He caught his breath.

"I'm Den Dillard, yes. If you know about Captain Conway's request, then you know all about me, what I'm here for."

"Not all." The voice again, humming like strings. "I have some small questions. I am AnnSmith. You will come with me, please." She turned and went away ahead of him along a passage that was a slow curve. He assumed that it followed the outer contour of the ship. She seemed to flow, so sleek was her movement, and he felt clumsy by contrast. In a moment she halted and gestured him into a compartment that was also all curves, like a section from a tube. There was a table, cushioned seats, the same red-tinted lighting, and everything covered in glossy waterproof stuff. He became aware of the humidity, and a faintly pervasive, not unpleasant smell of something like pine, or what is popularly called ozone. She sat, and he shrugged back and out of his flared poncho before copying her, but it didn't relieve the humidity much.

"Now, DenDillard," she said, running his name into one long sound, "I know that you are a sensor recorder, and I have heard of such, but I do not know what is involved. Explain, please."

He launched into a mechanical explanation of his apparatus, the while his inner attention was fixed on a host of new sensations. Never before had he been so vividly aware of another person. It was as if she were actually in contact with him, instead of sitting at the opposite side of a table. As if, and he had to hold back from believing it, he could tell what she was feeling. Now, for instance, she was intensely curious—but also fearful.

"If I understand," she said, "you want a recording of

what it feels like to be inside a Venusian ship, yes? But why?"

"Because it's my job, my function. I collect recordings of rare and unusual sensory impressions, that's all."

"For what purpose?"

"All sorts of things. First off the wires will be analyzed, typed, then stored against possible use. Then as background."

"Background? What is that?"

Dillard stifled mild impatience. After all, she *was* alien, in a way. "Did you ever see a dramatape, Miss Smith?"

"AnnSmith," she corrected. "A dramatape. Projected picture-illusions, for entertainment and amusement?"

"That's one way of putting it," he admitted. He had triggered his machine, by force of habit, as soon as he had started up that gangway, with one finger on the cut-out button to skip any dull bits. Now he flicked the switch to off and gave all his attention to finding the right words to explain to her. It was never easy, although he had tried to do it often.

"Look," he said, "the basic thing is pictures, scenes and actions and people doing things. Now, somebody has to work hard to contrive the right kind of scenery, and props, for each scene. Somebody else works out color-schemes, makeup, special effects, costumes, and so on. A storm at sea, for instance. You can't wrap that up and bring it to the studio. But you can take pictures and bring those. You can record sounds, and play them back. And you can, and we do, superimpose music scores to create the right impressions. But this gadget of mine does more. Tell me this—with your eyes shut, could you tell whether you were indoors or outside? Close to a solid surface, or stuck in the middle of an open space? High up or low down? In a crowd, or alone?"

"But that," she frowned thoughtfully, "is just sensory clues, like hearing, echoes and . . ."

"It's not, you know. It is actually skin sensors. Blind people can feel all sorts of things, not by hearing. And that's only part of it. I can feel this ship rolling, just a little, right now. My gadget records that feeling, and other things, and in such a way that the whole sense can be played back for somebody else to feel. If and when this recording is ever used, the audience, every single one, will actually feel they are inside a ship, this ship. You can't do that with words or pictures. I can't tell you how I feel, or what. There are no words for that. But I can feel, and record that feel, for others to share."

She seemed convinced, but he was aware of a small thread of suspicion still remaining. And she asked the inevitable question about sounds and pictures. He reassured her on that. People would never understand, he mused, that faked pictures and sounds were always much more convincing than the real thing. In drama, at any rate. She rose gracefully.

"What do you wish to see?"

"Just a normal interior. You know, where the crew would be in ordinary circumstances. And a scan of the control room, of course. That's where the human interest drama always is. Nothing technical. I wouldn't understand, so neither would the viewers."

"Very well." She moved to a wall and aimed a slim finger at a diagram pasted up there. He came to look, and it was as if he had taken her hand. The diagram was fine-line black, with areas of red. "These you cannot see, are for specialist people, are dangerous." She indicated the red patches, which took up a circular cross section of the interior. As he had guessed, the power-and-drive units lay along the core of the ship, top to bottom.

"I understand," he told her. "That's all right. You just lead on, and I'll follow. And thank you for being so understanding."

The simple courtesy seemed to surprise her. She turned to smile uncertainly at him and engulf him with her warm presence. Then she went away ahead of him, leaving him to follow and wonder over his peculiar impressions. Inside ten minutes he had lost all sense of direction and was following her blindly along and around a maze of curved passages, pausing to peer into oddly shaped spaces, some of which looked like living quarters, others like storerooms. They climbed ladders that were almost vertical. There was no break in the red lighting and the unrelieved yellow and brown tints of everything that wasn't black. His nervousness long gone, he became aware of another growing impression, of incompletion. As if the ship had been rushed together with no regard for final trim, the little details which make for comfort.

"It is not a ship for comfort," she explained, as if picking the thought from his mind. "You have seen workshops and laboratories, store spaces and living quarters. All is intended for practical use. We do not carry passengers, or provide entertainment." Her defensive tone stirred curiosity. Then it came home to him that, apart from the hatch guard, he had seen no one but her.

"I hope I'm not interrupting anything important," he said. "It seems as if everybody is keeping out of my way."

"All are busy with duties," she said sharply, and he knew she was lying, but couldn't understand why. She had to be lying. For all his confusion he had seen space enough, at least, for something in the region of a hundred persons. And they couldn't *all* be on duty at the same time. So they were keeping out of his way. He wondered about it as he scaled yet another steep ladder and guessed he must be reaching the top of the hull. *They are Venusian,* he reminded himself. *They don't like humans very much. So they are keeping out of the way, and what's so curious about that?* But then AnnSmith halted, her arm brushing his as she said, "We are now almost to the control room. You will wait here until I see if it is permitted for you to visit." And as she went away through a hatch he knew there was no dislike there. Not between her and him. He knew that as surely as he knew there was sweat trickling along his arm under the folded poncho he carried there. She was back in a moment, smiling like sunlight in the evening, convincing him still more.

"You may enter and look, but not to distract, because there is work in progress." She reversed, pushed open the hatch and stood aside for him to go in. For some time now he had kept his finger on the cut-off as there was no reaction within him worth recording, but now he let the wire run and used his eyes. He stood in a large chamber, the largest he had so far seen. He was near the roof, which went away from him in a curve like the underside of a dish, and glowed. Not pink, this time, but a cold blue light, almost like sky, and he knew by intuition that this was the viewpoint, the forward screening of the ship. *Venture Three,* he knew, used something similar, an arrangement of semiconducting surface and image intensifiers that served to make a whole area of hull as useful as a window without being in any way frail.

He drew his gaze away from that roof and scanned the

chamber itself. It was an enormous bowl, going away down there in regular circular tiers, down into a smaller space that was like an arena, or the focal point of a concert performance. He revised that first impression quickly as he noticed the panels and instrument controls on each tier. And the swivel seats. He boggled a bit at his estimate of how many people this place was designed to hold, all at one time, all functioning. Contrasting that with the apparently casual way in which Captain Conway had allowed a computer, the auto-helm, to bring in *his* ship, the only conclusion was that *this* ship didn't have that kind of computer. He tried imagining what it would be like with fifty or more alert people all in action at once, pulling, pushing and twisting various levers and buttons, and it just did not register. *Better them than me!* He thought, and cast his eyes down to the heart of the chamber, down there in the circular pit.

There were six people, enclosed in a ring-wall of consoles, staring at screens, all silent. Six people obviously engrossed, just to maintain one ship at anchor? Dillard stared, and noted something odd about those six. He half-turned to AnnSmith to ask a question but she, anticipating, shook her head and whispered, "You must not speak, except perhaps like this, very quietly. It is most important not to disturb."

Dillard shrugged it off, returned to his stare. Six people, four men and two women. Three of the men, and both women, were, like the hatch guard, hairless, greenish, lean and stone-cold queer. The one remaining man, though, was enough like AnnSmith to be her brother. As Dillard stared that man looked up, just for a glance, then looked away again, and he had the same deep purple gaze as she had. But then one of the stone-faces raised his head to stare, and this one had no tinted lenses to shield his eyes at all. For all the empty distance between them, Dillard felt the impact of that stare like a knife-thrust. Eyes as pale green and chill as ice-chips transmitted acid hate, a malevolence as immediate and full-throated as a tiger's growl. Dillard shivered involuntarily, tried to hold his own stare against that basilisk glance, and failed. Looking away, he muttered under his breath, "I don't know why you hate my guts, mister, but the feeling is absolutely mutual, believe me!" Mingling with the aftermath of chill came a warm query from AnnSmith.

"You said something?"

"Nothing. Just a reaction. Forget it. Not that I'm likely to. I've never struck anything like this before."

"It will be a good recording for you?"

"It certainly will be unique."

"Unique? What does that mean?" All at once her submerged uneasiness blazed up into consuming fear, stirring him. He wondered if she knew how open her feelings were to him.

"All recordings are unique, in a way. No two places, or experiences, are exactly the same, you know. For instance, I have a recording of the control room ambience of *Venture Three*, and it is totally different from this."

Her eyes were huge now, and smoldering. "Tell me, truly, if you had a recording of this ship, and another one just like it, could you tell the difference between them?"

"Why sure!" he told her. "That's what I meant. Look, back home I have my apartment suite. There must be a hundred exactly like it in the same building, but I know mine, would know it blindfolded, by the feel. Why should that surprise you? It's common enough!"

She didn't answer. He had hardly done speaking before she was off down the circular terraces of the chamber, running lithely, to halt alongside the man with the death-grudge eyes. She stooped over, muttering something. Dillard, completely baffled, watched the pair of them curiously, and ran full-tilt into another ice-cold stare of utter hatred as that stone-faced man looked up once again. The violence of it was fantastic. Dillard got the shattering sense that this man could knock him down with that glance, if he tried hard enough. Then the glaring eyes were averted and AnnSmith came leaping up the levels back to him, her agitation coming before her like a force-field.

"I bring the compliments of Commander Dekron, his hope that you have seen as much as you need, and his request that you leave the ship at once!"

"Was that Dekron, the one you spoke to?"

"Yes. Please, you must hurry."

"All right, but if that's his idea of a compliment, that look, I'd hate to get into his bad books. Lead on!"

She *was* in a hurry, too. She scuttled along the passageways and down ladders much faster than was comfortable for him to follow, and her agitation was an infection that he had to fight off or feel panic.

"What's all the rush?" he demanded at last, breathless

and damp with perspiration, reaching for her arm to slow her down.

"An unforeseen change of orders." She stopped quite still, but it was the stillness of an animal in flight, her arm trembling in his grasp. "We are to take off, soon. A lot must be done very quickly."

He had gathered that much already. Alarms were shattering the air with strident tones, and he saw now several lank and awkward stone-faces hurrying about various errands.

"How soon?" he demanded, releasing her arm.

"You must be off the ship in five minutes."

"Huh?" He swung his wrist to check, then ran after her. "You can't do that, honey. You can't!"

"But we *must* be clear for takeoff in five minutes!"

"And what am I supposed to do, swim?" He threw the question at her as he chased her around a corner and down another ladder. "I told that water-taxi to come back for me in a half hour, and it won't be that for fifteen minutes, at least. How do I get off?"

She halted, stopping and spinning so abruptly that he bumped into her, gently, and had to clasp her to avoid a tumble. This close, her eyes were pools of purple deep enough to drown in, and her terror washed over him in a warm wave.

"I had not thought!" she breathed. "Now what shall I do? You must be off the ship. You must!"

"Radio? The hydrofoil is equipped. Call him alongside!"

"Yes. If there is time. Come now, hurry!"

She ran again and he ran after, conscious of the slipping seconds and fervently not wanting to become an unwilling passenger on this ship, yet in all the turmoil still finding time to be stirred by the momentary contact with her. Alien. Venusian. All of that, and yet she was the very first female he had ever met to make him feel he would want to know her better. She moved in front of him like a deer. Other woman he had known all had sharp edges and minds like fangs, or stood behind barriers and put on impressions, like Miss Hunt, but this girl was as close to him, in some strange way, as his own skin. And the irony of it. As he ran he cursed it. Within scant minutes she would depart into space, and it was a million-to-one shot that he would ever see her again. There wasn't even time to speak, to tell her—what? What was there to say? He ran, belatedly remembering to snatch off his equipment and stuff it into its box. And here, at last, was the exit hatch. She halted, looking back as he pounded up, all breathless.

"The radio is busy," she said, tragedy clouding her face. "There will be no chance to call your 'foil."

"Oh! Ah!" he gasped, and then, "Hold on a bit, AnnSmith. I can step off onto the waterworks and wait there for the 'foil. Eh?"

"No. It is not possible. We are no longer alongside the desalination plant. Look! Already we have moved out into clear water for takeoff!"

Following her arm he looked out and down. There was the pontoon, and the end of the ladder, and the rest was open sea. His stomach heaved. As he resisted its upset he turned to her, made a stiff grin.

"I'm sorry, AnnSmith. I hope you won't get into trouble on my account. It wasn't your fault."

"You are sorry—for me?" The fear in her ebbed for just a moment, to give way to wonder. "Why should you care what happens to me?"

It was one of those questions no man can ever answer properly, not even with all the time in the world, and he had none. As he groped for breath and words there came a hoarse cry from the guard, and Dillard turned, followed a thrusting arm, and saw the hydrofoil coming across the water at the head of a foaming white wake.

"Looks like I'm just going to make it," he muttered. "I don't know, now, whether I'm glad or sorry. Goodbye, AnnSmith. Thank you for everything. I hope we can meet again sometime."

Then, clutching his kit-box to stop it from banging against his hip, he ran down the ladder onto the pontoon and stood there, balancing, as the 'foil ran in alongside. The seesaw motion was violent now. Dillard leaned, tried to time one movement against another, stepped off onto the 'foil as it was rising, felt his knee give under the sudden upthrust, tottered aboard in a scrambling heap, and heard the motor rave into power.

"Are you lucky I happened to notice that bolt-bucket getting ready to blow!" the pilot growled. "Don't they use radio at all?"

"Emergency orders, so I was told." Dillard gasped, se-

curing his balance and turning to watch the ship as the
'foil drew speedily away. "I'm grateful. I wouldn't fancy
being a supercargo on that."

"Thought you said they was friends of yours?"

"Did I? Well, one of them is. I hope."

"Where to now?" The pilot reverted to his trade, and Dillard frowned, not having thought that far yet. It had been a
queer day so far, in some ways a strenuous one. Logic indicated a fast trip back to *Venture Three* and a rest, but he
felt strangely disinclined for it. And there was only one
other spot.

"Take me in to Joytown," he said. "I might as well see
everything there is while I'm here." The pilot grunted, swung
his helm, and Dillard turned to keep the Venusian ship
in view, wondering whether he would ever see its like
again. And AnnSmith! Never in his farthest-out dreams had
he contemplated the possibility of falling for a Venusian
girl. But then, never before had he 'felt such an instant and
total rapport with anyone. He could recapture it now, quite
plainly, that sense of feeling her heartbeat, her breathing, the
start and tension in every nerve, the lift and pull of muscle
to move her arm, turn her head, even the sensation of
her smile. *Two hearts that beat as one,* he thought, and
jeered at himself for sounding like a stereotyped Gothic-tape.
And yet, it had been like that.

All at once reality broke through his mental vision and he
stared. The Venusian ship, from here, seemed to be sinking!
Settling down into the water. He rubbed his eyes and peered
harder. It was no illusion. That ship was lower, several
feet lower, than it had been. Then, all at once, the sea
boiled in a ring around the tapered base, spray spouted
high and the great bulk reared up, surging steadily and
strongly out of the sea. Now the spray was steam, and
the thin spindly stern lifted clear, spouting yellow fire. The
fire spilled out in a sheet over the rolling waves. Sound came,
a powerful deep-throated bellow of effort, spearing through
the billowing steam. The ship mounted higher, as if dragging
herself out of a gluetrap. Higher, and the flame-tail was a
rod now, stabbing down.

"There she blows!" Dillard said, and even as he said it the
whole scene changed with shattering speed. Around that
rod of yellow flame there sprang out a fierce white glare. In
one breath the glare lifted, surged up, engulfed the entire

bulk of the ship, blotting it out. In the next eye-blink the hovering white fireball erupted outward, changing swiftly from furious white to dark gray, to shot red, to a boiling pall of black through which spindly fragments appeared briefly and fell. The black monstrosity ballooned hugely. Then came the first shock-wave front of the immense explosion. An invisible hand shoved Dillard's chest and the hydrofoil—and an ear-blasting roar followed, stunning his senses. The frail craft leaped and plunged against the shock, the pilot cursing and hauling on his helm. Dillard got a hand-hold and clung. And stared at the boiling black cloud that rolled out and began to disperse over the sea.

"What the hell was that?" the pilot demanded, swinging his craft around to face the disturbance.

"The ship!" Dillard said stupidly. "That Venusian ship. It blew up!"

"It what?"

"It just blew up. One minute it was standing up away from the sea. The next minute it was all ablaze. Then it blew, just like that!"

He could barely believe his own words. It was impossible that a whole solid ship, full of people, could go so quickly, so entirely. All gone!

"Got to head back," the pilot growled. "Might be survivors in trouble."

"There won't be." Dillard said it with stunned certainty. "There just couldn't be. There was no time!"

Now he could hear the start up of sirens and hooters from several directions, and saw small craft of many kinds coming furiously over the water to investigate. The first shreds of stinking smoke touched his nostrils, and the hydrofoil lurched and heaved in the swelling aftermath of explosion. It ran back, joined the others who were combing the fumes and swells for anyone who might need help. But there was nothing, nothing at all. Here and there among the drifting trails of smoke could be seen patches of oil-slick, but that was all there was to show that a great ship had been here. Of debris, living or dead, there was nothing.

After half an hour of vain search, Dillard said, "I told you. Didn't I tell you?"

The pilot nodded, put his hand to his throttle. "I guess you were right, mister. This is a waste of time." The 'foil began once more to drive toward the distant island-town.

Dillard sat slumped alongside the pilot and let his thoughts sag wherever they could. The whole thing was just too much for him to take in. It was quite a while before it struck him that had he not been lucky enough to get off, he would have gone up with it, and when that idea did come it struck only a faint thrill. But then, on the heels of that thought, came another. It was fantastic that a whole ship could go, just like that, and he would never know how, but wasn't it just possible that he, by being there, had caused somebody to rush something, or make some vital error? That idea really did squash him down, so much so that the pilot had been talking to him for some time before he realized it and asked for a repeat.

"I said, mister, that I have to report this. And you!"

"Report? Report what? That the ship blew up?"

"No!" The pilot was heavily patient. "Everybody on Hydro knows about it by now. I have to report you. Look, your name and ex-card number are in my slot. I took you aboard. The *Venture Three* people know that much. And I got you off just two jumps ahead of the disaster. So I have to report that. There will be an inquiry. You understand?"

Dillard thought he sensed something more than just self-protecting routine in the pilot's tone.

"What are you really getting at?" he demanded. "Why the shifty look? Stars! You don't think I had anything to do with—with that?"

"Now look, mister, I didn't say that. But stand where I am for a bit. You go aboard, with some gadget or other, right? Now, I've been running this water-taxi here more than five years. I've seen maybe a hundred Veenie ships come and go. And I've never once seen a Veenie, not close. Never seen one leave the ship. Never seen anybody go aboard. Nobody. Not till you. Then, off you come all of a gallop, like the devil was on your tail. And then she blows. You add it up and see what you get."

Dillard didn't know whether to laugh or curse. He felt stomach-sick. But his pragmatic fraction had to admit the man had a point. The thought that he, Dillard, could deliberately destroy an entire ship—and all those people, alien or not—was insane. But only from one viewpoint, and that was Dillard's own. He couldn't expect anyone else to be sure about it.

"All right," he said wearily, and fumbled with his kit-box. "You have to do your duty as you see it, I suppose. Here, you'd better take this."

"What is it?"

"It's a wire spool. It carries all the recordings I've done today. It is worth quite a bit to me, so look after it, won't you. But it could be evidence of some kind, you never know, and if you have it, and turn it over to whoever you're going to report to, that will at least establish that I haven't faked it in any way. Go on, it won't bite."

"Look, mister, I'm not accusing you of anything!"

"That's just as well, isn't it?" Dillard felt a sudden spurt of anger. "See you don't. Keep that recording safe. Turn it over to the proper authorities. And be careful what you do say, or I'll dig you so deep in trouble you will never get out. You've seen my expense-card, so you know I have enough going for me to be able to do just that."

"I don't want any trouble!"

"Nor me, so we have something in common. Right? Can't this thing go any faster?"

V

BY THE TIME the 'foil had run in and under the nearest projecting rim of the floating island, Dillard realized the word "town" was no exaggeration. The great faceted dome was huge, easily half a mile across, and where the under half of the dish curved down into the water there was all of thirty feet headroom under the rim. What he had seen as slots from a distance now showed as miniature harbor mouths. The air-cushion ferry came billowing out of one just before they slowed to head in, and Dillard glanced back to see another spaceship up there, just a silver dot, readying in for planet-fall. The 'foil slid in and alongside a tiled wall, the pilot checked out on his card, and Dillard stepped ashore. Three more steps upward and he was on a broad, rubberized avenue, stretching before and behind in a long sweeping curve. And here, before he could decide which way to start walking, came a purring scooter in sparkling chrome, towing a wheeled chair after it. He stared, half-angry that the girl driver could be so breezy, beautiful and blonde, after what he had just seen. The machine purred to a halt

71

beside him and the girl swung long legs to the ground and saluted him briskly.

"At your service, mister. Name your pleasure and I'll take you to it, or something better."

He took time to study her, the better to get his feelings under some kind of control. No thought of recording occurred to him here. Sinful delights were not in his line, and this girl, after all, was only doing a job. She was petite and devastatingly endowed, none of it hidden. From the waist down spray-thin silver clothed her, yielding to mid-calf riding boots of the same color equipped with ridiculously large spurs. On her upper half she wore a scanty short-sleeved bolero that was no more than a gesture. It was unfastened. One glance was enough to show that it couldn't be fastened, not to contain what she had to put into it. She would, Dillard thought, have a weight problem very soon. She reminded him strongly of the type of female scenery regularly used to add "interest" to an otherwise insipid storyline. The silver-painted ten-gallon hat on her blonde mop was all part of the illusion.

"Supposing it had been somebody else?" he asked. "Not me. A lady?"

"Hah?" She blinked a moment then grinned broadly, fired her finger straight up like a pistol, and he looked to see the goggle-eye of a scanner watching him. "We have a headquarters," she explained. "The screen gets a picture of anybody coming ashore, and we select out according to who, and what. You look like the direct approach, couple of drinks and a good time, type. So me."

"So wrong," he said. "Maybe not your fault, though. You've heard about the disaster, just now?"

"Veenie ship blew up, so I heard. Say, you must've seen it!"

"I stepped off it about five minutes before it happened."

She gave a sudden shiver and seemed to wilt a little, made a shrill and quavering whistle-sound. "You some kind of nut, mister? You went aboard a Veenie ship? Nobody could pay me enough to do that."

"That's your problem. All I'm getting at is that I don't feel like any kind of good time just now. All I want is somewhere peaceful and quiet, maybe something to eat and drink, and time to think. Do you have that available?"

"Why not? What sort of class did you have in mind?"

For that question he had no ready answer, but let the problem solve itself by handing over his ex-card. Her flame-red mouth rounded into an "Oh" of appreciation at sight of his rating.

"Welcome to Joytown, Mr. Dillard. I think I know the very place for you. Climb aboard!" She gestured to the rickshaw-like chair, then grinned. "Or you could mount up behind me, piggyback. No extra charge."

She threw a slim leg over her saddle and turned up the voltage on her smile, but he shook out his poncho, slung it over his shoulders and said, "That chair will do me, thanks."

She looked hurt. "I didn't mean anything, mister, just being friendly. Besides"—she added acutely—"you've never been here before, have you? And a man like you will be full of questions, I guess. So how can I talk to you if you're sitting right back there?"

"What do you mean, a man like me? You missed my type once, sister. Don't you ever learn?"

"I reckon to learn something new every day," she retorted cheerfully, "and mostly by talking to people. You're a newsman, aren't you?"

"No. Sorry. This is not a camera. But you have a point, about learning things. All right, I'll take the piggyback."

"That's real friendly now." She beamed. "Climb on, and don't be scared to hug tight, I don't bruise easily. Ready?" She settled with a wriggle as he clasped her slim middle, and kicked her machine into throbbing life. They growled away along the wide ramp, swooped into a sharp turn and up a steep incline, then swooped steeply again and were out onto a glass-tiled roadway banked with raucous neon-lighted civilization. She kept her foot down and her blonde hair tickled his face as the breeze of their flight pushed it back at him.

"Don't pay too much attention to this bit," she called back over her shoulder. "This is mostly beer-joints, diners, flop-houses and gambling dens. Strictly for crewmen and bums. Right now it's only half-alive. Come nightfall it perks up some, but even then it's no great shakes."

"Where are you going to take me?"

"In a minute—whoops!"—she swerved dexteriously to avoid a straggle of pedestrians—"we strike an intersection. Coming up. Hold on tight!"

He needed no urging as she put the scooter into a forty-five degree heel to swoop into a four-lane highway. Purely by guess he estimated they were now heading in toward the middle, and she confirmed that as soon as she had jockeyed her way past a few minor roadrunners like single and two-seater cushion cars.

"We're now heading in to Center City. You'll like it. Very exclusive, quiet, nothing but the best. Whatever you want, the best." There didn't seem to be any comment called for, so he kept silent. In a moment or two her head half-turned again and she called, "Blue-true, Mr. Dillard, were you really on that Veenie ship?"

"Of course. Why not? According to what I hear, those ships come in here regularly. There's nothing weird about them."

"You don't mean that!" He felt her lithe young torso stiffen in quick revulsion as she spoke. "I wouldn't go within a million miles of them."

"Mean to tell me"—he let his irritation speak out—"that *you've* never met a Venusian either? They must come ashore here sometimes!"

"There'd be a riot if they ever did. Monsters!"

He snorted, got his retort ready, then let it go. What was the use? It occurred to him to tell her what Conway had said, that the Venusians found and built this place, but he thought better of that too.

"You know," she volunteered, "I always thought there was something queer about that ship."

"Queer? In what way queer?"

"Well, we get Veenie ships in here often enough, it's true, but it's always in and out again, pretty quick. Overnight. But that one has been here more than a couple of weeks now. Just sitting there!"

That certainly was queer. From what little Dillard knew of spaceship economy, it was insane. No one in his right mind keeps highly expensive machinery standing idle, and a spaceship is just about the most expensive assembly of machinery possible. To keep one bobbing at anchor for two whole weeks, doing nothing, was unthinkable. He was still trying to think it out in logical terms as the scooter slowed to a crawl and swung off into a quiet side street.

"This is it," she announced, and pointed. "The Hydro Palace. Best in town. You'll like it." He climbed down, waited

74

while she checked his ex-card again, and she grinned as she added, "If you happen to fancy some other place, or want something they haven't got, you just call me. My name's Stella, and that's my trade number. But you don't need to remember it, just ask Fodor. That's the commissionaire. Him, look. He knows me."

Dillard stared up the marble steps to where the uniformed attendant awaited him, then glanced back to Stella and smiled wryly.

"You never know," he said, "I might just do that. Not to take me any place special, just to give me one of your hair-raising rides on that. I hope you're insured?"

"Who, me?" She laughed. "Not on your life. I haven't hit anything yet, and don't intend to. Call me anytime. 'Bye now! Don't forget my cut, Fodor!"

As she stormed away, Dillard strode up the steps and the doorman threw him a salute fit for a general, at least. Resplendent in velvet-textured blue plastic ablaze with gold facings, he inclined his head graciously and murmured, "What is your pleasure, sir?"

"All I want is a table for one, me. With plenty of peace, quiet, and privacy. And service. Food, drink, the usual things. No entertainment, no diversions, nothing like that."

"Of course, sir. Are you familiar with the procedure for operating mechanical servers?"

"Hm? Oh, yes, certainly."

"Then allow me to show you." With a gracious gesture he pointed Dillard to a handy elevator door, and as the gate slid open he murmured, "Button Minus Five will deliver you to the Green Salon, sir. I'm sure you will find it exactly what you require."

Five was the last button on a long panel that went up to fifteen plus, and it struck Dillard with just a tweak at his nerves that by the time he got down five levels he would be underwater. Well under. Stepping out as the door opened, his first impression was a strong reminiscence of tropical monsoon, and he frowned, wondering where that had been. Then it came back. In Bombay, when he had been there making a documentary for a travel firm. But there were differences, now that he took a second look. The warm humidity was similar, but India had never been perfumed with mint. Or something like it, at any rate. Nor had it been steeped in an almost palpable green haze. Dillard stepped forward cautiously, expecting some kind of curtain, but the lambent green glow moved with him, and he realized it was some kind of interference screen effect. He nodded gently in praise. This was privacy indeed, to be wrapped in a tinted force-screen. But how did one find —and the question died unasked as there came a gently winking spot of red light, drawing near.

It loomed through the haze and resolved into a mechanical, a mobile attendant-machine, with an upright pole and hooks, a squat chrome and plastic body on tracks, and the red light blinking like a cyclops immediately above a radio grille. It halted a foot away from him.

"Your expense card please, sir or madam," it said gently.

"I'm male," Dillard told it, slotting his card into place. "I require a table and service for one, myself, please."

"Yes, sir. Should you be carrying any burdens, or wish to dispose of any garments or articles temporarily, please employ my hooks. I will proceed as soon as you are ready."

Dillard unloaded his tackle-box and poncho, hooked them, and felt just comfortably warm. "All ready," he announced. "Lead on."

It was ridiculous, he thought, how quickly one grew to think of the things as sentient. Expecting it to wheel around and go away. But it merely receded, still watching him with its red eye. He followed, and the curtain of green mist, now delicately flavored with citrus, went with them. It was impossible even to guess how big this chamber was. He became aware that he was ravenously hungry and guessed there was some chemical component in the air to help that kind of thing along. He strolled on a floor that was warm sponge and was aware of a winding trail, but saw nothing but the green fog. Then the guiding light halted.

"Your table, sir. Please program your requirements."

The light was subtly brighter now, and he saw the low table, and a chair, a long, low, inviting couch of dark foam-surfaced material. He sat, experimented a moment or two until he had a comfortable pose, locked the chair's flexibility to that contour, and then gave attention to the visi-screen the mechanical had extended for his benefit.

"I'll have a caffex immediately, and show me some wines, something dry and light." The list that rippled into view would have done credit to any cellar. Switching to solid food he ordered a meal light in starch and protein, conscious of incipient weight problems, and left it at that.

"Enough for the moment. I'll deal with anything else later; depends how I feel."

There was a click as the table sank into the floor and went away to fill his order. He grinned wryly, remembering the very first time he had encountered this kind of service, and how the table had been stuck because he, not knowing, had his elbow leaning on it and it couldn't move because it had protective circuits designed to avoid harming him. Dillard had been in many robotized restaurants since but never one quite on this scale.

"The green," he demanded, "is it compulsory?"

"What shade would you prefer, sir?"

After a moment's thought he requested a very pale, pearly pink, and got it. He wondered how it would affect somebody sitting close by. From that it was only a step to wondering whether there *was* anyone close by, or anyone else there at all. The mechanical explained.

"Each patron-area is secluded within its own polarized curtain, sir. There are other patrons present, groups and singles."

The table came back laden and Dillard started in, but after the first bite or two he felt something lacking and asked the servitor, "Can you do me some background music?"

It could. He selected thoughtfully and within a few seconds was softly wrapped around by lilt and the illusion of a surrealist ballet. It was well done. He knew something of the technique of hologram-in-the-round with 3D sound effects, and this was equal to anything he had met. They probably had sensor-accompaniment too, if he wanted it, but he chose not to. Those kind of sensations were not for him and he knew it. Music, rhythm and dance were mysteries as far as he was concerned. The sensor-craftsmen in that field got good money, and they earned it. To react evenly and totally on several sense levels simultaneously was exhausting for the operator. It was also insidiously narcotic for the audience, as the pop frenzies of the late twentieth century had proved beyond all doubt. Dangerous stuff. Like white noise, the total effect so overloaded the brain's channels that reason began to totter, and the outcome could be anything. He preferred just to watch. And listen. And eat. But not to get involved.

That thought triggered off the whole piled-up weight of the disaster he had just seen, and about which he had been resolutely determined not to think, until now. Here, alone, he could let the memories boil up. He bit and chewed and drank, filled his eyes with the movements of posturing bodies and his ears with Bartok, and so had something solid to anchor him while the Venusian ship blew itself to fiery death all over again in his mind. The complete devastation of a whole ship was something to stun his mind, but what really hurt was the thought of the people. There must have been a hundred or so of them, and they couldn't possibly have had a chance of survival. Not any of them. Not even AnnSmith. From there, as he went on doggedly chewing and swallowing, came the fearsome problem of responsibility. You could stretch coincidence just so far before it began to strain.

It was no use his rational fraction arguing the point, suggesting, as it did, that he had gone to visit Dr. Stanley also, and something queer had happened to him, hadn't it? Was Dillard feeling any pangs of conscience on that? He wasn't, but it did stir a moment's curiosity, enough to wonder just what had happened to Stanley, and what Miss Hunt was doing about him, if she was doing anything at all. So many strange things, open-ended problems, and no answers. Not only had he no answers, he had no hard notion what, if anything, he ought to do next.

He ended the meal feeling restless, programmed to have the ruins removed and a long, cold whisky sour brought, and sneered at the dancers and music. Dennis Dillard, pawn of fate, a straw in the wind, a nothing man. He poured scorn on himself lavishly, but it helped nothing. In common with most people, Dillard liked to think that he knew why he was doing what, at any given time, but this time it didn't work. All he could grasp was the vague conviction that he was being manipulated in some way that he couldn't understand. At last, in futile temper, he snapped at the mechanical, "Maybe I do need company, after all. What do you suggest?"

"I have a built-in switchboard, sir, if you wish to call someone."

"Such as who? I don't know anyone on this planet. At

least, no one who'd be likely to come running at my call."

"We have entertainers available on the premises, sir," the mechanical advised him, after a click that showed it had switched to a new level of circuitry. "I can show you pictures and details."

Dillard hesitated. Perversely, he said, "I'd far rather see just who is sharing this solitary jag with me, right now. Can you do that?"

This time there were several clicks and a hum or two. Then the robot servitor confessed, in a secretive tone, "I am permitted to show you the occupants of the other tables, with discretion."

"Oh! Are you, indeed? What discretion?"

"You may overlook any table for not longer than thirty seconds. After that period a warning is sounded and the view fails."

"Go ahead, show me."

There was another click, then the music ceased, the ballet dancers faded away and a glowing square hung suspended in mid-air. It was like peering through a drawn curtain. Dillard saw a large, fat-rolling man lolling on his couch, drink in hand, watching a pseudo-space opera. Click, and the man went, his place taken by a not-so-young couple disporting themselves in time to a frenzy of discordant noise they probably thought of as music. Dillard winced. Another click and he sat forward as he saw a dark-haired woman, black-frowning, staring right at him. Mara Hunt. And she had seen him!

"Hold it!" he commanded, as the picture went. "She was looking at me!"

"Possibly, sir, just as you were overlooking her."

"And no warning?"

"It can be circumvented by viewing in discrete periods of less than the permitted maximum."

"Somebody makes rules, somebody else makes holes in them. Be thankful you're just a machine. And mark that one, I may want to come back and do a bit of snooping myself." He considered it rapidly. No reason why Mara Hunt should not be here, of course. Call it coincidence. And maybe she hadn't been snooping at all. He decided to reserve judgment.

"All right, carry on and show me some more," he ordered. Up came another picture, a hole in the pink haze, and this time he caught his breath as if steel fingers had grasped his throat. There, life-large and startlingly near, so that he could almost reach out and touch, was the savage-eyed Venusian commander, Dekron. And, close-headed with him was another stone-face, almost certainly the hatchway guard. But it just couldn't be! The picture winked out and left him staring into nothing, his neck stiff and his teeth locked. With an effort he growled, "Show me that again. Again!"

"Yes, sir. Table-space G-5, two persons in conference, names withheld." The picture sprang into life once more. It was Dekron, positively.

"Take me to that table!"

"I am unable to do that, sir, without the express consent of the occupants beforehand."

"Then get it . . ."

But the order was not to be obeyed. Dillard's questions had overridden the mechanical's attention to time. A gentle chime shattered the quiet, and in that hanging picture Dekron snatched his head around, and glared, straight at Dillard. Searing hate lashed out from those chill eyes. Dillard cringed back in his chair, then scrambled to his feet. The picture blinked out. He put out a hand in aimless terror, not knowing which way to move, yet wanting desperately to run. The pink glow faded into the standard green haze, and that piled up the panic. Dillard tottered forward, hands out to grope, and a darkness in the green loomed suddenly, became solid, became Dekron with teeth showing in a snarl and his shoulders bulking huge.

Dillard swung away, ran two steps and smashed into something hard with his hip. The impact drove out his breath, flooded him with pain. He reeled to one side, hearing the growl and rustle of someone on his heels. A hard hand fell on his shoulder and he whirled, knocked the arm aside, threw a frantic punch at the face that loomed up again—and something hard and heavy slammed into the side of his head, sending him sprawling to his knees. He got up, half-blinded with the tears of impact, turned and ran—and smashed face-first into a solid upright, the shock almost knocking him down. Powerful hands grabbed him again. He whimpered helplessly as he was whirled around, right into an exploding blow in the head. The green darkened into black as he fell. He couldn't even put out hands to break his fall. Then something stung his arm. A needle-point. And all sensation slid away.

He came back to a conscious awareness of rhythmic explosions that hurt, that shattered, that were his head bursting, and realized first that he was still alive. He wasn't sure he was happy about that. Second, that his head was not really exploding, it just felt that way. Thirdly, as the crashing agony shrank to the point where it was containable, he discovered that his face felt flat, as if someone had stepped on it. And there was a sour-metal taste in his mouth. He remembered the needle. For dope of any kind he had a repugnance that amounted to phobia, as it posed a threat to his sensibilities, and thus his craft. By reflex, he attempted to twist away, and discovered that he was bound securely, hand and foot.

Stirred into full consciousness, he opened his eyes, the effort setting off new concussions in his skull. He stared at a near ceiling, dark and rugged, as if roughhewn from rock and lighted from the side with weird blue glare. By painful degrees he twisted his neck and head, becoming more aware with each passing moment. And the more conscious he became, the less he could be sure he was not dreaming. This place, wherever it was, looked like nothing he had ever seen before. So far as he could make out from his supine position it was a small chamber, possibly ten feet by six, and about eight feet high. He lay—had been placed—on a flat shelf that hinged out from one wall and was braced with cords to its horizontal position. As if it could be folded back to the wall when not in use. Like a bed? He wriggled, at some cost to the joints of his shoulders, which were strained against his bound hands beneath him, and determined that the shelf was covered in something resilient and slippery. So bed seemed a good guess. With considerable effort he managed to sit up without rolling off the bed, and took stock.

The strange blue light came from the walls—more accurately, from a pattern of interlaced diamonds on the walls. The light-strips seemed to have movement, a curious rippling effect, until he rolled close enough to the wall by his shoulder to see that they were, in fact, cut channels—and the light came from a steady trickling flow of liquid. The stuff had no particular smell that he could detect, nor was it warm. The liquid itself originated in a series of orifices close to the ceiling, all around. Scowling over this odd choice of illumination, he noticed an upright rectangular patch on the narrow wall at his feet, where there was no channeled liquid. In a moment it came to him that this must be a door. He craned over, precariously, and saw that the floor was all one blue glare, with ripples to indicate a steady flow.

The metal taste was almost gone now, and he was acutely aware of a growing ache in his arms and shoulders. In this light his pants looked black, and so did the stuff that was knotted about his ankles. The bonds at his wrists felt slippery smooth, like some kind of plastic, and he had more sense than to try either to burst the stuff or untie it. Only by careful straining could he take the pressure off his wrists enough to permit blood-flow, and the consequent pins-and-needles. And anyway, if this cord was the same as the stuff that supported the shelf, he hadn't a hope of snapping it. Still with caution he wriggled until he could swing his legs over the edge and down, and sit in comparative comfort. He lowered his feet gingerly into the blue. It was about three or four inches deep, cool, and felt just like ordinary water. Phosphorescence? Lifting his feet again he watched the stuff trickle off his scuff-proof plastic shoes, leaving them unaffected. Water with some kind of phosphorescence in it. A smart way of illuminating a place, provided you were not too fussy about the quality of the light. Or if you had supersensitive eyes! Venusians!

Now the shakes came. Dillard had no idea just where he was, but no doubt, now, that he was in the hands of the Venusians. And he could guess why, too. Somehow or other, he had contributed to the disaster that had wiped out that ship, and then added fuel to the flames by being caught in the act of spying—he stopped that notion flat. Couldn't be! He had seen Dekron. And Dekron *must* have been destroyed in that blast. Surely? Dillard felt his head start throbbing again. His stomach complained. And this was no sort of posture to sit in for very long. Plagued by too many distractions at once, he gave up trying to make sense out of anything. Except one thing. He was a captive and helpless, and whoever held him was not likely to be gentle.

He called on mental habits that he had developed over the years, and made himself relax. When you don't know, and have no way of finding out, why knock yourself out with wild guesses? Relax. Put it out of your mind. Be patient! Wait! Some of the tension began to drain away. He shut his eyes, got as comfortable as possible—and got the immediate and positive sense that he was inside, and deep inside, some immense and solid structure. And that it was inhabited. With care he tracked down the clues that could be defined. The silent hush, the sense of massiveness, of being deep—those were instincts, without rational tags. But the presence of life was something as tangible as the faint but regular vibration he could now feel, now that he was tuned to it. That was some distant but powerful machine. That argued people, an establishment, and maintainance. And this was no ship, on that he would have staked his life. And yet, when he compared the evidence of his trained senses with the knowledge in his mind, there was no match. Hydro didn't have any structures like this. It was all water, broken only by man-made things. And this cavern, or chamber, whatever it was, was far too solid to be a construct. But he couldn't be off Hydro and down on some other planet, not so quickly. Dillard tucked in his chin and scraped it against his bare chest, and there was a rasp of bristle consonant with some hours since his last shave, but nothing like long enough to transport him on that kind of journey.

He was on the point of forgetting his controlled relaxation under the irritation of so many contradictions when his ears picked up a new sound. At first faint, then growing louder, it was a regular slap-splash that baffled his imagination to interpret. Louder still, then it ceased, and that patch of wall that was free of light suddenly slid aside. It *was* a door, and now it framed two large stone-faced men as they moved in, one after the other, the blue-glow water splashing as they strode. Ugly enough by red light, they were creatures from nightmare now, with the shadows all wrong because the light came from below as well as the sides, and eyes so pale as to seem white, set in cavernous brow-ridges. Dillard cringed as one of them came close, drew a blade from the black plastic loincloth that seemed to be standard wear, and held it threateningly ready as his companion untied the bonds at Dillard's feet.

"Where am I?" he demanded. "What's this all about?"
They ignored him until his feet were free. Then the one

with the knife made a slicing gesture and spoke in that throaty whisper he had heard before. The words made no sense, but the command tone was obvious, as was the gesture. Dillard slid forward, tried his legs, managed to stand. One captor went ahead to the door, made a gesture to follow. Dillard braced his shoulders but made no other move.

"Where are you taking me?" he asked.

For reply, and entirely without warning, the other Venusian slid away the knife he held and brought his hand and arm back in the same movement but with the force of a flail. Edge on, it slammed against Dillard's head, to knock him sprawling, jolting down on to the edge of the couchbed and then to the floor, where, because his arms were still fast behind him, he could have drowned, except that the man who had struck him now took him by the hair and hauled him upright again. Once more there was that harshly whispered command, the gesture, an ungentle shove at his shoulder. Dillard went, utterly cowed and only half-conscious. The man in front did a quick left turn outside the door and went away down a gently sloping passage only just wide enough to have admitted two like him abreast. Dillard, reeling, followed on. Most vivid in his mind was the ease with which the stone-face had hoisted him up. That devil was strong, his hand and flesh almost as hard as the stone it resembled, and he was just two steps behind. Dillard was no stranger to fear, but this was the first time in his life he had known blank despair.

He stumbled on almost in a coma. The passage wound steadily to the left as if circling around some tubular structure, but always going down. The man ahead tramped steadily, with a peculiar high-stepping gait that made the slap-splash noise Dillard had heard. Three inches of glowing blue water ran steadily along the floor they trod. It caught at the feet, made walking a new skill to be learned. Dillard blundered into the walls a time or two before he managed to get something of the hang of it. He learned something else, too. Whenever this passage was joined by another, there was a water-step about an inch down. He found out the hard way, by falling over the first two, agonizing his shoulders and bruising his knees. The first time, shocked by the unexpected, he stayed down there a moment shaking the daze out of his head. The guard who followed had no time to waste on words. He kicked, hard and accurately, to send Dillard plunging forward on his face, then yanked him up by the hair once more. He repeated the lesson at the second step. Dillard began to conceive a murderous hatred, a savage rage that helped to drive out other distresses.

Someday, mister, he vowed internally, as he reeled forward from the second lesson. *Someday, it might be my turn!* But he learned to look out for the tiny furrow of ripples in the underfoot blue, and did not fall any more after that. But still the passage wound and descended, and back came the big problem. Where was this? He could devise no answer that made sense. He plodded on doggedly, and now the way ahead opened out into space under an arch. The lead guard slowed and stood aside, urging Dillard to carry on forward.

His first impression was of similarity with the control room of the Venusian ship, only now he was entering at the arena level and had to look up and around to see the circular tiers. It was difficult to estimate the size of the chamber because of the soft blue lighting, but there was no doubt at all about the concourse of people sitting there in rows and waiting in silence. Blue light trickled down the breaks between the series of steps, and in small channels around each layer, and it could have been a scene from hell. Dillard stared up at the impassive stone-faces and shivered. A solid door slid shut at his back. The two guards moved away on either side to climb to the first level and sit. He was left alone in the middle. The atmosphere was so patently one of trial that he never doubted it. Looking around again, he saw they were not *all* stone-faces. Curiosity stirred him just a little.

Dead ahead of him was one group of hard impassive people separated from the rest by a distinct gap on either side. And to right and left of this key group, about ten people, were two other groups, but these were the long-haired, lively, purple-eyed ones. Like AnnSmith! All the rest were stone-faces. He swung his head around slowly, taking them all in. Apart from the steady purling of the glow-water, there was silence. Just as he was on the point of shouting out something, anything, to crack the nerve-stretching silence, someone spoke out, a rich and vibrant voice, from the purple-eyed group to Dillard's right.

"You are Dennis Dillard, passenger on *Venture Three*, from Earth?"

It was a statement rather than a question. Peering through the wrong-angle shadows, Dillard was able to identify the young man who stood to speak. There was something familiar about him.

"I am," he said, as steadily as he could manage. "Who are you?"

"I am BilliSmith, of Hesperus."

Dillard fumbled with that for a moment until a fugitive memory came back. So far as Earth was concerned, the word was still Venus, but he had heard that the descendants of the original deportees had decided to rechristen their home Hesperus, the evening star. Getting that clear, he fastened on the other name.

"Didn't I meet a relative of yours, BilliSmith, on that ship?"

"That is correct."

"She was kind to me. I should hate to think anything had happened to her—but as I have seen others, survivors, from that ship . . ."

"I am fit and well, DenDillard, and I thank you!" That voice came from the left-hand group, and Dillard swiveled his head to see her stand. This foul light, coming from below, threw everything into reverse relief, but he was able to recognize her, and to spot the strong resemblance between her and her brother.

"I'm very glad to see you," he said, and meant it.

"DenDillard!" The young man's voice took on an edge. "You will attend me. This is no time for trivialities!"

Dillard felt an insane desire to laugh. "It's a triviality to be concerned about somebody's safety? To show common politeness? To try to act civilized? All right, I have to admit I'm not surprised. What am I here for?"

"You are in no position to offend." The young man pointed out the obvious with force. "You will cooperate or suffer. Tell me now, what have you done with the recording spool which carries the recording of the ship?"

"That?" Dillard forgot his wry amusement as he pondered the question. "What do you want that for?"

"Answer the question!"

"All right. I took it out of the machine. I gave it to the pilot of my hydrofoil to look after."

"Why did you do that?"

"Why? Something he said. When that ship blew up, we both saw it. He said he would have to make a report. About me. Just in case I had something to do with it. So I gave him the spool and told him to include it in his report, just to clear me of anything anybody might dream up."

BilliSmith received this in silence. Dillard saw him move, cross the gap to go into a huddle with the central group, and now that his eyes were adjusting to the light, he thought he recognized Dekron again. They all looked evil, but the ship commander stood out from the others in the way he kept aiming that deadly stare of his at Dillard. But he was listening to whatever BilliSmith was saying, and so were the others. Dillard wondered why they were so worked up about his recording? It looked as if the ship's explosion had been some kind of fake, or at least a deliberate business for some reason. Dillard chased that idea down the dark alleyways of his mind and reached the suggestion that maybe he had seen something they wanted hidden. But why? If they had something to hide, why let him on the ship in the first place?

He abandoned that fruitless cogitation, to latch on to something that had been nagging at him for some time, and now became a certainty. The stone-faces had not understood a word he had said. BilliSmith wasn't a spokesman, he was an interpreter! Now that he had the tail of it, Dillard saw all sorts of confirmation in the way they sat, the way the words were being transferred by whisper all around the audience. And something else struck him. This startling difference between the Smiths, and their kind—and the others. That stray thought ran into a spark, became a flaring light of surmise in his mind. Two different kinds of people! Venusians—and what?

Aliens! The word came by itself, rocked him until he forgot his perilous position and his physical distress. Could it be that the Venusians had succeeded where all other ships of Earth had so far failed? Was there, after all, another humanoid culture out there among the stars somewhere? That dream, half-hope, half-fear, had long been present in Man's mind, flourishing with the first mad leap into space, but diminishing fractionally with each ship that came back to report a negative. And yet, the wise ones maintained, the number of possible planets, the very vastness of space itself, made it virtually impossible that Earth alone had the privilege of spawning intelligent life. There must be others, even if we haven't found them yet. Had the Venusians done it?

Dillard rolled the stupendous idea around in his mind and knew bitterness. It would be the supreme irony if the outcasts of Venus, the disinherited, the group that had every reason to hate all that Earth stood for, should be the ones to make first contact with aliens. But it looked like it. It seemed to fit. And this obviously clandestine association on this unlikely water-planet argued no good intentions at all. They had to be hatching something. BilliSmith returned to his place and spoke again.

"DennisDillard. Who employs you?"

"Eh? Don't you know? I told your sister. Didn't I? Anyway, since you have obviously taken my gear, you should know. It's marked, 'Epic Dramatapes, Inc.' Check that, if you doubt me."

"We do not accept that. Why did you seek to inspect the ship?"

"I was *not* inspecting!" Dillard raised his voice in irritation. "I was just looking. I had never seen a Venusian ship before. Hesperian, if you prefer that. So far as I know, nobody has done a sensor-tape of that kind of ship. So it would be something new. And valuable, to me. It was only to get the feel . . ." He swung around to appeal to AnnSmith. "I told you all about it . ."

"Why?" BilliSmith demanded, the sharp monosyllable calling Dillard's attention back.

"Why not? I collect sensor-records! It's my job!"

"You said"—the young man's voice hummed now—"that such a recording would be unique, like no other ship. It could be used to identify one ship from another, *that* ship from others like it?"

Dillard stared wonderingly. "Why, yes. It could. If you had an expert, and recordings from other ships for comparison, yes! Don't you see, that was why I deposited that recording with the 'foil pilot, in case there was going to be an inquiry."

"There will be no inquiry. We want that recording."

"I don't see how you're going to get it," Dillard said. "Not without letting me go to get it for you. And I can't see that." He lifted his chin, stared up at the youth. "Not judging by the way you've treated me so far!"

Again BilliSmith crossed over to go into conference, and now it was beyond doubt that he was translating. Dillard turned in on himself in wild surmise. Aliens! They had to be. Language alone indicated that. System-English was the first tongue of three-fifths of Earth, and a second speech to everyone else. If these stony faced people didn't understand it they had to be from somewhere else. Just where else didn't matter for the moment. What was important was this choice of Hydro as a rendezvous planet, and what they were hatching. He quailed as he realized just how deeply involved he was now, through no choice of his own. This was an enormous thing, and the bigger it was, the smaller his chance of escaping from it. He watched BilliSmith with hawk-like anxiety, but the next question caught him completely unawares.

VI

"WHAT IS YOUR relationship with the woman, MaraHunt?"

For a thick moment Dillard had difficulty breaking up the polysyllable into recognizable fractions. Then he gaped.

"Mara Hunt? What's she got to do with anything?"

"Do you deny you are working together? You came here on the same ship. You went together to the desalination plant. Subsequently, instead of returning to your ship you arranged to keep a secret rendezvous with her in the Green Salon at the Hydro Palace. You cannot deny any of this. You cannot deny that you are working with her."

"I certainly can." Dillard shook his head to try and clear the confusion in it. The way BilliSmith put it, there was a connection, but that was just coincidence. "Just a coincidence," he said. "I didn't even know she was in the Green Salon. It was no rendezvous!"

"You were watched. Commander Dekron and Weaponeer Crade observed you, saw you establish visual contact with her. Then, when you saw you were observed, you tried to escape."

"I did not! You've got it all wrong! I didn't make contact. I was just looking. Sure I saw Dekron, but . . ."

"And you tried to escape, but you were caught and brought here. It is self-evident. You and the woman Mara-Hunt are associates."

"We're not! I never saw her before in my life!"

"Then why did she try to follow you here?"

"Hah?" Dillard was caught wrong-footed again. "Follow me? Here?"

"She was intercepted in the act. And taken. And brought here under guard. Do you still deny you are associated?"

"Suit yourself," Dillard muttered. "You have this thing so screwed up I don't know what's true and what isn't. All I know is that I never saw her before. Why would I associate with her, anyway?"

BilliSmith did not answer. Once again he went into conference with the chief members of the stone-faces. They were obviously that, Dillard realized. There was much guttural whispering, and then vicious snorts from Dekron, and harsh whisperings and gestures that proved to be orders to Dillard's recent warders. They rose and tramped on out by the door he had come in through. In short order they were back, one leading, then Mara Hunt, then the second. Again the solid door rolled across and the guards spread away to their places. She looked defiant but battered. There was the beginning of a blue bruise on her left cheekbone and red handling-marks on her forearms. She had lost her cape, and her snug-fitting dark blue slacks were soaked, clinging to her legs as she moved. It occurred to Dillard that he, too, was soaking wet, and he wondered why he hadn't noticed it before. But he dismissed that, just to watch her. Battered she might be, but her glossy black hair was neat, her head high, her back straight, and smoldering fury was in her eyes as she raked the assembly with her stare.

Just for one second her blazing eyes held on Dillard and there was a something in that stare that made him stiffen up a bit and lift his chin in instinctive desire to match her slim defiance. Then, as she swung to survey the rest of the audience, he saw that her hands were bound like his own, to drag her shoulders back. BilliSmith spoke, from his original position.

"You are MaraHunt," he declared, and her eyes snapped around to him like sword-blades. Her voice sang as she replied.

"I know you, BilliSmith, just as I know several of you by sight, just as you know me. Yes, I am Mara Hunt."

The stone-faces didn't understand a word. If confirmation was needed, Dillard had it now in the way they sat absolutely unmoved. But the other contingent understood, and writhed.

He could feel them seething under that lashing scorn in her voice.

"What is the nature of your association with this man, DennisDillard?"

The question came, and Mara Hunt laughed at it, throwing her head back. "So that's it! Yes, I can see why you think that we are associated. Very well, yes. I am very much associated with Mr. Dillard."

There was biting scorn in her voice still. Dillard half-turned to mutter a protest, but she ignored him and went on.

"Oh yes. Mr. Dillard is, as you know, human. Of Earth. So am I. So we have a relationship, in that much. You, BilliSmith, and you, AlanBrown, GregorHoffman, LizWilson, MaryEllis—and the rest of you"—her challenging stare swept the two wing groups of purple-eyes—"also are human. You are of Hesperus, which we call Venus, and you like to nurse in your breasts the idea that you are different. But only five generations ago your ancestors were of Earth, were human. You are human. Don't tell me you have forgotten?"

"We have not forgotten!" BilliSmith shouted in sudden anger, and there was a seething outburst, silent but very real to Dillard, from his companions. "We are not likely to forget that, not ever!"

"No?" she flung the word at him. "Then what in the name of sanity are you doing conspiring, hand-in-glove, with these—things? How do you justify allying yourselves against your own species, with aliens?"

There was a silence so complete that the running water sounded like a torrent. Dillard knew, now, something he had been steadfastly trying to deny to himself ever since he had walked into this arena. He was not going to get out of this alive. He knew it, and, somehow, it was a relief just to have it admitted and done with. BilliSmith swept his gaze to and fro to include his kin, then turned to face the prisoners.

"A century and a half ago," he said, "Earth cast out our ancestors. They were all, every man and woman of them, people of the finest kind. They were the cream of Earth's intellectual and philosophical development. They were people who could see, and did see, the way human culture was heading, into mass mechanization and materialism, accumulating neurosis, creeping death. And they gathered, in secret, to rescue humanity from that fate. Their idea was to restore the respect and the virtue of excellence, to bring back hopes and ambitions and goals . . ."

"To elect themselves as the rulers of all mankind." She interrupted him coldly. "Speak the truth, BilliSmith. They may have meant well, who knows, but they went about it the wrong way, in secret, just as you are doing now."

"Why argue?" he retorted. "The facts are beyond dispute. You cast them out, by the thousand, and you shipped them to Venus, a planet where you had never been able to establish a happy colony, or attractive conditions. You gave each one minimum survival equipment, and you left them to die!"

"Nonsense!" She scorned him. "You know better. They had maximum, not minimum equipment. And they did not die!"

"How little you know!" He smiled now, and it was not a pleasant smile. "A hundred thousand men and women, and half of them died in the first hundred days. But the rest survived. They were our ancestors. We are not likely to forget that. Would you?"

"Certainly not. BilliSmith, this has been talked out a thousand times since then. Mistakes were made on both sides. Your side did wrong to conspire in secret, and were misunderstood. Our side did wrong in casting out the cream of its intelligence, and Earth has paid a sore price for that since, I assure you. But that wasn't me, BilliSmith. Nor you. That was one hundred and fifty years ago. We have both learned wider sanity since then."

"Are you suggesting we should come together and forget our differences? Make peace and mutual forgiveness?"

"Have you ever thought of trying it?"

"Would Earth open its doors for us to return?"

"Not all of you, no." She was patient. "Be rational. You know that is impossible. We barely have room enough for our own people . . ."

"And we are no longer *your* people. You have admitted it. So what does it matter to you who we associate with? Why do you spy on us?"

"I could tell you a tale," she said, "about scientific interest, and the need to study an alien culture, possibly to mutual benefit—and all sorts of other possible plausible things. But I won't. You can have the truth, BilliSmith.

I think you are in cahoots with this crowd with some crazy idea of launching an attack on Earth. Conquest. Revenge. You name it, but it's still crazy." She said it flatly and with conviction. Dillard held his breath until the blood roared in his ears. The idea took a long time to get through. He had been taught in school, as had every other sensible citizen, that the outcasts of Venus could never mount a threat to Earth. They were too few. They lacked the technological know-how, being strictly academic types. And even if they had it, the planet lacked the necessary resources to support any such all-out effort. And so on. And he believed it. But add in an alien component, an unknown factor, and the whole idea went wild. Who could know just what kind of weapons, or technology, the stone-faces had? BilliSmith was in urgent conference again. Dillard edged close to Mara.

"Was that straight, what you just said?"

"Do you doubt it?" she muttered back. "Take a good look, Dillard. Do they strike you as amiable?"

The bruises on her face and arms were darker now. He recalled his ungentle shepherding on the way here, and his own bruises.

"You have a point," he admitted. "And you're right about the Veenies being crazy, too. I would just as soon make friends with a cobra as this lot."

He edged away again as Dekron stood and addressed the crowd in his nonvocalized, scrapy whispering. It didn't last long. As he sat the two warders rose and resumed their duties. The door rolled back. Mara went first, Dillard at her heels. He stepped close enough to demand, "What happens now?"

"Your guess is as good as mine. I don't speak the language."

The march this time was brief, and brought them to a cell similar to his first one, only larger and with six of the shelf-beds. Briskly the two aliens let down a couple of the shelves. Dillard was allotted one by the simple means of a shove in the chest until he fell. His legs were scooped up, bound securely, and dropped. The guards splashed out silently, and the door rumbled shut. Dillard wriggled up on his elbows to see that Mara was tied just as he was. But her reaction was utterly different. The door was hardly closed before she had arched violently and managed to hurl herself off the shelf into the water on the floor. Another furious effort and she was over, on her knees, then standing.

"Listen!" she commanded urgently. "When I say to, you roll over. That will get your fingers to my belt. See it? That ornamental buckle is no ornament. You grab it, twist it clockwise, and pull. That will get you a knife. Be careful with it, it's sharp. Ready?"

"Yes, hey! What do I do with the knife afterward?"

"You'd better let me take it in my teeth. That way I'll be able to see what I'm doing. I'd just as soon not get sliced by accident."

"All right." He rolled over and wriggled until his bound hands were close to the edge. His fingers met the firm flesh of her stomach.

"Down a bit! More! Right, now twist. And pull. Harder! You've got it. Now, just hold very still while I get it."

He lay still with the angular metal thing in his fingers, felt her breath on his wrists, and then a tug, the brush of her cheek, and let go but kept still otherwise. In a moment he felt movement at his bonds, and then a loosening, and freedom. He moved the upper arm, and had to grit his teeth to cut the groan from torturing sinews. But he was free. He levered himself up and over, turned to face her, to take the slim knife from her grinning teeth. It was a blade about two and a half inches long, and very thin and flat.

"Be careful now," she warned. "It's flexible. Has to be. The curved edge is a razor, the other a diamond-file. Ready?" She wheeled around and he sliced the black ropy cords at her wrists until she was as free as he. Moments later she had the knife again and their feet were free too.

"You must be a very confused man, Dillard," she said. "And I can't say I blame you. Enemy aliens are quite a thing to take in one mouthful."

"I had sort of guessed aliens," he said, "but you seem to know all about it already!"

"Not all," she denied, massaging her wrists. "Only bits and hints, and some guesswork. What I don't understand is how you came to be in the Hydro Palace. I thought you'd gone up with that ship. I never saw you leave it. When I spotted you in the Green Salon I thought I was seeing things. Spooks! I still don't get it."

He scowled in thought, reconstructing the scene. "I think

I know how you missed me," he said. "The ship was free-floating, ready to jump, so the exit hatch, and the 'foil, would be on the far side where you couldn't see. I damn near didn't get off, though."

He told her briefly what had happened and she listened intently. She took him back over a point or two about the interior of the ship, but she was obviously puzzled by something. When he was done explaining he said, "Look, you seem to have a fair idea what this is all about, but me—nothing! Can't you explain, just a little?"

"There's not much time," she said, flexing her wrists. "We didn't cut these ropes for the fun of it. Soon as I feel fit enough I'm leaving. I'm assuming that suits you too? Right, then you'd better limber up. Space only knows what we might run into." Seeing the sense in that he began stretching and flexing his arms, and trying his feet.

"You got on the ship in the first place," she explained, "because Captain Conway made the request, and they didn't dare do anything to excite any curious reactions. That's obvious, so there had to be something odd about the ship. They didn't know who you were, but once you said your recording was unique, that it could identify it, they flew into a panic, shot you away out of it, evacuated the thing and then blew it by remote. That also explains why they want that recording."

"But why blow the ship? What are they trying to hide?"

"That's something I don't know, yet." Mara Hunt made one more vigorous stretch, flexing her whole body, then declared, "I'm ready. Let's go!"

Dillard turned with her, then said, "What about the door? Suppose it has some kind of catch?"

"I doubt it." She stepped close, and as she moved her eyes in quick examination, it began to rumble. Before either of them could move it was open, to reveal AnnSmith standing there, frozen in surprise. Next moment the surprise broke into quick movement. AnnSmith started to duck back, Mara Hunt struck forward with outstretched hands, grabbed and heaved, dragging the girl inside, spinning her, clamping one hand over her mouth.

"Fix that door, Dillard!" she rapped. "Quickly, before someone comes by to surprise us."

Dillard fumbled for just a moment, until he found a slot cut in the surface where a hand would naturally go. His fingertips encountered a lever within. Heaving on it slid the door shut, and the lever moved, then settled. Some sort of catch, he guessed, and spun around to see Mara still holding the girl securely. AnnSmith did not seem to be offering any resistance.

"It's all right," he said urgently. "We aren't going to hurt you."

"The hell we're not," Mara disagreed. "If she lets out one yell for help, or anything else foolish, I'll break her neck!"

"Then you'll have to break mine too," he declared, surprising himself by his sudden determination. "She's not going to do us any harm, I tell you. Let her go. Give her a chance to explain."

"All right, but let me get my back to the door first." Mara swung her captive around, shoved her away and put her back to the sliding slab. Dillard noted the razor-sharp knife in her hand, then looked at the Venusian girl.

"Why did you come here?" he asked. There was no fear in his mind now. This close, he could once more feel her emotions. He knew she was disturbed, even frightened, but not threatening. Her first words confirmed that.

"I wish you no harm, DenDillard," she said. "I had to tell you. The Roggans say you have discovered too much, and that you must die, both of you. They will kill you. But I had to come and tell you that it is not my wish, person-to-person. Our quarrel is with Earth."

Dillard was confused again. He felt sure there were values and meanings here that were going over his head, but there was no doubt in his mind as to her feelings. Seen now, in this weird blue glow, she looked like a silver goddess. Only the larger irises, and the lambent violet glow of her eyes, served to make her different from any other Earthwoman, and she had a vibrant poise, and a shape, that any Earthwoman would have sold her soul to own. But what was the subtle stress in the way she spoke of "person-to-person?" Mara Hunt seemed to understand.

"I know about your strong community sense, AnnSmith," she said. "It developed in the bad days, when you had to band together for survival. It was during that time that you all learned to think on two levels. For the communal welfare—and for your own personal satisfaction. And to keep the two in separate compartments in your minds."

"It was necessary then. It is still necessary, sometimes, that

I as a member of the group shall agree to and permit things which I as a person do not approve. I am one. The group is all."

"Yes. I know. But it won't work now, my dear." Mara's voice was unusually gentle. "In the name and tradition of Hesperus, you hate all Earth people. But I am an Earth person. Do you hate me? Do you hate Dillard, here? Enough to stand by and let him be killed?"

"For the good of Hesperus—yes!"

"You really mean that," Dillard said slowly. "You'd go along with something you don't agree with, for the sake of a principle. I can understand that. I've done it. I have to do it, often. I have to drive myself into things that I knew were going to scare the hell out of me, because I'd be unable to look myself in the face afterward if I didn't. And so long as I know the outcome is going to be worthwhile."

"You, too?" AnnSmith's eyes were huge as they met his.

"Oh yes. I know what it's like. But you're away off on just one bit of it. The outcome has to be worth it."

"Restitution! My people will walk the face of the Earth again!"

"They won't. Look, if you're really tied up with these aliens—what did you call them, Roggans?—and even if they have something really hot in the line of weapons. And even if you get organized, and attack Earth, you don't stand a chance of winning. Not a chance!"

"If you mean many people will be killed on both sides, I know. I do not like that. I do not like killing. But if you say we cannot succeed, you are wrong. We can. Earth has grown fat and lazy, overcrowded and anarchic. You could not scrape up an army, or a space-force, of any power, not without a lot of time and trouble. And you will not have that time."

"I didn't mean it that way. If you go ahead with your plan there will be people killed, sure. On both sides. Far more than you think. But you can't possibly win. Ann, there are five billion of us. And, if you've read any history at all, you must know that we know how to make war. We may not be much good at anything else, but we do know that."

"We have weapons, too," she declared, but he could feel her pain, the way her mind cringed away from the thought of slaughter.

"Weapons?" Mara Hunt joined in. "My dear, you have no idea just what you could run into. At the time your ancestors were being captured and shipped away to Venus, the armed forces of Earth had weapons powerful enough and awful enough to fry the entire surface of the Earth into a cinder, and to insure the end of all possible forms of life on its surface for ever and ever, amen—ten times over! That very knowledge was one of the reasons why the major powers were so eager to get your ancestors away out of it, before they triggered off doomsday. It looks now like you're all set to do it again!"

"We have weapons!" the girl repeated stubbornly. "And ours are now, not yesterday!"

Dillard stretched out a hand to touch Mara on the shoulder. "Let me," he said, very gently. From some hitherto unsuspected inner resource he felt an upsurge of warm confidence. He knew that AnnSmith, for all her outward assurance, wanted desperately to be persuaded out of her elected role, wanted a good honest reason to change her mind. And he felt sure he had one.

"You have no weapons," he said. "Not really. The Roggans have them. They have the know-how, and, from what I've seen, the right kind of personality. They are the warmongers, aren't they?" She didn't reply, but he knew he had the right answer. "You can do the rest of the sum just as well as I can, now. All right, you go past us somehow. You carry out your plan. You attack Earth. It's one of two things. Win—or lose. Even suppose you win, and inherit what's left of Earth, how long d'you think you'll keep it? Do you really think the Roggans will go away? Or be content with a fair share? You know them better than I do. Can you really believe that?"

He had her. He knew he had her suppressed fears and anxieties pushed to breaking point. But he was as surprised as anyone when she suddenly wilted, her eyes flooding with tears. What came next was automatic, and as natural as drawing breath. Her face went up to his chest, her cheek snuggling close, and she clung to him like a lost child. He put his arm around her gently, stroked the shaking silk of her shoulder.

"I have felt this a long time," she choked, "but the others are so hotheaded, so eager to grasp at anything that will offer revenge, they have lost the ability to feel, where the

Roggans are concerned. Because the Roggans have no feelings. They have cold blood, no emotions. They know only efficiency and results. What shall I do, DenDillard? I cannot betray my people!"

He held her securely, his hand idly patting her shoulder, and gave thought to her question. But the more he thought, the more he ran into a dead end, and into concern that grew rapidly into tension. He stared at Mara over AnnSmith's shoulder, surprised a savage gleam there that vanished as fast as he saw it, and then Mara shook her head.

"It's too late for that, AnnSmith," she said. "You're already betrayed. Let me put it to you." Her voice was steel hard now. "As you see, we are on our way out. Escaping. You've walked into it. We have to think of our own necks. So what else can we do but eliminate you? Or take you with us? We can't just leave you here."

AnnSmith turned her head. Dillard felt her stiffen. He said, "She wouldn't betray us."

"She doesn't have to. When the Roggans find us gone and her here they will make the obvious conclusion. Wouldn't you?"

AnnSmith swung her head back to stare at Dillard, and now she was full of terror, her face a mask of dread.

"You'll have to come with us," he said. "Help us. There's nothing else for it, not now."

"But—that will mean the destruction of everything we have worked for. I can't do it!"

"You have to. You're dead if you stay, now."

"And we're dead unless we get moving fast," Mara snapped. "We've wasted enough time as it is." She exhibited her knife. "Make up your mind, AnnSmith. Come with us, or we leave you here—for the Roggans to find."

Dillard sensed a moment of extreme tension, then the Venusian girl sagged.

"Very well, I will come with you. I will help as much as I can."

"Right. Lead on, then. You know the way out of here?"

"Yes." She moved to the door, slid it open cautiously and peered out. "There are several ways. Come!"

"You follow her, Dillard. I'll bring up the rear, just in case we meet opposition. Go ahead, AnnSmith."

Dillard went out into the blue-glare passage close on the heels of the Venusian girl, and for the first time it came home to him that so far they had only escaped from bonds and a cell. They still had the unknown hazards of the building to pass. Whatever it was. AnnSmith had turned right, and now the gradient was upward, but that was the only change. It was still narrow stone walls and rippling blue water all around. She halted, peered around a corner, went on by a side-passage, and he followed, wondering what any of them would do if they suddenly encountered one of the stone-faced aliens. He remembered how strong they were, and how ruthless, and he felt cold. Pressing up close on the girl in front he asked, "They were going to kill us, you said? How?"

"Drugs first," she whispered over her shoulder, "to make you talk, to discover how much you know and how many others share the knowledge. And then you would be cut up for food."

"For food?" He echoed, hardly able to believe his ears.

"It has been the Roggan custom for many generations, to use their convicted criminals for food. They live in a harsh environment. They cannot afford to waste anything."

He fell back a pace or two and ordered his stomach to stop heaving. Something like this was to be expected, he told himself. The clues were at hand, now he had been alerted to them. For Venusian and Roggan to meet on any equable basis the backgrounds had to be similar, and the Venusian environment was stringent enough. But cannibalism? Cringing away from that thought, he came up close behind her again as she halted at another intersection, and an old question came back to him.

"Where are we, anyway?" he asked. "What is this place?"

She turned on him in amazement, but before she could answer, Mara Hunt moved close enough to whisper to him, "We're under the sea, Dillard. Where else?" The shatteringly obvious answer struck him silent. She went on: "Could you think of a better place to hide, on a water-world? Go on, she's away again."

He shambled forward following AnnSmith, feeling suddenly that he was walking through a nightmare. And yet, thinking it over, it fitted such a lot of pieces together. Venusians were well accustomed to a watery world, to constant damp. "They swim the way we walk." Mara had said that. And if the alien Roggans came from a similar kind of planet, they too would be at home here. But it must have taken time, and a lot of effort, to build this place. He didn't know the full extent of it, but the parts he had traversed so far would add up to a considerable size. But that slotted something else into place.

"I'm beginning to get it," he muttered over his shoulder to Mara. "You know there's a Venusian ship in and out of here regularly?"

"So?"

"So, does anybody count how many ships depart from Venus, and come back? Does anybody count all the ships that splash down on Hydro, and where they're from? And compare?"

"You're getting smart," she hissed, showing her teeth a grin. "You can see this underwater rabbit warren wasn't put together overnight, can't you? And the Venusians couldn't have done it alone. This controlled water-flow illumination, for instance, is some kind of specially-bred algae, and that means dosing equipment somewhere, and powerful pumping machinery to get the accumulated water out of the basement. That's technology, Dillard, and the Venusians are weak on that."

"With spaceships?"

"Prefabricated parts, built on Earth and shipped out to them. Didn't know that, did you? But if the Roggans have technology, and the wit to make a few of their ships look like Venusian craft—you get the idea?"

"So that's why they blew the ship?"

"And that's why they want your recording, and your hide, Dillard!"

He gasped, then cut it off short as AnnSmith hissed a warning and fell back, flattening herself to the wall. He did likewise, and heard the regular splash-slap of feet approaching.

"Back up and in here!" Mara muttered urgently, and he turned, touching AnnSmith. They scattered to a side alley and cowered there, to see five impassive Roggans come striding past, three men and two women. Dillard realized all over again how utterly alien they were and his insides shrank at the thought of what would happen if they fell into those hands again. The aliens went on into the dim blue and the fugitives started moving again, treading cautiously through the purling water. It seemed a lifetime to Dillard

since he had seen sun and breathed dry air. A long-forgotten
question came to him.

"What about Dr. Stanley?" he asked. "Where does he fit
into this?"

"*Fons et origo,* if you recall any Latin," Mara whispered.
"He came here, in the first place, to do some highly important research. That's genuine. But he is by nature a
highly inquisitive man. And he can count, add and sub-
tract. He counted the Venusian ships. He knew, as I know,
that Venus has only a score of ships altogether, and has to
strain to maintain even those. Also, that water-plant processes something like fifteen million gallons of water every
hour. It all has to be screened. The perfect spot for finding
any debris that might be sculling about. There's quite a bit,
naturally, but some of it was queer stuff. Plastics and other
materials that did not originate on Earth, or Venus either."

"That file!" he gasped. "Artifacts native to Hydro—"

"A cover only, in case anyone got curious. But there had to
be something funny going on. He checked, for instance, the
recorded appearances of Venusian ships on other planetary
colonies like Castor, Pollux, Lyra, Vega—everywhere there's
any excuse for a ship to go. And compared numbers. And
they didn't add up. So he sent for me." -

Dillard absorbed that in silence as he tramped on. They
had been going steadily upward for some time now along
a straight gallery, and he thought he could see an open
chamber showing ahead. AnnSmith was moving faster now.
He slowed, turned his head.

"Dr. Stanley sent for you? Who are you?"

She met his stare with a wry grin. "I don't often get asked
that, and it's just as well, because it isn't easy to answer.
You never heard of the Philosophy Corps, did you?" His
blank stare was enough answer. "Never mind. Perhaps
I'll be able to explain to you sometime. We're a bunch of
people who make it our business to keep a careful eye on
various unpleasant things. It's just a job. Leave it for now.
I think we're about at the end of our trip."

He moved on to close up to AnnSmith. She stood in an
archway that led to a chamber reminiscent of the trial arena,
but with differences. It was a lot smaller, for one thing,
and from the dished roof descended a thick column of what
looked like copper-bronze alloy. The lower end of the column lost itself in a basin some fourteen feet across that was

full and steadily overflowing in a chatter of water. Staring in wonder, Dillard saw that the water cascading from the basin was clear, and fell into an annular channel which, in turn, overflowed into another, and then another, descending like an ornamental fountain. But at each leap it grew progressively more luminous, until it ended in a broad circular bed, from which it flowed away through several narrow cuts. As the fugitives stood under the archway they had to go down a few steps to that pool, and where they stood was comparatively dry.

"That the way out?" Mara demanded, and as AnnSmith nodded, she added, "All right, what are we waiting for?"

"There is someone coming," the Venusian girl said, and Dillard started, because he had felt exactly the same intuition. "We had better hide," AnnSmith warned. "Here, in this other archway. It is a tank storage, where the flame-seeds are kept." She led them swiftly to a dimlit chamber where there were several broad-bellied jars of glossy black stuff, and where the only light came from the intense blue glare that spouted up from the jars' mouths. Turning, pressing against the wall, they waited. Mara fidgeted.

"How do you know there's anyone coming?" she demanded, and Dillard frowned. Obviously she couldn't feel it, so there was no point in trying to explain. But he could, quite distinctly. In a moment the intuition was justified. There came a disturbance in the regular chatter of the water, and agitation in the basin as heads bobbed up. For an awful moment Dillard thought he was seeing yet more aliens, of a different kind, until he realized that these were people wearing some kind of aqualung. He watched them climb out and down the cascading terraces, and then begin peeling off the odd harnesses they wore. A transparent face-mask that clung from brow to under the chin was secured by a headband. It fed two tubes that curled back over the shoulders to a small and compact unit between the shoulder blades. From there, like shapeless wings, fell a flapping and saturated quantity of gray-white filmy stuff, secured at either wrist and with a waistband.

The six newcomers were all Venusian, all sober-faced and intent. Their worry was as apparent to Dillard as a strong smell would have been, and he knew AnnSmith could feel it too. He put out a hand to touch hers, to grip gently in reassurance. Within a minute or two the six, four men and two women, had shed their swimming gear and went away by a distant arch, on the other side of the chamber.

"You know anything about a cape-lung?" Mara asked, and Dillard shook his head. She eased out into the chamber, looking around, then beckoned him to follow. "This is where you'll have to learn fast," she said. "Not that there's a lot to it, so long as you keep your head and don't pant. You check me, AnnSmith, just in case I get something wrong. It's been a while." They were across the blue pool now and on the first tier of the cascade. The recently departed Venusians had dunked their equipment in the water, each set secured by a fine line to a hook apparently there for the purpose. Mara hoisted out one. It looked like nothing at all except a gray-white mass of slime until she carefully freed the face-and-tube section.

"Now," she said intently, "this part over the face, make sure the seal is good all around the edge, and the unit square in the middle of your shoulder blades, right? Then you shackle the belt around your waist, here, and these straps around each wrist, so that the rest of it is free to hang in back. In the mask"—she parted it wide to show him—"this ridge sits on your nose, for location. This stiffener tucks against your chin, is a bone-conduction talk unit. That's all the works. This unit merely adjusts the mixture so you won't get CO_2 chokes or nitrogen narcosis. The slimy stuff is permeable membrane, is a lung in actual fact."

"You need to inflate," AnnSmith put in. "You press here, on the right-hand tube, which holds open a non-return valve. You take two or three breaths in, breathing out into the filter-cape with the valve shut . . ." She paused, stared at him. "What is wrong?"

"You know damned well!" he choked, staring from her to the clammy thing she held. "I can't! I can't! I'm scared! I can't even swim!"

"Oh no!" Mara growled. "Dillard, this is no time to go neurotic on us. You have to swim, there's no other way!"

"You do *not* have to swim!" AnnSmith corrected, suddenly firm. "You just put this on, remember not to pant or gasp quickly, because the filter-membrane cannot handle that, and just drift. There is this line, see? You will be linked with myself and MaraHunt. You will not have to do anything at all, except be passive."

"You don't know how I feel—all that water out there—!"

104

"I know. Your feelings are mine to share. But feeling and doing are different, you know? One cannot help feeling, but one *can* control one's doing. Be afraid, but come. I was afraid, but I came with you."

Her steady words helped him realize that this, after all, was no more than he had done many a hundred times before, cringing inwardly from some fearful prospect, yet driving himself into it just the same.

"All right," he mumbled. "Check me while I put the thing on."

"And move!" Mara urged. "Every moment we lose means the Roggans are that much closer on our heels."

"They will not come this way," AnnSmith contradicted. "I chose it for that reason. They use lower exits and entrances than this, because they go up to the surface very seldom, and then only at night." She watched Dillard get into his mask, saw him breathe enough to inflate the cape-lung at his back, and patted his shoulder in approval. Then, swift and supple, she copied him and went ahead up the cascade terraces and over the edge of the basin. She had the trailing end of his line. She looped and knotted it to her own and let him see it done, then down she went, out of sight. Stiff-kneed and inwardly cringing, he followed, clambered over the edge and felt Mara's hand at his belt. She was knotting her line there, jerked it tight, made a hand gesture to him to go on. He let himself down into the water, felt it rise up and over his head, and the panic was a bursting pressure in his chest. He saw the open end of the column—which was really a tube—and ducked to get under it, then kicked and tried to spring upward. There was no sense of movement, only a plunge into darkness.

Banded constriction gripped his chest, the feeling of being caught and crushed. Then his head nudged something solid, and the panic doubled. A door or something! A tube was blocked! In that instant, before he could scream out, a voice said, flute-clear in his head, "It is all right, DenDillard. There is an S-bend in the column. It is an air lock. Follow the line."

"Ann?" His nervous question came out a high-pitched quack that shocked him. He tried again and the result was the same.

"You must pitch your voice low," she said, "because sound-speed in water is fast, much faster than in air, and the tonal values are distorted." To prove it he heard another quacking, shrill and almost impossible to understand, and it was an effort to realize that it was Mara Hunt, urging him on. Forgetting his panic in the novelty, he managed to scrape around the bend, saw ahead of him a ring of blue flame and struggled toward it, through it, and then he was out. He knew, instantly, that there was vast space around him, even though he could see nothing but blue-black void at first. Then, dimly, he saw AnnSmith, in front and moving, looking like a silver dream against the blue twilight. He made motions, tried to swim as he had seen people do in drama, and drew up close to her.

It had a dreamy quality, this sense of hanging poised and without motion in a limitless blue-black space. AnnSmith looked like something from a fairytale, the black of her brief loincloth invisible against that backdrop, and her torso and legs like shimmering silver but solid, whereas the cloud of her hair and the billowing gray of her cape-lung were insubstantial mist. Now Mara came to join them and they hung there, all three, slowly revolving. Mara was just a mask with filmy wings and a white body, the rest invisible. Over her shoulder as they spun he saw the blue circle that marked the end of the tube. And as a huge black shadow darker against the blue, he saw the place they had just left. A hillside, irregular and jagged, where long-haired weeds and plants waved in the ceaseless currents. And he was no longer afraid.

"It's a strange feeling," he said, remembering to sink his voice into a growl, and intrigued by the way it came out tenor. "Is this why the Roggans talk the way they do? In that whisper?"

"Not a whisper," AnnSmith corrected, in that flute-like treble her voice was now, "but subsonic, or almost. From twenty to a hundred cycles per second, in air. Low-pitch travels further and more coherently in water."

Mara squeaked. Then she tried again, just a note. And again, but now it was better. "Ah—ah—ah—I think I'm getting it, but I shall have a sore throat if I talk too much like this. I'm no contralto. You know where we are, Ann. Better get moving before they miss us and come looking."

"We *are* moving. Look behind!" Dillard wriggled around in mid-air—it felt like mid-air—and saw that the dark hillside was gone out of sight. "We are in a current flow that will take us part of the way."

"How do you know where we are?" he asked. "It's the middle of nowhere to me. No marks, clues, anything!"

"It is a sense one develops, under pressure of circumstance." He sensed bitterness, although there was none in her voice. "I have many senses you do not have. I am Hesperian!"

Now he felt more than just bitterness. He was suffused by a wash of chokingly lonely, outcast, angry-lost feeling from her that brought sympathetic tears to his eyes in a moment. And he knew why she felt like that.

"It's not true," he said impulsively. "The way you're feeling, it's not right."

"How do you know what I am feeling?"

"But of course I do. You're feeling sick and empty inside, and lost, because you're different from us and all alone, now that you have deserted your own people. And that's just not true, Ann!" Clumsily he propelled himself near enough to be able to offer his hand to grasp hers. "Look, this ability to share my feelings—if that is one of the senses you have that you think makes you different, then you're wrong. I have it, too. And I know people who have orientation sense. You're stuck with this notion that because you're the fifth generation on Venus you are somehow *not* human, and it isn't true."

"She doesn't share my feelings!"

"Mara? Maybe not, but that's only because she hasn't developed the gift. I have. I suppose it's because I work in that field anyway, sensor-recording helps to fine it up. Ann, you have certain talents. Your home environment helped to *develop* them, but you had to be born with them in the first place. And they are human, those gifts. Quite well known!"

"He's right!" Mara chimed in, sounding like a very small schoolboy just out of choir practice. "You had me baffled for a while there, you two, but I think I've caught up now. He's right. We humans have all kinds of talents we hardly suspect, because we seldom need to use them. But when it comes to survival, we manage to turn on all kinds of things. Incidentally, survival can be bought at too high a price. How far down are we?"

"About one thousand feet," AnnSmith said. "We are rising

slowly. You are quite right to remind me that we should not rise to the surface too rapidly. It would be uncomfortable, even for me."

"The bends, just in case you didn't know, Dillard," Mara explained. "These lung units overcome most of the hazards. They're designed to do just that, but even they have limits."

Dillard breathed in carefully, suddenly very conscious of the vast waters around him. "Where abouts are you taking us? Where are we, anyway?"

"If we follow the drift for some time longer and then strike off, we will come up by the water-plant. As for where we are"—AnnSmith extended her arm back the way they had drifted. "You saw that hill we came from? That is one extremity of an island continent about five hundred miles long. The water-plant stands on just such another submerged mountain. Long ago, before the ice caps melted and raised the sea level, there were two large island continents on Roggan. One was called . . ."

"Just a minute!" Mara's voice sailed up into a squeak of astonishment. "You mean—*this* is Roggan? The aliens belong here?"

"Of course. You didn't know that?"

"I certainly didn't. How long have *you* known?"

"Ever since this planet was first discovered by Solarian ships. It was a ship from Hesperus that found it."

"That's true," Dillard put in. "Captain Conway told me that himself. And that it was your people who built all the establishments."

"My father was a young man on that first ship, was one of the men who planned and built the water-plant basis, with the idea of establishing a base and a fueling station. Our people did all the pioneer work. We tried to claim rights on Hydro in the name of Hesperus. It was hard work, and dangerous, but we did it. And then there was a legal dispute over territorial rights. We were cheated, somehow, out of everything except a minimum royalty on the operation of the plant. A legal quibble about sovereign rights, and territorial rights. Now it is owned and operated by an independent body of profiteers!"

"Conway told me a bit about that, too. You had a raw deal, Ann!"

"There's quite a lot about this whole thing that is raw," Mara snapped. "Earth has much to be ashamed of. I can only assure you, my dear, that we are not all cursed with the same idiocy. There are quite a few of us working to bring about some kind of understanding between us. You could help a lot, if you will."

"So you say. It does not matter very much now, one way or the other. My life is forfeit. I cannot go back." AnnSmith said it quietly, then put out her arm again, in another direction. "It is time to strike away from the current now," she said. "Follow me."

She spun and then leaned forward into flight, her slim arms reaching out and stroking the blue. It *was* flight, Dillard realized, as he made an awkward attempt to mimic her movements and fell into a lazy, dreamlike action in which he was weightless, but without the falling terror of zero-gravity. His breathing no longer troubled him. Now that his eyes were adjusted he glided at the indeterminate interface between a dark purple "sky" and bottomless blue-black. And—surely—those were lights, away down there?

"That couldn't be a city down there, beneath us?" He asked.

"It is. At least, I can tell you only what I have been told, not what I have seen. Some of our people have been down there, with special equipment, but the strain is very great and we cannot endure it for long."

"You mean the Roggans can stand it, down there, *without* pressure suits?"

"They have had two thousand years and more of learning how. It is not easy to work out the time scale exactly, but it must be that long since they fought their last war. Two nations, one against the other. Fire-bombs melted the ice caps and Roggan died. All except one ship, a warship that had been crippled and blown into cometary about their sun. When it got back, Roggan was wiped out. But that handful of people refused to give in. They took the ship down, made landfall down there, lived in it—and learned, by degrees, how to reclaim their submerged city. They sealed it off, bit by bit, restarted industries, food supplies, relearned technology. They hollowed out whole mountains and hills. It was on one of those that our people lowered the first pylons and embedded them, for the water-plant. That's where we met the Roggans for the first time."

"And for fifty years you've been dealing with them, swapping secrets with them, and not saying a word about it?" Mara accused.

"Why should we tell you?" AnnSmith demanded, very simply. "What would you have done? Would you have had any mutual sympathy for a people who had lost their home planet through hazards of the distant past?"

"You learned their history," Dillard put in. "You knew they had wiped themselves out in a suicidal war. And yet you made friends with them?"

"Ancestors," AnnSmith retorted. "Theirs, and ours. History! Must I suffer for what someone did a hundred years ago? Or a thousand? Two thousand?"

"Yes, but," he argued, "surely you can see what the Roggans are?"

"We know that they are a hard and ruthless people. They would not have survived otherwise. And we Hesperians tend to be soft. Did you know that? We come from a line of thinkers and idealists, not workers and pragmatists. We were a defeated and hopeless people until we met them and learned how it is possible to survive far worse things than we had known. And fight back."

"Ye-es," Mara commented. "We'd better talk about that a bit more later on. Frankly I think you were psychologically ripe to be fooled. You had a raw deal from Earth, but it's nothing to what the Roggans will do to you, once you've served their purpose."

"So you say," AnnSmith retorted. "You are judging them in human terms, and they are not human. For one thing, they have no dreamers, no theoreticians. No parasites. Everyone earns a living somehow. No one is idle."

"Like an anthill? And they do have dreamers, believe me, if they think they are going to take over Earth. Whoever started *that* crazy nonsense?"

"I am not sure." AnnSmith sounded indifferent as they swam steadily on. Dillard kept staring down, seeing the tiny, faraway lights, trying to visualize cities similar to those on Earth, but all watertight and populated by hordes of stone-faces all busily working. All he could get was a blurred vision of swarms of gray beetles squirming through ooze.

"We met and talked," AnnSmith said. "In the process of learning their tongue we exchanged ideas, and a few skills. These lung-capes are an improved form of something we had, but the sonic units are theirs entirely. We had a few solid-state tricks new to them. They have fabrication processes adapted to underwater and high humidity which are completely new to us. They also have biological techniques we do not have. A fecundity serum, for instance, which gives them total and positive control of breeding and population. And they know a trick or two about getting power from water. And minerals from water, too. And we compared histories; in telling them about our world as it is, we had to tell them how it had been once. The idea that one day we would earn the right to walk the Earth again—hush!" Her gentle tone sharpened suddenly in warning. "Please be absolutely still, and silent. There's someone near."

VII

DILLARD DIDN'T ASK how she knew. He wasn't even curious. The utter certainty in her voice was enough to make him freeze at once. In the same instant the beautiful blue-violet vastness that had seemed so wonderful now became a trap. He was defenseless, out in the open, vulnerable. Then, over the hammer of blood in his ears, he heard a distant rhythmic noise, a steady thumping for all the world like a crowd of people hand-clapping in unison with gloves on. It grew louder. He saw, not too far below and ahead, vague movement that at first was no more definite than a curtain fluttering in a breeze, but solidified, by degrees, into a wedge-shaped formation of things. White bodies. People swimming.

They swam in perfect stroke like a squad of marching men, arrowing in the dark blue like so many white geese. It was the beat of their multiple arms and legs that he heard, and his mind served him up the answer to the riddle even as he stared and froze and tried to wish himself invisible. That steady beat was well below the audible range, but the bone-conduction speakers were designed to alter that, to facilitate speech under water. So he could "hear" that squad swimming by. And now he remembered reading, somewhere, that the larger predators of the fish world could also hear their prey in the water. But these were Roggans. He counted them. Fifteen, all in step, and dragging something in their midst that was not a man at all, but

111

some kind of cylinder. They went by down there, cold and intent about their business, and Dillard found time to be glad they hadn't been Venusian. Had they been, they would have sensed the fugitives. That thought stayed with him as the marching beat faded slowly into the distance, and AnnSmith murmured, "They are gone. It is safe to move again."

"If that had been a squad of your people," he said, "we'd have been detected. They'd have felt us."

"That's right. Empathy works even in water."

"I wasn't thinking along those lines," he retorted, stung by her mocking. "I was thinking—they can't feel you, or me, at a distance, can they? Can you feel them?"

"No," she said. "Not in the way you mean. I can sense something there, but only as you would be aware of a solid object like a stone, or a wall. Not personally, not with feelings."

"That's what I thought. And it only goes to point up the thing. We are human, all of us. All the same kind. They are different, alien. Do you still think you'd get a better deal from them than you would from us, your own flesh and blood?"

"That is a silly argument, and a stupid question," she answered. "An appeal to the emotions. I give you facts: we have been cast out by Earth; the people of Earth have robbed us, cheated us; even now they believe us to be monsters. These are facts. From the Roggans, however, we have had understanding, sympathy even, in their style, and help. These also are facts. I prefer them to your talk of what might be."

With that she rolled over vigorously and began to swim, reaching for the distance with long powerful strokes, her cape-lung shimmering above and behind her shoulders like the stardust robe of some Valkyr, the twin curves of her bosom lifting and sliding to the pull of her pectoral muscles. He rolled and scissored and tried to emulate, but was aware of his awkwardness. Then Mara came up and to one side of him, drew ahead, and he was in the humiliating position of being towed by the pair of them. Below—he snatched a glance—it was now as black as midnight. He couldn't keep up. He struggled to remember that he must not gasp and pant, but it was effort piled on effort, and he was on the point of calling out for a rest when he realized they were heading into the side of another hill, swooping up to it. Ahead, he saw AnnSmith disappear into a gully fringed with waving weeds. He followed, into the steep-sided cleft that must have once been a swiftly flowing stream-bed.

It was black-dark here, with only now and again the glint of blue from a cluster of writhing fronds, or the quick scuttle of a cloud of little fish all alight, but he knew they were climbing steadily. His groping hands met weeded rock again and again. Then, overhead, the water was brighter blue and he could see as they arched over an edge and on to a gently sloping plain. The blue brightened, faded into vivid green. AnnSmith slackened her pace.

"Soon," she said, "we will come to a pylon-foot. We go straight up. The water-plant is directly above."

"We should take it easy," Mara warned. "Give time to adjust."

"If you think it is wise," AnnSmith agreed, but with a bite in her voice. "You should know that the squad we saw must have come from here. There is nowhere else they could have been in this direction. Where one squad is, others may be, or may come. If we are caught in the water the end will be certain, and violent."

"We don't seem to have a lot of choice. And there's the pylon now. What do you say, Dillard?"

"Are you asking me?" he panted, shaking with the effort to keep his breaths long and steady. "That's a laugh. Nobody has bothered about my opinion so far. For what it's worth, I can't get out on to dry land fast enough!"

"All right. Lead the way, Ann. Better the devil we know."

He saw AnnSmith reach out to touch the silvery column of the pylon-leg and then dart upward, paddling along its surface. He followed, using the rivet-heads like hand-grips to propel himself after her. The water grew more and more bright, a green that was a flame and dazzle. But then, all at once, the light went out, became a dim twilight, and he reasoned that they were now in the shadow of the plant itself. His fingertips hurt from the constant shift along the metal. Then it was his whole hands. And his toes throbbed, and there grew a steel band around his neck just above his shoulder muscles. Now he was seeing dancing fire-spots on his retina, like the grandfather of all the bilious attacks he had ever had. Cramp knotted his fingers, locked his elbows and knees. And wrists and ankles. It was as if some invisible demon had hold of all his joints and was crushing them in a vice. He wanted to scream, but his throat was bloated so that every breath was a scorching agony.

Past the streaking fireballs in his vision he saw the twilight green changing to blue again, to ripples and movement. And then his head broke the surface and he peered, half-blind, at a weed-stained wall of rubberized concrete. His shoulders screeched rustily as he hoisted his arms, got his knotted claw-fingers over the edge, and heaved. And almost passed out from the hellish pain, plus the shattering fact that he now had weight again, that his bent and broken body weighed like lead. Strong fingers grabbed his wrists and pulled. He scrambled out and lay helpless as those fingers ripped the mask and fittings from his face, dragged away the belt and straps. He could do nothing to help. His entire body was one huge wire-tight convulsion of fiery agony, each breath a torment, movement a torture. Through a red haze he saw Mara come out and flop and writhe into spasms as AnnSmith stripped her of her cape-lung. He knew exactly how she felt, and wished he didn't.

From some buried source he recovered enough sanity to remember what to do, what he had always done to rescue himself from nerve-knotting tensions. There was a certain hillside that he knew, where the sun always shone kindly and the breezes coolly whispered, where the grass was thick enough to sink into and there was no alarm. In his mind he went there, relaxed in that peace, made himself relax, melt, go so limp that the nerve-tension could get nothing to grip on, the ache nothing to bite into. The therapy worked. It was like surrendering teeth, but it worked. The agony lessened, became bearable, and then subsided to the point where he could face it, and struggle up on to an elbow to take notice. His lungs felt red-raw on the inside, but he could breathe.

He saw Mara arched backward like a bow, wrenched into a spasm as if she had swallowed cyanide, with a rictus grin of torment on her face. By her side, squatting and impassive, AnnSmith watched, looked up to stare with her violet eyes as he moved, achingly, to come near.

"Relax!" he advised, his voice a croak. He grasped Mara's

shoulders and said it again, firmly, "Relax. Don't fight it. Yield. Forget effort. Go slack all over!"

Her eyes slit open to stare, and the tendons stood out on her neck as she gasped, "I can't—breathe! Can't—"

"Breathe out! Deflate. Let go!" he ordered, and massaged his fingers into her shoulders, into the soft places at her neck. By grudging degrees her wire-taut tension slackened, her splayed nostrils twitched and she began to snort and gasp, her chest heaving mightily as she managed to get her throat working again. "Whoa now!" he warned. "Never mind about filling up. Get it all out. Breathe out—out—out—as far as you can. Breathe out all the knots, the aches, the agonies, breathe them out. Let go. Melt! Like a soft jelly." For a moment longer her instinct fought his advice, then she got it and surrendered all her tensions in one huge sigh. And another. And again, and she was quite still for a moment. He released her shoulders, watched, saw her pull in a tremulous breath, and then another, and then a mighty heave that stretched and lifted the firm contours of her bosom until they threatened to burst. Within moments after that she was able to sit up, and to stare at Dillard in open curiosity.

"I owe you, for that. Thank you. Where did you learn it?"

"All sorts of places. I'm the original coward. I get scared even at my own imagination. But that is exactly what the customers are paying for, so I have to go through with it, whatever it is. As much as ever I can stand. So I need a rescue technique, and that's it. Panic, nerves, fear and pain, they all use tension one way or another. Can't happen if you relax." He rocked back on his heels and turned to AnnSmith. "Where are we, anyway? This doesn't look like the water-plant to me."

"It's water level. A kind of basement. These are some of the intake pipes, see? And look there!"

Where she pointed he saw that the rubberized concrete flooring, a narrow walkway between the bulky pipes, was wet. Splotchy wet, as if many wet feet had walked there recently. He looked back at her.

"You didn't make those patches?"

"No. Apart from taking the cape-lungs to sling from the handrails, there—they should be kept moist, you see, and they are now hanging in the water—no, I haven't been along there."

"That swimming squad which passed us," Mara declared.

"What the devil were they after? What was it they took away?"

"That's right." Dillard nodded. "They were towing something."

"Let's go see." Mara climbed to her feet. "That way to the elevator shaft, I imagine. Very convenient, that. Come on."

As they rode upward Dillard realized that, although all his wracking agonies were gone, he was utterly and staggeringly exhausted. And hungry, too. He wondered how long it had been since that meal in the Green Salon. In terms of experience, that was almost a past life! As they left the elevator at the top, Mara marched straight into the office, but Dillard stayed where he was, waited for her to return.

"Wet feet went thataway," he told her, pointing to the laboratory and feeling slightly light-headed at the thought of a squad of Roggans robbing Stanley's laboratory. Of what? She had the same thought.

"What the hell would they take from here?" she demanded, as she stared angrily around the gleaming glass and chrome. The answer came to Dillard in a bright flash of nonsense.

"Your friend Dr. Stanley, of course," he said. "You can't find him. No one knows where he is, or why he should go away. So what else? The Roggans have got him!" He was definitely light-headed now, not caring what reaction Mara turned on, a silly grin already settling itself on his face. But then he saw AnnSmith's expression, saw a curtain fall across it, and felt the way she drew in her reactions as if hiding. The truth shocked him into clarity, into grabbing Mara's arm, as she was framing a violent retort. "By the stars!" he muttered. "Look at her. She knows! It's true. They *have* got him!"

Mara whirled, and from somewhere she had that knife again, so smoothly that Dillard never saw it done. A breath later and it was aimed meaningly at AnnSmith's naked stomach, and the corded intensity of the arm holding it left no doubt as to intention.

"All right," Mara said, very softly. "Dillard's intuitions have a way of being accurate, I've noticed. I'm buying this one. You have some talking to do, AnnSmith. Better start!"

The Venusian girl held quite still for a moment, then she curled her lip and moved forward until the razor tip of the blade touched her flesh. Mara inched back. AnnSmith smiled more coldly.

"You will *make* me talk? You will cut me if I don't? You human!"

"Your friends would have drugged us to get the same result!" Mara shot back at her, furious at having her bluff called. "Have you forgotten which side you're on, traitor?"

"You forget what little you know of our ways, MaraHunt. You cannot *make* me do anything. My life is mine, or for Hesperus, not for anyone else." AnnSmith hesitated, and Dillard sensed the simmering indecision under her sneering calm. "I came with you because I felt our plan, with the Roggans, was all wrong. But now—with this"—and she flicked a gaze down at the knife—"I am not so sure that humans are any better."

"Hold on!" Dillard spoke up from inner conviction. "Suppose you put away the knife and we all act like reasonable people. Will you tell us about Dr. Stanley, Ann?"

Her violet eyes swiveled to him, lingered a moment, then, "Of course! Why not? There is nothing you can do about it."

Mara sucked in a furious breath but before she could speak he carried on the line of thought. "All right, then. Suppose we all relax, get out of these wet rags, have something to eat, act civilized, huh?"

"No!" Mara snapped. "I want to know about Stanley. Now! We can relax later. Now!"

Dillard sagged back against the wall and felt his knees begin to tremble with deflation and fatigue, but AnnSmith nodded calmly.

"Very well, I will tell you. My people caught Dr. Stanley some time ago, caught him underwater, snooping about the water-plant. We turned him over to the Roggans as a sample of what humans could be like."

"You lie! What about those wet patches? He hasn't been gone that long!"

"Hold on again," Dillard said wearily. "Whatever else, she's not lying. Don't ask me to explain how I know. I know, that's all."

"The wet patches are recent, yes. But a wet foot makes a wet mark. You can identify Dr. Stanley's footprint? I have not seen or met him. I know only by report at second- and third-hand. Apparently Stanley has told the Roggans a lot.

117

We knew, for instance, that he was expecting assistance, which is why we were suspicious of you two. We have heard rumors, even, that Stanley is cooperating with the Roggans!"

Mara's knife-hand trembled. "You bitch!"

"Cut that out!" Dillard shouted in sudden rage. "How the hell do you expect to get information if you keep threatening to chop her when she gives it? She's telling you the truth. And it makes sense to me, too. That's why I'm in this mess up to my eyebrows. You and your damned Stanley. I thought I was through with him years ago, and now look at it."

"Stanley wouldn't cooperate with them!"

"No? What're the odds he sent some of them to get apparatus for him, from his laboratory? That's what the footmarks are. Want to bet?" For all the indignant heaving of her breast he saw that she was shaken. "Why don't you go and look? Me, I'm going to find out what this place has in the way of food and refreshment. Ann?"

The Venusian girl nodded and followed him as he shambled wearily into the living section. Mara, presumably, took his advice and went to study the laboratory. He wasn't too interested. By the time she reappeared he had shed his pants, delivered them along with AnnSmith's loin-cloth to the auto-clean, and the pair of them were nakedly debating program recipes on the autochef.

"I can't be sure," Mara confessed. "It looks as if there's a thing or two missing but I can't tell what. You checked in there, Dillard. Go look, will you, and see if you can spot what's been taken?"

"All right, anything for peace. Mine's the citrus juice, cereal and mixed grill. Suspend it if I'm not back in time. She seems surprised that it is all syntho. What did she expect?" He went away heavily, clutching a tall and cool vodka-and-lemon in one hand. Though wobbly from almost total exhaustion his mind was pinpoint clear. A quick stroll up and down the benches showed him that two items *were* missing, but nothing else he could define. He went back frowning, and found the two females in a momentary truce as they handled and held out various pieces of wispy fabric at each other. The sight snatched him back into the insane values of a society only recently absolute, a society he knew better than most because Epic Dramatapes had a regular line of so-called "historical romances" that he helped

118

work on when he wasn't out on an assignment somewhere else.

Dress. Fashion. Drapery. Prudery and taboo. Exposure and neurosis. Insecurity and identity-failure. Jargon terms had been tossed about with great freedom by many a wiseacre in the attempt to explain why such things had lived so long, and why they had so suddenly all vanished. Dillard knew the jargon, didn't believe half of it, but he did know the facts. He knew the headaches that went with trying to supply sensor programs to match a cast all dressed up in those old clothes. The constrictions of collars and belts and gripping elastic, the awful hamper and drag of many-layered trappings, had to be toned down for modern audiences. Players complained bitterly and audiences were put off unless the story-line included long stretches of comfortable undress to compensate. But those old-timers had worn clothes on top of clothes all the time, even in bed! They wore clothes under clothes, and called them, uninspiredly, "underclothes."

But then, almost overnight, sanity had come. Some said it was the impact of new materials available, new synthetics with new versatility. Or the overall spread of better environmental control. Or the new age of leisure. Some pointed to the long delayed end of the sex war and quoted the shrinking and final disappearance of the skirt in the late 1970's as a sign that women, at last, were no longer second-class citizens. Emancipation and the truth about sex—whereas others, more prosaically, called it only simple economics. Who could afford, nowadays, to carry a whole wardrobe of various social uniforms, half of which would go out of date regularly every few months? To be thrown away? But you couldn't throw away modern stuff, either in fabric or packaging or anything else, because there was no longer any spare space left to throw it!

Arguments from hindsight, he thought, and doubted all of them. What he did know was the fact that everyone, nowadays, wore one simple day-cover to fit the job, occupation or conditions—and in leisure hours there were no rules at all, but only the free dictates of fancy and inclination. Mood colors, mood music, mood styles—there came a gentle *ping* of completion from the autochef to break his reverie, to bring Mara's head around. She saw him, swirled a cobwebby handful of green stuff about her shoulders toga-style and came to demand, "Did you spot what it was?"

"Eh? Oh. Yes. There was a small demonstration model of the water-plant. A trick model. It's gone."

"The water-plant?" She stared at him blankly. "What would anybody want that for?"

"How would I know?" He shrugged, and turned to take his platter from the machine. "Look," he said over his shoulder as an idea came to him, "you're supposed to be some sort of associates, aren't you? Philosophy Corps, wasn't it? Well, wouldn't he leave some kind of trick clue for you, something that you'd spot and I would miss?"

For his guess he had the reward of seeing her total discomfiture.

"I'm a fool!" she snorted. "You're quite right. Where the devil are my wits? Stick mine in the warmer, will you? I'll be back!"

She went away at a trot. Dillard shrugged, took his platter over to the table to sit by AnnSmith. She had chosen a shimmering gold cloud of stuff to drape around her shoulders and it suited her, but he was more interested in what she'd said earlier.

"Don't you have syntho-food on Venus, then? I'd have thought you'd need it more than we do. On Earth, I mean."

"For technology one needs hardware," she said, chewing none too happily on a syntho-steak. "That's not very practical in our hot humid climate. You should see what airborne fungus can do even to sealed-cabinet electronics. Even if we could afford the devices in the first place, we couldn't maintain them afterward. We learned that in the early days, when our survival gear perished so quickly."

"You have a point. But what do you do for food, then?"

"We grow it, of course. Hybrid strains, mutations, successful adaptations, all sorts of ways. We have fresh eggs from waterfowl. Fresh meat from a kind of whale we have domesticated fairly well. The females yield us milk. We have many kinds of fruit. Even a kind of coffee bean, better than this stuff!" She sipped at the turgid brown liquid in her cup and made a face. Dillard's stomach protested momentarily at the thought of eating things that had grown from dirt, or lumps cut from dead animals. He knew it had once been commonplace, but all the same—

Mara came back wearing a black frown and radiating

angry suspicion. She took her platter and sat, eating with little regard for the food. Dillard gave her a moment to settle then asked, "Did you find your message, clues, anything?"

"Yes," she muttered. "You were right. And you." She flashed a hard glance at AnnSmith. "Stanley *is* cooperating with the aliens. But not against Earth. As far as I can figure it."

"Whatever that may mean." Dillard took his platter over to the washer, ditched it, dialed himself another vodka-and-lemon. "You and Stanley and the Philosophy Corps can sort it out among yourselves. Me. I've had it." He took a healthy sip of his drink and wandered across to the bed nook, patted the resilient surface, then sat on it. "This is for me." He finished the drink and had reached up for the deep-sleep headset that hung on the wall over the pillow, when he found Mara standing before him, feet planted astride, hands on hips and eyes blazing down.

"What sort of thing are you?" she demanded. "A man, or what?"

"Back off," he told her. "Biology doesn't come into this. I'm male. That's as obvious as the fact that you two are female. What you mean is am I a crusader, a death-or-glory hound, a hero? The answer is no!"

"You're in this mess, up to your eyebrows. You said so."

"I was. And who got me in? You and Stanley between you. Who got me out? Me. And I'm staying out. I've been slugged by cold-blooded aliens, lined up for drugging, interrogation and destruction. I've escaped. I've had the bends. I've lost valuable equipment and some unique records, and all my personal documents. That's enough, sister. I'm out. You want to go ahead and save Earth, or rescue your comrade, you do that. But leave me out, huh?"

"Resigning from the human race now, eh?"

Her acid scorn got through, stung him into irritation. "I was never invited into the race the first place, nor have I been welcomed by it, nor impressed by it, since. You'll have to find another arm to twist."

"You spineless louse!"

"Cool it!" he warned. "I came up to where I am now the hard way. I'm no idealist. Prod me with that kind of needle and I am just capable of smashing your pretty face in. Don't think you can ride on your big bust and your curves. They

don't mean a thing to me." He warmed to his subject as long
pent irritations spilled over. "You and your Philosophy Corps!
Phony ideals. Empty abstractions. Earth! The human race!
What the hell do you know about it? You had the good
life, position, security, comfort, something to lose. What do
you know about somebody like me? I'm a nobody-nothing
who got caught in the machine. I have a built-in sensitivity
to phenomena which is another name for a talent for suffering. And nobody to give a damn."

He sat up angrily. "This is no play for sympathy. You
can keep that. I'm one of the lucky ones. I made it up
and out. But I've been down there among the pointless,
hopeless, brainless and futureless millions, and I *know*. You
think you know. There's a difference. Do you think they
give a damn for, quote, the human race? If you do, all
right. You do something about it!"

She backed off half a step, startled by his vehemence.
"You know what will happen, don't you, if the Roggans
have their way?"

"I know." He looked from her to AnnSmith, who stood by
in distressed silence. He spoke to her now. "With, or without Stanley's help, if you and the Roggans start any kind of
offensive against Earth"—He hesitated, feeling for adequate
words—"millions of people will be killed and millions more
will be injured, maimed, crippled, ruined, made miserable,
homeless and wretched. There will be misery and starva-
tion, disease and bloody riots, a reversion to savagery. It
will set back the story of mankind a thousand years and
more."

"That's not true!" the Venusian girl cried out in pain, but
he shook his head slowly at her.

"You know it's true, what I'm saying. And here's why.
Earth, right now, is one vast village, a sprawling slum,
strangling in pollution, shambling over piles of refuse,
barely managing to get along, and very very slowly hauling
itself back from the edge of total collapse. I know. So do
lots of others. The main mass doesn't, because it is tranked
and doped up to the gills to make the misery bearable. But
that's the truth. Isn't it?" He threw the question at Mara
Hunt and she nodded silently.

"So," he went on, "if you put a firecracker under that lot
it will all fall apart. And that's just one side. Why do you
think anybody who can scrape the cash and the permits

together is madly heading out into the stars? Why do you imagine we have syntho-food? Why do I serve a firm that makes total-sensation dramatapes for a bottomless market? Life isn't worth living anymore. Nor is it worth saving, in my opinion, but the responsibility isn't mine, thank the stars! You go ahead!"

"But we do not intend all that destruction, that killing!" AnnSmith argued desperately. "We want only our right to live on Earth again!"

"Never mind what you want. I know what you'll get. Remember this, that a hefty percentage of Earth's production and occupation goes into the military. It has to. There'd be economic collapse, otherwise. So we have immense war potential. Enough to destroy Earth entirely ten times over. I mean destroy, just like that. You strike at us, and you'll get it. Venus would be annihilated as a place for life in a matter of hours. Totally and for evermore. And as for *this* planet, there wouldn't be anything to it. A concentrated rain of depth bombs and goodbye Roggan. Forever."

Where she had been the white of warm ivory before, she was now chill as marble, cringing away from the awful picture.

"That's not what we want," she mumbled.

"You wouldn't be the first to start a war for some good reason, some ideal concept. But that's what will happen. Venus destroyed. Roggan destroyed. Earth crippled and spinning back into barbarism. Just like that."

She went back and back until her seat nudged her legs and then she sat heavily, stunned and shaking. Mara heaved a deep breath.

"You know all that, and you still think it's none of your affair. You won't raise a hand to save it?"

"Save what?" he snarled. "A planet-wide blight? A biological error? You make me tired. Have you seen the suicide figures lately?" The shaft was a good one. The steady increase in suicide rates was Earth's number one headache for those who concerned themselves with social matters, ranking just a little ahead and closely linked with the accelerating use of dream drugs. "You want to save something? You do that, and the best of luck!" He reached for the deep-sleep headset again, slid it over his head and swiveled to extend his legs and stretch out. "Good night!" he said firmly, and pushed the button. In a matter of seconds he was fast asleep. Two hours under the machine were more than equivalent to eight hours so-called normal sleep, so Dillard expected to awake refreshed. He did not expect to find the two women stretched out on the floor beside the bed, each on an air-mat, each wearing a spare headset.

In the scant seconds before switching out he had hoped they would manage to decide on something and be gone. But there they were, still, Mara flat on her back with one knee flexed, the posture of the confident personality, while AnnSmith was curled up instinctively on the defensive. He sat up, slipped off the headset and racked it, feeling refreshed physically but realizing that his problems had not gone away. Catlike, Mara came awake as soon as he moved. She yawned, stretched luxuriously, and said, "I needed that. Coffee, Dillard?" He nodded, saw her nudge AnnSmith awake then go over to the autochef and start dialing. She looked at him over her shoulder. "We talked, after you switched out. We decided something. You might be interested."

"Cooperation? You two?"

"We have common interests," AnnSmith murmured, sitting up and shaking the pleats out of the gold gauze she had wrapped around herself. "We have to go back down there."

"To do what?"

Mara handed him a steaming cup, passed one to AnnSmith, held one herself. "Ann feels she must, if only to try to get it across to her people what a disaster they are heading for. Very few of them realize the way things really are, the way you told it. You made an impression, there!"

He chose to ignore that. "And you, I suppose, have to be loyal to your colleague, Dr. Stanley?"

"Old-fashioned, isn't it? Put it this way. I know him very well. If he really has thrown in with the Roggans, then he is either doped, brainwashed, under some devilish kind of duress, completely off his trolley, or something. And he needs help."

"But just you? Don't you call up the heavy brigade, reinforcements?"

"We don't work like that. We move in where authority and force have failed, where there's a situation getting out of control, building up to danger. We use brains, initiative, inspiration, knowledge, whatever. And we are thin on the ground. Stanley sent for me, for help. So I'm going to help."

Sleep, and recent practice, had sharpened his intuitive faculties.

"You know it's virtually suicide, don't you?"

"I'm going to help, Dillard. The odds are stupendous, yes, but you could pull them down just a bit, if you helped too."

AnnSmith came to sit beside him, to put a hand timidly on his arm. "You *can* help a great deal. You could convince my people of their error, the enormous crime they are contemplating, just as you convinced me. Please?"

"You heard me on that," he said, making the words with difficulty, his inner senses in turmoil because of the warm embrace that came from her aura. "What do I care, one way or the other?"

"Perhaps you have nothing to care for. Or no one who cares about you? Nothing to look forward to? But I care. Hesperus is a strange place, in some ways a hard place to live, but I think, from what I have learned from you about Earth, it is a happier place to live than that unfortunate planet. And you could live there, DenDillard. With me. . . ."

He wrenched up and away, shaking off her hand, to march out, along the corridor and into the silent sterile sanity of the laboratory, his emotions in chaos. Stalking over to the great window he stared out unseeing for a moment, until the sheer beauty of the purple and gold sunset claimed his eyes. Then he saw that *Venture* was gone, on her way, without him. His link with the raw-edged and ugly real world was gone. And so was that world, like a lifetime past. All was different now. He was in love with a purple-eyed Venusian girl, and there was no future in it, not for him, nor her, nor anyone. She did right to sneer at an Earth stalked by the three plagues of population, pollution and psychosis, but how could he help it? What did she want?

He started at the breath of a presence at his elbow, and knew it was Mara. Her hand touched his shoulder, and her feeling was kind.

"You need to know something," she said, very gently. "Not about the way she feels for you. You'd have to be stupid not to know that for yourself. Nor about the way you care for her, because that's your business. But you do need to know who she is."

"Who?" he grunted.

"Her father is AlastairMcLarenSmith. President of Hesperus, just to fill in the fine lines. He has tremendous influence with his people, even if he is something of an idealist, and ineffective in himself. They respect him. Now, you've made a hell of an impact on Ann. She's close to her father. He listens to her—and to her brother Billi, who is something of a firebrand, like most young men. Through her you can get to the old man, and, through him, all the rest. That makes you a pretty important person, Dillard. You are involved in this whether you like it or not."

"That is just what I needed," he growled. "For the first time in my life I run into a girl I care for. I'm in love. And she cares for me, too. And it gets snarled up in a political issue!"

"Not just a political issue. This is life and death. Your life, if you want to be narrow about it. And a stake in the future."

"But what can we do? Three of us!" He turned on her, and she met his stare soberly.

"We can try. On your own showing, what is there to lose?"

Over her shoulder he saw AnnSmith come in at the far end of the laboratory and stand there, just watching. There was no need for her to say anything.

"All right!" he surrendered. "We can try. I might as well go all the way with this crazy pitch. What do we do?"

Mara wheeled and went away, leaving him to follow. AnnSmith touched his hand as he went by, caught it and went with him. Words were unnecessary.

"First of all," Mara declared, rummaging in her bag, "we get rid of the bare-handed image. I've had to co-opt local aide before. I always carry spares. Here!" She held out a broad black belt similar to her own. He took it, watched as AnnSmith got one too.

"Only time for one quick run-through, so pay attention. Knife!" She produced it dexterously. "This edge is razor sharp, the other is diamond-dust studded, makes a very useful file against almost anything. These"—the knife went away and out came what looked like a string of plastic beads—"are Detonite. Extremely powerful. You nip one off, dispose of it, and it explodes exactly thirty seconds later. This"—a slim plastic tube no bigger or impressive looking than a ball-point pen—"fires mini-darts. Accurate up to about thirty feet. Absorbent. Knockout dose for a full-sized man. Fast. You thumb this end. And these"—she zipped open a slim compartment to show silvery blobs like peas in a pod—"are retch bombs. Smoke and gas, and nothing that breathes air can get past them. That's the crop. Questions?"

"No questions," AnnSmith murmured, "but I have a contribution." She brought her now dry loincloth, groped in a pocket and produced a small vial of greenish-blue fluid. "This is a skin-friction inhibitor. You need a drop or two, like this," she said as she shook the vial against a finger tip and applied it, "on hair, shoulders, elbows, knees—and it spreads itself from there to make a body-covering film in about ten minutes. It reduces drag in the water by a factor of thirty to thirty-five percent."

"That's something I've heard about," Mara said, taking the vial and using it. "First time I've seen the actual product though."

"This is one of the things we have not as yet revealed to the Roggans. We do have some secrets left."

Dillard took the oily stuff in turn and was dabbing it on his knees when it occurred to him to ask, "Surely clothes will hamper the effect?"

"That's more like it," Mara approved. "Your mind will work, once you get around to it, Dillard. I suggest we wear just the battle-belts. We'll move a lot easier."

He had it in mind to utter something trenchant on a paraphrase of an old saying, something like, "Never was so much risked by so few wearing so little," but it didn't sound so very keen anyway, so he saved it. And then there was nothing more to do but go. On the way down in the elevator, Mara asked AnnSmith, "Do you know where Dr. Stanley is likely to be?"

"Oh yes. He is in The Ship." The capitals were obvious in her tone. "It is the preserved hull of the original ship the ancestors went down in. The Roggans maintain it as a sort of memorial. And it is fairly high on the side of a hill. Since their relationship with us it has been a kind of gateway to them and us. A common ground."

Dillard was only half listening, still bemused by the fantastic plight he had walked into, but there came a note into AnnSmith's voice now that made him prick his ears.

"You say Dr. Stanley is cooperating with the Roggans. He left you a message about that? How?"

"Very simply. It was coded into the computer-store. It's an old dodge, and I'm a fool for not having thought of it quicker. There was a sequence of messages. First the suspicion that you people were up to something, and that it had to be underwater, somehow, then that he was going to investigate. Then a brief note to the effect that he had detected signs of an alien kind of intelligence. And the last one was in number-code. He must have punched it in while they were there watching him, while he was pretending to do something else. Translated, it said that he had been caught, but was in process of working a deal with the aliens. The way it cut off short, I suspect it was incomplete. That's what has me worried. Ah, here we are. Now, where did you cache those lungs?"

Ten minutes later the three of them sank into the oily water, with AnnSmith leading the way. On the surface it was almost dusk. Underneath it was blue darkness, but Dillard had no difficulty sensing where he was now. Neither had he any of his habitual tension and fear. Instead his mind was clear, with a harsh, tight-nerved edge. They moved steadily along just below the bulk of a water tank, heading for the billet-space usually occupied by visiting Venusian ships. Ann Smith's mellow whisper explained, "There is an access tube five hundred feet directly below the billet. It leads directly into The Ship."

With the cape-lung sizzling quietly in his ears and the ghost-touch of body-warm water all around him, Dillard's whole attention was constricted into the immediate now. His mind refused to look even a little way ahead. He sensed AnnSmith, in the lead, surging up to the surface for a final check. And then a blast of urgent fear from her, and a shout as she turned and arrowed back.

"Go down!" she screamed. "Go down! A ship is coming in to land!"

VIII

DILLARD TURNED INSTANTLY, forewarned by her alarm even before she spoke. He clawed his way frantically through the water in pursuit. Within seconds he felt the link line come

taut and knew he was holding her back. He struggled harder,
trying not to get in a panic about his breathing. A ship!
How close was it? he wondered. In another ten seconds he
had his answer. Faintly at first, but rapidly growing louder,
came a deep throbbing shudder through the water. It climbed
from a subsonic growl up into a scream and beyond, itch-
ing his skin, stabbing painfully at his ears. He abandoned
any notion about conserving his breath and hurled himself
down crazily, flailing at the water, plunging into the dark.
There came an almighty crash that hurt him all over,
like a multiple giant fist punching him from all directions
at once. That murderous punch came again, and again,
savagely now, hammering him cruelly to the accompaniment
of a hellish slam-bam barrage of shattering explosions. Above
him, white-hot jets ripped the water into instant steam,
which collapsed in the next instant in condensation, and
sent out a pulsating series of shock waves that drove him
down and around, helpless, stunned, reeling and only half-
conscious. In the inferno he caught a blurry eyed glimpse
of a ghostly blue something down there and he struggled
crazily toward it, racked with cramps and spasms as the fiend-
ish barrage diminished, fell away into separate bangs,
and then pops, and then an echoing stillness. Pops and
squeaks lingered in his head and ears as he dragged
himself painfully down to that blue thing. It grew, became a
ring of cold light, and then, as he came close enough, was
a domed metal surface.

A drifting, spinning shadow crossed between him and the
light, and he knew it was AnnSmith, reached out a hand to
touch, and her panic burst in on him like a scalding flood.
Instantly he knew she was in trouble with her breathing,
that she was trying to say something.

"Tell me what to do," he demanded, grabbing her arm.
He heard a choke, a gasp, and the one word, "Squeeze!"

The picture formed in his mind and he accepted it without question. No time for doubt. Hauling her around, kicking madly, he took her shoulder in a firm grip, scooped the
slimy surface of her lung out of the way and passed his
other arm across and around her back to seize the other
shoulder. The mass of the lung billowed up against his
chest, obscured his view. He drew her close, squeezing the
lung between them, to drive enough pressure into her face-
mask to lift it clear. He heard her gasp, and knew that he

had done right. She coughed once and was able to say, "Good! Thank you. I can breathe now."

"Sure you're all right?"

"Yes. In a moment. And this is the entrance."

"Hang on a bit. Where's Mara?"

He probed the swirling dark frantically, then remembered his line and hauled on it, the stolid resistance telling him what his senses had already guessed. AnnSmith coughed once more then went arrowing past him to grasp the lifeless figure as it spun down on the end of the line. In a moment she called, "Help me, Dennis. My arms are not long enough."

He let go his grip on the metal edge and kicked upward, groping, to grasp a limp ankle.

"Just as you did with me," AnnSmith gasped, "and I will squeeze from in front, try to knock out a breath. Quickly!"

In the almost total darkness it was a nightmare. Mara floated absolutely limply, her arms trailing up over her head, her lung billowing, getting in his way. At last he was able to get himself properly positioned at her back, and reaching around in front, managed to match his fingertips over her rib cage, then to link them. And squeeze, gently, to gain enough to be able to lock his hands, and squeeze again. And he heard bubbles escaping from her face-mask.

"You'll have to bump her, Ann!" he gasped. "She's not breathing at all!"

He held on, sensing AnnSmith's actions, the way she backed off and then launched herself, head down, at Mara's midriff. He felt the impact, felt also the sudden shudder and convulsive gasp in the ribs he held. She began to kick and struggle. He held on grimly.

"Take it easy!" he snapped. "Little breaths, damn it!"

She was strong. In the frenzy of choking and struggling for breath she threw herself about until he almost lost his grip. Then there came a sound of impact, and stillness, and then a grunt from Mara.

"Gark!" she said. "Kark! Hark! Whoo! All—right! Who-ever—Dillard? All right. You can—let go, now. I'm all right! I think!"

A minute later they were all three clinging to the metal edge, in a blue glow, while she coughed and whistled and got her breathing under control again.

"That was close!" she muttered. "Damn near died. Be in

your debt for evermore, Dillard. And you, Ann. What the hell was it, a ship?"

"It has just landed. We cannot risk being caught here. My people may be coming down at any minute. It must be something urgent, because there is no ship scheduled for this time, to my knowledge. Can you manage?"

"I'll have to, won't I? You lead on, I'll try to keep up."

AnnSmith went down and under. Dillard, following, found himself at the mouth of a tube some seven feet in diameter, with the metal dome acting as a cupola for it. She went down into it headfirst. He followed, found that there were handholds, barred loops of metal, at regular intervals, each one suffused with the phosphorescent glow. He began to climb, moving rapidly to keep up with AnnSmith. It was like climbing, at first. But then, very soon, he lost all real sense of direction. And time. And speed. And he was moving in an unreal Alice-well where a blue thing showed up and he pushed it past, and another and he pushed that, and so it went on. And he might have been at rest and shoving the world past him for all the difference he could feel. He had time to wonder where all his nervous fears had gone. Perhaps, he mused, that incredible hammering, the knowledge of near annihilation, had finally smashed all his responses into numbness. He didn't know whether to be glad or sorry at the thought. It would be a relief not to feel terrifying fear any more. But then, surely, the world would become a dull, neutral gray sort of place?

An urgent warning thrust from AnnSmith snapped him out of his waking dream and he slowed just in time to avoid running into her feet.

"We are almost there," she said, in that silver piping that was her voice in water. "You stay here a moment. There is a U-bend into the reception pool. I will go ahead and check up to see if it is clear."

She went away out of sight but not out of range of his empathy. Mara surged up to grasp his shoulder.

"Hold it," he told her. "We're about to land. It's just around the corner from here." In a moment he felt AnnSmith's relief, and a quick tug on the line. "All clear. Here we go!" he said, and surged forward. He groped around the bend into a mauve glow that became pink as he broke surface. He lifted arms that were suddenly heavy, grabbed a rail and hauled himself out of a basin very like the one by which they had all escaped from the hill, only this one was of some white stone like marble, and was flush with the floor. He heaved himself upright, acutely aware of his body weight, then lent Mara a hand to scramble out after him. She winced as she straightened out to a standing posture on the dull gray metal floor, and he saw the first beginnings of purple bruisings on her chest and stomach.

"Sorry about those," he said, pointing. "There was no time to be delicate back there. Hurt much?"

She inflated her chest, reached down to test the marks with fingertips and then grinned. "Forget it. I'm glad to be here and know about it. What now, Ann? This place seems to have nothing but doors!"

AnnSmith opened her mouth to answer then shut it again, rapidly. He felt it too, almost as fast as she.

"Somebody coming!"

"The pump room, quickly!" She pointed and ran. All three of them dashed to an arch and inside, into red gloom where a squat machine purred busily to itself and took up most of the floor space, leaving them just room to turn around and peep out of the opening. That pool, flush with the floor, overflowed steadily into an annular gutter, which drained back to this busy machine. The whole of that room there was curves and bends. Like a nosecone? Dillard forgot the speculation as he saw movement in an archway on the far side. A Venusian youth appeared, followed by two gaunt and impassive Roggan females. Dillard stared hard.

"That's BilliSmith. Your brother. Isn't it?"

"Infold!" she hissed, grabbing his arm. "Infold!"

He guessed what she meant, could feel her doing it, contracting her living aura until he hardly knew she was there. He had no idea how to do it himself. Fortunately the youth out there was too engrossed in his own thoughts to be paying very much attention. The two aliens swung open a wall locker and produced a light metal structure which they opened out, with clicks and snaps, into a ladder and platform. This they lowered into the pool and locked into stability. Dillard was horribly fascinated by their movements, by their alien quality. It wasn't so much their ruggedness, the overdeveloped brow-ridges, the pallor of their skins, or even the tint of color. Nor were they ugly. They had shape and curve that would have qualified them as attractive, had it not been for the stonily repellent way in which they moved. He was reminded of the guard who had kicked him. Not from cruelty or sadism, but simply because it was the most efficient way. And Stanley was cooperating with these?

There was a rippling movement in the pool. Heads appeared. AnnSmith's grip on his arm tightened as she saw the first faces come out from under the lung masks.

"Oh, no!" She sounded betrayed.

"Oh, yes!" Mara muttered, beside her. "It's the big man himself, the McLarenSmith of Venus."

"Your father?" Dillard turned to her wonderingly, and her eyes were mauve pools in this light as she nodded.

"There must be something desperately urgent here to bring my father."

Dillard watched the dignified old man stand and sigh, waiting for the six oldsters who had come with him. They all wore a simple gold band on the left wrist. BilliSmith placed the back of his left hand to his brow in some ceremonial greeting, then said, "I'm sorry it was necessary to send for you, sir."

"Was it necessary?"

"Yes, sir. The Earthman, Stanley, seems to have driven some kind of wedge between us and the Roggans. I can't find out just what."

"It's enough. Will the Rogganor see me?"

"The conference is all arranged to start as soon as you are ready." The small gathering began to move toward the far arch. They heard BilliSmith going on faintly, "There is another piece of bad news, sir. There were some interfering Earth people . . . prisoners . . . escaped. . . ."

Then the words were too faint to catch. Dillard felt her grip slacken. He reached for her hand. "Your brother will tell him about you?"

"It doesn't matter," she mumbled, but her words were hollow.

"No time for grieving," Mara said. "Let's get going."

AnnSmith moved out into the chamber again. "This was the forward gun room, once," she explained, as they passed through, "and the pipe comes in by what was a gun port. Below this is an ammunition store, and the next deck is crew living quarters. None of it is used now, of course, and it's all closed up. I've been around it, but that's all." They followed her along narrow corridors and down steep zigzag ladders. At every turn there were mysterious boxes and fittings embedded in the walls, strange and massive hatchways, old and faded marks and instructions in oddly angular characters. "The next deck below is a huge chamber, originally intended for crushing rock and extracting metal ores. This ship used to go asteroid mining. Roggan is poor in metals. That was, partly, what brought about the final war. That, and pressure on living room."

"It has a familiar sound," Dillard muttered. "Earth all over again, except that we have stopped short of destroying ourselves."

"So far," Mara qualified. "It could be altered once the Roggans step into the overall picture."

"The big chamber will be used for the conference, by long tradition," the Venusian girl explained. "So we must go carefully as we pass it by the side galleries. On the level below that is what used to be the hospital and sick quarters. That is where they have Dr. Stanley installed. Because there is space there for equipment."

She went ahead as cautiously as a cat stalking birds, stopping to test the environment and listen at each intersection. Dillard's own perceptions seemed to stand out from his skin like porcupine quills, probing the mental ether. Yet, for all their wariness, they were surprised. Dillard got the message as Mara spun around and thrust away from the metal wall alertly. He wheeled in time to see her fall into a crouch with her hands advanced, and, over her shoulder, two stone-faced Roggans came stalking forward. She surged to meet them, veered to plunge full-tilt at the left-hand one. Her left arm came up and across her chest, then flailed out in a palm chop straight for a Roggan throat. The alien croaked, reeled aside, and she spun, using the blow as a drive, aimed for the other. But this one was fast, had reached out for her arm, grabbed it, and poked out his other hand for her throat.

By this time Dillard, remembering certain kicks of the recent past, was mixing in. He launched a balled left fist, rejoiced as it thudded home on alien ribs, then whirled his right hand in an arc, smashing at the junction of neck and shoulder. Mara, clinging to the arm that held her, ran around, heaved, and the Roggan buckled forward rather than dislocate his shoulder. Dillard reached up for that ridgebrowed head, dragged it down to meet his upswinging knee.

The first Roggan lumbered back into the fray, but staggered as AnnSmith sprang on his back and locked her fingers at his throat. As he staggered, Mara swung her foot like a dancer to trip him. Down he went, hard, face-first, AnnSmith clinging, using ears to grip and hammer that face into the floor. Then Mara stood back, her dart-pistol ready. Seconds later both aliens were taken care of, and she grinned at Dillard as she slid the weapon away again.

"I enjoyed that," she said. "Cancels a grudge or two."

"True," he said. "But as soon as this pair is missed there'll be hell to pay, and us in the middle of it."

"We can hide them in here for a while." AnnSmith indicated a niche in the bulkhead where stood some ancient piece of equipment, a canister, but which afforded enough room to stuff the two unconscious Roggans. They went on in haste, and at last she halted them by a door where there was a capstan-lock. The spokes gleamed from recent usage.

"He is in here," she said. "And this door seems to be free. The outer bars are not in place."

"You mean he isn't a prisoner, don't you?" Mara made a grim face, then grabbed a spoke, spun the wheel, heaved, and the door swung silently open. She darted in, Dillard at her heels. This was a long low-ceilinged room, glowing pink, and with more of the wall-beds, six this time. At the far end was a sturdy bench littered with gadgetry, but Dillard had time for only one glance, then his attention went to the man stretched out on the first bed to the right, a man who stared up in amazement at their precipitous entry. That first glance took Dillard back into his juvenility. Dr. Edmund Stanley, lean and awkward, sour-faced, with a disconcerting trick of tucking in his chin and glaring up at the world from under jutting eyebrows. He did it now as he sat up.

"I'll be damned! Mara! What the devil are you doing here? Like that? And—you're AnnSmith, aren't you?" He scowled in thought. "The grand Council has been searching for you."

"You know me?" she cried, backing off a step.

"Of course. You're too much like your brother to be any-one else. But what is this . . . ?" Stanley swung his legs down from the bed and stood. Dillard felt a moment's disadvantage, because his former tyrannical tutor was fully clad in poncho and pants, but then the sensation reversed itself in a most odd way, because he could not look down on this insignificant man. Years had given him an advantage in sheer size. Stanley was a *little* man.

"You left me a message," Mara put in, "that you were trying to pull some kind of deal with the Roggans."

"So?" he craned his head around to her.

"So you must be out of your mind, chief. That, or you've been doped, which amounts to the same thing. I'm told the Roggans are good at that."

Stanley stared at her, then moved slowly to the door, shoved it shut, came back, swept the three of them with a sour gaze, and snorted.

"I'm a scientist. My training is to accept facts as they stand, and I try to. But this is well-nigh unbelievable. Am I right in assuming that you three have come here with some insane notion of rescuing me?"

"That's no more insane than your collaborating with these gooks, chief. If that's the way you see it then we're taking you out of here for your own good!"

Now there came that acid smile that Dillard remembered so well. "You really mean that, don't you? Lord knows how you managed to get this far, but to imagine you can take me out, by force . . ." He began to snigger, and Dillard moved forward, boiling. He balled a fist in readiness.

"We came down here to get you, mister, and that's what we're going to do. It would be a pleasure for me to slug you." Mara touched his arm but he shook off her fingers angrily. This was the acme of farce, that the man they had risked life and limb to save should stand there and snigger. "It would be a pleasure, I assure you," he repeated.

"Don't be ridiculous!" Stanley backed off warily. "I tell you I don't want to be rescued. You'll ruin everything if you try anything so silly. I am about to conclude an agreement with the Roggans . . ."

"You can't mean that," Mara interrupted in anguish.

"Would you rather they went through with their plan in cooperation with Venus?" Stanley snapped. "Do you know about that?"

"They know." AnnSmith spoke up. "I told them. I did not approve. I do not approve now. I have come with these two in the hopes of being able to turn my people away from such a suicidal path."

"Indeed?" Stanley had his skin-scraping tongue going now. "Do you really believe the Roggans will *let* you back out, now? You know what they are after, don't you? Land. Dry surface. Somewhere to live. Do you really believe they will forget all about it, abandon a drive that has inspired them for more than two thousand years, just because *you* change your mind?" He sneered at AnnSmith as she backed away. Clasping his hands at his back he hunched his shoulders in a familiar pose.

"What about the half million Roggans already settled on Venus? What are you going to tell them?"

"Half a million!" Mara cried. "But that's impossible. They can't have transported that many in the time. They haven't the ships!"

"No, but the Roggans have bio-genetic skills and techniques for breeding control and accelerated development. They can, and do, control their numbers precisely according to capacity. You fools!" He withered them with a look, settled his bleak eyes on Mara. "You!" he scorned. "You should know me better than this!"

"I still can't see a deal with the Roggans," she said stubbornly. "I wouldn't trust any one of them as far as I could spit!"

"And you're a sociologist? Use your brains! Think!"

"You don't change much," Dillard growled. "I'm not surprised that you'd find the stone-and-ice Roggans congenial. Just your mark, they are."

Stanley swung his head to frown upward. "Yes, I thought we'd met. No, don't tell me. There's something about your choice of emotionally loaded words—Good Lord! It's young Dillard!"

"You're not so smart. You saw my name on that equipment over there. That's my sensor-recorder, and it has my name on it."

"Distrustful as ever, I see. So that's yours, is it? Pointless to say I never even looked at the owner's name. You wouldn't believe it. But it's exactly what I would have expected of you. If I can quote one of your outbursts, 'Feelings are more important than facts. Facts just are. It is we who make rights and wrongs out of them, and you can't do that without feelings.' Am I right? I think so. And, of course, it's a point of view. But it stands or falls on whether one really has the facts in the first place, doesn't it? And for those you have to depend on unfeeling people like me, you know." He made his sneering grin again. "But that's a fascinating toy you have there. I think you, and it, may be able to help me. Do you know how it works?" He wandered away to the bench as unconcernedly as if he were lecturing in some classroom. Dillard followed.

"How did *you* get it?" he demanded.

"That was inevitable, wasn't it? The Venusians took it from you—they said a suspected spy, and of course I didn't know any different—but they are shockingly inept at technology. Brilliantly intelligent, of course, but with almost no practical application. We did wrong to expel them, you know. Earth needs dreamers and idealists as never before, now. But, as I was saying, they could make nothing of it. Nor could the Roggans. Oh, they could comprehend the mechanics of it readily enough, but not the use. They have glandular and sensual reactions, of course, but totally different from ours. For this to affect them, it would have to be modulated—"

His thinly pedantic tone stopped abruptly. Engrossed in his own ideas, he had not noticed Mara stealing up by his side. He never saw the flailing blow that snatched him into insensibility. Mara caught him as he slumped.

"We'll have to carry him," she snapped. "It's a good thing he's no great size. Try the door, Ann."

"We'll never make it," Dillard protested.

"We've got to. Look, Dillard, doped or not, Stanley is a brilliant brain. With him in their pocket the Roggans are ten times as dangerous as they were. We have got to get him out, or kill him!"

AnnSmith went to the door, and it heaved open in her face, sending her reeling back. In surged a grim-faced swarm of massive Roggans. Dillard saw the Venusian girl go staggering away from a blow. He charged forward desperately and met a crashing fist with his cheekbone. His angry blows were blocked. Another exploding fist smashed into his ribs, and one at his back. He went down, retching. A foot took him in the belly, lifting him up and over, and something very hard slammed against the back of his head. The room went dark and foggy. Something needle-sharp bit into his arm, and the room went away altogether.

The shattering ache in his head was painfully familiar. He lay still and waited for it to gather into a lump. There was a bitter taste in his mouth. He stirred cautiously, and felt the bond at his wrist. *Here we go again,* he thought, and tried his other hand, but it was free. Surprised, he made a great effort, squeezed his eyes open and sat up. A blue-glow room. A wall-bed. A black plastic cord fastened to his left wrist. But the other end went away, was clutched in a massive hand. The hand belonged on the end of an arm, to a Roggan guard who squatted at the end of his bed, impassively. Dillard shook his head carefully, swallowed, and said, "All right, I'm awake. Now what?"

The muscle movements to produce the sounds brought lancing pain to his face, made it feel as if he had been stepped on. The Roggan turned to stare at him in ice-eyed indifference. A shaky voice closed by said, "Dillard? It's me, Mara. I've been awake some time. Far as I can tell there's just the two of us. What do you suppose happens now?"

"You took the words out of my mouth," he mumbled, and then the guard stirred, stood, and he saw that there was a black cable in both hands, the other one leading to the next wall-bed. He just had time to notice that, then the Roggan heaved powerfully, and Dillard slid down from the bed to his feet. It was that or be dragged off in a heap. He saw Mara descend in a similar scramble. The alien marched for the door without any attempt to warn or explain, and they had to go along.

"Taken your belt," she muttered. "Mine too. Stanley seems to have gone. AnnSmith, too. I'm none too steady, Dillard. Drugs, maybe?"

"I have a queer taste in my mouth." He tucked in close to her as they negotiated the door in the wake of the Roggan. "If you've any idea of muscling this character, leave it, huh?" He felt his face loosening up a bit, and went on. "Let's see what they want with us first. Admit it, if they wanted to kill us they could have done it long ago."

"Corny line," she muttered, "but there are fates worse than death."

Their captor marched on as sublimely indifferent as a machine hauling freight. He led them up a steep ladder, through an archway, and into a huge room thick with the surf-roar of many voices. As they marched unwillingly down an aisle between packed benches and into a central, clear space, the roar of gossip halted momentarily, then swelled up again on a different note. Dillard looked around with sinking heart, sensing the inimical atmosphere. To his right was a highly ornamented rostrum where sat a group of hard-faced aliens. They had color stripes painted across their foreheads, just above the brow-ridges. Most were blue. The man in the middle wore gold. Off to one side of him was the hatefully familiar face of Dekron, glaring under a double blue stripe. It was not a time to ask for explanations. This was, had to be, the ruling body of the aliens.

Straight ahead stood another rostrum, not quite so ornate, and here Dillard saw the massed might of Venus. He recognized McLarenSmith and the other elders. And BilliSmith. Backing them a solid gathering of Venusian people stared at the prisoners. Then there was no time for more, as their guard led them a quick left turn and up to yet another rostrum, in dark stone and smooth plastic stuff. The stone-faces were here, but ranged at a wary distance, leaving the center place clear. Here, rising from a seat, was Dr. Stanley. By his side, gloomy faced, was AnnSmith. One look at her and Dillard estimated they were all in the doghouse, so he did his best to radiate a sense of encouragement and cheer to her. To his gratified surprise she smiled instantly and sent back spontaneous affection like the shivering of a struck gong.

"At last!" Stanley snapped at the aching pair, fussy with impatience. "I have been stalling like a lunatic, here. Fortunately there was quite a deal of formal ceremony to go through."

"Waiting for us?" Mara muttered. "Why? Is this some new crazy idea of yours? Are you going to co-opt us into the Roggan cause too?"

"Shut up and listen," he ordered. "I had a tentative scheme worked out, but you and your insane heroics have upset that, so I've had to modify. You don't seem to know very much. For instance that it has taken me hours of hard work to get it into the Roggan heads that we humans can be just as logical—and reliable—as they are. They are, believe me. They keep their word. It's not honor, not as we understand it. It's more that having once worked out the log-ical thing to do, they declare it, and do it. And it would never occur to them to do otherwise. And just when I had got it across to them that we can work like that too, *you* had to come and spoil it. Fortunately you attacked me, otherwise they'd have believed I was trying to escape. They're a very interesting phenomenon . . ."

His nervous chatter cut off as a stentorian whistle-scrape voice began from the center of the floor. As they turned to watch, AnnSmith interpreted.

"This is the Astrogator, asking if all the data is in. It means, are you all ready to present your cases. Including us."

"We'll be ready, when it comes to our turn. You hear that? Astrogator, the man who gives the signal to proceed according to data. Relic of ship-life values. But never mind that for the moment. Listen!" Dillard found himself torn by contradictions. Stanley was still the acid voiced and sneering pedant he had hated from long ago, but there was something else too, discernible under the appearance and manner. It was an urgent flame, a sizzling drive of power and ability. And it commanded respect. The petulant sourness, the irritating mannerisms, those were the outcome of having to live with a bunch of people who dragged their mental feet and couldn't keep up. This was a frustrated man, but working at top output right now. Dillard listened.

"I am not mad. Nor a traitor. Nor anything undesirable, believe me. I urge you to play this exactly as I give you the cues. If you do, we'll walk out of this with honor, maybe even glory. But try any tricks, and we will all wind up as edible protein. Understand?"

Mara still had an edge of resistance. Dillard nudged her. "We'll go along, Mara. We have to. And I think he's got something."

"You and your intuition. All right, chief. This once!"

"Thank you." Stanley sounded relieved. He shot a sharp glance at Dillard. "This young lady has told me a good deal about you, my boy. I hope it is at least substantially true. Now, we'd better sit and look as if we are ready."

The seats felt like stone under a thin layer of slippery stuff. Stanley had AnnSmith on one side of him and Mara on the other. Dillard found a seat at the end alongside Ann. In the middle of the floor a tall Roggan with blue and yellow blazons across his forehead swung away from his own contingent and put a finger out toward the Venusians.

"He has called all the 'officers' of Roggan to judgment, to

decide on a course. The ship faces hazard. There is a decision to be made which concerns all. The Captain will hear all the data and ask for a decision. That's him. His name is Orsonon. At any other time he is the Rogganor, the ruler of all Roggan. Now, however, he is the captain of The Ship."

"Traditional," Stanley leaned across to whisper. "Fascinating instance of one-culture evolution. Fascinating!" he leaned back as BilliSmith started.

"McLarenSmith, our leader and representative, comes in person to the conference chamber to remind the Rogganor of Roggan of the long-standing agreement between his people and the people of Hesperus. There has been cooperation between us, understanding between us, obligations shared by both sides, agreements entered into for the furtherance of both and the assurance of a brave future. President McLarenSmith at this time wishes also to warn Roggan to be on guard against those who profess to speak for Earth, and those who are of Earth. As we know and can prove, they are a treacherous and untrustworthy people, seeking only their own gain."

BilliSmith stopped there, took a breath, and started repeating what he had just said, but in the grotesque speech noises of the aliens. So AnnSmith said. Dillard was fascinated to learn that any human throat could make such unlikely noises. Then, thoughtfully, he leaned across to Stanley.

"They have a case, sir. They have their own history as evidence!"

"I know, but there is also the opposite side. Better than two thousand years of Roggan history. And drive. You'll see."

BilliSmith ended his speech and sat. The commanding finger swung and AnnSmith said, "It is now for us to say. What do you wish me to tell them?"

"I'll say it. You translate as we go, right?" Stanley stood up and took a moment to scan the audience, as confidently as if he were addressing a faculty dinner group.

"Captain of The Ship, Rogganor; President McLarenSmith; people of Roggan; people of Hesperus . . ." He halted, and Dillard was again astounded to hear those noises coming now from AnnSmith's throat. "It is my intention to show you, here and now, to your satisfaction, that, first of all, your proposed Roggan-Hesperus plan to ally and attack Earth by force is doomed to failure." When the buzz from that had abated he added, "I shall show that if the plan is followed, Roggan, the planet and the people, will be destroyed utterly. That Hesperus, the planet and the people, will be destroyed utterly. That Earth, the planet and the people, will be so badly hurt that it may, in turn, be destroyed. At the least it will be plunged into chaos and be unfit to occupy for several decades. This I propose to show, so that you may all reconsider the merit of a plan that will surely bring disaster, and will benefit no one."

He gave that time to settle, time to build up a tension, then went on as calmly as before. "I will then show you a different plan, and offer proof of a way in which the people of Roggan may once more have a planet fit to live on, fresh air to breathe, dry land to walk on, and with no one to dispute the right, or to fight them for the privilege. I intend to show how, with the cooperation of Earth, the people of Roggan may regain their own planet!"

Dillard sagged back, dumbfounded, as AnnSmith labored through the translation. His new-found confidence in Stanley began to shake, but before he could get it into acceptable words, Stanley sat, his eyes gleaming. AnnSmith offered to translate the general hullabaloo that had broken out, but he shook his head at her.

"Quite all right, my dear. I can follow it well enough. Can't speak the stuff, but I can understand it."

"You can?" She stared in wide-eyed amazement. "But it took me three years to learn . . ."

"I did it in three weeks. Never mind. Listen carefully, I need you and Dillard here for this next bit. It could be tricky, so let me check up. You can tell, can't you, whether Dillard here is lying or not? Can't you?"

"Oh yes!" She nodded. "And you, too!"

"Just as well I'm honest then, isn't it!" He grinned, and Dillard was staggered by the difference in the man now. All the bitter pedantry was gone. Stanley was literally enjoying this crucial moment, a challenge to his abilities. And he simmered like a potent brew as he swung on Dillard.

"I need you, my boy," he said. "AnnSmith will be right beside you. Her people will be tuned in to her. They will know, through her, that you are telling the strict truth. They will feel it, through her. They will *know!* But there's more. Here!" He produced from a box between his feet Dillard's own sensor headset. "It's your own gadget, but I've modified it a bit and I've managed to rig up a mass transmitter that is beamed right at the Roggans right now. It's all been tested out, quite safe. Never again will I say hard words about emotional values, Dillard. They are going to turn this trick for us, you'll see. Put it on!"

"What do you want me to do?"

"Put it on. Stand up. Tell them, tell me, tell his Eminence over there and all the other benighted Hesperians, exactly what you told AnnSmith—and *feel* it, man—about what will happen should they launch a war against us. Just that. Take your time, make it good. AnnSmith will translate for the aliens—but this gadget will give them your feelings in terms they can really understand. All right?"

Dillard cringed. He had never addressed an audience before in his life. He had never wanted to declare his feelings to anyone before. Always he had tried to hide them, to mask them. "I can't do it," he muttered.

AnnSmith touched his arm. "You can," she said softly. "You told me, once. Just tell me again. Come on, stand up and tell me. And I will tell them."

BilliSmith had just completed a passionate rebuttal, repeating his warning about lies and deceit. As he sat, Stanley rose, urging his two helpers to stand with him. He aimed his stare at the Venusian delegation.

"Pay attention," he said. "AnnSmith is known to you, is one of you. It is within your power, right now, to tell whether she speaks true or not. This young man is of Earth, yet he shares something of your sensitivity. You can tell whether *he* lies or not, too. You can say, with words, as loud as you like, that it is all lies—but you will know, inside, that it isn't. I ask you to listen, now, and, if you value anything at all, be honest with yourselves."

He turned to tap Dillard on the shoulder. "It's all yours, my boy. Give it to them hot and strong."

It took a moment to get his voice going, and he would never have started at all had it not been for the warmth by his side, but once he did start the passionate convictions boiled up in him of themselves. Because it was the way he felt, he made no secret of the fact that he didn't care, personally, whether civilization survived or not, but once that declaration was out of the way he felt sufficiently detached from the issue to be able to call up the horrid realities with all their hideous impact. He threw gigantic figures at them, population densities, transport snarls, mass production miracles of achievement slowly but inexorably falling behind the remorseless law of logarithmic progression, the creeping blight of pollution and waste—and then the enormous slumbering potential for destruction, the war machine that each major power had to keep in motion simply to sop up otherwise surplus manpower, to provide employment—the whole fantastically insecure structure of an economy stuck in the rut of expansion, when there was nowhere to expand to.

He painted them a spine-chilling picture of the results that would come from invasion, or the threat of invasion. And then the crazy retaliation of a war potential almost beyond imagining. He pictured for them two immense nations shaking atomic doom at each other, suddenly diverted toward an outside enemy. And then Venus, scantily populated, hampered by technoligical ignorance, handicapped by climate—Venus ripped apart by weapons from which there could be no escape, and against which there could be no defense. Then he switched to Roggan, calling on his own experiences of depth, and pressure, and darkness down there; the agony of a few shock waves from a ship in splash-down; magnify that a million times, and then a million times again, as the vengeful ships of Earth orbited the planet and released multimegaton depth bombs. Roggan dies. The people die, smashed into pulp by incredible forces released before they have so much as a chance to call out. He was limp and sweating when he sat down.

There was a silence within the chamber that could have been cut into cubes, it was so dense. BilliSmith heaved to his feet, but his face was gray and his eyes glazed. He tried, once or twice, to make sounds, but nothing would come. The entire Venusian contingent looked stunned. Dillard stared at them, then swung his gaze to the Roggans, as he slipped off the headset. He could make little of the hard faces, but he did see that Dekron was leaning back with his eyes shut, as if in thought. Then the Rogganor spoke, just a few brief sounds. AnnSmith stirred, but Stanley already had it.

"I think we've got them," he muttered. "He's asked to hear the alternative suggestion. Nice work, Dillard. It's up to me, now. Ann, tell those two characters there to bring in the apparatus." As she made the necessary noises Stanley stood again, and his manner was still confident, but Dillard felt the cracking tension in him, just under the surface.

"I'll take this easy," he said to Ann. "Give you time to get the right terms. Technical stuff. Ready?" As she nodded, he faced the Roggan bench.

"As you know, I am skilled in scientific and technological matters. You have such people also, and I have had dealings with them. We understand each other. Your technical people are very skilled and have my admiration for the things they have achieved and their capabilities. Quite naturally, you have a highly developed technology for the use and handling of water. You can purify it, extract valuable substances from it, derive power from it, just as we do. This apparatus"—he gestured to the trolley the two aliens were hauling in—"is not in any way strange to you, except for one thing. It is, as you see, a miniature model of the much larger plant which floats on the surface up there. In many ways it is similar to plants you already use. Seawater enters here"—he was down on the floor now, demonstrating —"and passes through a series of carefully designed membranes which extract minerals, also power, and discharge pure water. A power source is needed to start the cycle, but once that is done the reaction is self-sustaining, driven by the power extracted from the water itself. It is a well-known principle. It gives water, mineral extracts, power. But—please observe!" He took hold of the trolley and pushed it back to the edge of the arena, then did things with a series of quick movements. The trolley separated into two. He pushed half of it all the way across to the other side, some fifteen feet, and everyone present could see, now, that the water-plant model was in two halves, separated by thin air. And that the seawater level diminished in one half, and grew in the other. Dillard stared. This he had seen before. It was a trick, surely? But Stanley was going on.

"You are seeing something quite new, a discovery with which I had the privilege to be associated, although I do not claim the honor of discovering all of it. Two lines of research came together here. One, the search for a better membrane substance; the other simply to feed back the generated power into the cycle to see what would happen. What did happen is what you see. The two membrane sheets are a perfectly tuned transmitter-receiver couple. The recycled power breaks down the water molecule into micro-wave patterns at this end. The microwaves are transmitted, coherently, and converted here into water again. The theory behind this is not too well developed at the moment, but that need not concern us now. Nor the speculation that it may be possible, eventually, to transmit other molecular patterns. For the moment all I want to show you is the fact, that it is possible to transmit water, by radio wave, from here to there. From here to any point within the effective micro-wave range. And that, as far as has been established, lies far beyond measurable distance. The theoretical estimate is that it compares with the transmission of coherent light."

He left it there, turned and stalked back to the rostrum, sent his gaze around the silent audience again. "The applica-tion is obvious. You call your system-debris the Million Moons, I believe. There was a time when you used to travel among them, seeking minerals and rare substances. You can do it again, with Earth ships to help out. Only, this time, you will be planting water-receivers on every moon-let you touch. And over the seas of Roggan will float gigantic water-transmitters, self-powered. I have discussed this with your technicians and skilled people. We have performed cal-culations. We agree that within one year the mountaintops of Roggan will once more raise above the sea. Within ten years you will have all the land your ancestors had. And it is entirely up to you how much more you can have. The polar landmasses? Other islands? It is within your own choice. Your own planet. And we of Earth will help, this I guarantee."

IX

DILLARD MISSED almost all of the debate that followed. He was distantly aware of the argument the Venusians tried to put up, an argument that was hopeless right from the start. He knew that Stanely had made it inevitable that the Roggans would overwhelmingly accept his proposition. He knew relief, even a small degree of pride, that he had helped to avert a catastrophe. And he had the happy, warm feeling from AnnSmith to make everything that much more worthwhile. But there was a small cold worm down inside him that would not rest, would not be comforted. Nobody knew it but him. No one saw the worm in the apple but him, or so he thought. So he sat on it, choked it down as formalities were observed, as the Roggans did what they believed to be friendly things and the Venusians did their best to hide their discomfiture. Through it all AnnSmith clung to his hand as if she were afraid he would vanish should she let go. And she knew, but she didn't say anything until they were all foregathered in the main lounge of the Venusian ship that had so nearly been their destruction.

They were six. They had been escorted back to the ship in style and comfort, with much whistle-croaking and assurances of cooperation, and the Roggans had gone back. The elders had dispersed. There was only McLarenSmith and his two children, Mara Hunt, Dr. Stanley, and Dillard.

"Within this group," McLarenSmith said bitterly, "I can speak openly. Again we have been betrayed by Earth. You feel self-satisfied, EdmundStanley, but you have betrayed us just as surely as my daughter there."

"You mean you didn't believe Dillard? That *your* plan, if you'd gone on with it, would have been a total disaster?"

"No. I accept that. We were criminally foolish there. No, Billi, it is only the hot blood of youth which believes in death before dishonor. A nation cannot afford such gestures. We were wrong to think that we could be allied with the Roggans in such an insane enterprise. There is no doubt in my mind of that, thanks to you, young man." He nodded to Dillard, who appreciated the thought but said nothing.

"Exactly how have you been betrayed?" Stanley prodded deliberately, and his attitude was one Dillard knew from old times, that of provoking the other person into a statement, only to crush him with some logical contradiction. As if the President of all Venus were no more than a thickheaded student.

"You have given the Roggans back their planet," McLarenSmith said. "I do not doubt that for one moment. I know what applied technology can do. But—Dr. Stanley, why couldn't you Earth people have offered *us* this minor miracle? Venus, too, has a water problem. You could have come to us with this technology. You could have said to us, 'We will help you reduce the perpetual humidity of your planet until it is tolerable, so that you will be able to live like reasonable beings, to look at the sun and walk the dry surface, and hold up your heads again.' You could have done this. But no, you kept the secret in reserve. And now you give it away, to aliens!" His voice was bitter with the history of long years of struggle against inclement conditions. "I call that betrayal. Don't you?"

Stanley lolled back in his contour chair perfectly at ease. The mess steward of the Venusian officers' quarters had provided them with refreshment. Stanley took a contemplative sip from his glass now, and smiled. Dillard knew that smile, too, the way a cat would smile before pouncing. If a cat could smile. McLarenSmith shifted uneasily in the light of that smile, and adjusted his silks. The Venusian ship had been able to produce suitable covering for the unexpected guests. Dillard himself was in dark blue silk, the natural stuff, and he was still strongly aware of its unusual tactile impression. Mara Hunt was openly luxuriating in her swirling robe of some shimmering pearly stuff. AnnSmith looked completely at home in a brief grecian of paper-white satin. But Stanley was still in his own clothes, just as he had been all through. A formidable and unpredictable man.

"If the matter was just as you have stated it, sir," he said now, "I'd agree that my action was unethical, at least. Nor would I want to defend it by pointing out that I had to use whatever I could to prevent a wholesale disaster, because that is bad ethics too. Circumstances do not justify cases, any more than the end justifies the means. But it isn't quite like that. The microwave conversion effect is very new. Although I am an official of an obscure and clandestine power group of Earth's security services, I am also a research scientist. When I have the chance. And I did, perfectly honestly, leap at this chance to perform some basic research, here on Hydro. And the microwave transmission effect *was* that research. So it is very new." He paused to take a sip from his glass again.

"The full potential is immense, of course, and others have speculated on various aspects of it. One of those speculations had to do with beaming water to Mars. As we all know, that planet has been singularly difficult to colonize, much more so than Venus. With a copious supply of pure-by-definition water, most of the difficulty will be canceled. And what better place to take it from than Venus?

That proposition is already in the pipeline. So you're wrong to think that we kept it from you." He paused again, and then grinned.

"You know, it is refreshing to debate with a man who you know can tell whether you're trying to deceive him or not. It cuts out a whole spectrum of dialectical tricks. But it also serves its purpose. You know that what I just said is true, don't you?"

The president nodded uncomfortably. He also knew, as Dillard knew, that there was more to come, that Stanley had a brickbat up his sleeve.

"Now, then. The process has been developed to the point where we can apply it, where we—meaning Earth Government—can approach you and your people, and make the offer I have just outlined. But can we?" Stanley put an edge on his voice now. "Can we deal with you? You know, better than I can tell you, the climate of savage distrust that exists among your people against anything of Earth. I will admit that, among the masses of Earth at least, a similar feeling exists toward you. But not at executive level. Our higher executives would be only too willing to meet you, to offer the hand of common friendship and welfare. But how far would we get?"

"You would break down on one thing, Earthman!" Billi-Smith burst out angrily. "For all your clever talk, you know this, that if my people ask the one thing that is theirs by right, that they be allowed to return to the planet of their origin, to return to live on Earth, you would refuse. You know this, so how can you pretend that you come in friendship?"

"Exactly!" Stanley nodded as if some point had been made for him. "You have one fixed idea. Almost a neurosis. You want to come back to Earth. And we can't have that."

"The hand of friendship!" BilliSmith snarled.

"No, not at all. The dictates of common sense. You were there. You heard Dillard speak out. You felt the truth of what he told you, about our disgusting planet. And you still want to come and live there?"

"Amplified suggestion and exaggeration!"

"No it wasn't!" Dillard objected, stung in his professional capacity. "The amplification was for the Roggans, not you. You got what I was feeling through Ann, here. Your own sister!"

"Face it," Stanley advised. "You got the truth. There just is not the room on Earth for any kind of considerable contingent from Venus. At all! I'll go further. Never mind that you'd be acutely miserable if you did come to Earth to live, to sniff up stinking air, huddle in noisy, close quarters with millions of others, chomp your way through syntho-food and drink recycled water. Never mind that. Think of this. I've visited your planet, as a touring lecturer. So has Mara, there. Check us on this: if the people of Earth knew what a pleasant place Venus is to live on—in the few places you have been able to convert, that is—they would be flocking to go there. And I mean just that!"

Into a thick silence McLarenSmith said, "There is a great deal of rethinking to do here. If I understand you, Dr. Stanley, you are saying that we can have the water beaming technique, and technical assistance, but only if we can convert our people into a more rational attitude toward Earth."

"It will have to be like that, sir, otherwise, before you know it, the story would be about and raging, that we of Earth are once again imposing some sort of tyranny on your people. You know that. But it's up to us, too. We have the job of selling the truth about Venus to our people. There are lots of odds and ends to be tied off, too. We shall have to recompense you for the loss of your percentage, here. We have to make adjustments in giving Roggan back to its rightful people. There will be swarms of scientists here to meet and study real aliens. A thousand things. But those two stand above the others. We have to chance the attitudes of our two peoples."

There was another thick silence, and a sigh from McLarenSmith. "It will not be easy, that."

"Let me offer a suggestion." Stanley spoke casually, but Dillard became tense as he detected the underlying simmer of cynical amusement there. "You have a powerful weapon to your hand, right here, Dillard."

"What now?" Dillard growled. "No more heroics for me."

"Not at all. Just your job that's all. Make him your chief propaganda merchant, sir. I feel sure his parent firm will back him to the hilt once the idea takes root. Do you see it? Dillard established on Venus, sending back dramatapes complete with sensory effects, to let Earth people know exactly what kind of place it is, and what kind of people live there. You could do that, Dillard, couldn't you?"

"Me? Live on Venus?"

"Yes," AnnSmith said, very softly. "Oh yes. With me to help."

Now, for the first time, McLarenSmith realized how it was between his daughter and the Earthman, and he stared. And then surrendered to what he could sense. But then he nodded, thoughtfully. "It would work, Dr. Stanley. And, like all good coins, it has a reverse side. Dillard could import dramatapes from Earth, to let us see and know what conditions are like there. It is a good thought. You have a real talent, young man. What say you?"

Dillard didn't know what to say for quite a long while. The chaos in his mind was without pattern, but two things held fast in it. One was the nerve-tingling clean warmth that surged from the girl by his side to envelop him in a glow of total rapport. The other was the canker-worm that he still held, down deep. At last he said, "All right, I'm willing to give it a try. But . . ."

"Something has been worrying you all this time," AnnSmith said gently. "You must tell us what it is."

"All right. What about the Roggans?"

The question was aimed at Stanley, who half-closed his eyes and took on a crafty look of anticipation. McLarenSmith spoke into the breach with great confidence.

"You need have no fears about them, my boy. They will be eager to leave Hesperus—I suppose we must cease to use that silly name now—but anyway, they will be keen to return to their own planet. Nothing to worry about."

"I mean," Dillard said it stubbornly, "the Roggans right here! On this their own planet."

"What about them?" Stanley purred, and Dillard frowned, sensing he was being outguessed again. But he went through with his worry just the same.

"I'm no sociologist, let's face it. But I do know people. And I know a bit about our aliens down there. They *are* alien. You know that, too. You can't feel them, can you? They don't think the way we do. Don't talk to me about logic. That's not thinking, or feeling. That's a set of values, a mathematical thing. A machine can do that."

"Go on!" Stanley urged.

"We don't know how they think. But we do know this,

from their own history: for more than two thousand years they held fast to one supreme drive. To get back to the surface somehow. They were prepared to do it the hard way, via Venus, and a smash attack on Earth. They've been talked out of it, for the moment. They are going to get back their own planet. That's fine. But how long are they going to stay content with that? They've seen Venus, and Earth. They know about us, and how vulnerable we are. They have a hell of a drive. How do we know what they will do, once they've got their own culture going again? Remember what they did, long ago? They destroyed themselves in a war. They could do it again. Or us. So —as I said—what about the Roggans?"

The ship's lounge went chill as his reasoning took hold of the rest. All except Dr. Stanley, who smiled.

"You have a very good point, Dillard. A very good point indeed. I always said, did I not, that you had brains? And you can use them, when you choose to do so."

"Forget that," Dillard snarled. "What about the issue? You've handed the Roggans back their planet. You're responsible for what they may do in ten, twenty, fifty years' time. To us!"

"You're quite right." Stanley nodded, and sat back. "Responsible is the word. I accept it. I'm a scientist, Dillard. Like you, I know a little about people. I believe the Roggans to be logical. Or, shall we say, they have been, so far. They chose their own planet by way of peace, rather than an abortive effort to take ours from us. That was rather obvious. What they will do in time, in new conditions, with development and change, I don't know. But they will be watched, I assure you. And if they show the signs you quite rightly point out, they will be destroyed." All at once this lounging little man was cold, like inexorable fate. "We talk a lot about human nature, and the sanctity of human life, and so on. But are the Roggans human? Do they feel as we do? I doubt it."

"You're building up to another war," Dillard accused. "More accurately, you've simply postponed it."

"No. I didn't say we would fight them. I said they would be destroyed. In fact, they will destroy themselves. I will tell you how, with your assurance that the knowledge must not be repeated outside this room. Not until the right moment. Yes? Very well. It has to do with rock, and pressure, and the process of planetary core-formation. It's highly technical, but I can give you the simple facts. Like this. Above a certain gross mass, all planets have a core. The characteristics are common, the process well-known —to those who study such things. Above a certain given pressure the rocks which form the interior body of a planet are forced—deformed—into a closely packed lattice pattern. This is quite standard. Earth has a core. So does Venus. Venus, in fact, is just slightly more massive than the lowest critical possible. Mars, on the other hand, does not have a core. Nor does the moon. Nor Mercury. Now, this planet we call Hydro happens to be very close to the critical limit. It has a core. But should it in some way lose sufficient mass—to decrease the internal gravity pressure, to reduce it below a certain point, to upset the balance of pressures —should that happen—"

"Yes?" Dillard forced the word through a dry throat.

"The core will disappear. The molecular collapse will reverse itself. The overall energy release will be on the order of ten to the thirty-sixth power ergs. I know that's an unthinkable figure. It's enormous. It will be enough to shatter the mantle, to throw the entire surface into chaos, even to throw off continent-sized landmasses into space."

Dillard sagged into his chair, completely stunned by the prospect, as Stanley went on: "I had this all worked out. By my calculations, the Roggans have something like ten years. In that time they should have reclaimed all the land they had before, and a trifle more. I shall stay here, of course, to guide and assist. And watch. Let's hope they change their ways. That's up to us. All of us, human and Venusian alike. We have a big job ahead of us. You've lived with the Roggans, sir, a lot longer than I have. Your people have a part to play, here. We all have a part to play. We can start in a small way, by showing the Roggans that *we* can cooperate, forget our differences, work together. Do you agree?"

"I have to." McLarenSmith sighed. "It looks as if I am going to have an Earthman son-in-law!"

CLASSICS OF GREAT SCIENCE-FICTION

from ACE BOOKS

F-375 (40¢)   **THE WORLDS OF ROBERT A. HEINLEIN**

M-153 (45¢)   **THE WEAPON MAKERS**
by A. E. van Vogt

M-154 (45¢)   **INVADERS FROM THE INFINITE**
by John W. Campbell

F-422 (40¢)   **SWORD OF RHIANNON**
by Leigh Brackett

F-426 (40¢)   **THE GENETIC GENERAL**
by Gordon R. Dickson

F-429 (40¢)   **THE WORLD JONES MADE**
by Philip K. Dick

G-627 (50¢)   **THE BIG TIME**
by Fritz Leiber

G-634 (50¢)   **WAR OF THE WING-MEN**
by Poul Anderson

M-162 (45¢)   **EDGE OF TIME**
by David Grinnell

M-165 (45¢)   **WORLDS OF THE IMPERIUM**
by Keith Laumer

G-649 (50¢)   **THE WORLD SWAPPERS**
by John Brunner

G-661 (50¢)   **BIG PLANET**
by Jack Vance

H-30 (60¢)   **CITY**
by Clifford D. Simak

G-676 (50¢)   **THE SECRET VISITORS**
by James White

G-683 (50¢)   **THE BIG JUMP**
by Leigh Brackett

H-39 (60¢)   **EYE IN THE SKY**
by Philip K. Dick

Available from Ace Books, Inc. (Dept. MM), 1120 Avenue of the Americas, New York, N.Y. 10036. Send price indicated, plus 5¢ handling fee.

HEROES IN EXILE

Three explorers returned to Earth after nine long years en route to Proxima Centauri and back. You would have supposed that they would have been greeted as the heroes of the century, feted, honored, rewarded. But Earth was rewarding the trio in a strange and terrible manner—with permanent exile in orbit, never to touch any planet's surface again.

If Earth wanted that crew isolated so badly, it ought to be worth a lot for someone to learn the reason, because the powers that ruled the world were not talking.

The *Scorfu*—the Martian equivalent of a Mafia—had the idea that the three exiles might prove winning pieces in their endless competition with Earth. And therefore the somewhat unscrupulous but absolutely fearless operative, Slade, could be persuaded that the three from Centauri might mean a million for him—Cash on Delivery, Mars.

Turn this book over for
second complete novel

C.O.D. MARS

MARS

by

E. C. TUBB

ACE BOOKS, INC.
1120 Avenue of the Americas
New York, New York 10036

I

Martin Christopher Slade, detective extraordinary, rested the tips of his fingers together, admired the sheen of his nails, and spoke to a bowl of orchids on his desk. "You may speak quite freely," he said. "This room is proof against violation."

"And against your own recorders?"

"That too." Slade dropped his hands and stared at his visitor. The remark had been crude in its implication. *The man is a crumb*, he thought. *A weasel. A flagging lump of nurd.* But, apparently, he was rich. "If you would care to activate your own safeguards," he said pleasantly, "I have no objection. But I assure you, my word is generally considered to be safeguard enough."

"I am aware of your reputation." Herb Jasker, second-generation Martian, shifted uncomfortably in his chair. The seat was too soft, the air too close, the gravity too high. Even though it was night and the air-conditioning was on at full blast the humidity was appalling. And the people! He felt smothered, choked by a sweltering mass of humanity. He tugged at his collar. Slade watched, silent, an aging idol of weathered stone. The Martian had bought five hundred solars' worth of his time. In ten minutes he would have stated his business, arrived at a satisfactory conclusion, or Slade would have him thrown out. He had six minutes to go.

5

"You know of the Prox expedition," said the Martian abruptly. "You know that the *Hope* arrived back more than two weeks ago."

"I know it."

"Do you know that the crew of the *Hope* is now in strict quarantine?"

"I heard the broadcast," said Slade. "Tomorrow every paper will carry the news. You will be able to buy it for twenty cents."

"But I have information that you cannot buy for twenty cents—or for twenty thousand solars!" Jasker was annoyed. He forced himself to be calm. Anger was not the weapon with which to deal with Slade. "Do you know what decision has been reached by the UP regarding the disposal of the three surviving members of the crew?"

Slade knew but said nothing. His agents in United Planets could rely on his discretion.

"They are to be blasted into space," said Jasker. "Sent on an unending journey into the unknown."

"They are diseased," said Slade. "UP can't risk the infection running wild on a habitable world."

"Diseased!" Jasker snorted his disgust. "What kind of disease are they supposed to have? What disease is it that modern medical science cannot cure? Why must they be blasted into space? Why can't they be kept in controlled isolation for long-term tests and study?"

Slade glanced at his watch. The man had three minutes to go.

"Those questions were asked by the Martian delegate in the United Planets Supreme Council," said Jasker. "They weren't answered to our satisfaction. The representative from Callisto asked the same questions and received the same vague answers. It's time Earth stopped treating us like irresponsible children and told us what we wanted to know."

Two minutes—Jasker was going to find that propaganda could be expensive.

"All right," he said. "That's why I'm here. I want you to find out the truth about the *Hope*."

"What's it worth to you?" Slade believed both in shock tactics and getting to the heart of things.

"The truth?" Jasker hesitated. "Well—"

"I'll give it to you for free," interrupted Slade impatiently. "The crew is diseased. We cannot cure the disease. Rather

6

than run the risk of a planet-wide epidemic we are sacrificing the lives of three men. They are spacers and should be able to accept the decision. So should you."

"And if they are not diseased?"

Slade leaned back and lit a pale green cigar. His instincts were working overtime and they told him that Jasker was holding something back. *He knows something,* he thought. *Something worth money. If it weren't he wouldn't be interested. He cares as much for the welfare of the crew of the* Hope *as I do for some alley cat down in Mexico. And he must be fighting a time limit. If he weren't he wouldn't have come to me. Not with the Scorfu to call on. Those Martian hellcats would stop at nothing if they thought it to be in their interest.*

"You are suggesting," he said aloud, "that the United Planets' examination teams conspired to lie. That the story given to the public is a pure fabrication."

"It could be."

"But why? Why should they lie? What do they hope to gain out of it?"

"I don't know," said Jasker. "Without proof we shall never know."

"And you want me to find the proof." Slade drew thoughtfully at his cigar. "You claim to have special information," he said casually. "When is the *Hope* to be blasted into open orbit?"

"As soon as they have completely wrecked the engines and made certain that the life-maintainence mechanisms are fully operational," said Jasker. His eyes narrowed with suspicion. "How did you know that they were to be sent off in the *Hope?*"

"Logical deduction," lied Slade. "If they are diseased then their ship must also be suspected of being contaminated. When?"

"Soon. Three days, maybe four. Not much longer than that."

"It's not long enough," said Slade. "I won't have time to make a thorough investigation. Listen." He explained, "The examination teams are still up in orbit with the *Hope.* They are the only ones who know the real truth. Maybe some high official in UP knows it also and maybe not. And, for all you know, they could be telling the simple truth. It

takes as long to determine one thing as the other. Truth or
lie, the investigation has to be the same."

"I don't see that," protested Jasker.

"You wouldn't," said Slade. "You're not a detective." He
drew again at his cigar. "And even if I discovered the real
truth," he said, "no matter what it is, it wouldn't do you any
good. There wouldn't be time to stop the blasting. Once
the ship is lost in space any investigation becomes pointless."

"True—that's why they are in such a hurry."

Slade shrugged.

"It wouldn't be because it's the United Planets, would
it?" said Jasker. "I mean, you aren't afraid of them or anything?"

"No."

"I thought not." Jasker looked down at his hands, they
were hard, calloused, the hands of a worker, but he looked
at them to hide his eyes. This was the moment he had
led up to and now he had to gamble that greed and
curiosity would weigh against indifference and caution. He
hoped the psych-breakdown on Slade would prove correct.
He filled his lungs with wet, clammy air. "I asked," he
said slowly, "because there is still something we could do.
One way in which we could be certain that a dreadful
mistake wasn't being made."

Slade concentrated on his cigar.

"The only way we can discover the real truth is to release those men from their ship," said Jasker. "If they can be
rescued and taken to a place of safety—"

"Against the patrol?"

Good, thought Jasker. *He is still listening, still interested.*
"A way could be found," he said. "And there would be
no risk. On Mars we have facilities for total isolation. We
have doctors and medical equipment of all kinds. We could
find out just what is wrong with those poor men and maybe
help them back to a normal life."

*And do the United Planets one in the eye at the same
time,* thought Slade sourly. Well, he had let the nurd talk
long enough. Now was the time to scald his tail.

"One million," said Jasker quietly.

"What's that?"

"I'm offering you one million solars for the crew of the
Hope—C. O. D. Mars."

It had been a heavy night and he'd overslept, waking just in time to avoid being nipped as the bed swung up tight against the wall.

"What the hell!" He stood, looking and feeling foolish with his rumpled hair and gaudy pajamas. The bed sighed pneumatically as it settled into its niche. "Mary! What did you do that for?"

"Time to get up, Ed Taylor," snapped his wife. She was three years older than himself, and had a hard, flat uncompromising voice. She was already dressed, probably had been for the past hour, in her Purity League uniform of black pants, jumper, cummerbund and shoes. She wore the red flashes of a captain. Her hair was cropped, she wore no makeup and her only perfume was soap. She stabbed again at the convert-button and the utiliflat. A flap opened and a table slid into the center of the room. Ed had to squeeze past it on his way to shower and shave.

Cleaned, dressed, his head still throbbing from the night before, he sat and waited for breakfast. Mary kept him waiting. She stood and glared accusingly down at him.

"You were drunk last night."

"I'd had a few drinks," he corrected. "Sam Keyson, one of the men at the office, was celebrating. He's won fifty acres on Venus."

She sniffed.

"It's the truth," he insisted. "He won a competition. Fifty acres, living dome, power-plant, flitter, a genpurpose ag-machine and two paid passages to his farm. It's somewhere near Aphrodite," he finished weakly. "He leaves next week."

"With his wife?"

"Of course with his wife! Who else would he be taking?"

Mary didn't comment but he knew what she was thinking. And she was wrong. Eunice Keyson was all woman and a man would be content with her no matter where he went. Sure, Venus was tough, what with the terraforming still in its early stages, but that was half the fun. The necessity to meet and conquer the challenge of each day. And, after the work, Sam would have Eunice to provide comfort and understanding. Ed sighed, wistfully remembering how her breasts had shown through the lace-topped gown she'd worn at the party, the long curve of her thighs. With a woman like that hell itself would be a picnic. He blinked at what Mary was saying.

" . . . immoral." She sneered. "I've heard all about Venus and what the settlers get up to for amusement. It's no coincidence that everyone who goes has a tart for a wife."

"Eunice is no tart!" He was stung. Damn Mary and her flagging mouth! Ever since she had gotten bitten by the Purity League, sex to her had become a dirty word. Not for the first time he wished the organization would be outlawed. It had wrecked his own sex life and, if it had its way, it would wreck everyone else's. "She's just a nice, normal, friendly girl."

"As her new Venusian friends will no doubt discover," she snapped acidly. "It's due to women like her that the world is in the condition it is."

Which was another wild exaggeration. Overpopulation was due to the fact that normal women wanted babies and that was all. But arguing with Mary was a waste of time.

"Where's breakfast?" he demanded. He could have reached the carton himself but, damn it, a wife had to be good for something.

The offer that week was for a scale model of Sebastian Cabot, circa 1497, the build-it-yourself kit delivered for a top and half a solar. Ed studied it as he spooned up the sugary pap. His luck was in; he only needed one more of the Men of Action series to entitle him to enter the big competition. He already had Christopher Columbus, Marco Polo, Leonardo Da Vinci and Francis Drake. Cabot would make the necessary five. They, twenty tops and ten solars and he could send in the filled out coupon and hope for the big prize. Sam had done it and Sam had won.

But Venus? With Mary?

Venus or anywhere else with her would all be the same. A more uncomfortable purgatory than what he had. But if he won and could find someone like Eunice?

"Eat hearty, mate!" The booming voice from the light-activated panel of the carton matched the colored similacrum of Long John Silver complete with peg leg, hook and raucous parrot. He came stomping forward, eyes shrewd yet twinkling, staring directly at Ed from the carton. "Fill up with delicious Chompies and make like me. Know what I do? Sight, grapple, lay 'em alongside." His wink was suggestive. "Chompies puts an edge on your cutlass, fills your pistol with powder, lets you aim straight and hit dead-center every time." The scene dissolved into a close-up of a BB girl. She leaned forward, smiling. "A girl just can't help loving a Chompie-man," she purred. "I find them irresistible."

"That's right!" Long John Silver came back as Ed triggered by the subliminals, reached for the carton. "Eat hearty, mate! The girls will love you for it."

"Pieces of eight!" screamed the parrot. "Pieces of—awk!" The voice died as he gripped the box, tilted it, refilled his plate with soy-cereal. " . . . eight!" yelled the parrot as he put down the box.

"I won't be home when you get back tonight," said Mary. "There's an important meeting of the League."

"Another?" Ed felt something foreign in his mouth. He probed and discovered a small envelope. It held the usual free gift—an inter-uterine deterrent. He flipped it at the carton. "What about dinner?"

"Get something out or fix it yourself."

"All right." He wasn't displeased. It would give him a chance to finish Marco Polo; he still hadn't completed the head, and the models had to be good to pass scrutiny. If he entered the competition, that was. He still hadn't made up his mind, though last night he had been tempted.

"You'd better get moving," she said. "You don't want Slade to fire you."

"He won't," said Ed absently. He could have a talk with Carson, the firm's legal adviser, maybe he would know the best way to set about getting a divorce. Then, when he was free and had won the competition, he could go to one of those marriage brokers and fix himself up with a new partner. Someone like Eunice, say, or the girl on the carton. A BB type in any case—he'd had enough of synthetic males.

"It's getting late," said Mary and then, just as he reached the door, she added, "you can clean up the place tonight. And you needn't waste time looking for those toys of yours. I've thrown them out with the garbage."

"My models!" He felt as if he were choking. "All of them?"

"The lot."

"You bitch!" he yelled. "You flagging bitch!"

"Pieces of eight!" screamed the parrot.

"Go to hell!" he yelled back.

And slammed the door.

He bought a paper on the way to the comtube and looked disinterestedly at the headlines. PROX CREW QUAR-ANTINED! they screamed, but he had troubles enough of his own to have sympathy for the adventurers who had returned from Proxima Centauri.

So they were in quarantine, so what? They weren't married to a neuter-wife. Their models hadn't been thrown out with the garbage. They didn't live in a ten-by-ten utiliflat with shared toilet and shower and built-in kitchen. They didn't have a lousy job servicing electronic equipment for the Slade Detective Agency. They had memories—to hell with them.

He reached the comtube, jumped aboard, found an empty seat. He felt the weight of someone settling beside him and turned to scowl at his fellow commuter.

"Good morning, Mr. Taylor." She had blue eyes, light gold hair and a smoothly rounded bottom and bust. *About twenty-five,* he thought, *which makes her ten years younger than I am, but women mature faster than men so there's no real difference.* He frowned, feeling that he should know her.

"Susan Weldon," she said. "I work in the same block as you."

"The Slade Agency?"

"Imperial Credit. We met at an inter-office Christmas party, but I don't suppose you remember me. You were a little high."

"I must have been stinking not to have remembered," he said gallantly. "How is it that I haven't seen you in the tube before?"

"Coincidence," she said. "Or maybe we work different shifts. Isn't it dreadful news?"

"Uh?"

She pointed to the paper, folded so as to display the headlines. "Those poor men. After all those years in space to come back home and be treated like rabid dogs."

"Yes," he said.

"That's no way to treat anyone," she continued. "Especially heroes. The UP should be ashamed of itself."

"I guess they should," he agreed. And tried not to feel jealous. "But I guess they know what they're doing."

"Maybe," she said. "But I don't think it's right. Nine

12

years, that's how long it took them to get to Prox and back. That's a long time to spend all alone in space."

He nodded.

"They say that two of them died during the journey." Her eyes grew pensive. "I wonder if they quarreled about something and had a fight? They must have been under terrible strain. Maybe they went crazy or something. It could have happened."

"I doubt it," he said. "They spent most of the time asleep. Well, not exactly asleep but under a drug. Hagan," he explained. "I read about it. You take it and you get all sorts of hallucinations. Harmless ones, of course. It's like a waking dream in which you think that you're back home or wherever you want to be. It stops you from getting bored."

She nodded, white teeth biting her lower lip. "Do you ever get bored?"

"Sometimes." He felt his pulses begin to race. She was unmistakably a BB girl and Mary always claimed that girls with her development were promiscuous. This could be his lucky day. "You?"

"Often," she said. "Sometimes I feel as if I've got to do something about it. What do you do?"

"When I'm bored?" He brooded. He couldn't tell her about his models and he didn't think she'd be interested in his activities at space school. The same with the fencing class he'd had to leave because no one would fence with him. Not after he'd got carried away during a bout and earned the reputation of being dangerous. "Well," he said slowly, "I go on the town a little. Drink. Gamble. You know."

"Girls?"

"Sometimes," he lied. "You?"

"Things," she said vaguely. Then, "That drug you were talking about. Hageen?"

"Hagan." He spelled it. "What about it?"

"From what you say it would be fun to try."

"Sure, if you could get it."

"I could get it." She smiled into his face. "My brother works in the United Planets' dispensary. He has access."

He waited.

"Shall we try it?" She squeezed his arm. "Together?"

13

II

THE SCREEN WAS DEAD. Instead of showing the misty ball of Earth a hundred thousand miles away it showed white words on a black background. THIS SCREEN IS OUT OF COMMISSION DUE TO A TECHNICAL FAULT. Balchin slammed it with the heel of his hand and cursed with mounting fury. "The flagging scum! They've cut off our view!"

"Take it easy," said Bland.

"For what?" Balchin strode across the compartment, twenty-five paces—the builders of the *Hope* had been generous. He turned, strode back, a heavy, squat man with flaming red hair and a face ridged and mottled with anger. "Because they could be listening? Damn them, I hope they are. I want them to listen. I want to tell the lice just what I think of them." He halted, glared at the screen, the wall beyond, the compartments beyond the wall. "Hey there! Are you listening? You've cut our view," he roared. "It isn't enough that you stinking nurds have cooped us up like rats in a trap. Now you cut our view. Damn it," he raved, "we aren't going to stand for it!"

"Yes we will," said Bland. He was a thoracic type, slim, flat-muscled, lithe with a serious, scholastic face. "We have to. They've got us here and they're keeping us here and there's nothing we can do about it. Now relax and quit beating your head against a wall."

Elgar said nothing. He sat, slumped in one of the form-fit chairs, eyes closed as if asleep. Balchin paused in his restless striding, looked down at him, resumed his pacing.

"Nine years," he said bitterly. "Nine stinking years in this can and when we get back what happens? Are we treated as heroes? Are we even treated as ordinary human beings? We are like hell! Lepers, that's what. Those nurds treat us as if we were lepers. They can't get away with it."

"They can," said Bland. "They are." He stretched in his chair. "Who's going to stop them? Us?"

"Someone," said Balchin. He looked bewildered, a little lost. Tiredly he slumped into one of the chairs. "Someone's got to do something," he said. "It isn't right what they're doing to us."

14

Bland shrugged.

"There's nothing wrong with us," said Balchin. "There can't be anything wrong with us. We haven't even been sick. Ken and Ty got sick but we didn't. They died but we didn't even catch a sniffle. Not then and not during the journey back. How can we be diseased?" He glared again at the featureless screen. "Why do they keep telling us we are?"

"They're afraid," said Bland. "We've been out to where no one's ever been before. Way out to another star. To them, now, we're somehow alien; somehow no longer quite human." His muscles tensed as he thought about it. "Alien by association," he said. "We've got interstellar dust in our hair."

Elgar muttered and stirred in his chair.

"Xenophobia," said Bland. "That's what they're suffering from. A simple fear of strangers."

And now they're giving us the old xenelasia, he thought, *excluding and maybe expelling the aliens in their midst. And it doesn't seem to matter to them that we aren't aliens at all, but just three people who've traveled a long way and are tired of traveling and who want nothing more than to be allowed to go home.*

Home, he thought, and felt a terrible hunger for the teeming billions of Earth, the crowded cities, the towering blocks of apartments. *Dogs,* he thought, *cats, rats and mice, birds and snakes and sheep, pigs and cows and turtles. Insects, even, and fish in the sea.* A multitude of living creatures just waiting on the planet of his birth.

Space is too bleak, he thought. *Too barren. Too damn sterile and too damn cold. And there was too much of it. Nine years too much.*

We made a mistake, he told himself. *We should never have contacted Earth as we did. We should have landed somewhere else, on Titan or Iapetus, Ganymede, Callisto, Io, Rhea, on any of the terraformed outer satellites. Or on Mars. Anything but heading straight for Earth and what we thought would be a hero's welcome. We were wrong,* he told himself. *They didn't treat us like heroes at all.*

Instead they had turned the *Hope* into a jail.

Elgar stirred again, muttered, opened his eyes. "No," he said thickly. "No!"

"Did you get anything?" Balchin reared from his chair

and crossed to his side. "Come on, Saul, did you get anything?"

"I'm not sure," said Elgar. He was a thin, Egyptian-faced Negro, his hair a cap of black crinkled wool. "There's so much noise out there," he said. "So much confusion." *And so many minds,* he brooded, *so many thoughts.* All tangled in space and time like multicolored skeins of wool, an abstract tapestry made of a near-infinite number of threads. "You know how precog works with me," he said. "I can't tell when it is going to happen. A minute, a week, a year, even. I just don't know."

"But you got something?" Balchin was eager.

Elgar wondered if he should tell. They wouldn't thank him for it, but they were all in this together and they had a right to know. "They've decided," he said. "Or they will decide. And they will tell us."

"Tell us what?" asked Bland.

"That we have to stay here," said Elgar. "That they're going to keep us here until we die."

"I can do it," said Slade. He sat at his desk, bare now of orchids, the aged pattern of his face stark in the glare of the light which threw a cone of brilliance over the immediate area. "There's a way in which it could be done." He smoothed the sheets of paper before him, a thick pile of sheets, the building plans of the *Hope*. "I can release those men."

"Why should you?" Carson, plump, shrewd, calculating, sat at the edge of the light and smoked a Martian cigar. "For a million? You've got a million. More." He flipped ash from his cigar. "Anyway, what good is money to a man in jail?"

"I won't go to jail," said Slade. "That's why I pay you."

"You pay me for legal advice," said Carson. "Not as a partner in criminal enterprises. All right," he conceded, "I'll admit you've got a thin case. The *Hope* is orbiting at a hundred thousand mile altitude. Planetary jurisdiction ends at ten diameters—thirty thousand miles as applied to the Terrestrial legislature. Technically you'll be breaking no Earthside law. But the United Planets have jurisdiction between the worlds. How are you going to persuade them to lay off?"

"Without evidence," said Slade, "what can they do?"

"They'll have evidence."

"Not against me, they won't," said Slade. He leaned back in his chair, feeling the old, familiar thrill of excited anticipation. It had been years since a problem had interested him so much. "And even if they try to bring the case to court I'll be safe. They've been too cagey," he said. "They've told too little. They claim that the crew is diseased —but do we blast our sick into open orbit? If they are telling the truth then their action is morally indefensible. And don't forget that space-law demands that, at all times, one man must go to the aid and assistance of another. If they try me I'll wind up a hero."

"Maybe," said Carson. Slade had a point.

"No doubt about it," said Slade. "That's what I'm paying you for. That's why I'm telling you all this—so that you can be a witness to my incredulous indignation at what the United Planets propose doing to those poor men in the *Hope*."

"Sure," said Carson. He drew thoughtfully at his Martian cigar. "Even so, why do it?" he asked. "You don't really give a damn for those men."

"I care about money."

"Don't we all?" Carson examined the spiraling blue smoke. "Why?" he asked softly. "Why should that Martian be prepared to pay so much?"

"I don't know," said Slade. Carson was getting close, too close. He jabbed at a button on his intercom. "Did you get that information yet?" he snapped at the face which showed on the screen.

"Almost, Mr. Slade," said the girl. "I'm about to contact UP headquarters now." She looked to one side. "A moment, Mr. Slade."

"Call me back," said Slade. He looked at Carson. "Herb Jasker knows something," he told the lawyer. "He could only have learned it from a fellow Martian or a relative of one. So—" He broke off as the screen came to life. "Any luck?"

"No, Mr. Slade." The girl was regretful. "Seth Ingram, the only Martian on the examination teams, died shortly after contact."

"From disease?"

"They didn't say, Mr. Slade."

"All right." Slade turned from the graying screen. "He must have been the leak," he said to Carson. "Ingram contacted Jasker somehow, maybe by telepathy—a lot of Martians have psionic power, and told him enough to make him willing to pay a million for those men."

"But Ingram died," said Carson. "UP could be telling the truth."

"Not all of it," said Slade. "They can't be. No diseased crew could be worth a million to an economy like Mars. Not even if they had a disease which was turning them into solid uranium." *And I'm going to get them,* he thought. *If they're worth a million to the Martians they must be worth far more than that to me. Ten million, perhaps, a hundred, even more. But it isn't just the money,* he told himself. *It's what is behind the money. Power, real power—and I want it.*

"Listen," he said, smoothing out the blueprints. "I've found how it could be done. Not now, not at this minute, but later when the time is ripe."

"Before they blast the ship into orbit," said Carson. It had to be then.

"Right." A thin film of sweat shone on Slade's mummy-like face. He dipped into a drawer, took out a dispenser, shook a couple of tablets into his palm. He gulped them down without water. He was on his third day without sleep. "Just before they blast," he agreed. "They're fixing boosters to the *Hope.* Just before they touch them off the area will be cleared. Then, and only then, a man could get aboard."

"And go with them?" Carson crushed out his cigar. "How will that help?"

"It won't," said Slade irritably. "But he won't go with them. He'll take them out and away."

"Without anyone noticing?"

"Did I say that?" Slade leaned back in his chair. Blinking, he looked like a poised eagle, waiting before it struck. "They'll notice, all right. But what the patrol will see will be a news-ship after a story. A ship with its radio on the blink. A ship which will touch the *Hope,* wait, then leave—and then vanish."

"With the crew," said Carson. He didn't ask for details; it was better that he didn't know. He raised no further objections. Slade would go his own way. But one thing he had to ask: "And the crew? Of the rescue ship, I mean. What about them?"

"One man and automatic controls. One lone, single operator with a taped radio."

"Nice," said Carson. He could fill in the rest. "Very nice," he said. "If you can find the man."

"I'll find him," said Slade.

The sergeant was tired, irritable, hungry and impatient. "Listen, lady," he snapped. "Just what is it you're complaining about?"

"It's my husband." Mary Taylor didn't like the local precinct house, the harshness, the scurry and bustle of too few men trying to do too much, conscious of their failure and angry because of it. "He hasn't been home," she explained. "Not last night and not this morning. I want you to find him."

"Just like that?" The sergeant raised his eyes toward the ceiling. "Listen," he said, and gestured toward the street. "Out there is murder, rape, mugging, theft, mayhem, fraud —you name it, it's there. And you want us to drop everything to find a man who stayed out all night? Hell," he said. "Be reasonable."

"It's your job," she said stubbornly. "It's what you're paid to do."

"Sure," said the sergeant.

"My husband is missing," she insisted. "I want you to find him."

"All right," he said, and reached for a book and a pen. "Let's have some details. Name?"

"Edward Taylor, thirty-five, six feet two inches, a hundred and ninety pounds, dark hair, blue eyes, pale skin, no distinguishing scars or features." She hesitated. "And no money."

"Are you sure about that? Have you checked with his bank?" The sergeant waved toward a row of phones. "Check now. Go on, check!"

He waited, booked in a drunk, took details of a mugging, listened to a tale of fraud. He sighed as Mary returned. "Well?"

"He drew out some cash," she admitted.

"So he has money." The sergeant looked down at his book. "Is he at work?"

"No," she said. "I checked three times," she added. "I thought he might be working late but he wasn't. Then—"

"I get the picture," interrupted the sergeant. Work was piling up, he really had no time to waste. "Look," he said, "your husband is an adult. Maybe he decided to hit the town, take a powder, anything. Lots of people stay out all night. Hell, lady, that's no crime. Give it a week and then come back."

"But—"

"A week," he said firmly. "Who's next?"

A woman was waiting when Mary got home. She was dressed in dark, severe clothing, wore no makeup and her dark hair was cropped close to her head. Corsets flattened her BB attributes. Chameleon-like, Susan Weldon could adapt her appearance to suit the occasion.

"Mrs. Taylor?" she said. "My name is Hardcastle. I represent the firm of Thomas, Thomas and Dewey. We specialize in divorce."

"Yes?" Mary opened the door of the utiliflat, pressed the convert-button for "lounge," and waited as the table vanished and chairs came from the wall. "Won't you come in?"

"I'll make this brief, Mrs. Taylor," said Susan. She rummaged in her handbag, produced a thick envelope. "Our client is suing his wife for divorce and naming your husband as corespondent. The evidence against him is incontrovertible. My client will, naturally, ask for costs and damages. I am sure you can realize the position in which you find yourself."

"My position?" The blow had come too quickly.

"The communal property laws will affect your liability as to monies demanded," explained Susan. "Is Mr. Taylor a rich man?"

"No." Mary swallowed. "No, he isn't rich. This is my flat." Then, "What evidence?"

Susan held out the envelope. Mary took it, opened it, examined what it contained. The photographs were cruelly sharp—the participants unmistakable.

"Our client has suspected his wife for some time," said Susan. "He has had her followed. These photographs were taken last night. Would you like to know just where and how?"

"No!" Mary looked at the pictures with mounting revulsion. *The fool,* she thought. *The stupid, sex-mad fool! This will ruin him,* she told herself. *And, if I'm not careful, it will ruin me too. Not just as regards the money but my*

*position in the League. How can I ensure respect with a
goat for a husband?*" "No," she said again, and flung down
the photographs. "I don't want to know."

"I understand." Susan was all sympathy, one woman com-
miserating with another. "It's a dreadful thing to happen to
any woman, but for one so prominent in the League—"

"What can I do?" interrupted Mary. "How can I protect
myself?"

"One way." Susan gathered up the photographs. "If you
were to file a counter-suit for divorce against your husband
then you would not be liable for his costs or damages.
My firm would be happy to act for you in the matter. The
expense would be low—we have all the necessary evidence,
and the charge would be against your husband, not yourself."
She paused, waiting. "Well, Mrs. Taylor?"

"I'll do it," said Mary.

"You are being very wise." Susan produced papers. "If
you will just sign here . . . and here . . . and once more
here, please. Thank you." She gathered up the papers, the
photographs, replaced them in her handbag. "One other
thing, Mrs. Taylor. It would not be wise to allow your
husband to return here. There is always a danger of con-
donation."

"I'll take care of that," said Mary. "I'll pack up his things
and have the janitor change the lock on the door." She
hesitated. "You'll notify him?"

"Of course, Mrs. Taylor."

"You know where he is?"

"At the fifteenth precinct. He is charged under section
five, subsection three—unauthorized use of drugs. Goodbye, Mrs. Taylor."

Outside Susan made two calls, one to Thomas, Thomas
and Dewey, the other to the Slade Agency, speaking directly
to the seamed visage of the owner himself. "Phase two
successfully completed, Mr. Slade," she said.

"Good girl," he answered. "Send me your bill."

It had to be a dream. It had to be a hangover from that
stuff Susan had fed him last night when they had met after
working hours and they had gone to her brother's apartment. Hagan, that was it, the hallucigenic drug which had
turned the world inside out and dappled it with fantastic
colors. But how long was the dream supposed to last?

Ed Taylor sat on the edge of the narrow metal bunk, head resting in his hands, elbows balanced on his knees. in his mouth. The tang of disinfectant, of sweat, vomit, blood and fear. *Jail*, he thought. *I'm in jail. Locked up like an animal and for what? What did I do for them to take me in?* He looked at his wrist but his watch was missing together with his belt and tie. *To stop me dutching myself,* he thought. *As if I'd do a thing like that! I'm not crazy. Sick, maybe, but not crazy. But what the hell happened last night?*

Some of it he could remember. The apartment, Susan, the sharp, acrid taste of the drug. Then there had been movement, new surroundings, new company. Female company, strange and exhilarating despite the illusion it must have been. *It's worth being a spacer,* he thought, *just for the drug they take to stop getting bored. With hallucinations like that who'd want anything else?*

He lifted his head as a guard unlocked the cell. "All right," said the man. "Out."

"I can go?" Ed stood up.

"Your fine's been paid," said the guard. "You can pick up your stuff at the desk. Now get out and don't come back."

There was an envelope with his things. Ed looked at it as he checked his money, keys, identification papers, the usual junk a man carried around. He donned his belt and tie, strapped on his watch before ripping open the envelope and reading what was inside. He couldn't believe it.

Divorce. May was divorcing him. He was forbidden to return to the utiliflat. It doesn't make sense. She must be joking or, more likely, teaching him a lesson for being out all night. Or maybe this was a part of the hallucination—whatever it was it couldn't be real.

He looked at his watch and decided against phoning her. He was late already and with the way things were he needed his job. First he had to get to work and then, later, he would clear up this misunderstanding with his wife.

A flitter took him to the agency. An elevator lifted him to the office. Mr. Quiss, his immediate boss, stopped him as he entered.

"Taylor! Just a minute."

"Sorry I'm late, Mr. Quiss," said Ed. "I got held up."

"In jail," said Quiss. "We know all about it."

"You do?" Ed felt a sinking in his stomach. "How?"

"They contacted us. They knew where you worked from your identification. Mr. Slade ordered that your fine was to be paid."

"That was decent of him," said Ed. "I'll pay it back from my salary."

"You already have," said Quiss. He held out a check. "This is the balance owing you. Collect your stuff and go. You've got fifteen minutes to get out of the office."

"I'm fired?"

"You're fired."

"But why? Just because of a lousy mistake? Maybe the union'll have something to say about this."

"They won't," said Quiss. "They've already been consulted. Look," he said confidentially. "You're engaged on delicate and important work. Mr. Slade has to know that he can trust you. How can he do that when you've turned into a junkie?"

"I'm no addict!"

"Maybe not—not yet, but you were found raving in the street and taken in for your own protection. Who knows what you may have told and to whom? I'm sorry, Taylor, but that's how it is. Fifteen minutes."

Disconsolately Ed went to gather his tools and personal belongings. He'd liked working for Slade; there had been a hint of mystery and excitement in the devices he'd serviced, the bugs and directional miniature radios, the taps and secret eyes. Now it was over.

I'm finished, he thought dully. *The word'll get around and I'll be lucky to get a routine job doing repairs in a service station. Mechanic's work, that's what, and low-paid at that. Mary'll blow her top when I tell her.* Then he remembered.

"Yes?" The girl on the screen was coldly distant, she didn't gush over artisans.

"Get me 24-15-67-71," said Ed. "Hurry."

"Is this a personal call?"

"Business," he snapped. "Now get moving." Impatiently he waited, standing beside the bench-phone, not caring if Quiss or Slade himself saw him breaking the rules. "Hello, Mary."

"So it's you." She stared hard at him. "What do you want?"

"That joke of yours," he said, and wondered if she had been crying. Her eyes were red, as if she had. "I—"

"It's no joke," she interrupted. "Your stuff is with the janitor. Try molesting me and I'll report you to the police."

"But why?" he yelled. "What have I done?"

"You can read, can't you?" She snapped the connection. Slowly he turned from the screen. Slowly he reread the contents of the envelope.

Baffled, he shook his head. *I didn't do that,* he told himself. *At least I don't remember doing it. Not consciously anyway. Can hallucinations be held as grounds for divorce?*

At least, he thought, *I didn't have to pay for the stuff;* he'd drawn some money just in case. It was a small consolation.

III

DOCTOR HILDA GOOTMEYER stared at the screen in her makeshift laboratory and suddenly felt as if the very props of normal existence had somehow dissolved and left her hanging unsupported over an abyss. *They hadn't reacted! They knew,* she thought. *They knew!* Somehow, someone had told them or somehow they had learned so that the bombshell on which she'd relied had had simply no apparent effect.

And yet who could have told them when she controlled all communication with the three adventurers? They must have learned by other means: telepathy, precognition, something like that. They'd had years of isolation in which to develop their paraphysical abilities. Or perhaps she was assuming too much? They could be acting, or perhaps they simply didn't understand. Or believe.

"Listen to me," she said, and leaned closer to the screen. "It is important that you fully realize your position. You will not be allowed to leave this vessel. You will remain in the *Hope* until you die." Surely, this time, there could be no doubt. "Do you understand?"

"Sure," said Balchin. His broad face was hard with anger. "What do you want us to do, weep?"

"Are we to be left wholly alone?" asked Bland.

"So you have decided to abandon us," said Elgar. As usual the dark one sat slumped in one of the chairs. "On whose authority?"

"That of the United Planets."

"Which means they are acting on your recommendation." Elgar lifted his head, meeting her eyes. "Why do you hate us so much?" he asked softly. "Why?"

The question was irrelevant. As a scientist she was concerned only with facts and the thalamic processes of her brain could not be allowed to influence her judgment. Could not and did not. Decisively she released the record-button and switched off the screen. She had tried and failed. There was no pretense. They had known all the time.

Which meant they were even more dangerous than she had previously suspected.

A bell chimed on her phone. She looked at the face of her first assistant. "Yes?"

"Company, doctor," he said cheerfully. "I've just had notification from the guard-patrol. Senator Keeway of the Northwestern Quadrant, Terra, is coming up to pay us a visit."

"Damn!" Scientist or not she knew the therapeutic value of expletives. "What the devil does he want?"

"At a guess I'd say that he wants to have a look at our problem."

"Why?"

"The senator is a politician," said Ross cynically. "Need I say more?"

"The UP isn't concerned with local politics," she snapped. "At least the Health Organization isn't. My orders were explicit. No visitors, no sightseers, no news-services. Refuse him entry."

"I wouldn't," said Ross seriously. "Not if I were you and wanted to continue in my career. Keeway is connected with the General Space Equipment Company. They had a big hand in building the *Hope*. Maybe he wants to find out what is happening to their investment."

"They've lost it."

"Sure, but they don't have to be happy about it. Maybe they think that the UP has been a little high-handed over this affair. That could be why they've sent their boy to investigate."

"Damn him!"

"I agree," said Ross. "Thirty minutes?"

"Damn him," said Hilda again.

Senator Keeway was round, short, beaming and with the cold eyes of a praying mantis. He came bursting through the lock and jerked to a sudden halt. They had already dressed him in the thin, near-invisible plastic envelope, and he plucked at it as he stared around.

"What the hell?"

"The burn-marks?" Hilda had correctly guessed his thought processes. The *Hope*, while never a luxury vessel, had been designed with the thought that five men had to live aboard and remain sane for a long period of time. So it couldn't be a slum. It couldn't be a coffin. It had to have some resemblance to a home. Now it was a slum and, while it would end as a coffin, it made a hell of a place in which to live.

"Vandalism!" stormed Keeway.

"Essential prophylactic procedure," corrected Hilda coldly. Surely the fool knew that the ship had had to be sterilized, and what better method than with flame? Hot, cleansing flame which had to be applied to every inch because who knew what alien microorganism might be present—or be disguised as something apparently innocuous? The whole ship should have been dumped into the sun, in her opinion. Should still be so disposed of. It was the only sane method. "In any case," she said, "it doesn't really matter. The ship will never be used again."

Keeway grunted as he followed her from the lock and into the cramped rest room of the investigating team. He was a man who liked room in which to move. Irritably he plucked at the envelope. "Do I have to wear this thing?"

"No," she admitted. "You can take it off if you wish— and if you have no objection to joining us in quarantine."

He caught the irony and stared hard at the woman. A *proud bitch*, he thought. Tall, about five ten, touching forty but well kept, slim though not mannish. Neat, too, in her uniform of surgical green. *And a joker*, he told himself. *Well, maybe I'll have the last laugh. I'm on her territory now, but one day she'll be on mine. These eggheads of the UPHO seem to think they're God annointed,* he thought furiously. *But when you come down to it what are they but paid servants of the public? And I represent the public.*

"Is that still necessary?" he said coldly. "You've seared the ship down to bare metal. You've cooped up those brave boys who've done so much to expand the frontiers of knowledge. You're taking every medical precaution. Why are you so afraid?"

"Perhaps because, to date, twenty-three personnel of the Health Organization have died," she said abruptly. "I would prefer not to make it more."

"From disease?"

"Yes—from the disease carried back from Prox by the men we have been forced to quarantine."

"And now whom you want to shoot into space," he said acidly. "Where are they?"

He stood before the screen, operating on one-way view, his round face thoughtful. "They seem healthy enough," he said finally. "Fine specimens of the human race. I'd be proud to go in there and shake them by the hand."

"If you did you would collapse in shock within two hours and be dead within six."

He didn't answer.

"From the first moment of contact you would be contaminated," she pursued. "Every living thing you touched would also die."

"No period of incubation?"

"None." *He has done his home-work,* she thought. *At least some of it. But why the hell hasn't he read my reports?* "The disease seems to follow the attributes of the sporoza but with the characteristics of the myxomycetes," she said. "I realize that this is apparently a contradiction of terminology but the thing is alien and has a life-cycle of its own. The fact is that those men are carriers of something against which we have no natural or artificial defense. Contamination is by contact and is instantaneous. The—germ— is extruded on the skin and from there can pass by contact to any inanimate structure. There it lies dormant until picked up by a host. Propagation is terrifyingly fast and seems to follow the pattern of the mycorrhiza. Massive physical shock follows contamination. Death is one hundred percent."

"No," said Keeway.

"I beg your pardon?"

You're annoyed, he thought. *Good. But you aren't as clever as all your words seem to signify.* "Not one hundred percent," he said. "If it were those three men wouldn't be alive." He looked at the silent, mouthing figures on the screen. "The other two died," he said. "They didn't. Why not?"

"I don't know," she admitted.

"But if they managed to survive there could be a cure?"

"Not necessarily," she said. "Not that we have time to discover. Not that we have need to discover. The disease is alien."

"Yes," he said. "But what happens when others go out to Prox?"

"They won't," she said. "They mustn't. Never again."

Keeway grunted and turned up the sound from the screen.

"Diamonds," said Balchin. "Do you remember that field of diamonds we found? Big. As big as your fist, some of them. Stuck in that blue clay like peanuts in a candy bar."

"Uranium," said Bland softly. "The geigers almost shook apart over that plain. I'll bet there's more uranium there than in all Earth."

"Never mind that," said Elgar dreamily. "I like to think of all that open ground. A world of timber and soil, rivers and mountains, snow and seas, all alive with game and nothing artificial in sight. Eden," he said slowly. "The Garden of Eden. Enough real estate to give every man and woman of the Northwestern Quadrant a hundred acres and still leave enough for the next twenty generations. Paradise, that's what it is. Paradise!"

"Coal," mused Balchin. "Oil, iron, copper, you name it and it's there. Why did we come back?"

"No women," said Bland.

"Duty," said Elgar. "We came back to bring the word and for reward they're going to shoot us off into space. To let us die like rats in a tin coffin."

"Nice," said Balchin.

Hilda switched off the screen. Liars, she thought. Dirty, underhand liars! They were saying all that for the benefit of Keeway, trying to arouse his sympathy and greed, appealing to his political nature. Land, she thought, a world ripe for exploitation. *By whom?*

She became aware of Keeway's eyes, hard, cold, speculative. "They were lying," she told him. "I've read the reports, the logs, the automatic recorders. Prox isn't like that."

"Isn't it?" He looked thoughtfully at the screen. "Then why were they talking that way?"

"To appeal to you."

"Is that so?" He touched the screen controls. "But how did they know I was here listening to them? Telepathy?"

She sensed his antagonism and said nothing.

"Listen," he said coldly. "The company which I represent spent millions on the *Hope*. They have a right to know the truth. The people I represent also have that right. I want to talk with those men."

"The screen communicates with their quarters."

"Face to face," he said. "I am aware that recordings can be faked. I am also aware that actors could be taking the place of the real adventurers. I want the truth, Doctor Gootmeyer. All of it!"

For a moment the temptation was almost too much. To let the fool have his way. To send him in with the others, unwarned, blind in his ignorance—and then to watch him die. *He might just learn the truth then,* she thought. *He might look into their eyes and see what I've seen, the taint of strangeness, the alienness of what lies behind their smiles. Actors,* she thought. *If you only knew.*

"I cannot allow that," she said firmly. "There must be no personal contact."

"Who says so?"

"The United Planets Health Organization. The safety of worlds cannot be endangered to satisfy the curiosity of one man—even though he is a senator, even though he does represent vested interest. In this matter my word is law."

Your word, he thought furiously. *And who the hell are you? God? Damn it, woman, I represent a quarter of Terra.*

"I insist," he said. "The people have a right to know."

"They do know," she said. "Good men died so that they should learn. Other good men died trying to save the first to go. There is no cure, barely any defense, nothing to be done other than what has been decided. There must be no delay."

"But surely I can talk to them," he said. "They've been to another star. They've seen new things. That knowledge should not be lost."

"We have gained all we can."

"And the ship," he pressed. "It was the first of its kind, what can be done to improve the design? They can tell us that."

Abruptly she switched on the screen. It had been a futile hope. They were as they always were, Balchin striding the floor, Bland thoughtful, Elgar slumped, eyes closed, apparently asleep. *Doing what?* she thought. Trying to read a mind, predict an occurrence? Was he probing at Keeway this very moment, at Ross, at herself? Could he reach as far as Earth? And again, how *did* these three manage to survive?

"They can tell us," Keeway repeated. His eyes were hungry on the screen.

"Yes," she said. "They could—but they won't."

And in twelve hours it would be too late.

"All right," said the man. He was small, wizened, with a prosthetic arm and mechanical ears. His breath smelt of medication and he was as bald as an egg. "The rudder controls left and right, the left-hand lever up and down, the right-hand lever forward and back. Got that?"

Ed nodded. He'd tried to explain that none of this was new to him, that he'd handled spaceship simulacra before, but the man had been adamant. "You've got to do it right," he said. "In space there's only one mistake—the last. I learned that the hard way." And he'd touched his arm and ears. *Radiation,* Ed guessed. *He was old and probably had ridden in the early ships. It couldn't happen now. At least,* he corrected himself, *the chances were that much less.*

"I'm ready," he said, and settled himself in the chair, hands and feet on the controls. "Let her run."

The man grunted. "You've got to hit those two points of light together," he said. "You're coming in at two-G. Go!"

The screen shifted, flickered as old film slipped over worn sprockets. Points of light, red and green, glowed. Ed's was the red one. He had to match it to the green. The red dot shifted as he moved the controls.

"Not bad," said the man. His name was Carl and he was a member of the Friends of Space. "Try it again."

Ed tried it again, and again, and again. He got so that his hands and feet moved automatically and he could match the points every time. He turned as a pimple-faced youth stuck his head into the booth.

"Time's up," he said. "You want another session?"

Carl hesitated, looking at Ed. Ed thought of the ten solars it would cost and shook his head.

"All right," said the youth. "Out."

He stepped back to give them room to pass and ushered in a man of about sixty.

"I want the real thing," said the man. "I've always wanted to be a spacer and it looks now as if this is the closest I'm going to get. The real thing, mind."

"How about the Callisto-Iapetus war?" said the youth. "I've got a hot tape on that. You against the enemy. Lasers, the works. You let yourself get hit and the screen turns red."

The man hesitated.

"Or simulated landings on Venus," urged the youth. "Running blind and operating strictly by control? Or how about can-maneuvers? You've got to aim 'em right and let 'em go. Or match position and speed to pick 'em up. Real work, mister, they're doing it all the time." He busied himself with the machine. "And you're not too old to stand a chance at the real thing. Not if you can pass their tests, that is, and how do you think they learn how to do that? Listen, mister," he said confidentially, "you'd be surprised at just how many can-jockeys got their basic training in this establishment. Shall we say twenty solars' worth?"

Carl pulled Ed away before he could hear the answer. The old spacer's face was twisted with disgust. "Hear them peep," he sneered. "They don't know from nothing. Space isn't a damn machine with a wash-out for a mistake. Space is a monster just waiting to feed. Don't you forget that."

"I won't," said Ed, and wondered what was happening to him. It didn't seem real. The meeting with the old spacer, the talk, the offer of a job. And the training—his head still ached from the hypnotutor. And for what?

For ten thousand solars, he thought, that's what. The chance to make a pile and get something out of life. A real chance of adventure and, if it seemed odd, what of it?

Fate worked that way. Coincidence couldn't be ignored. The Friends of Space were looking for a man and he was the one they'd found. A man with electronic training, space school experience and the willingness to take a chance. *Ride it,* he told himself. *Ride it all the way. What the hell have I got to lose?*

Some time, he thought, and that was about all. A short sentence at the most if he was caught and there was no reason why he should be. A protest, Carl had said, a gesture against the inhumanity of those in authority. The men in the *Hope* had a right to be heard. The publicity of their rescue would give them the opportunity to do that. And, for himself, ten thousand solars plus what extras he might pick up in the way of endorsements, interviews, write-ups.

A gift, he thought. *I can buy a farm on Venus or Mars, marry a BB girl, get some fun out of life for a change. To hell with Slade and his agency. Who needs Slade?*

IV

THE PILOT SAID, "Position achieved, sir. Your orders?"

"Get as near to the *Hope* as you can," said Slade. "Take it easy and halt if ordered by the patrol."

"Of course, sir," chided the pilot. "My programming makes it impossible for me to disobey such a command."

"You talk too much," said Slade.

"Yes, sir," said the pilot. "Would you like a running commentary on external affairs or would you prefer to spend the time in quiet meditation?"

"Keep it up," said Slade, "and I'll switch you off."

"Yes, sir," said the pilot.

Damn machine, thought Slade. *I'm going to switch you off anyway. I don't want any nosy snooper probing around in your memory banks. But that can come later,* he told himself. *After the thing's done its job.*

He relaxed in his chair and idly played with the screens. The sun flashed past, a flaming ball of eye-bright fury. The moon, pale beside the full-blown glory of Earth. Tiny lights winked far below, the working lights of the can-jockeys, the flames of their tugs.

A hell of a job, thought Slade. From Earth rose a continuous stream of wheat, rice, maize, oil, lumber, manufactured goods, supplies of all kinds. Lashed into bales of five thousand tons, skinned with iron-sprayed plastic, inflated so that they looked like giant sausages rising into the sky. The staples to keep the colonies alive. The life-blood of trade. Passengers too, those who could afford no better passage, doped and half dead for the duration of the trip.

The can-jockeys grabbed them, aligned them on their various targets, sent them on their way. They grabbed the traffic from outside, slowed it down, sent it into landing orbit. A tough job for tough men with ruptured kidneys, burst capillaries and strained hearts as minor occupational hazards.

A light winked attention and Carson stared from the screen.

"Is everything all right, Mr. Slade?"

"Why shouldn't it be?" Slade scowled at the lawyer. "Everything is going according to plan, isn't it?"

"The leak has spread," admitted Carson. "The news-ships are on their way. Others too. The sector should be crowded pretty soon." He hesitated. "Are you quite sure that—"

"I know what I'm doing," snapped the detective. "I'm safe enough. Space is free so what law am I breaking? If I miss out then I'm in the clear. If I get what I'm after, and get intercepted, then I'm only doing my duty as a citizen by taking them in custody. If I get away with it then I'm safe. How can I go wrong?"

How indeed? He thought as he cut the connection. He looked back toward the rear of his ship. The accommodation was ready, a sealed room with cans of air, food and water. He had an infection-envelope. They would enter the ship from the external loading hatch. How could he go wrong?

"Attention," said the pilot. "I have received warning from the patrol to proceed no further."

"Ignore it," said Slade. "Get as close to the *Hope* as you can."

"This is it," said the pilot. The ship slowed, came to a halt. "I must obey the orders of the patrol. We can advance no closer." The mechanical voice sounded pompous.

"Go to hell," said Slade, but he had expected no better and this was close enough. He hunched forward, eyes on the screen and the distant shape of the interstellar vessel silhouetted against the stars. It jumped toward him as he stepped up the magnification.

They were almost ready. Even as he watched a ship left the side of the vessel and drifted free. That would be the medical team leaving; the engineers would already have left. All that remained was for the patrol to clear the area and then fire the boosters clamped at the base of the *Hope*. They would fling the ship on its last journey and, if he had planned it correctly, no one would know that the coffin had been robbed of its prey.

"Now!" he breathed as a flurry of ships came streaking past. Newshawks intent on a last minute scoop, ignoring the patrol warnings, putting their safety in numbers. "Now, Taylor. Damn you, now!"

It was incredibly easy. Incredible because most of the time he didn't seem to have to think of what he was doing. Easy because the computer-brained ship took all the guess-work from the maneuver. Ed grunted as the ship dived between two of the giant boosters, magnetic clamps gripping fast. Immediately he threw a lever. An iron-sprayed plastic balloon inflated from the body of the ship, became a frail simulacrum of the vessel, darted away with both lights and incorporated radio signaling its presence. It would register on the radar of the watching patrol both in size and shape. They would mistake it for the original ship. Unsuspecting, they would allow Ed to work in peace.

His hands checked his suit, spilled air from the cabin, threw open the hatch. He grabbed a laser and climbed from the ship. He had maneuvered well. Squinting against the glare he burned a hole in the hull of the *Hope*, blinking as molten drops of metal threatened his suit, dumping the plate when it came free.

Beyond lay the main pump and beyond that the reactor mass tanks now filled with water. Between the tanks, writhing through the guts of the vessel, was the main conduit for the control wiring. Beyond that waited the three condemned men.

He thought about them as he thrust his head into the opening. His belt caught and he snarled with impatience as he backed, freed the belt and tried again. This time he made it, advancing by inches, writhing his way like a worm in a too-small hole.

The pump blocked his path. Tools scraped against metal as he extended them forward and up past his head. The helmet spread his arms and made working a mechanic's nightmare of fumbling touch and continual frustration. Sweat ran into his eyes and tasted salty in his mouth.

Time! He had so little time!

Savagely he ripped the pump into its component pieces. They struck his helmet with little ringing noises, blocked his arms, gouged at his suit. He reached forward, gripped, dragged himself higher up the angled tube. Pieces of the pump jammed his legs. He tensed his muscles and pulled until red sparks flashed before his eyes. Something gave. He moved deeper into the tube, past the remains of the pump, his body twisted in impossible angles. He felt a constriction of his chest, a grinding ache in the small of his back. He swore as his helmet rang against metal.

It was the inner inspection port for the pump. It was meant to be opened from the inside in case of emergency but the bolt heads were available and he had both wrench and torch. All he needed was room to work. He had no room.

"Damn it," he gasped. "Damn it to hell!"

Fire sparked before his eyes as he switched on the laser. If he slipped or aimed it wrong it would burn a hole in his suit or helmet before he knew it. Death was only an inch away.

Twisting, he guided the beam to one of the bolts. It glowed red, white, dissolving like sugar in boiling water. Little droplets of metal spurted from the area, red-hot globules which had nowhere to go. He shifted the beam to a second bolt, a third. Again he twisted, ignoring the pain in his chest, the dull ache spreading from his kidneys.

This is the hard part, he told himself. *Once past this and the rest will be easy. I can handle electronic equipment in the dark and wearing gloves. A little more effort*, he thought, *and that ten thousand solars is as good as won.* Ten thousand good reasons for hanging on.

Three more bolts dissolved in the beam. He killed the laser and pushed.

The plate refused to move.

The ship held air; almost three thousand pounds of pressure fought his strength. It wasn't even a struggle. The plate was as immovable as if welded to the structure; it was impossible for him to shift it. He switched on the laser again and burned the edge of the plate, cutting a long, narrow opening. A thin wind blew toward him, raining his suit with a mist of molten metal, dimming his visor with a reflective film.

The wind grew, became a rush of air, a miniature hurricane, a solid force as the plate yielded, swung down at his head on a hinge of twisted steel. The shriek of escaping air drummed in his helmet, the impact of it smashing against his body wedged in the opening.

The game was zoltan, played with sixty-six pieces on a hundred and twenty-one square board. They had invented it on the way out to pass the time. Now they played it to kill the same thing.

"Your move," said Balchin. He glanced at Elgar, slumped in his chair. The Negro took no notice. "Your move," he repeated.

Bland moved a piece: a sniper.

Balchin grunted and moved without caution, uncovering his general to the sniper's attack. He couldn't concentrate on the game. "When?" he demanded.

"It can't be much longer now," said Bland. He scowled down at the board. "We caught their vibrations as they left the ship. They're all gone now," he said. "They must be getting ready to send off the *Hope*."

"And us with it!" Balchin rose, kicking back his chair, his knee striking the table and upsetting the board. "Unless Saul is in phase." He stared at the man in the chair. "How about it, Saul? Is it now? Can he make it in time?"

"I don't know," said Elgar slowly. "I don't know if it's now or in a months' time, or when. But someone will rescue us." He kept his eyes closed, his face strained with concentration. "It's hard," he complained. "I can't get a clear picture. It's all blurred and uncertain."

"But it's now?" demanded Balchin. "Now?"

"I think so. It could be."

Balchin grunted and strode to the wall. He pressed himself hard against it, a living diaphragm, alert to catch the slightest vibration. They waited. "It's now!" said Balchin triumphantly. "It's now, Saul. You hear that?"

"I hear it," said the Negro. He frowned, projecting his mind. "He's managed to get past the main pump and into the conduit. He's tired," he said. "Ill. I think that he might be suffering from internal bleeding."

"To hell with him!" stormed Balchin. "Can he make it in time?" Impatiently he strode the compartment, beating his hands against the walls, looking for the ten thousandth time for a way out. There was no way. Later, when the ship was far on its journey, timed relays would open the electronically closed doors and give them the run of the ship. But that was later and, for all he knew, the doctor could have been lying.

They could all have been lying, he thought savagely. *For all we know this ship is going to head smack into the sun. They want to get rid of us,* he told himself. *And what better way than that? Damn them!* he thought. *Damn them all to hell!*

His rage was so intense that the compartment blurred before his eyes.

Earth, he thought. *Mother Earth! God, how I hate you! If there's anything I could do to hurt you,* he told himself, *I'd do it. You've got so much and you give us so little. Let me out of this trap,* he prayed. *Just let me get out and Earth will have reason to regret what she's doing.*

And they had a chance of getting out. If Elgar's precog was in phase with the present time—if the vibrations he had caught belonged to the same man. But would he be in time?

"He's making it," said Elgar. "He's found the circuit box and managed to seal the doors behind him. Now he can take off his helmet if he wants to." He waited, sweat beading his ebony skin. "He hasn't taken off the helmet. Not yet. But he's having trouble breathing. I think that maybe he's damaged his air supply. Bent the feed, perhaps, something like that."

"Help him," said Bland. "Can you help him?"

"I'm trying," said Elgar.

Then try harder, thought Bland. *Get inside his skull and show him what to do and how to do it. Guide his fingers the way they should go. Damn it, you know this ship like you know your own skin. You can do it. Get us out of this coffin while there's still time.*

Time, he thought desperately. They had so little time. Already that doctor and her crew must be well clear of the vicinity. Allow the normal period for fussing and within minutes, seconds even, a five-G thrust would kick them on their way. *We should get into the chairs,* he told himself. *We should take every normal precaution.* But for what? For why?

Please, he begged the unknown stranger. *Hurry! For God's sake, hurry!*

"He's close," said Elgar suddenly. He stood up, opening his eyes, shaking with anticipation. "Real close."

"That's right," agreed Balchin. He was pressed tight against the wall. "I can hear him."

"Now," breathed Bland urgently. "Let it be now."

A door slid open at the end of the compartment. A suited figure staggered through the opening. He stumbled, almost fell, then clutched at the edge of the panel for support. Throwing back his head Ed Taylor squinted through the almost opaque visor of his helmet at the dim shapes standing before him.

"I've come to rescue you," he said. "There's a ship waiting outside. If you'll just follow me . . ." He coughed, tasting blood. *I'm hurt,* he thought. *I took a beating back there. A real beating. But it's all over now. At least,* he told himself, *the worst part is over.* He coughed again and suddenly vomited into the helmet. Without thinking he snatched it off and stood blinking in the light. His eyes widened at what he saw.

"God!" he said. "Dear God!"

Bland smiled and, with infinite tenderness, stroked him gently on the cheek.

V

SLADE WOKE WITH a sour taste in his mouth and a ringing in his ears. The ringing was from the phone; it died as he slapped the button, the smooth, young face of his secretary smiling from the screen.

"Sorry to disturb you, Mr. Slade," she said, "but there is an urgent call from the Secretary General of United Planets."

"Put him on," said Slade. He reached for a cigar as the girl went through the normal secretarial procedure. Status, he thought sourly as the fragrant smoke cut some of the taste from his mouth. The little man has to wait on the big man's pleasure. Small victories in a narrowing world. To hell with him! But he was smiling when the bland face of Chen Yu looked at him from the screen.

"Slade," he said. His eyes drifted past the detective to the rumpled bed. "Did I disturb your rest?"

"No," lied Slade. "I was about to rise when you called."

"I am glad of that," said the Secretary General. "At our time of life tranquil rest is a very precious thing. Are you busy, Slade?"

"I am always busy," said Slade. "Why?"

"I would like to see you. There is a matter in which I feel you could be of great service to the United Planets. You have special talents which we could usefully employ. In two hours, then? At my office?"

"I'll be there," said Slade. He sat smoking for a while, feeling the recent exertions tearing at the lowered vitality of his body. *I'm getting old*, he thought, *and slow. I didn't ask Chen Yu what he wanted. Not that he would have told me but it wouldn't have hurt to ask. Well, we'll have to wait and see.*

He crushed out the cigar and went into his bathroom. He stripped, showered, thrust his face into the maw of the depilatory-massage machine, stung the perspiration areas of his body with anti-odorants, dusted the rest with perfumed talc, finally brushed and dressed his thinning hair. From a cabinet he took fresh clothes. From another he took and swallowed three hundred milligrams of vitamin B complex, his normal dose of nortriptyline hydrochloride, and a generous shot of thirty-year brandy.

The doorbell chimed as he returned to the bedroom.

Jasker stood outside and he wasn't alone. A younger man stood beside him, tall, thin, with a hooked nose and deep-set eyes. Those eyes held a smoldering impatience—the stigma of the fanatic, the hallmark of the Scorfu.

"We want to see you," said Jasker. "Now."

"Come in," said Slade. He turned and walked away, facing them from a safe distance as the young Martian closed the door. "It was a bust," he said curtly. "A flop. A washout."

"You didn't rescue the crew of the *Hope*?"

"No." Slade lit a cigar. "I waited," he said. "I was at

the rendezvous all ready to pick them up and head for
Mars. I waited until the *Hope* kicked off. I waited until
the patrol started getting nosy. Then I left." He blew a
thin streamer of smoke. "Sorry," he said. "I guess you keep
your million."

"Liar!" said the young Martian.

"Steady!" Jasker rested his hand on the young man's
arm. "He doesn't believe you," he said to Slade. "His name
is Ephraim Osmund and he belongs to a rather select
fraternity. He—"

"I know about the Scorfu," said Slade. "Come to the
point."

"We were talking about the crew of the *Hope*," said
Jasker. "You claim that you failed to rescue them?"

"Yes."

"And yet you must have tried," continued Jasker. "You
must have had some plan by which you hoped to release
those men. If not," he pointed out, "you wouldn't have been
waiting at a rendezvous. What went wrong, Mr. Slade?"

"I don't know. I had a plan, yes, but the less you know
about it the better for all of us. It went wrong. It must
have gone wrong. Why I don't know. As far as I'm aware
those men are still in the *Hope*. As far as I care they can
stay there."

"No," said Ephraim coldly. He respected all Terrestrials
as he did a Martian ryken—to be deceitful, dangerous and
utterly poisonous. "You must do better than that," he said.
"Much better."

"How?" Slade carefully put down his cigar. "Just what
are you getting at?"

"It is very simple," said Jasker. "To be frank, Mr. Slade,
the Scorfu don't trust you, and with reason. They think
that you may have those men hidden away somewhere. They
would like you to earn that million by delivering them to
Mars."

"They're crazy," said Slade. "Those men are still in the
Hope."

"No," corrected Jasker mildly. "That is the whole point.
They are not—and where else would they be but in your
keeping?"

"I'll make this brief," said Hilda Gootmeyer. She looked
at the assembly gathered in Chen Yu's private office: Kee-

way, Slade, Ross, Prentice, Chen Yu himself. Keeway and Ross she knew, Slade she had heard of, Chen Yu was an old friend. Only Ron Prentice was a total stranger and the Chief of UP Security was a very strange man.

A superman, some called him, but they were wrong. He was simply a man trained to a point of near-perfection, an orphan, taken shortly after birth and exposed to the pressure of a skilled, scientific environment. A brain, was what Hilda would have called him, an emotionless brain capable of extrapolating the course of events from scanty data. Better than a computer, for a machine could deal only with facts— he had the benefit of human intuition.

Hilda met his eyes and realized that she had been staring at him, realized too that he had guessed her thoughts. He smiled, a facial expression without warmth or humor, a polite gesture to put her at her ease. Annoyed, she turned to the cinescreen which had been set up in the office.

"You have all heard of the *Hope*," she said abruptly. "You may have wondered at the necessity of quarantine and the decision to send those three men on open orbit into space. I am going to explain that decision." The screen flared with light and color, a long shot taken of the interstellar vessel from the examination ship.

"From the first moment of contact," she continued, "we acted on the assumption that the *Hope* could be contaminated with some alien disease. We were right. Twenty-three medical personnel died to establish that fact beyond all suspicion of doubt."

The view changed. Dying men filled the screen. The photographer had acted with clinical detachment. Keeway made strangled noises and grabbed for his handkerchief. Ross pushed a carafe of water toward the senator.

"If the disease had been a normal sickness and the three men unwitting carriers of that sickness, we should have been able to handle the necessary isolation methods without difficulty," she said. The light from the screen touched her face and gave it a warm, far-Eastern touch, an idol dreaming in the sun. "Unfortunately the disease was not of that nature. In fact I think it correct to say that it is not a disease at all. Not in the true, medical sense of the word."

"Not a disease?" Keeway had recovered from his sickness. "But you told me—"

"—what you had to hear," she said coldly. "You were

41

too concerned about those 'brave boys' to realize that they were neither brave nor boys. But I did not lie to you. My terminology was correct. However, since you are so concerned and since you represent the people, it is right that you should know the truth." Her eyes traveled over them, one by one. "All of you should know the truth," she said. "The real truth."

All right, thought Slade, get on with it. He began to have an inclination of why he had been invited to attend this lecture. What had happened on that damn ship? Where was Taylor?

"The truth," said Doctor Gootmeyer, "is really very simple. "Unfortunately it took me a while to gain concrete proof of what, until then, had only been a suspicion. A very strong suspicion, true, but that was not enough to convince others." She looked at Keeway.

"I'm listening," said the senator. He drank more water. "What are you getting at?"

"This," she said. And pointed at the screen.

It showed the sealed compartment of the *Hope*, the chairs, the table, the scattered pieces of the zoltan game. It showed the occupants. Three of them. Frozen in a moment of time as the film halted its run.

"God!" said Keeway sickly. "Dear God!"

They aren't human, thought Slade. They can't be. They've changed. They aren't men at all, not real men, no human could look like that and live. Like rubber, he thought. Like wax too near a flame. Like a memory plastic which is in the process of reversion.

"They're clever," said the doctor. "But I tricked them. I left the recorders running when we left the ship. After the initial thrust the rockets died and we caught up with the *Hope* and recovered the film."

And got the proof, she thought. *The one thing which will convince men like Keeway that what I decided was the right and proper thing to do. But too late*, she told herself. *Too damn late.*

"The men," said Keeway. "Those things—can't you plunge them into the sun?"

"No."

"Why not?" He reared to his feet, unconsciously adopting his platform voice. "In the name of the people I demand that you rid them forever of the threat of this ghastly danger. These aliens"—he gestured toward the screen—"must be destroyed. They must not be allowed to run free."

"Sit down," said Chen Yu tiredly.

"But I demand—"

"You can't demand anything," interrupted the Secretary General. "You are here to be educated, not to make speeches. When you've listened and learned you can call off your friends in the news-services. If you don't I'll crucify you—and that is not an empty threat."

Keeway sat down, shaken, dabbing at his face. "But those things," he said. "Something's got to be done. Can't we atomize the ship?"

"It's too late," said the doctor. She ran the rest of the film.

The only good thing about it was that Taylor hadn't mentioned his name. Not that he had any reason to, but it helped. Suspicion was one thing, proof another, and Slade knew how to handle suspicion.

"I know the man," he admitted. "He worked for me. That is true and that is all I know about it. Why he should have got himself mixed up in this is beyond me. "Listen," he said. "I realize how it must look but you've got to believe me. I had nothing to do with it."

"You were out there," said Prentice. "Your ship was seen and the pilot confirms the time."

"So I was there," said Slade. "Along with how many others? I wanted to see the ship leave. I saw it and I came home. Is that a crime?"

"You saw the ship leave," said Prentice. "Anything else?"

"No," said Slade truthfully. "If the crew left the *Hope* then I didn't see them." But why he hadn't was a mystery. The ship Taylor had used, the one in which they'd escaped, had been programmed to go at once to the rendezvous and wait there. They must have tampered with the pilot, he thought. Overridden it in some way so they could use it on straight manual. They were spacers; they would know how to do that. "Didn't the patrol spot them?" he asked. "They were watching."

"They spotted something," admitted Prentice. "They even got the number. A newshawk ship, they thought. We'll trace it."

"Yes," said Slade. But they wouldn't. They couldn't. False

43

numbers were only a matter of a little paint. "So they got away, is that it?"

"That is it," said Chen Yu quietly. "Now you know why I asked you to come here, Slade. Those men have to be found. I cannot overemphasize the urgency of the problem. I think perhaps that Doctor Gootmeyer could clarify the details a little. Doctor?"

"It is essential that you realize what we're up against," she said tightly. "It isn't just a question of three disease-carriers loose among our worlds. Those men are, as you saw, no longer human. One of them, at least, has extrasensory perception. He is able to either read minds or see the future. And they have a tremendous lust for life—an overwhelming yearning to be among a crowd. It is a survival characteristic. The yearning is their drive to reproduce. You must understand," she said. "These facsimile men are really alien life forms from Prox."

"Tell them," urged Chen Yu. "Explain."

"You said that it was an infection," said Keeway. "You tried to blind me with words. A fungoid infection which acted with parasitic characteristics. How can that make a man an alien?"

"Let us rephrase the question," she said. "When does a parasite stop being a parasite? Answer—when it becomes larger than its host. That is what happened to Balchin and Elgar and Bland. The others too, but we have no proof of that. Somehow they became contaminated. The thing which attacked them grew, mainly along the fibers of the central nervous system, into the brain, throughout the body. It grew and it replaced. *Replaced!* Those things in the *Hope* were really a form of slime mold. A sophisticated form, yes, adaptable, very, but an alien growth for all that. And it wants to reproduce. To do it, it must contaminate other, intelligent life."

"Why must it be intelligent?" asked Slade. "I would have thought that any host would be useful for a parasite."

"I used the word loosely," she admitted. "We don't have the correct word in our vocabulary. The drive to reproduce will cause a man to inseminate any female—the desire to be a father will make him selective in his choice of mate. The analogy is rough but illustrative. The thing replaces, remember, and is, for all practical purposes, the entity it has taken over. It would not like to be hampered in the confines of a dog, say, or an insect. The continual sporifulation, the 'germs' which it extrudes through the skin, are almost a by-product, nature's method of determining maximum survival." She made a helpless gesture. "This is difficult," she said. "Too academic. Look at it this way. There are three things loose among the worlds. They can spread a killing disease anywhere they go. Each victim they claim also becomes contaminated and can also contaminate others. Imagine, if you can, the result should any one of them manage to land on Earth."

"Decimation," said Ross from the background. "And that's a conservative estimate."

"The Black Death would be a picnic by comparison," said Keeway. He glared at the doctor. "You knew this? All the time you knew it and said nothing?"

"She said nothing to you," corrected Chen Yu. "I knew and so did the Chief of Security. Did you really believe that her authority alone was sufficient to determine the fate of the *Hope*?"

"I had no proof," she confessed. "Scientifically I had a case but there was nothing to show the public. Did you suspect them?" she asked Keeway. "You saw them and spoke to them. Would you have believed?"

"No," he admitted. "I wouldn't."

"They were cunning," she said. "More than that. All the time we watched they acted just as if they were human beings. And it couldn't have been all acting. They *were* human beings. They had the personality, the memory, the attributes of their original hosts. Only at the last, when tension and fear and terror had weakened their control, did they change. Survival probably demanded that they adopt another shape; adopt a different form. It was a pity they were released," she said. "A pity in more ways than one."

"It was a damned shame," said Slade dryly. "Just think of what you could have learned."

"Exactly." She didn't catch his irony. "The *Hope* would have been attended," she said. "By remote monitoring, naturally. We just didn't want the public to know. They would have become curious had they known that the ship was in closed, not open orbit. That, together with the arrested firing, had to be kept a secret. Even I couldn't know.

It would have been a wonderful opportunity for study," she said regretfully. "Now it's all gone wrong."

"Pandora," said Slade.

"I beg your pardon?"

"Nothing," said Slade. He caught Prentice looking at him. Well, let him look. The doctor still reminded him of the female of classical mythology who couldn't let things alone. And, like her, she was left only with hope.

The chauffeur was an old fighter, the seams of knife-scars puckering his face. He looked into the mirror and spoke without turning his head. "We're being followed, Mr. Slade. You want I should lose them?"

Slade twisted, looked back at the following vehicle. It was an ordinary flitter painted with cab-colors. Jasker, he thought, or his young friend. Hot on his tail in the hope that he would lead them to the men they were after. The men they thought he had and which he knew he didn't.

"Don't bother," he said. They were a nuisance but they could do no real harm. "Take me home," he ordered, and settled down to think.

He brooded as the flitter swept across the sky. In a way the situation was ironical, almost amusing. Chen Yu wanted him to find the missing men and was willing to pay him for doing it. Ten thousand. Peanuts!

Peanuts when Mars offered a million.

And what was that against the real worth of the prize? What was the potential value of a monopoly to trade with and exploit a brand-new system?

Slade didn't know but he could guess. It would be the commercial killing of all time. The stream of wealth and power would be endless—and all because three etees had come back from Prox. Three humans who had turned into etees, he corrected himself. But it made no difference. They were the dominant life-form, had to be, and so could be bargained with. No wonder Jasker was so eager to get his hands on them. They would save the Martian economy for all time. And Chen Yu? He probably only wanted to see them lying dead.

"Landing in half a minute, Mr. Slade."

The flitter touched down on the roof, halted by the elevator. Slade climbed out, turned as if to give an order, caught a glimpse of the following flitter as it hovered to land. Thoughtfully he walked to the elevator, dropped to his floor, entered his apartment. He was ready for the bell when it chimed.

"I've been expecting you." He stepped back, allowing Ephraim Osmund to enter. "Does Jasker know you're here?"

"This is Scorfu business," said Ephraim. He leaned back against the door until the lock clicked. "We want the men from the *Hope*," he said. "You are going to take me to them. Now!"

Slade raised his eyebrows. "And if I don't?"

"I will hurt you. Not too badly and not too dangerously, but you will never want to look in a mirror again."

"You will cut my face to shreds," said Slade evenly. "Is that it? Remove my ears, my lips, the lids of my eyes, my nose, my cheeks." He slowly took a cigar from his pocket, lit it, breathed smoke. "I suppose you will never believe that I don't know where they are?"

"You are wasting time."

"Have you checked with Jasker? Before you do something you may regret I would advise it."

"Stop wasting time!" Steel glinted in one slender hand. "For your own sake I must insist on no further delay."

"All right," said Slade. He walked toward the young man and stumbled, the cigar falling to the carpet. He stooped to pick it up—and jammed his ring-needle hard against the other's leg.

Picking up the cigar he ran into the bathroom and returned with a hollow, flexible probe. It contained something small and covered with fuzz. Standing beside the Martian, Slade inserted the probe into one nostril, triggered the anesthetic and pushed. There was a slight resistance then the probe entered the sinus cavity. He sent the burr on its way. It was an organic explosive sonic-keyed to a special sound. The charge would shatter the young man's brain.

"All right, my young cockerel," said Slade. "That settles you." He snapped his fingers before the staring eyes. "Listen," he said. "In a few seconds I'm going to give you the antidote. When I do you are going to wonder just what you're doing here. You will change your mind, turn, leave without argument. You will remember nothing of what I have done or said at this time. You will just go."

He stooped, holding the cigar as if he had just picked

it up, and jabbed in the antidote. The Martian blinked, unaware of any passage of time, unconscious of any violation.

"I shouldn't have disturbed you," he said. "If you will excuse me?"

Slade nodded, locking the door after his visitor. The miniature bomb was for later insurance if he needed it. The man hadn't been joking when he'd made his threats. The credo of the Scorfu was that one living example was worth ten silent corpses.

Impatiently the detective strode the apartment, his mind busy with plans. He would put out the word to all his contacts, the grapevine would carry it to the underworld. Ten thousand for information leading to the crew of the *Hope*. Ten thousand and no questions asked. Better make it twenty, he told himself. It was no time to be ungenerous.

VI

THE ROOM had a clinical smell, the indefinable something composed of antiseptics, soap, filtered air and scrupulous cleanliness. A hygenic smell, thought Ed Taylor. A hospital smell. Remembering, he tried to sit up.

"Steady!" The shape at his side was blurred by the plastic of the tent in which he lay. More blurred by the plastic film he wore. Like a pound of hamburger, thought Ed. Something untouched by human hands, sterile, barren, cold. Almost like a machine. A robot. He tried to say so but could only make a gurgling noise. Startled, he tried to touch his throat and found his arms immobilized. Frightened he tried to scream.

"Steady!" said the man again. His voice was soft, muffled. "There's nothing to be scared of. You're sick and in a hospital. That's all."

Sick, thought Ed. Sick? Then he remembered the ship and the beating he'd taken wedged in the hole, helpless against the rush of escaping air. That had been a bad moment but he'd done the job. Or had he? He frowned, trying to remember. He recalled the taste of blood in his mouth. He recalled the way he had vomited. He'd taken off his helmet and . . . and . . .

The disease, he thought. *Dear God, the disease! And I've been among them. I must have caught it,* he told himself. *That's why I'm in a hospital. But what manner of disease could alter men so much?*

Terrified, he shrank back against his pillow. *Maybe they got to me in time,* he thought. *Maybe it won't be so bad seeing as how I'd got immediate medical attention.* Maybe it's just something that will pass in a little while. Then he would be up and about, he thought. He could concentrate on spending that ten thousand he'd earned.

But why did everything look so strange?

"He's rational," said Ross excitedly as Hilda entered the room. Like himself she was wearing a plastic envelope. Like he and Ed and the rest of the staff she was in a ship orbiting a hundred thousand miles above the Earth. The *Hope* was in a closed orbit around the sun. When the engineers had finished the *Hope* would go to feed the primary. "He spoke," said Ross. "Or tried to speak. But he understood what I said."

"Are you certain of that?" Hilda stooped over the cot, examining the pipes and tubes which buried themselves in the patient's body.

"I'm sure," insisted Ross. "He was as scared as hell but I managed to calm him. Then I put him to sleep."

"To minimize shock?" Hilda nodded, it was correct therapy. It was the reason why they had bypassed his heart. Even though they had tried it before, and failed, yet she had to try it again. This time, apparently, with success.

"We could have hit the jackpot," said Ross, echoing her thoughts. "With him the disease must be progressing as it did with those three in the *Hope.* It is possible that there is a unifying factor—something they have in common."

Hilda nodded, knowing that Ross was talking to release strain, to ease his own tension. She stood looking down into the cot. *You poor devil,* she thought. *You poor, misguided fool! You probably thought you were doing something heroic. Instead you've loosed a terror and become contaminated yourself. Why did you do it?* she wondered. *Why?*

"Keep a close watch on him," she ordered. "Call me the moment he shows signs of awareness."

Ross nodded. "I'll do that," he said. He glanced at the

flickering needles of an electroencephalograph. "He's dreaming," he said. "He dreams all the time."

Dreams of what? she wondered. An alien planet beneath an alien sun? Does he realize what is happening to him? Not on the conscious level, of course, but way down deep where his primitive emotions lurked together with his primitive fears. Possession, she thought. Literal possession. A host of microscopic invaders growing, assimilating, spreading, changing what was to something utterly different. Every cell, every fiber, all changing. Would any of the original man be left?

She thought there would. The others acted like men, she told herself. They spoke, walked and ate like men. Maybe the id is left, she thought. The distilled essence of the being. The nub of the personality. The soul, for want of a better word. Something, anyway.

She turned away and found herself fuming at what could not have been avoided. But if they had only returned to the *Hope* sooner they would have found him before the initial shock had thrown him into coma. *We could have gained time,* she thought. *We might even have been able to save him from the coma itself.* But that was nonsense. *We couldn't save the others,* she reminded herself. *How could we have saved him?*

But he could have been questioned. It would have helped.

"From the available data it seems clear that the rescue ship could have taken only one direction," said Prentice. He had a dry, precise voice. An emotionless voice which made him sound older than he could have been. "Do you agree, Mr. Slade?"

"It's obvious," said Slade. He was inwardly amused. They sat in a room at UP headquarters, the Chief of UP Security and himself and Chen Yu probably thought that they were working in close harmony and full collaboration. Collaborate hell! He would suck what he could, grab what he was able, use anything he could find. For himself, naturally. He was no idealist when the prize was so glittering. "To Earth, naturally."

"You surprise me," said Prentice. "Why do you say that?"

"They wanted somewhere to hide. They wanted to get home. Earth was the nearest place to get both." And they

50

were short on food, air and water, he thought. He'd taken no chances in stocking the rescue ship.

"If they'd landed here the disease would be in evidence by now," said Prentice. "It is not. I have also checked all ship-movements during the critical period. All are accounted for. All but one, that is, and that must be the rescue-vessel. It left Earth," he continued. "It was plotted as being in the vicinity. It was plotted again as having left it. Yet, later, that same vessel was again in the vicinity of the *Hope*. Leaving at full speed in the direction of Earth."

"With the escapees," said Slade. "They had friends working for them."

"Obviously. But I wonder," said Prentice, "if those friends are still working for them?" His eyes were hard, direct. "The Martian, Jasker," he said abruptly. "You know him?"

"We've met."

"On more than one occasion. What was the nature of your business?"

"I am interested in ancient Martian ceramic art," said Slade easily. "Jasker is also interested."

"In selling?"

"I assume so. He seems interested in money."

"And you?"

"I have money." Slade decided that this had gone far enough. "Is this an inquisition?" he demanded. "If so I will send for my lawyer. I understood that we were to compare notes, merge our skills, so to speak. The Secretary General gave me to understand that the prime object was to discover the whereabouts of the missing men. Was I wrong?"

"No, Mr. Slade. You were not wrong."

"Then shall we get on with it?"

Prentice nodded and looked at something on the table before him. Papers of some kind, coded as if coming from a computer. To Slade they made no sense. "It seems logical to discount the possibility of their landing on Earth," said Prentice. His dry voice hadn't changed. "I think it reasonable to assume that they would be limited as to supplies. In that case, what would they do?"

"Head for the freight-cans," said Slade. He was giving nothing away; a child could have found the answer. "They could have joined the stream and hooked onto a can. That way they wouldn't be detected."

"And they could, with luck, even manage to replenish

their supplies," said Prentice. "A shrewd deduction, Mr. Slade."

"What are you going to do?" asked the detective. "Check all the cans?" It was impossible and Prentice must know it. There were too many cans, not enough ships and men. Not enough time. And they could be can-hopping, trusting to luck to remain undetected. It would take very little luck.

"They must eventually arrive somewhere," said Prentice. "When they do they will leave a trail. We must wait for that trail to appear. In the meantime we can tackle the other aspect of the case. The 'friends,' " he reminded. "The ones who arranged for the ship, the pilot, the furniture of rescue. Have you any ideas on the subject, Mr. Slade?"

"The Scorfu. They're crazy enough for anything."

"True, but the Scorfu has little power and less influence on Terra. We must try closer to home." He paused, waiting. "Have you nothing to contribute, Mr. Slade?"

"Do you want a confession?" Slade switched on a pretense of anger. "Just because that man, that Taylor, worked for me? Is that what is worrying you? Hell, can't you even backtrack a man now?"

"We can and have," said Prentice. "What do you know of the Friends of Space?"

"Nothing. What have they to do with it?"

"That is what I would like to find out. A man, claiming to be from that organization, contacted Taylor shortly after he left your employ. Among other things he took him to the Starbright Amusement Arcade and gave him tuition on a spaceship simulator. The attendant remembers the incident because he wanted none of the usual tapes. He thought it odd at the time."

"Training him for the job," said Slade. He wasn't worried. Carl had woken up half a world away with a thousand solars in his pocket and no memory of the incident.

"Exactly," said Prentice. "Don't you think it a strange coincidence?" he asked. "I mean, Taylor getting fired and, almost immediately, being trained for a special job?" His eyes were bland. "Well, Mr. Slade?"

"Well, what?"

"I thought that you might feel you had a personal interest in the case. Taylor working for you, I mean."

"I'm not interested in that nurd!" This time Slade's anger was real. "I'm interested only in finding those men and I won't do it squatting on my rear listening to you making speeches to yourself. You're supposed to be good," he sneered. "The Chief of UP Security! Hell, I wouldn't give you a job as an office boy."

Prentice said nothing.

"Those men are hooked onto a can of some kind," stormed the detective. "Find out which cans were in that section of space at that time. Find out where they are heading. Get there before they do. That's the way to catch those men."

"Are you sure, Mr. Slade?"

"Of course I'm sure!" Slade checked himself, asked cautiously. "What do you mean?"

"You are a clever man, Mr. Slade. Would you stake your reputation that those men are to be found hooked onto a can?"

"Yes." Slade sensed danger but it was too late to back down now. "Why do you ask?"

"No reason," said Prentice. And smiled.

The suit was patched, worn, harsh against sweat-softened skin but Sam Laurie had long since stopped worrying about it. He didn't worry about the soft, continuous hiss from the air-supplier either. He would worry about it only when it stopped. The chances then were that he wouldn't be able to worry about it for long. When it stopped he would be five minutes away from death.

A hell of a life, he thought. *Why did I ever leave Earth? They should do something about those lying nurds and their flagging propaganda. Come out to the Asteroids, they said. Be a rock miner. Tear riches from space and live like a king. Pigswill!* he thought. The only wealth out there was in the hands of those who sold air and water and food. And living accommodation, of course, and light and heat and the rest of it. Out there a man was the helpless victim of a grinding capitalistic society, a peon, in Sam Laurie's view.

He shifted in his saddle and looked anxiously around. Nothing. Just the sun, small and harsh. The distant rocks of the Belt, jagged and treacherous. The stars, cold and indifferent.

"See anything?" Jud's voice echoed from the helmet-phone.

"No." Sam turned again, squinting through his visor, looking for the telltale lights of a patrol ship, a prospector,

an asteroider on his way home or to work or paying a
visit. Anything or anyone with eyes to see or instruments to
register. "She looks clear, Jud."

Webster grunted. Like Sam he straddled a sporse. A jet,
fuel tank, instruments, tools with which to dig, to grab,
to bind. And a saddle to ride on. The saddle had given the
space horse its name.

"You think it's safe, Jud?" Sam was anxious. "You think
that it'll be all right?"

"Sure," said Webster. "It'll be as easy as falling off a log.
Kick off now."

He jerked the phone cable from Sam's helmet and touched
his controls. Fire licked briefly from the rear of his machine.
He swayed, guiding it by the weight and balance of his
body. The flame died. Silent, almost invisible, he coasted
through space.

"Jud," called Sam. "Where are you, Jud?"

"Shut up!" snapped Webster. The stupid nurd! Didn't
he know better than to use open radio at a time like this?
He flashed a light, risking the glow to soothe his companion.
Sam drew alongside, awkward on his mount. Deftly Webster
connected their helmets. "Listen," he said. "Never do that
again. You wanna get caught can-raiding? Then you get
caught on your own. Me? I'm too young to serve life in some
stinking prison."

"I'm sorry," said Sam.

"All right," said Webster. "You remember now. Do as I
say and everything'll be smooth. Goof and you'll be sorry."

"I'll remember." Sam looked up and ahead to where the
cans glinted silver in the light of the distant sun. They
looked like a string of beads strung against the stars, orange
fluorescence bright on nose and tail. A string of sausages,
he thought. Dipped in ketchup. Cargoes for the outer
worlds. "Which one, Jud? You know which one?"

"It don't matter." Jud was a realist. "Any of them with
stuff we can use or sell. Keep a sharp lookout, now. You
see anything you tell me fast. Got it?"

"Yes," said Sam. Jud made him feel as if he were a
criminal and, technically, he supposed he was. *But it's
not my fault*, he told himself. *They tricked me into coming
out here. They didn't tell me that it would cost all I earn
just to stay alive. A man hasn't got a chance unless he can*

*make a lucky strike and that happens about once in a blue
moon.*

To hell with them, he thought. *So I'm taking a chance
in raiding the cans, but what harm am I really doing? That
stuff won't be missed. It's not as if we were robbing some
poor devil of his air or water. All we want is enough to
provide a few essentials, some amusement, some decent food,
some drinkable liquor.*

Enough to buy a girl a dress, he thought wistfully. To
buy himself a decent suit so that he wouldn't risk his
neck everytime he stepped through an air lock. To pay off
what he owed on the sporse and to settle his air and water
bills. Enough, perhaps, to buy a passage back home.

"Let's look at this one," said Webster over the wire. "Rice,"
he read as he studied the markings. "For Io. Five thousand
tons of it."

"Any good?"

"Hell, yes, the Chinks'll go for that stuff. But it's bulky,"
said Webster. "We'll wait for another." And wait to make
quite sure that no one caught that nurd on the radio, he
thought. Damned amateur! But Sam had muscle and good
eyes and, if it ever came to it, he could always be thrown
to the wolves.

"This one?" Sam was getting nervous. They were too far
from the Belt and who knew who could be looking.

"Maybe." Webster grinned as he studied it. "This one for
sure! Canned fruit, pickles, spices and sauces. Luxury goods,
man! Money in the bank!"

"We take it?" asked Sam.

"We take it." Webster sobered. "Now listen. When we
hit I'll go inside and you watch. Understand? You watch.
You see anything you tell me at once. Don't try to make
a run for it. Don't panic. Just freeze. Got that?"

"All right," said Sam.

"Let's go," said Webster.

He led the way, passing under the can to rise on the
other side. Sam followed him—and almost died as he saw
the waiting ship.

It rode, hugged tight against the can, and Sam shriveled
as he looked at it.

The patrol, he thought. *They were waiting for us.
They've caught us in the act and now it's life for sure. I
didn't mean it,* he babbled to himself in quick rehearsal.

I'd just come along for the ride. I was curious and wanted to take a close look. That's all. But it was useless. They won't believe me, he told himself. *It won't make any difference what I say because getting too near a can is considered proof of intent to raid. The first time,* he thought drearily. *Caught before I'd even a chance to touch the loot.*

"It's not the patrol," said Webster suddenly. His voice was high as it came over the phone. "No markings, see? No lights."

"Let's get away from here," pleaded Sam. "Quick, before it's too late."

Webster grunted his irritation. He wanted to think. The ship looked dead but that's just how it would look if a gang of can-raiders were at work. They could be ruthless when it came to dealing with witnessess, but, on the other hand, they might be willing to accept another recruit. It was worth a chance to find out—they were too close to escape now.

"Come on," said Sam.

"Take it easy," said Webster. He frowned, trying to remember something he had heard or read. "I can't see anyone," he said at last. "Let's take a closer look."

They bumped lightly against the hull.

"Earth registration," said Webster thoughtfully. He felt a rising excitement. "I'm going inside," he decided. "You wait out here." He lifted his hand to pull free the phone cable.

"Wait." Sam was nervous. "How will I let you know if anything turns up?"

"You can't." Webster was disgusted; didn't the nurd realize the door would cut the wire? "Just freeze," he said. "Don't radio—just freeze." He lifted a laser-cutter from the sporse and kicked himself free. "I won't be long," he said. And pulled free the wire.

Sam watched as he entered the ship, feeling suddenly very alone and horribly exposed. This was wrong, he thought. It was stupid to hang about like this. The ship could be a disguised patrol vessel; a Q-ship just waiting for raiders and Jud walked right into the trap. Or perhaps he's working for them, Sam thought, leading him right along the line to a life in jail. *That's crazy,* he told himself. *Jud knows what he's doing.*

Restlessly he shifted in the saddle, conscious of the passing minutes. He grunted with relief as the outer door opened.

It was Jud. Sam could tell by the suit. He held the laser-cutter as he gestured for Sam to come closer with the other arm. Sam smiled as the laser centered on his helmet. Trust Jud to have his joke.

He lost the smile as the laser punched a hole through his helmet and brain.

VII

THE REPRESENTATIVE from Callisto held the floor and was determined to hold it for his full fifteen minutes. "I must emphasize the unfairness of the allocations," he thundered. "Callisto may have a relatively small population but the pro rata needs of that population are almost double those of Rhea, for example, and certainly far greater than those of Mars or Venus. Not," he said graciously, "that we begrudge our friends their supplies. It is only that Earth, with all its tremendous resources, should, nay I demand, must give more to . . ."

Chen Yu resisted the desire to yawn. The representative from Callisto was taking fifteen minutes to say what could be better put in three. He wanted a bigger slice of the cake.

They all wanted a bigger slice, thought Chen Yu. Men have always wanted more than their brothers and have always been able to find good, logical reasons why they should be so favored. Once they had gone to war over it. *Well*, he told himself, *we've stopped that at least. We've got to keep on stopping it.*

He felt like a juggler: tossing the balls of hunger and greed and fear and hate into the air and keeping them there with tricks, compromises and playing both ends against the middle. And the balls had to be kept in the air. For a generation at least, he thought. Until education could mold social mores and overpower the natural instinct to procreate. Until the feverish, yeast-vat of fecundity which was Earth could be brought under control. A generation should do it.

A generation or a virulent disease.

Prentice wouldn't feel this natural horror at such a prospect, he knew. Prentice was of the new school of administrators. It was time they had turned to the development of trained, educated politicians.

The representative from Callisto sat down. The one from Titan climbed to his feet.

"May I ask the Secretary General if there is any further news of the men from the *Hope?*" he asked coldly.

"The matter is under full investigation," said Chen Yu blandly. "But I must point out that it falls within the province of the Security Council, not the General Council which is here assembled."

"But—"

"You are out of order," said Chen Yu firmly. "Please be seated. If the representative from Ganymede wishes to take the floor . . . ?"

The session lasted another two hours. At the end of it Chen Yu hurried to his private office where Prentice sat waiting for him.

"You look tired," said the Chief of Security. "A hard time?"

"Bad enough." Chen Yu hadn't missed the point of the representative from Titan's question. The leak had grown into a flood—and the men from the *Hope* could be regarded as the most compact and formidable weapon the outer worlds could hope to find. "What news?"

Prentice didn't have to ask about what. "Slade was responsible. We'll never be able to prove it but he was the engineer of the escape. I've tracked back on what Taylor was finally able to tell us. He doesn't connect his ex-boss with what happened but there can be no doubt. And Slade condemned himself out of his own mouth. I tricked him," explained Prentice. "The escape operation was well-planned. There had to be a second ship waiting to take those men to a place of safety. Slade was in that second ship—we know he was in the vicinity at the time."

"And?"

"Something went wrong. Slade was left standing. I got him to deduce where those men must be. He backed his deduction with his reputation. The only way he could have been so certain was to know that the original plan had failed. Therefore, he must have been connected with the original plan."

"Logic," said Chen Yu dryly. "There could have been another set of rescuers. The Martians seemed interested."

"True," admitted Prentice. "But where could they have found a workable instrument? No. They may have hired Slade or he could have been working on his own. But he is our man."

"I believe you," said Chen Yu. "But it will get you nowhere in a court of law." He restelssly began to pace his office. "Knowing Slade is involved doesn't help to find those men," he said. "That is the important thing. Finding them before someone else does." Someone who had paranoidal delusions of grandeur, he thought grimly. Someone who maybe hated Earth. The population problem would be solved then, he told himself. Maybe solved for all time. "Where is Slade now?" he demanded. "What is he doing?"

"He's looking for those men."

"And?"

"I'm letting him look. He is a noted detective," said Prentice calmly. "It would be illogical not to use his skill."

They had taken the pipes from his chest and the wounds had healed, but they still wouldn't let him move beyond the confines of the cabin. It was as bad as being back home, thought Ed Taylor. Back in the utiliflat. At least there he could step outside, mingle with others, see more than the walls of a cabin. And how could he claim his ten thousand unless he were free?

I'm not going to claim it, he told himself. *I'm not going to get free. I caught something off those men and it nearly killed me. But I'm all right now,* he thought. *Never mind what they say. I'm as fit as I ever was. It's just that I broke some law and they're going to jail me for it. They must be keeping me in here until it's time for the trial.*

Disconsolately he sat down, elbows on knees, hands supporting his head. It was no good lying to himself. He was in a hell of a mess and there was no way out. Hilda had told him that and she wouldn't lie. Not to him, she wouldn't. Somehow he knew that.

Odd the way he felt about her. She was a long way from being a BB girl but that was all show anyway and not really important. What was important was the other thing. The warm comfort of seeing her around. The feeling of security she gave. The wanting to touch her, to know where she was and to know that she would always be there close to him. *Reliable,* he thought. *That's it. I know where I am with a woman like her. She's not like Mary. She wouldn't go all puritan and strange. She wouldn't kick me out because of a stupid mistake.*

She would stand by a man, he told himself. *She is standing by. I can trust her. God help me,* he thought. *I've got to trust her. There's no one else.*

He heard a sound and turned and there she was standing behind the big sheet of glass set in one wall of the cabin. He rose and stepped toward her, automatically following his desire to be close to her, then stopped with a conscious effort.

"Hello," he said.

She wasn't alone. Ross was standing beside her and he felt a sudden jealousy at the close proximity of the assistant. Then the emotion died as it began to happen again.

The thing. A distortion of the eyes. A subtle alteration in his objective point of view.

The two figures became mechanical. They ceased to be soft, round creatures of flesh and blood. They grew angular, hard, stiff-jointed as puppets. The muscle and sinew visualized beneath the clothing seemed to belong more to the factory than the farm. The light changed, dropping toward the infrared. Sounds became louder, extending beyond the normal aural spectrum. He shook with a sudden, overwhelming urge to rush forward, to smash the barrier, to touch what stood beyond.

"Hello," he said again. "Aren't you coming inside?"

"No, Ed." The doctor, he saw, now stood alone. "I just want to talk to you. I want to know everything about you."

"Everything?"

"Well, everything from say, a week before you entered the *Hope.*"

"Again?"

"Yes, Ed. Again. Do you mind?"

No, he thought bleakly. *I don't mind. I like telling you just how big a fool I was. How I met that girl and went to the party and wound up in jail. And got fired and cited for divorce. And took a job which landed me here. Like hell I mind.*

"You know it all," he said. "There's nothing left to tell."

"Yes there is," she insisted. "You've left something out. Why did Slade fire you?"

"I was picked up and thrown into jail. They said that I was under the influence of drugs."

"Drugs?"

"It was a drink," he lied. "I'd had a few drinks. Maybe someone spiked one of them. It could have happened." How could he tell her about the BB girl, the party, the seeming hallucinations? "Must I talk about it?"

"It's important," she said. "Very important." Suddenly she realized what the trouble could be. "I'm a doctor," she reminded. "Nothing you could say could upset or shock me. You don't have to be afraid of that."

"You're a woman," he said curtly. "If you want the truth I'm afraid of losing your respect. That is," he added, "if you could have any respect for me anyway."

"Why, Ed?"

"Because I'm in love with you," he blurted, and wondered where he found the courage to say it.

"We'll arrive in fifteen minutes, Mr. Slade." The stewardess had the big-chestedness of all third-generation Martians. Her legs were slender, her face shaped like a heart. "Are you quite comfortable, Mr. Slade?"

"I'm all right," grunted Slade. He was far from that. It had been a hell of a journey, what with having to shake off his followers, and he'd run out of nortriptyline. His emotional cycle was on a down-swing and, freed of the dampening influence of the drug, would be a trial. "Has anyone been asking after me?" he demanded. "Anyone at all?"

"No, Mr. Slade."

He thought that she was lying, as he watched her move down the aisle. Or she could be telling the truth. Which didn't mean the ship's radio-officer hadn't let the Scorfu know that he was aboard. And which could mean a patrol ship had monitored the message and passed it on.

To hell with it, he thought. *A man can only do so much. Just as long as I can stay one jump ahead*, he told himself. *That's all I need.*

He hunched down in his seat looking at the rest of the passengers. Those not taking their turn in the bunks, that was. Tough, acid men mostly with a sprinkling of softer types eager to make their fortunes in the Belt. Half of them would be dead within three months. The rest, having learned, could last for years.

"This your first time to the asteroids, Mr. Slade?" The woman beside him was painted, aging, desperate to please. Slade wondered what it had cost her to ensure the seat next to his. Whatever she had paid was too much. "I've lived here for years," she said. "Rock Eighteen. That's where we're landing. You must have heard of it."

Slade didn't answer.

"It's as big as Ceres," she said. "Well, almost, and it's getting bigger all the time. But it's so terribly crowded. They tell me people are having to sleep in the passages but that's dangerous, what with thieves and all. I've a little place of my own," she confided. "Good food, decent water and"—her elbow nudged his ribs—"a soft bed. Interested?"

"I'll think about it." Slade didn't believe in making enemies. "You got a card? Thanks." He thrust it in his pocket as the ship swept in to land.

Without luggage to worry about he was the first through the tube. A cluster of touts stood at the dome-end. They pushed forward as he advanced.

"Wanna guide, mister?"

"Hotel Acme's the best, mister."

"Carry your bag, sir?"

"Got anything to sell? Candy, cigarettes, old clothes?"

"Spare a solar, mate, I'm starving!"

He looked it. Slade grabbed him by the arm, pulled him to one side away from the throng. "Your name?"

"Paul. Paul Ely."

"You a guide?"

"Try me."

"Stoneman's Joint. Know it?"

"Over on R21? I know it."

"Take me there." Slade pulled a ten-note from his pocket. Paul grabbed at it. Slade jerked it back and shook his head. "Later," he said. "When you've done the job. This and two more just like it. Deal?"

"We'll need transport," said Paul. "You wanna go public or have you cash for a private hire?"

Stoneman's Joint was on the third level, second decant of Rock Twenty-one. It was the usual combination of inn, store, post office and general focus of gossip in the area. Slade walked in, saw what could only be the owner, jerked his head as he walked to the far end of the counter. Behind him trotted his guide, the little man determined to hang onto his catch.

"Give him a drink," said Slade. "And a meal," he added. "A sandwich anyway. You got somewhere we can talk?"

"The office." Stoneman yelled orders to his assistant, a pasty youngster with a dragging leg. "Got caught in a crunch," he explained as he led Slade to the office. "Missed his timing and got caught between two stones. It was lucky he had someone with him," he said as he opened the door. "Or you could look at it that way."

"Do you?"

"A crip's not much use in the Belt," said the owner. "No chance to earn a stake for regrafts or corrective surgery." He slammed the door and produced a bottle and two glasses "Drink?"

"A small one."

"You look like Slade," said Stoneman. "Can you prove it?" He squinted at the papers the detective produced. "Anything else?"

"You sent word. A man named Barsac relayed your message. Good enough?"

"I guess so." Stoneman swallowed his drink. "That offer," he said. "The one you made. Twenty thousand for information. It stands?"

"Steer me to the men and you get it. Can do?"

"Maybe. Maybe not. Anything for trying?"

"A knife in the guts," said Slade evenly. "If you've dragged me out here for a giggle I'll put a price on your head. A big one. Catch?"

"No need for that." Stoneman refilled his glass. "It's no giggle," he said. "A couple of the boys dropped in here a while back. Strangers. They sold me their mounts. I heard later that a couple of miners from Twenty-three had gone fishing and hadn't come back. Same mounts. Maybe they got themselves hijacked."

"Fishing," said Slade. Thoughtfully he sipped at his drink. The liquor was strong, a by-product of the yeast vats which supplied most of the local food. "Can-raiding," he mused. "One of the local sports. Maybe they got cold feet and took a powder?"

"Could be," agreed Stoneman. "Sometimes they get too deep in debt and try for a fresh start somewhere further along the Belt. Sometimes they make it. Not often." He finished his second drink. "But the two I'm talking about weren't like that. They were pressed, sure, who isn't? But the pressure was light and their credit good. Sam Laurie and Jud Webster. Sam was a little green but Jud was as wide as they come. Too wide to lam out. He'd know better."

Slade nodded. It fit, he thought. It fit too damn well. A couple trying to steal from a can and they hit the wrong one. The wrong one—for them. "These men," he said. "Did they act normal?"

"Funny you should say that." Stoneman poured himself another drink. Slade shook his head as the bottle moved toward his glass. "I didn't pay much attention at the time," said the owner. "You know how it is. But they kept on their suits. They kept on their gloves and had their visors on half-filter. They didn't talk much either. Just asked what I'd give, took it and went."

Cunning, thought Slade. *They've learned, damn them. They must know of the trail they would leave if they weren't careful. So they had been careful. But, only two?*

"That's right," said Stoneman. "Two."

It fitted. Two men, two suits, two mounts. The third man had either been left behind, was dead, or had somehow been smuggled into one of the rocks. It was important that he discover the truth.

Slade finished his drink hoping that the alcohol would give him a lift but knowing it would only increase his depression. At times like this it was hard to think, harder still to act. Apathy gripped him in smothering folds of indecision. The temptation to say to hell with it all and catch the first ship back to Earth was resistible only because it required mental and physical effort. He was far down on the manic-depressive curve of his emotional cycle. He needed help.

"You got a doctor around?"

"Sure." Stoneman was curious. "Something wrong?"

"Nothing important."

"Glad to hear it." The owner guzzled more liquor. "Do I get the money?"

"When I get the men." Slade dug into his pocket, frowned as he felt a card. He had forgotten the woman on the ship. He produced money, counted out a thousand solars. "This on account. The rest when I get what I came for. Can do?"

"Leave it to me," said Stoneman, and reached for the money.

The woman's papers said that she was Mrs. Osprey, address, room fifteen, sector four, decant nine, level six, Rock Eighteen. It was a long way from the landing terminal and it was some while before she reached her door. She inserted her key, turned it and entered. A man sat up from where he had been dozing in a chair. He held a laser in his hand, lowering it only when she had closed the door and switched on the light.

"Well?" said Jasker.

"I gave him a card," she said. "He didn't seem interested but I did my best." She stooped, slipped off her shoes, shrugged off her thin coat. "You look tired," she said. "Been here long?"

"We arrived six hours ago." He was tired; a fast passage from Earth had knocked the stuffing out of him. "Couldn't you do better than just give him a card?"

"No. He was in his bunk most of the time," she said. "The opportunity for contact was limited." She unzipped her dress and let it fall to the floor. Padding had disguised the youth of her figure. She released it, sighing with satisfaction as it joined the dress. "We've planted a seed," she said. "Given him an address, a place to go if he needs it. A quiet, discrete kind of place where money talks and kills curiosity. Did Ephraim manage to pick him up at the terminal?"

"He knows Ephraim."

"Someone else, then. Did he?"

"No," admitted Jasker. "Joachim did his best but the odds were against him. Slade picked up a man named Ely. Paul Ely.

"Do we know him?"

"He isn't one of us," said Jasker. "But I think he can be bought. Joachim learned that they went to Twenty-One. He called me. I told him to stay on their trail."

She nodded, studying her reflection. The thick coating of makeup both aged and degraded her heart-shaped face.

It looked ludicrous over the young lines of her body. The wig was an added insult.

But necessary, she told herself. *We need Slade to find what we want. He can do it if anyone can. He has contacts and a reputation in the underworld. Men will talk to him, trust him, where they would fall silent if questioned by strangers or the patrol. We let him guide us,* she thought. *And then we'll move in.*

Aloud she said, "This could have been a mistake. He might have been more attracted to a younger woman. Let's face it. I look like a raddled tart."

"And, as such, of no real importance," said Jasker. "Not to Slade. He would have been suspicious of a younger woman. He would have expected someone like Mrs. Osprey to say and do what she did. He might feel contempt and even a slight disgust, but he would not sense danger."

"We hope," she said, and suddenly felt dirty, unclean. "Have you any money?" she demanded. "I've got to have a bath."

VIII

THE LIGHT WAS BLUE-WHITE, harsh, revealing, killing all shadow and painting the interior of the ship with a luminescent glare. Little things took on an exaggerated importance. A scratch, a chip, the trail where something had traveled over the seamless plastic.

Something or someone, thought Ron Prentice. He stood in his suit, the suit covered by a plastic envelope, the envelope coated with a gummy substance which ensured that all fragments would be safely trapped. Two others stood with him, their armored shapes bulking huge in the blue-white glare.

"It checks," said Colton. "The registration's the same. This is the ship they escaped in."

"They didn't get far," said Lambert. His gloved hand pointed to what lay on the floor: three bodies sprawled in the relaxation of death. They were all horribly mutilated but one retained a recognizable face. Elgar looked very peaceful. "Lasered," said Lambert. "Burned to a frazzle."

His foot kicked the laser-cutter on the floor. "A hell of a way to go."

"They must have been desperate," said Colton. "On the run with nowhere to go. Maybe they'd had all they could take." He looked around the cabin. "No water, no food, bad air. Alien or not they had to eat and drink and breathe."

"They had the can," said Lambert. "They could have broken in, found something to drink, something to eat. They could even have used the trapped air." He shook his head, the movement grotesque in the light. "You know," he said, "in a way I feel sorry for them."

"Don't," said Prentice shortly. He stooped, examining the one recognizable figure. The laser had charred the entire region of the chest, the burned flesh crisp at the edges. The ebony face looked at him, the eyes upturned, the cheekbones prominent. The face was calm. Elgar had not been afraid to die. "It's a plant," he said. "A setup. These are not the men from the *Hope*."

"But?" Colton pointed at Elgar.

"He was left to convince us," said Prentice. "He is genuine, the others are not."

It was clever, he thought, *but not clever enough. Surely they didn't expect us to swallow it? But they did the best they could*, he told himself. *They had to use what they had.*

"Assuming they had a laser on board," he explained to the others. "Why would they kill themselves in such a way? Who killed whom and in what order?"

"Elgar burned down the other two," said Colton. "Then he turned the beam on himself."

"After burning the others into unrecognizable ash?" Prentice pointed to the bodies. "Those men were mutilated for a reason. The reason being to throw us off the scent. If we accept this charade, call off the search, what then?" He didn't give them time to speak. "They're still alive," he said. "Balchin and Bland. They must be." He paused, thinking. "The Belt," he said. "Slade is there. He knows."

But we know that he knows, he thought. *We can afford to be patient. We have to be patient. The last thing I want is to scare those men so that they panic. Let them think they are safe. Let them stay in one place long enough to be caught.* Then, he told himself, *we'll strike. And the danger will be over.*

Back in the patrol ship he stared somberly at nine blazing

points of atomic disintegration. The ship, the can to which it was attached, four other cans in each direction. It should be enough. They would hardly have had time or opportunity to contaminate more.

"Get me the Belt," he ordered. "Patrol headquarters. Have them check all rocks and installations. I want to know if any of them have ceased communication. And," he added, "if any of them have reported an outbreak of a mysterious illness."

One down and two to go, he thought as he looked again at the dying, man-made stars. But he knew that in this war numbers weren't important, only success mattered.

The drumming of her fingers had long ceased to be an irritation and had now become a source of amusement. Casually Ross leaned back in his chair and watched the movement of her fine, well-kept nails. *Our Hilda isn't the ice-maiden she would like all of us to think,* he told himself. *Taylor has upset her. He's managed to hit her where she is weakest. That's the trouble with these middle-aged women,* he thought. *They go through life, apparently untouched, and then, suddenly, whaml They're in love.*

"Hagan," she said suddenly.

"What?" Ross wasn't with her.

"Hagan," she repeated. Her fingers ceased their drumming as she turned to face her assistant. "That's the unifying factor. It has to be. He took hagan approximately twenty-four hours before attempting the rescue," she explained. "He finally told me about it."

"Taylor?" Ross pursed his lips. "How did he get hold of hagan?"

"Someone gave it to him. The thing was a put-up job—something to get him into trouble. He was ashamed," she said. "He didn't want to tell me."

"How much?" Ross was practical. "The dose, I mean. How many milligrams?"

"He doesn't know."

"But—"

"It doesn't matter," she interrupted. "We know that hagan works directly on the central nervous system and the thalamic regions of the brain. It gives rise to hallucinations, daydreams, of a particularly vivid nature. The crew of the *Hope* must have used it. It could be the reason why three of them survived. Why Taylor has managed to survive. It makes sense," she continued. "It is a unifying factor, the only one in common."

"You are forgetting something," Ross pointed out. "Two of the crew died. They must have taken hagan too."

"We can't be certain of that." She paused, frowning. "They could have taken it in turn," she surmised. "The ones that died could have either been in hallucination or long out of it. I am inclined to believe the latter. The shock of possession would be lessened to someone under influence of the trug. You see what this means, of course?"

"Tell me," he said cautiously.

"It is a defense against the Prox plague," she said. "Not a real defense. Not a vaccine. But a means to ensure that catching it does not automatically mean death."

"Wouldn't death be preferable to possession?"

"No." Impatiently she rose and crossed to where the window to the other room showed in polarized darkness. She adjusted the control. The pane cleared in one-way vision. Taylor, awake, was lying on his bed. "Would he be better dead? Look at him," she commanded. "He is fit, healthy, in full command of his faculties. Without hagan he would be dead."

"So?"

"What do you mean?"

"What has he to live for?" asked Ross deliberately. "A lifetime in quarantine? A freak to be prodded and probed in a hope that he will be able to help medical science? What else can he be but a guinea pig? No normal life," he continued relentlessly. "No wife, no children, no intimate relationship with any woman. He can't even shake hands," he said. "Everything he touches is contaminated with potential death. Would you wish that on anyone else?"

"Stop it!"

"And you can't be sure," he insisted. "You don't know the dose, the effective time, the critical period. Maybe there is just one moment, a certain level of hagan in the blood, when you would be safe. Against that chance is the risk of certain death."

"We can experiment," she said. "The procedures are well known."

"Sure they are," he agreed. "But what's it all for? What do we hope to gain? Taylor is contaminated and we know what is happening. He is being possessed by an alien form of life. All right, so he looks human. Maybe he even thinks he's human, but he's not. And we know it."

Know it but refuse to accept it, he thought. *At least you do. God, but you must have it bad. Any first-year psychologist could read you like a book. You give yourself away. Subconsciously you want to be with him, to touch him, take him to bed. All the rest is justification. You don't really give a damn about medical science. You're a woman and your glands have taken over.*

"There is a difference," she said coldly. "The crew of the *Hope* was in isolation, unaware what was happening to them. The human ego isn't so easily conquered. It is possible that we can use the invader; turn it into a symbiote instead of yielding to it as a parasite."

"Nonsense!" exploded Ross.

"Is it?" She darkened the window, turned, stared him directly in the eyes. "You must have noticed how fast he healed. The gain in the speed of his reflexes. The apparent widening of his aural and visual range. These things must be investigated. Order three dozen rhesus monkeys from Earth right away. And a supply of hagan. A large supply."

"Yes, Dr. Gootmeyer," he said woodenly.

"Right away," she repeated.

Alone, he cleared the window, stood for a long time looking at the man on the bed. *Why?* he thought. Why did an intelligent, sophisticated woman have to fall in love with a man like that? *It's the Galahad-syndrome,* he told himself. *The gallant rescuer facing impossible odds to right an imagined wrong. The fool who doesn't know better than to stick his head where it isn't wanted. But it isn't just that,* he thought. *The mother-complex comes into it as well.*

Hilda should have got married, he thought. *Had a child or two. Got rid of the romantic nonsense which lurks way down deep inside all of us. But even that isn't all the answer. The true reason is more simple: it's just a matter of biological reaction. The reproductive urge triggered off by the proximity of a compatible type. It happens,* he told himself. *It happens all the time. But why the hell did it have to happen now?*

The doctor had helped a little. Drugged, his depression on the wane, Slade tried to book into a hotel.

"Sorry, sir," said the receptionist. "We're booked solid. Try the Earthman's Rest."

The Earthman's Rest was equally sorry but why didn't he try the Ceres Arms?

The Ceres Arms was full but they thought he could manage to squeeze in at the Paradise Central.

At the Paradise Central he got a room and mist-shower for fifty solars a day. It was worth, at the most, ten. Scowling, he moved into the expensive slum. Rock Eighteen was a terminal landing point with traffic coming in from all sides. Any terminal point would be equally as busy, but Slade had no choice. He had to stay where he could get a ship in case of need.

He called Stoneman and told him where he was. He called two other contacts and passed the word. He sent down for all ship schedules, a map of the local sector of the Belt, a list of major supply houses. Paul Ely knocked on his door as he finished compiling a list.

"You sent for me?" The guide still looked as if he were starving, slept in the corridors and would kill a man for the sake of his shoes—if he could find a man small enough both to kill and to be sure his shoes would fit.

"I want to hire you," said Slade. He threw the man a list. "Contact each of these places and any that I may have missed. Find out if they have sold any large quantities of plastafilm or hermetic sprays. Collodion, even, anything which could be used to make a transparent, flexible seal. Spread the word to look for a man or two men who stay inside, wear gloves and remain aloof. Check to see if there's been any irregular crime, mugging, theft, stuff like that."

"Anything else?" Ely was ironic. Slade produced money, threw it to the little man.

"You'll need help. Get it. Get lots of it. I want the answers fast and I'm willing to pay for them. Move!"

Alone Slade rested on the bed and reviewed what he had done. Stoneman would be looking and he could do it better than a stranger. Ely would see to the leg-work. The men he was looking for, if they hoped to remain undetected, would have to seal in their lethal skin exudations. To do that they would have to buy something he'd mentioned. To get money to pay for it they would either have to work or steal. If they were on Rock Eighteen finding them was only a matter of time.

He forced himself to relax, closing his eyes, letting his mind drift. He had set wheels in motion to find the men but that was the hard, slow way. There was another method. That was to place himself in their position and figure out what they would do. What they had to do. *You can do it,* he told himself. *You haven't come so far that you've forgotten what gave you your start. The edge you had over others. The little extra which succeeded where others failed. It should be simple,* he thought. *Damn it, they are strangers in the Belt. They don't know what to do or where to go. they have suits and a little cash. And the ability to deal almost immediate death,* he reminded himself. *Never forget that.*

But any man had that ability if he were ruthless enough. Or scared enough. It was the one weapon they would hesitate to use because if they did it would be a red light showing where they were.

Finding them should be a simple problem in logical reasoning.

He opened his eyes and looked at the man standing beside his bed. Looked at the laser in his hand. "You," said Slade.

"Me," agreed Jasker. He let the door close, leaning against it, letting it take his weight. He looked older, tireder than when they had last met. "Who are you working for?" he asked the detective. "Who's side are you on?"

Slade sat up, not answering. He found a cigar and lit it, squinting at the Martian through the smoke. Jakser wore a loose jacked with wide sleeves, each of which could easily conceal a knife. But he didn't think the man had come to kill him.

"Put away that gun," said Slade. "I don't like talking to men with guns."

Jasker shrugged and holstered the weapon.

"We had an agreement," said Slade. "As far as I'm concerned we still have it. You?"

"We made a mistake," admitted the Martian. "We thought you had crossed us. The Scorfu thought that," he corrected. "They wouldn't listen to reason."

"Hotheads never do," said Slade agreeably. "How did you know where to find me? Never mind," he said. "I can guess. Money dropped in the right places can do wonders. And you, of course, have money."

72

"That's right," said Jasker.

"A lot of money, I hope," said Slade. "A million at least. A million plus expenses. This thing is turning out dearer than I imagined."

"A million," said Jasker. "Cash on delivery, Mars."

"That's right." Slade put down his cigar, locked his hands behind his head, looked up at the Martian. "Why are you here?" he asked abruptly. "What have you got to tell me?"

"They've found the escape ship," said Jasker. "The patrol, I mean. They burned it with atomics. There were three men in the ship; one of them was a Negro."

"Elgar?" Slade frowned, thinking. "You intercepted a message, I suppose," he said. "Have they called off the hunt?"

"No. Prentice thinks it was a plant."

"He could be right. Anything else?"

"Only that he's concentrating on the Belt."

"He would." Slade unlocked his hands. "Prentice is no fool. He can add two and two as good as the rest of us. The Belt is the only place they could have headed." He paused, wondering just how much the Martian knew as against how much he guessed. Not too much, he thought. If he did he would have sent the Scorfu after the quarry, bypassing the detective and saving both time and money. The intercepted message had stampeded him, sending him in panic to this confrontation.

"You've got to hurry," said Jasker, confirming Slade's suspicions. "You can't beat the patrol. No one man can do that. You've got to find those men before Prentice does."

"Naturally." Slade rose from the bed. "I may need help," he said. "Can you have a ship ready and waiting? A fast ship?"

Jasker nodded.

"I'll be taking them in alone," said Slade deliberately. "Just leave word where the ship is to be found. Better still, I'll call you. Where are you staying?"

"I'll leave word," said Jasker. He stepped to the door and hesitated, one hand on the catch. "You'd better not take too long over this," he said flatly. "And you'd better not fail. If you do the Scorfu might get the idea that you've been playing a double game. They wouldn't like that."

"I'm crying," sneered the detective.

"You may have cause to," said the Martian. He was

73

grimly serious. "Think about it," he said from the passage.

Slade kicked shut the panel and picked up his cigar. It had gone out. Savagely he threw it to the floor.

IX

THE COMTECH WAS a slim girl of Asian extraction, flower-like, incongruous against the severe functionalism of the operations room. Colonel Weatherby was proud of her. He reminded Prentice of a gnarled oak towering protectively over a delicate fern as he made the introductions.

"This is Miss Tsin Ashaki," he said. "Tsin, this is Ron Prentice, Chief of UP Security."

"I know," she said, and came immediately to business. "I've run the problem," she said. "We know exactly when the cans you destroyed passed over the Belt. Assuming that the raiders traveled by sporse we can identify the maximum effective area from which they must have originated. More important, we can determine the area to which the wanted men must have escaped."

"Assuming that they used the same method of transport," said Prentice. "Is that a safe assumption?"

"I think so," she said. "Can-raiding is a local enterprise and depends for success on absolute secrecy. A sporse is small, almost impossible to see and equally impossible to identify at a distance. The raiders have to be local men. They need to know of a safe market for the disposal of their loot and the buyers have to know and trust the raiders. Ninety-nine percent of such thefts are conducted by sporse-riders. Seventy-eight percent of such raids are successful. To lower the success-rate patrol surveillance would have to be increased by three hundred percent. The cost would be prohibitive."

She turned, touched a control, and stood looking at the panorama depicted on a screen.

"This is the relative area," she explained. "There is a ninety-nine percent probability that the remaining two men from the *Hope* are here somewhere."

Prentice nodded and looked at the screen. The Belt, he knew, was not a homogenous collection of planetary fragments orbiting the sun. Gravitational forces had been at work for countless years and had resulted in clusters of varying size and density. The area depicted was one such cluster. Beyond it lay empty space, aside from a few rogue asteroids. Her extrapolation was correct as far as it went but it did not go far enough. She had shown him a haystack and was probably confident that he could find the needle.

"The initial problem was elementary," she said. "To run a cone from the determined position of the cans, defined only by the limitation of assumed transport and probable markets, wasn't hard. More difficult is to determine just where within that area the men could be."

"Yes," said Prentice. He stood, frowning at the screen, letting observed data build up so that he could assess the overall pattern. "Those men are strangers to the Belt," he said finally. "How would they navigate?"

"Each rock has its own radio and visual pattern," she said. To her the question was so elementary that she hadn't thought of volunteering the information. "Each installation the same. They could either navigate manually or by mechanical pilot."

"Remember they are strangers," said Prentice. "They wouldn't know just where to go. The only thing they could be sure about was that it would be suicidal to return to the original base. They would be recognized as having stolen the sporses," he explained. "You said that the can-raiders had to be local men." He brooded over the screen. Identifying lights glowed on the pattern. Rocks Eighteen, Twenty-one, Twenty-three, Nineteen, Sixteen and, at the edge of the area, Rocks Seventeen and Twenty-four.

Rocks were asteroids with permanent habitable installations. The rest, regardless of size were stones. Among them men fought to earn a living. As often as not they died doing it. There were a lot of stones; too many to search one by one.

"Has any area ceased communication?" he demanded. "Have you run a continuous radio-check as I ordered?"

"We have." Colonel Weatherby thrust himself forward, like a father protecting his daughter, it seemed to Prentice. The veteran shielding the novice. "It's a big job," he said. "We have other work, you know."

"Forget it," snapped Prentice. "This is of prime importance. Well?"

"Three areas failed to respond." Weatherby snapped his fingers at a radiotech. "Tell him," he ordered.

"Connors', Freemain's and Hebron's," said the man. "Connors came through later, some fault in his set but my bet is that he just didn't want to answer. Freeman answered on the second try. Claimed an emergency had forced him to abandon radio communication."

"And Hebron?"

"Answered the first two times—nothing since."

"Try again," said Prentice. "Immediately." He looked thoughtfully at the screen as the man hurried away. "This Hebron," he demanded. "Tell me about him."

"A nurd," said the colonel. "He runs a camp out among the stones. He's in the prospecting business and provides bed, board and basic on credit. Freelance stuff too. He'll stake a man, send him out looking, buy what he finds—at his price."

"A nice arrangement," said Prentice dryly. "For Hebron."

The colonel shrugged. "His workers are peons," he admitted. "But what can I do? Out here the system protects men like Hebron. One day he'll wind up with his head bashed in but it won't make any difference. Someone else will take over. They always do."

"How does he recruit?"

"Simple. He can always use labor and asks no questions. Turn up with a suit and you're hired. Turn up without one and you're hired just the same. You're deeper in debt, that's all." He turned, shouted at the radiotech. "Made contact yet?"

"Not yet," said the man. "Still no answer."

"All right," said Prentice. "Let's get over there."

Hebron's camp was a rough collection of inflated plastic balloons anchored to one of the larger stones. Supplies stood in untidy heaps. Off to one side, hanging in space, a cluster of ore-bearing fragments had been welded into a composite whole. When large enough it would be towed to one of the big smelters and sold to the company owning it. They would refine the metal and pass it down the line. Everyone would make a profit, but Hebron would make the highest percentage.

Would have made, corrected Prentice to himself. Looking at the camp growing large in the screen he had the mounting conviction that the entrepreneur had made his last solar. The conviction deepened as the radiotech reported from where he sat at his instruments.

"Still no reply from the camp. No local noise either."

"Keep trying." Prentice turned to the colonel who had insisted on accompanying him. He hadn't objected. Local knowledge was of prime importance. "Spot anything unusual?"

Weatherby nodded. "The place is too quiet," he said. "There should be men working on that ore-cluster. More men shifting the supplies. The place looks dead," he complained. "Deserted."

He was right the first time. Suited, protected, Prentice entered the largest of the balloons. A part of it had been walled off to form an office. The main area was a combination mess and recreation hall. A bar stood at one end. Gambling machines lined the sides. Hebron hadn't missed a trick.

Prentice passed through the double doors leading to the dormitories, the ruinously expensive showers. He returned to the office and looked down at the owner. He was quite dead.

"Prentice?" Lambert, scouting outside, spoke over the suit radio.

"Here. Find anything?"

"Some men, suited, by the local transport. There are some sporses and a freight-carrier. The men are dead."

"The same here," said Colton. He had gone to investigate the ore-cluster. "Three of them all cold. You?"

"The camp's a morgue. Weatherby?"

"Here."

"Send out word for all available patrol craft to enclose this area. I want every stone searched and everyone found taken into protective quarantine. Spread the net wide. Get every prospector, every visitor. Understand?"

"It'll be a hell of a job!"

"Do it. Colton?"

"Yes?"

"Snag those men you found and bring them down. I want you and Lambert in here with me. The files have to be checked and the dead identified. With any luck at all we can contain this to a limited area. I don't want to sterilize more than is necessary."

Sterilize, he thought. A smooth word for utter destruction. The atomic burning of a portion of the Belt with all it contained. But it had to be done.

They'll love me for it, he thought. The people who lived out here would see the destruction and remember all the blood and sweat and tears which went into tearing a living from space and stone. And they'd curse the patrol and blame it all on them. *With reason,* he told himself. *If we hadn't let those men escape in the first place this wouldn't have happened. Destruction wouldn't be necessary.*

Slowly he looked around the office, at the staring eyes and round, twisted face of the dead man. Hebron had been fat, the victim of low gravity and little exercise; now he looked like a sagging, half-inflated balloon. He thought of the others he had found, too many of them, dead in their bunks or lying on the floor throughout the camp. An unmistakable trail.

They were here, he thought. *They did just what I suspected they would do. What they had to do.* They'd found work, somewhere to live, camouflage of a kind. But they had walked into a trap without knowing it. Hebron had them in a financial stranglehold. He controlled transport so they couldn't escape. And they grew careless or perhaps simply desperate and, suddenly, they were the only ones left alive.

Their camouflage has gone, he told himself. *They're on the run again. They've had to move—to where?*

He should freeze the sector but if he tried it the patrol could never make it stick. Not with life itself depending on a steady flow of air, food and water. Not with the freedom-loving asteroiders determined to do as they wanted when they wanted. He didn't have enough men to enforce such a demand. He had to guess and guess right. But it didn't have to be wholly a guess.

"Get me patrol sector H.Q." he said into the radio. "I want to know where Slade is."

The voice was noncommittal. "The ship is at slip fifteen, gate seven," it said.

"Who is this?" Slade glared at the blank screen.

"Slip fifteen, gate seven," repeated the voice. Then there was a click and the empty hum of a broken connection.

Slade hit the button and the hum died. He hit another and a face smiled from the screen. It belonged to the receptionist of the hotel and it could afford to smile. At the rates the dump charged it was a wonder it didn't laugh outright, thought Slade. "Your pleasure, sir?"

"Are there any messages for me?"

"No, sir."

"Anyone asking for me?"

"No, sir."

"All right," said Slade. He hadn't really expected Ely to have come up with anything yet. The little man was covering a long shot; he doubted if the two men from the *Hope* would be found on Rock Eighteen. But his time was running out and he could no longer afford to wait. "Get me a flitter," he ordered the smiling face. "I want to go to Rock Twenty-one."

"Yes, sir. With chauffeur?"

"No," said Slade. "I want to travel alone."

On his way the detective leaned back in his chair and closed his eyes. He was physically tired but his mind was active and now he was working under added pressure. Jasker hadn't been joking. Out here the Scorfu was a real menace and they would have little mercy should Prentice find the men before he did. Even on Earth he wouldn't be safe, not unless he could bring down the Martian hotheads—and even the patrol had failed to do that. One man with a knife, he thought. That's all it would take. Just one flagging nurd with a fanatic's determination. And the Scorfu were all fanatics.

They arrived at Stoneman's, he decided. They sold their sporses and took what he gave. They went somewhere—where and what for? To work, he thought. To hide. To accumulate some money. But, in the Belt, money was in short supply. Cash money, that was. Trading and paying was mostly done with checks. Useless to anyone hoping to bribe a skipper for an unregistered passage.

They would need cash and would know of only one sure place to get it.

The ship jerked and he snapped open his eyes, seeing warning lights and gripping the arms of his chair. "What the hell?"

"Your pardon, sir," said the mechanical voice of the pilot.

"I had to take evasive action to avoid a stone. The danger is now safely past."

Slade grunted.

"Fortunately such danger is extremely slight," said the pilot conversationally. "I have been carefully programmed to take full care of both ship and passengers. You can always trust the equipment of the Peerless Space Service. You may be interested in mentioning this incident to your friends."

"Shut up," said Slade.

"Our rates are very competitive," said the pilot. "We may not be the cheapest but we do guarantee your safety, which is more than some of our competitors can honestly claim to do. Travel with Peerless and arrive in one piece."

"All right," said Slade.

"Remember that," said the pilot. "Always travel with Peerless for safety, comfort and discretion."

"In a pig's eye," said Slade.

"I assure you that what I say is correct," said the pilot chidingly. "I have an erase-button incorporated into my circuits. For the sum of one hundred solars fed into my receptor that button may be activated. When pressed, the details of my last journey will be eliminated from my memory. This service," continued the pilot smugly, "almost unique to Peerless, is made possible by the Free Enterprise Laws governing the Belt economy. I quote the First Freedom: 'A man has the right to do what he likes, when he likes, how he likes—providing he is willing to pay for it.' Unquote."

"End of commercial," said Slade.

"Yes, sir," said the pilot.

There was trouble at the landing. Suited, sealed, Slade waited as a guard thrust his head into the cabin and spoke to the pilot. "Where are you from? Make any detours? Pick anyone up? All right." He turned to Slade. "You're clear."

"Something wrong?"

"Nothing that need concern you." The guard was abrupt. "Are you going inside or do you intend hanging about?" he demanded. "Make up your mind."

Inside Slade ignored the checker eager to mind his suit and, still sealed, made his way to Stoneman's Joint. The place was closed. Slade banged on the door but got no answer. A man, passing along the tunnel, halted and looked curiously at the detective.

"It's shut," he said. "It happens sometimes."

Slade made no answer.

"He could be sick," mused the man. "Or maybe he's gone off on business. If you want something maybe I could fix you up. Marcis," he said, and held out his hand. "I run a nice place."

"I want Stoneman," said Slade. His voice echoed flatly from the helmet diaphragm. "Know when he'll be back?"

"No," said the man. He peered at the closed visor of the helmet. Suited men were normal in the Belt but usually they doffed their suits before entering the residential areas. "Say," he said. "Don't I know you?"

"You've never seen me before in your life," lied Slade. The man had been in Stoneman's during his last visit. "Where did you say your place was?"

"The next level down. Ask anyone." The man lingered. "Want me to guide you?"

"I'll find it," said Slade. "I'll give Stoneman five more minutes."

He waited until the man had gone and then kicked open the door. Inside it was empty. He closed the door and stood looking around. The long bar was bare, chairs still stacked on tables, only a few lights burned. Brighter light came from the glass transom of Stoneman's office to the rear. Slade crept toward it, halting as he reached the panel, listening. He heard nothing. Gently he tested the catch. The door was unlocked. Throwing it open, he stepped inside.

Stoneman stood against the far wall, one hand resting on his desk. His eyes widened as he recognized the detective through his visor. The pasty-faced youngster with the game leg sat on the floor, his back to the wall. A purple bruise stood ugly against the whiteness of his temple. His eyes were closed and he breathed raggedly through a thin froth of spittle. A shadow moved against a wall.

"Hold it," said Slade quickly. "Hurt me and it'll be the worst mistake you've made so far. I know who you are," he said. "I know why you're here. I know what you want. I can help you."

81

The shadow hesitated.

"Trust me," said Slade urgently. "What the hell can you lose?"

He turned, feeling the sweat on his face, the prickle between his shoulders. A suited man stood in the angle between door and wall. He held a laser-cutter in gloved hands. Slade knew better than to argue with the tool which doubled as an effective short-range weapon.

"He came busting in here a while ago," said Stoneman. "Just as we were getting ready to clear up. He made the crip lead him back here. Once inside he conked him. Then—"

"He wanted money," interrupted the detective. "Lots of money."

"You know?" Stoneman looked surprised.

Of course I know, thought Slade impatiently. *Does the nurd think I'm a fool? Why else would he be here? But where is the other one? Outside, maybe? Somewhere inside? But one man acting alone didn't make sense: he had no insurance in case things went wrong. They've split up,* Slade told himself. *It has to be that. They've each decided to go it alone.*

"Listen," he said to the suited figure. "You're in a spot and I can get you out. But you've got to trust me all the way. You can start by putting down that laser." He grunted as the man obeyed. "Good. Now I want the owner to take the boy outside and fix him up. They won't send for help. They won't do anything but what I say because there's money in it for both of them."

Lots of money, he thought. Enough for the boy so that he could get himself proper treatment and enough for Stoneman for him to develop a bad memory. He would do that to save his own neck—the last thing he'd want would be the patrol sniffing around his goods.

And he would know a way out of the rock. Can-raiders had to have such means of egress and entrance away from the official gates and it didn't take much to burn a tunnel and fit it with locks.

I'll send him to Rock Eighteen, thought Slade. *The boy can take him. He can hide out there. Not in the ship Jasker arranged—I'm not such a fool—but somewhere else. Somewhere he can wait until I can fix other transport. A place where, if he is found, I wouldn't be involved. That woman,* he thought. *The bag on the ship. She'll do anything for cash.*

And who cared what happened to her?

X

SHE WOKE AND STRETCHED and wondered why she felt so happy. Doctor Hilda Gootmeyer, she thought. The unfortunate victim of an extra-terrestrial disease, the host to an invading parasite which would cut her off from all close communion with her own kind forever. It was a sobering thought but she refused to be sober. *I feel too good,* she told herself, *too euphoric. Like a young girl on her wedding day—or an old maid venturing on her first affair.* But she was neither. She was a scientist who had made a mistake. An investigator who had become contaminated with the thing she was investigating.

A shadow fell over her. She turned and saw Ross. He looked odd, sterile in his protective clothing, devoid of human warmth and understanding. She laughed at the seriousness of his expression.

"I feel wonderful," she said, anticipating his question. "The tests with the monkeys proved what I had suspected. Hagan does minimize the initial shock and can serve as a prophylactic to the lethal effects of the Prox plague. How long have I been unconscious?"

"Eight hours."

"Progress?"

He lifted a chart from its hook and showed her the tabulated data. "An extremely high temperature to begin with, falling off to a point two degrees above normal. Heart and respiration, at first slow, later speeding to a little faster than usual. Metabolic tests show a slight regression in cellular breakdown. It is, of course, too early to be positive."

"About what?" Her voice was sharp.

"Whether or not your metabolism will follow the same path as that of Taylor. You are a woman," he explained. "We have no data but that obtained from males. There could be a difference."

"*Vive le differance!*"

Ross made no comment.

"I'm sorry," she said, instantly contrite. "I expect I've been a nuisance. I still don't know how I became infected. Just one of those things, I expect. I'm sorry."

"Yes," he said.

"I mean it," she insisted. "I must have been careless."

Like hell, he thought. *That was no carelessness. That was a Freudian motivaton if ever there was one. A classic, textbook example. You wanted to become contaminated. Well,* he thought, *you've got your own way. Taylor is no longer something to be kept locked away in maximum isolation. Not as far as you're concerned. Not now.*

"I've notified Chen Yu," he said. "He had to be told."

"Naturally. What did he say?"

"He was annoyed," said Ross. "He didn't like the idea of losing one of his top scientists. He'll speak to you about it later." He paused. "He put me in command."

She nodded.

"I've also told Taylor. I thought that he should know."

"Why?"

"Because he has a personal interst in what has happened to you," he said. "He blames himself."

"That's ridiculous!" She half-rose in the cot. "How can he think such a thing?"

"Because it's true." Ross could have elaborated but he didn't think it fair. It was too late for recriminations and regrets. But he found it impossible to remain calm. "Damn it!" he exploded. "You are supposed to be an intelligent woman. Didn't you ever stop to think of what you were doing?"

"What are you talking about?" Her face grew hard. "I don't understand. Explain yourself!"

"Is that really necessary?" He recognized the futility of the argument. "Never mind. What has happened cannot be rectified but, as Chen Yu pointed out, we now have to face an urgent practical problem. Urgent to solve, that is. This ship is far too small to contain two separate isolation installations. To use a second ship will double the contamination-risk for the staff and crew. Also it will make it that much harder to maintain secrecy."

"That is obvious," she said coldly. "Is that all?"

"No, there are the political implications. The crew of the *Hope* is still missing. As yet Taylor's illness has been kept a secret—as far as Keeway and Slade are concerned he died in the *Hope*. Should it become known that the Prox plague is spreading, and it is, there could be trouble for the United Planets. It is possible that the Secretary General would be impeached for criminal mismanagement."

"So?"

"You and Taylor will have to get married." He saw the young-girl expression on her face, the look of happiness. "It will solve the first part of the problem," he said. "We shall not need a second ship. You can both share the same quarters and, as a medical officer, you will be able to conduct all necessary tests. The marriage can be regarded as a matter of convenience," he added. "Insurance, if you like. A protection against the accusations of the Purity League and other bluenoses if the facts are ever made public."

"Is this Chen Yu's idea?"

No, he thought, *it was yours. As if you didn't know. As if you hadn't worked it all out way down deep in your subconscious. But did you work it out far enough?*

"We thought of it together," he admitted.

"And?"

"And what?"

"Does Ed agree?"

"Of course," said Ross. "I should have told you. Taylor wants me to be his best man."

"Then," she said firmly, "what are we waiting for?"

Stoneman moved restlessly, his face anxious. "I don't like this," he said. "It's getting in too deep."

"Shut up," said Slade.

"But calling the patrol! From here!"

"What have you got to be afraid of?" demanded Slade. "I asked you to help me. You've helped me. Now I'm passing on the information. That's all there is to it." *And all there's going to be to it*, he thought grimly. He wished Stoneman were somewhere out of the way—preferably dead. Balchin should have killed him before he left. It would have made things so much simpler. For a moment he was tempted to do the thing himself but it was too late for that now. He couldn't get rid of the body and there were tests which could prove embarrassing.

"Listen," he said. "The patrol is breathing down my neck. I was checked on arrival and that means there's a general alert. If I'm not careful I'll be in trouble and so will you. Bad trouble," he added. "Or do you want them asking a lot of awkward questions?"

"They can't touch me. I'm a citizen of the Belt."

"Sure, but what if they find some can-raided stock? What if they made sure they found some? The patrol might let the Belt handle its own local affairs but when it comes to something serious they step in. Get wise, man, what have you got to lose?"

"Nothing," admitted Stoneman. "But plenty to gain, eh, Slade. Plenty to gain."

"That's right," said the detective. "Remember that." He swtiched on the phone. "Get me patrol headquarters," he said to the operator. "Patrol? My name is Slade. Connect me to Ron Prentice, Chief of UP Security." His lips tightened at the alacrity of the connection. "Prentice, this is Slade." He thrust his visor close to the scanner. "I've got some news for you about you-know-what. No, I can't be more explicit. Pick me up at the main gate—you know where I am. How long? Thirty minutes. I'll be waiting."

He killed the phone and looked at Stoneman. The man was sweating. Slade was glad that he was suited and had stayed sealed all along. Not that he thought there was any real danger of either the boy or his boss having been contaminated. Balchin had been sealed too.

He glanced at his watch. Prentice had said thirty minutes, which could mean that he would arrive in fifteen and have time to do some snooping. Well, it couldn't be helped. He had given the boy all the time he dared. It should be enough. That and the fact he had too much to lose if he didn't make it.

"All right," he said to Stoneman. "I'm going. You know what to say if anyone should ask."

Stoneman nodded. "What about the money?"

"Do you want a check?" Slade was bitter. "How would we explain that away if it should be found? You'll have to trust me. I'll settle before I leave if I can. If not I'll send it later. But you'll get it. That's a promise."

Twenty minutes later a fast patrol ship dropped down and picked him up. Prentice was in the cabin. He was fully protected. "Talk," he said.

"Rock Twenty-four," said Slade.

"Are you sure?" Prentice looked thoughtful. "Out at the

edge of this cluster," he mused. "Relatively small population. Little trade or shipping—what makes you think they're to be found out so far?"

"Information." Slade was deliberately curt. "I've a contact. He's been keeping his ear to the ground. Word drifted back that a couple of men, strangers acting queer, are on Twenty-four. Maybe they're the men from the *Hope*. Maybe not."

"Two men?"

"That's right." Slade was defiant. "I know all about Elgar," he said. "A friend told me."

"Jasker." Prentice nodded. "I know all about him."

You know too damn much, thought Slade viciously. *Or you think you do. But this time I know what you don't. I know that Balchin's sold out his friend. Bland's on Twenty-four. Get him and you'll maybe waste time looking for the other one. That's what Balchin's hoping. That way he gets time to escape.*

It always happened that way, he reflected. When the pressure got really tough it was each man for himself. Or each thing; it was just the same. Survival had the same old rules no matter what shape or skin you have to wear. *I know that,* he thought. *I learned that the hard way. That's why I've succeeded where Prentice failed. I know where those men are and he doesn't.*

"I am puzzled," said Prentice suddenly. "When you phoned me you were suited and sealed. Why?"

"Because I like my skin the way it is," snapped the detective. "Those men have been in the Belt too long for comfort. How do I know what's lying around. And what about you?" he demanded. "You're protected and you're in a patrol ship."

"I've been working," said Prentice quietly. "Cleaning up a mess. You know," he said, "you should have been with me. It would have taught you something. All those dead men, killed without knowing what hit them, dying from a touch. It makes you think."

"About what?"

"Relative values, for example. Just how much money is really worth. How many dead men are worth a solar? A thousand solars? A million? When you stand among them you begin to realize just how much some people will pay for money. The people who arranged to rescue the men of the *Hope,* for example."

"You're saying something," said Slade tightly. "Or you think you are. What the hell is a bunch of stiffs to me? I didn't kill them. I didn't even know them."

"No," said Prentice. "That's the worst part of it."

"You're crazy!"

"No," said Prentice. "Just tired."

It was like Christmas, thought Ed Taylor. *Like New Year when everything is supposed to be bright and exciting but, somehow, never was. I'm married,* he told himself. *Married to a real, honest-to-God woman who loves me and isn't afraid to say so. I was lonely,* he remembered. *Lonely and a little scared, but not anymore. Not now that I've got Hilda and she's got me.*

He looked up at her from where he sat in a chair. His left arm was bare, resting on the arm. His right hand reached for her, touched her with an intimate familiarity. She didn't pull away as Mary would have done. Instead she smiled, understanding and reciprocating his need to display affection. Her kiss was warmly possessive.

"Are you ready for the tests, dear?"

"Sure. What do you want me to do?"

"Just relax." She took a scalpel from a tray and poised it over his bared arm. "I want you to tell me if this hurts." Blood spurted as the blade made a long, deep incision. He yelped. "Did it hurt?"

"Not much." He looked curiously at the blood. "I guess it wouldn't, with the blade being so sharp." He didn't take his eyes from the cut.

"Heal it," she said.

"Just like that?"

"Think about it," she ordered. "Think of it as healing, as having healed. You can do it. Please, dear," she urged. "For me."

He nodded, concentrating. The blood ceased, became a red smear, vanishing as it was absorbed by the flesh. Beside him he heard the sharp sound of indrawn breath. He looked at his unmarked arm. "All right?"

"Wonderful!" She made notes on a pad, looking up as the signal light flashed from the phone. Rising, she hit the button. Chen Yu stared at her from the screen.

"Dr. Gootmeyer," he said and then, remembering. "I'm sorry, I should have said Dr. Taylor." His eyes, shrewd, understanding, probed her face. "You are looking well, my dear. Marriage seems to suit you."

"It does." She looked fondly at Ed where he sat in his chair. He tried not to look smug, managing instead to fairly radiate pride. It was really something having a wife who was on friendly terms with the Secretary General of the United Planets.

"How are your experiments progressing?"

"Well." Enthusiasm added to the sparkle in her eyes. "As I suspected hagan has a repressive effect on the alien intelligence—if you can call it that. There is a pronounced bolstering of the human ego, seemingly at the expense of the alien sentience. The results are fascinating. There is a tremendous increase in the mental control of cellular tissue so that healing is accelerated to an amazing degree. I suspected that, with further progress, regeneration will be as automatic."

"I see." Chen Yu was thoughtful. He knew as well as she did what could be the logical outcome of such a discovery. "You are hinting that the end product of this mating of human and alien tissue could well be immortality?"

"Extreme longevity," she corrected. "An end to the crippling effects of injuries and death caused by mechanical and unnatural disturbance of the metabolism. An end, too, of the fatal effects of disease. The body seems to have become self-repairing to an incredible extent," she added. "The alien tissues seem to work as a fantastically effective form of antibiotic against all bodily malfunction." She paused. "As yet," she ended, "we have no way of telling if these peculiarities are hereditary."

"That seems to be merely a matter of time," said Chen Yu dryly. He looked at something on his desk below the range of the scanner. "I have news," he said, abruptly changing the subject. "Prentice caught up with Bland on Rock Twenty-four in the Belt. He had to be destroyed."

"Why?"

"Prentice had no option. When challenged Bland refused to surrender. He chose to fight. It took a surprising amount of force to subdue him. In fact he was lasered to ash." Chen Yu's eyes drifted from the woman to Ed and then back to the woman. "He had regressed to an incredible extent," he said quietly. "I leave it to your imagination to guess just how far."

"I see." Suddenly she remembered that she too had the infection which had transfigured Bland and the others. She and Ed, both. But she was a scientist—unpleasant facts could not be ignored because they were unpleasant. "I do not think that it will happen to us," she said. "The crew of the *Hope* was untended for years. They had no knowledge or defense. We have both."

"Perhaps," said Chen Yu evenly. "But the problem is the same, is it not? Come now," he said. "You must have considered the situation. You represent, in your way, exactly the same threat as did those three men. More. Your discoveries could have terrible repercussions if ever spread abroad. Rich men would do much to live on to enjoy their wealth. Longevity, now, would be as bad for Earth as untrammeled disease."

She said nothing, waiting.

"I have ordered the *Hope* to be refitted and put in full operational order," said Chen Yu. "You will be transferred as soon as it is ready."

You're disowning us, she thought. *Expelling us from the system. Getting rid of us just as I wanted to get rid of the original crew of the* Hope. *And for the same reasons. But it was my decision,* she told herself. *I can't protest now.*

"It isn't as bad as you think," said Chen Yu quietly. "You aren't going to be sent on open orbit into space. That would be a waste. We wanted to do it before because of fear, but now those reasons no longer apply. We can't hide forever," he added. "Sooner or later we've got to reach out to the stars and be able to handle what we find. You can help us. You and your husband and the children you may have. Those potentially immortal children."

"To Prox," she said.

"Yes. To the one place where you should be able to settle and grow. To our nearest star." He smiled then, for the first time. "It won't be so bad," he consoled. "What nicer ship could you have than the *Hope*—for a good, long honeymoon?"

But they both knew there would be no coming back.

XI

SLADE ARRIVED AT Rock Eighteen in a fever of impatience. *Damn Prentice,* he thought. *The nurd didn't have to take me with him after Bland. He didn't need me and could have handled things alone. Had handled them,* he reminded himself. *Say what you like about the patrol, they were efficient.* But he couldn't have done anything else, he told himself. You made your protest but Prentice wouldn't listen. To have insisted would have aroused suspicion. All Slade could do was to wait and get away as soon as he could.

But it had wasted time.

Inside he checked his suit and grabbed a guide. "Know where this is?" He thrust the woman's card into his face. "Take me there."

"Cost ten," said the man hopefully.

"Five," said Slade. "It should be one. Get moving."

Mrs. Osprey lived in a quiet passage at the edge of the habitable area, well away from the main arteries and junctions. Slade maintained his pace as they neared the door, passed it despite the protests of his guide.

"It's back there, mister. We've passed it."

"Shut up." Slade gave him money. "Beat it."

Waiting until the passage was deserted, he then returned to the door and gently tested the catch. The panel was locked. He beat on it, waited, knocked again with mounting impatience. The door clicked and swung open. He stepped inside. The door closed behind him. He turned and saw Ephraim standing before it.

"It's a pleasure to see you again, Mr. Slade," said the young Martian. "I have been waiting for you. What kept you so long?"

Slade stepped backward, well away from the man, searching the apartment with his eyes. A bedroom opened off to one side, a small kitchen and bathroom with metered taps were on the other. The place had a disheveled, lived-in appearance. The bed was unmade. Aside from the Martian and himself the place was deserted.

"I'm afraid our hostess couldn't stay to greet you," said

Ephraim. "You realize, of course, that she was working for us?"

Slade made no comment. Now that the trap had been sprung it was obvious.

"Your friends reached here just as you planned," continued the Martian. "They arrived just before the rock was sealed on orders from the patrol. That is why I am here," he explained. "We couldn't get away until a short while ago. It was decided that I should remain to teach you that the Scorfu means what it says."

"What about the boy? The one with the crippled leg?"

"The guide?" Ephraim shrugged. "He had a regrettable accident. We didn't want him to talk, did we?"

"You killed him." Slade was contemptuous. "It figures. All you flagging nurds can think of is the knife and gun. Stinking cowards the lot of you. Where is Jasker?"

"Jasker obeys the orders of the Scorfu."

"That isn't answering my question. All right, then. Where is Balchin?"

"Safe."

"On a ship bound for Mars," said Slade. "He has to be. That's why you're here. You stinking nurds can't help but crow when you've got the chance. The Scorfu!" He spat. "A bunch of fanatics who should get their tails well and truly beaten. How far would you have got without me?"

"You're so clever," sneered the Martian. "The great detective from Earth who has no time or respect for Martian bumpkins. But who is really the cleverest, Mr. Slade? You, trapped like a child with nothing to show for your expense and effort, or us, the Scorfu, who have used you all along the line? Used you until you are no longer useful." He paused, breathing fast, his right hand clenched inside the wide sleeve of his left arm. "Used until you would serve a better purpose dead than alive."

He stepped forward, young, confident, hungry for blood. Steel glimmered as he drew his right hand from the wide sleeve. "You were warned," he whispered. "Jasker warned you what to expect if you disobeyed the Scorfu."

"Go to hell," said Slade. And screamed.

It was a soundless scream, the air whistling through the specially constructed denture. Dogs would have heard it but there were no dogs in the Belt. Ephraim jerked, a dull report echoing from within his head. Blood showed at ears and mouth and eyes. He fell, instantly dead, his brain shattered by the charge Slade had inserted back on Earth.

Slade jumped over the body and reached for the door. He jerked it open. Outside, in the passage, Jasker stood waiting. He stared at the detective with undisguised shock.

"All right," said Slade grimly, and dug his fingers hard against the nerves in the other's arm. "I can guess why you're waiting but you're wasting your time."

"Ephraim?"

"Dead," said Slade. "As dead as you'll be, you nurd, unless you decide to see things my way." His fingers dug even harder. "Well," he demanded. "What's it going to be?"

The ship was small, cramped, an ore-boat from the Belt, functional rather than luxurious. But it had power. Power enough to haul masses of rock from their age-old orbits. Power enough, Slade hope, to catch up with the ship carrying Balchin and his lone Martian crewman.

"You must have been crazy," he told Jasker. "To send him off with one man like that. What made you do it?"

"Joachim's a good man," said Jasker.

"He's a fool," corrected Slade. "The rest of you weren't. At least you weren't such fools as to stick your heads in a noose. Suppose he breaks free? Suppose Balchin decides to take over? What then?"

"He won't," said Jasker. "I spoke to him. He knows that we mean him no harm."

"Like hell you don't." Slade was disgusted. "Did you tell him all about that nice, clean, sterile jail you've got waiting? Did you tell him how you hope to use him?"

Jasker didn't answer.

"Why the hell do you think they broke free in the first place?" continued the detective. "I had a ship all nicely fitted out ready and waiting to take them somewhere safe. They didn't keep the rendezvous. Instead they overrode the programming of the rescue ship and went their own sweet way. One of them died doing it. Another got himself charred trying to find somewhere to hide. And you think that Balchin's going to do exactly as he's told?"

"What else can he do?" demanded Jasker. "With us he'll be safe and he knows it. On his own he'll be hunted down like a mad dog. The man's got no choice."

"Wrong," said Slade. "There is always a choice. Do you want to make a bet?" he added. "I'll bet that Joachim doesn't get out of this alive. Two to one in thousands. Yes?"

"No."

"All right," said Slade. "Keep your head stuck in the sand. But when you tried to cross me you did more than you guessed. You killed Ephraim for one thing. What makes you think that it's going to stop there?"

"Your attention," said the mechanical voice of the pilot. "A ship is approaching from the direction of the Belt."

"So what?" snapped Slade. "Space is full of ships. Why tell us?"

"The vessel in question is a patrol ship," said the pilot reprovingly. "It is following a flight-path which will intercept our own within one hour. I thought you would like to know."

"The patrol?" Jasker looked at Slade, his face white. "After us?"

"Us or Balchin," said the detective. "You don't think Prentice is a fool, do you? He probably had me followed from the moment I hit the Belt. You too, most likely. He's let us go our own way. Now he's closing in." He spoke to the pilot. "Get a move on. Hurry and catch that ship we specified."

"The ship bound for Mars?"

"That's right."

"There is a problem," said the pilot thoughtfully. "The ship previously specified is no longer bound for Mars. A course-correction was made a short while ago. The ship is now bound for Earth."

"Earth?" Jasker swallowed. "But that's impossible," he whispered. "Joachim would never disobey orders like that. It can't be heading for Earth."

"It is," said the pilot.

"Follow it," ordered Slade. "Top speed. Catch it and fast!" He steadied himself against the acceleration-surge. "It's happened," he told Jasker. "What I suspected would happen all along. Balchin doesn't intend being your prisoner. He's decided to take a hand in the game."

"But Earth?" Jasker shook his head. "Why there? It doesn't make sense," he complained. "That's the last place he'd want to go."

"Wrong," said Slade.

"But—"

"Shut up," said the detective. "I want to think." Scowling he looked at the controls of the ship. The ore-boat had been designed as a working vessel. It carried external tools, among them a laser which could be used to drill, weld, slice and fuse. It was the only weapon they had aside from Jasker's gun. But it was ideal for his purpose. "All right," said Slade. "I know what to do. This time we'll cook his goose but good."

Chen Yu looked anxiously from the screen. "You're sure that everything is under control?" he said. "There can be no mistake?"

"No." Prentice leaned back in his chair, conscious of the smooth efficiency of the patrol ship in which he rode, the small noises of working men and working machines. A part of his mind assessed, correlated and dismissed it. Another part wondered curiously how much longer he could operate without sleep. Long enough, he knew. The chase was almost over, the mess about to be cleared up and swept away. "How are things at your end?"

"Satisfactory," said Chen Yu. "They are both intelligent people," he explained. "They accepted the fact that what we proposed is the only humane solution. Anyway," added, "they are very much in love. To be alone when you are in love is the reverse of punishment."

"So you tell me," said Prentice. He wondered what it was like to be in love and what made the emotional madness so important.

"It's true," insisted the Secretary General. "Don't concern yourself with the matter. The new crew of the *Hope* is, and will be, very happy." He returned to more urgent matters. "So both ships are now headed for Mars?"

"Yes." Prentice threw a switch and read the figures thrown on a panel. "Slade's been clever," he admitted. "He used the external laser of his ship to wreck Balchin's drive. He then welded the two ships together. I'm wondering what he intends to do about landing. My guess is that he'll cut the ships free and rely on the emergency coils to get Balchin down in one piece."

"And you?"

C.O.D. MARS

"I'm following," said Prentice. "I want to have a few words with Mr. Slade."

"I know," said Chen Yu. "I had a report from the Belt," he said. "Rock Twenty-four had to be sterilized and the personnel dispersed. The compensation will run into millions and, of course, the United Planets will have to pay. But I suppose we were lucky," he admitted. "If those men had managed to land on Earth or one one of the terra-formed outer satellites—!" He shook his head. "I've never seen a world atom-burned," he said. "I don't want to see it. But what else could we have done if they had reached Io, say, or Ganymede?"

Prentice didn't comment. The Belt had been bad enough but, if it had had to happen anywhere, it couldn't have happened in a better place. The rocks were isolated and suits were worn as a matter of course. The chances of contamination were that much less and isolation and quarantine were things easy to apply. But it would be a long time before he would forget the things he had seen.

And the danger still existed.

His eyes narrowed as he read the figures on his panel. "We're getting close," he said to Chen Yu. "What are we going to do about Slade?"

"There's not much we can do," said the Secretary General. "The legal department is working on it but they aren't hopeful. The man has been too clever. I'm afraid that he's going to get away with it."

"I don't think so," said Prentice. "He killed a member of the Scorfu before he left the Belt. Nothing we can prove and it was probably self-defense, but that won't matter to them. They'll want his blood and they won't rest until they get it. I don't think we need worry too much about Mr. Slade."

"Good," said Chen Yu.

"He's going into planetary orbit," said Prentice. "I want to make sure nothing goes wrong."

"Has he cut free?"

"No. The fool!" said Prentice. "He's trying to land double."

"You could stop him," said Chen Yu. "Freeze his pilot and send him into continual orbit. He could kill himself if you don't."

"That's right," said Prentice. "That's why I'm not going to interfere."

It was one of those things, thought Slade. A good idea which had blown right back into his face. It happens, he told himself. It just can't be helped. It happens, he told told himself. It just can't be helped. Welding the ships had been easy, cutting them apart proved impossible. The external laser lacked maneuverability. Using it only made matters worse and threatened to weaken their own hull. There was only one thing they could do.

"Emergency landing," he told the pilot. "Take all necessary precautions. Hit something soft and hit it easy."

"That will be extremely difficult," complained the machine. "My balance is completely unstable. I have little fine control. I simply cannot recommend such a landing."

"Get on with it," said Slade.

"There is an alternative," suggested the pilot. "I can maintain orbit until help arrives. There is a patrol ship not far away. I could summon assistance."

"No."

"I feel it my duty to insist," said the pilot. "It is against my programming to allow you to jeopardize your lives as you propose. I assure you that it would be best to do as I suggest."

"Land!" yelled the detective. "Now. You flagging thing," he raged. "Much more of your lip and I'll tear your guts out and take over myself."

"Maybe we should do what it says," said Jasker. "Why take chances when we don't have to?"

"Are you soft in the brain?" Slade made an effort to control himself. "Listen," he said. "That's a patrol ship out there. Prentice is on it. You know what we've got welded to us. What do you think happens if he finds it?"

"We're within ten diameters," reminded Jasker. "The patrol has no jurisdiction so close to Mars."

"You tell them that," said Slade. "After they've done what they intend doing. They might even listen to you. They might even apologize—like hell they might."

"All right," said Jasker. "But we could call help from below."

Sure, thought Slade. *You'd like that. You call help and where does that leave me?* "We land," he said. "Now. Get in a chair and strap yourself down. This is going to be rough. Hurry," he shouted as the Martian hesitated. "Or do you want to wind up a skinful of broken bones?"

Hastily he followed his own advice. Strapping himself tight in a pneumatic chair he forced himself to relax. "All right," he said to the pilot. "What are you waiting for?"

Air whined thinly over the hull, deepening into an organ-note as the coupled ships plunged further into the atmosphere. The note rose to a scream, a maniacal shout, then there was a horrible jarring, a scraping, an insane combination of movements.

"Landing accomplished," said the pilot weakly. There was a click and the instrument died.

"You all right?" Slade unstrapped himself, jerked himself free, dragged the limp figure of the Martian from his seat. Jasker groaned. He had an ugly bruise on the side of his face and blood trickled from his nose. He wiped at it and stared at his stained hand. "Only a nosebleed," said the detective. "Let's get outside."

The lock was warped, jammed solid. He hit the emergency release and built-in explosive charges blasted it open. Outside a cloud of dust drifted over the wrecked vessel. Further back, looking like a dented tin can, the other ship lay on its side.

"They broke apart," said Slade. He coughed and spat out a mouthful of dust. "Damn planet. I wouldn't live here for a fortune."

"You wouldn't be given the chance." Jasker threw back his shoulders, regaining his self-assurance now that he was back on native soil. He looked up as something cut across the sky.

"The patrol," said Slade. "Prentice is up there. You'd better hurry before he comes down for a closer look."

He followed the Martian to the other ship. Fire and noise spurted from it as the lock was blown free. Together they stood and waited.

"It's Joachim," said Jasker as a suited figured showed in the opening. "You were wrong, Slade. Joachim's all right."

"No," said Slade. "Look again."

The suited figure stumbled, regained its balance, turned to face the two men. It was tall, too tall; the suit showed rips where it had yielded to internal pressure. Something pressed against the visor of the helmet. Metallic fabric, almost indestructable, ripped like paper as it lifted its arms.

Balchin stepped from the ruined suit.

"No," whispered Jasker. "My God! No!"

It wasn't human. It was anthropomorphic but that was all. A dull gray rind covered it, protection, Slade guessed, against the shock of impact. The alien growth which had possessed the original human shape had reverted to a more suitable form.

It began to walk toward the two men.

"No!" Jasker screamed as Slade caught his arm, held him firm. "Let me go, damn you! Let me go!"

"You've got a gun!" yelled Slade. "Kill it, you fool. Kill it while you've got the chance!"

Jasker whimpered, tearing at his jacket, jerking the laser from its holster. He aimed and fired, using both hands, the beam cutting a charred path across Balchin's face. Tissue boiled as it sought to repair the wound. The rind grew thicker, harder.

The beam cut again, again, crisscrossing in a series of slashes, drilling deep as Jasker managed to control his fear and held the gun steady.

The thing changed. It crouched, began to sprout wings, grew a long, prehensile tail. Smoke rose from it, the thick, oily smoke of burning flesh, the acrid odor of smoldering vegetation. Then, when the gun was almost exhausted, the movement ceased, the column of smoke grew thicker, rose straighter into the dust-laden air.

"It's dead," said Jasker. He looked at the empty gun in his hand. "Dead."

"And you killed it," reminded Slade.

"I didn't know," said the Martian. "I just didn't think it would be like this. How could I?"

"That was the last of the crew of the *Hope*," reminded the detective. He looked up to where the patrol ship was readying for landing. Prentice would be after his hide, he thought, but so what? There was nothing they could do to him. Nothing at all. Quarantine, maybe, but aside from that nothing.

He looked at the little heap of still-smoking ash.

"That was Balchin," he said. "I delivered him. Right?"

Jasker nodded, eager to absolve himself from blame.

"He was the last surviving member of the crew of the *Hope*," said Slade. "That was our agreement, remember? The crew of the *Hope* delivered to Mars."

"Yes," said Jasker dully. "I remember."

"Good," said Slade. "You owe me a million."

Here's a quick checklist of recent releases of
ACE SCIENCE FICTION BOOKS

G-titles 50¢   H-titles 60¢

If you are missing any of these, they can be obtained
directly from the publisher by sending the indicated sum,
plus 5¢ handling fee per copy, to Ace Books, Inc. (Dept.
MM), 1120 Ave. of the Americas, New York, N. Y. 10036